THE
Memory
of
Music

OLIVE COLLINS

POOLBEG

Published 2016
by Poolbeg Press Ltd
123 Grange Hill, Baldoyle
Dublin 13, Ireland
www.poolbeg.com

A catalogue record for this book is available from the British Library.

ISBN 978-1-78199-873-1

Printed and bound by CPI Group (UK) Ltd. Croydon, CR0 4YY

www.poolbeg.com

About the Author

Olive Collins grew up in Thurles, Tipperary, and now lives in Kildare. For the last fifteen years, she has worked in advertising in print media and radio. She has always loved the diversity of books and people. She has travelled extensively and still enjoys exploring other cultures and countries. Her inspiration is the ordinary everyday people who feed her little snippets of their lives.

Acknowledgements

A big thanks to Paula Campbell and the team at Poolbeg for bringing this to life, especially Gaye Shortland for meticulous editing and support.

To Eileen Keane, for friendship, input and advice. For reading every single draft and listening to the many unwritten plots, and only occasionally yawning!

A special thanks to those who read early drafts and gave great encouragement: Tom Ryan and Pat O'Brien.

Thanks to Newbridge Liffey Circle Writers for support.

To my friends and family who regretted asking how my story was unfolding, and patiently listened as they were met with a barrage of too many details.

And finally a heartfelt thanks to you, the reader.

To my grandmother, Ciss (1911 – 2000)
and every child living in a time of war

Prologue

Saint Gabriel's Nursing Home, Dublin 20

April 2016

The story and time of Isabel's birth was an omen of things to come, so her mother said. It was many years later that Isabel understood the importance of her mother's words. Now, as she lay in her nursing-home bed, her mind constantly brought her back to scenes from the distant past. The black-and-white pictures that dotted her home came to life. For years, names and eventually faces eluded her, but suddenly she recalled conversations and minor details from almost one hundred years before. The lucidity of her recollection was overwhelming. The sheen from a new violin, the clip-clop of a horse's hooves, penny sweets from Mr Hartmann's hat, Mona Daly's raucous laughter, each name of Mona's ten children – all of it returned to Isabel. Occasionally she thought of the tremendous changes that had taken place in Ireland in those turbulent years since her birth in 1916. Isabel's mother, Betty, had often told her how she had prayed for a quiet dignified birth. But the onset of Betty's labour pangs coincided with gunfire from the GPO and gunfire camouflaged her final birthing cries. Many times Betty told Isabel how she had arrived alert and eager, as if she was ready to join her father in the battlefield that raged outside her door.

Isabel marvelled at how she could recall the stories told about her birth, yet couldn't recognise the woman before her. Of course she should know her. The young woman addressed her as 'Nana'. She wore footwear with a lift that resembled brogues for a club foot. Her slacks were tight, shaping her thighs and bottom. She had a short jacket and a large scarf, white with splotches of red – so much red running through the scarf that Isabel could feel her heart gather speed.

She could never banish it. The image remained vivid and haunting. The intensity of the colour never faded. Red and white. The blood from her father's neck. How it seeped into his white shirt. The small red stain grew, swept onto his chest and abdomen and sullied the floor. From her hiding place, she watched her father's blood trickle along the uneven surface. Like a red serpent intent on catching her, it meandered between the grooves in the ground. When her ears stopped ringing from the gunshot she heard her father moan. Sometimes she could hear her father's low moan here in the nursing home. Other times she could smell the blood, the metallic odour that suffocated her. It haunted her, the senselessness of it. For the most part, she saw his stained shirt, red and white, striking.

'What will become of us, Nana?' the woman sighed as she took Isabel's hand in hers.

Isabel smiled. Nobody took offense when she smiled.

The woman squeezed Isabel's hand before getting to her feet.

Isabel watched her statuesque frame saunter from the room. The white and blood-red scarf was trailing down her back. Isabel would forget the lady. The red-and-white colour in the scarf was the indelible memory that would never fade.

Part one

Chapter 1

Dublin, January 1916

When Seamus took Betty to their first home in Dublin, she was horrified. The once-gorgeous Georgian house was a miserable sight. Seamus promised faithfully that the rooms in Middle Abbey Street were only a temporary stopgap.

'A few months at the most,' he swore as he led her into the hallway.

The formidable staircase was battered and colourless with so many missing banisters it gaped unattractively. With each step Betty took, her horror was as great as the wafting smell of Lavender Wax Floor Polish that could never mask the true stench of poverty.

'It isn't much but it's a start for us – at least it's our own,' Seamus said with optimism as he opened the door.

Since their hasty marriage the previous August they had been staying in cramped conditions with a cousin in Ringsend. These rooms were not crowded but nothing could have prepared Betty for their dismal condition. There were two rooms: a bedroom and kitchen. She noticed that someone had left an empty bottle of stout and a broken looking-glass on the mantelpiece of the large fireplace. A discarded bicycle tyre lay on the bare wooden floor. The wallpaper was patched and stained and most of what remained

5

was peeling. There was a rickety table and only two well-worn wooden chairs. Seamus proudly pointed out the old stove which was as good as new, according to him. The window-frames of the tall windows were stuffed with paper to stop the draught. The racket on the street below was ceaseless: loud accents and a din so alien that she closed her eyes in protest.

She felt a sudden longing for her rural home in Tipperary, for the comfort of the quiet boreen flanked with trees gently whispering, swelling fern and wild thyme – the smell of burning turf and of fresh bread rising in the bastable. Where had Seamus taken her? What kind of landlord would rent a room without cleaning it first? If Seamus noticed the tears in her eyes, he pretended he didn't, continuing to point out the advantages of their new home.

'These are the best rooms I've seen. Two rooms,' he enthused, 'so we can have a separate bedroom. The only other real option was a room at the top of a man's house with no banisters and a leaking roof.'

Betty looked around again at the high ceilings and missing coving. The large regal windows were reminiscent of a bygone era when Middle Abbey Street housed the wealthy. What remained of its former glory was agonising, like an elderly forlorn woman waiting for a passer-by to find beauty beneath her hollowed wrinkled face.

'Some places I looked at had no outhouse. Another fella offered me a basement room – 'twas reeking of a putrid smell from the pipes. This is a palace compared to most of them.'

Momentarily Betty was torn between hysteria and hilarity that her husband could find hope within these crumbling walls.

'With a bit of scrubbing this will be a home to behold,' he said with a smile.

Betty didn't remove her hat or coat. This 'home' was not a place she would even have liked to loiter in. They were only a stone's throw from the affluent Sackville Street, and she found it peculiar that such poverty and prosperity could live side by side.

On the corridor outside she heard loud footsteps, a crying baby, two women talking, a man calling for 'Mona Daly', a child singing, and everywhere the unfamiliar inner-city accent.

She felt foolish for spending so much of the money her father had given her on clothes. What remained of the handsome furtive parting gift was tucked into the back of her suitcase. What good were new blouses with matching skirts and patent shoes from Clerys amidst such scarcity?

Seamus took Betty's hands in his. 'It's the best we can do for now. But time will fly – we'll be out of here by May, before the baby is born.'

She allowed him to hold her hands before she snatched them from his gentle grasp and slapped him.

For the next few weeks Betty refused to go along with Seamus's notion of a 'home'. Each morning she rose to prepare his breakfast but refused to humour him. Not only had she gone against her parents' wishes by marrying Seamus Hopkins but she'd left the security of her extended family in Tipperary. In hindsight she realised that she had left a life that was more than comfortable. She'd worked three mornings a week in the office of her father's small musical-instrument workshop, taking care of the books, and she'd learned the value of well-crafted musical instruments.

Betty had heard about Seamus before she met him. He was employed as an apprentice violinmaker in her father's workshop. When she first started to work there she was drawn to the only employee who refused to fawn over her. Although polite, he remained distant and wouldn't enter into gentle banter like the other men. She noticed his puckered brow as he toiled at his tools and wood. He was handsome, strong and rugged, with messy blond curly hair and light-blue eyes. At twenty-three, he was just one year older than her.

She sought Seamus out at every gathering. She persisted in trying to get to know him, attending forbidden Wren dances where boys killed wrens and pinned them to branches. Betty joined the men and women and danced around the boy deemed King of the Wrens, her eyes always on Seamus. Finally, at a local dance, she was the one to ask him to dance during Ladies' Choice.

He was a wonderful dancer and musician. He played several instruments, his favourite the fiddle. When he played, his strong body appeared serene and agile, the strings on the fiddle dancing to his command, lending an air of beauty and mystique.

The pensive and distant craftsman finally warmed to her and, each day at noon, when her day's work was done, she delayed until lunch to speak to him.

Only once was she in Seamus's home in Tipperary. It was a well-kept cottage in a tightknit community called Borris. Seamus's mother died when he was a boy, leaving his father with four sons to raise. A few times a week his aunt called to ensure the men were looked after. On one wall of their kitchen was a picture of the Sacred Heart, on the others pictures of Ireland's martyrs, Robert Emmet and Wolfe Tone. When she commented on them, Seamus proudly told her how his ancestors took a prominent role in the Fenian Rising in 1867 and the following uprisings.

'My great-granduncles took part in the 1798 Rebellion. One was hanged and another transported to Van Diemen's Land.' He smiled when he said that. 'Would you like to live in Van Diemen's Land where the heat would melt you and giant spiders would devour you?'

'I'll settle for Dublin,' Betty said.

Afterwards they had tea in his Uncle Bart's home. Bart's passions were music and republicanism. He insisted Betty have a drop of sherry while he had a glass of whiskey and sang a humorous song about a bachelor besotted with a magpie called Polly. She clapped loudly when he'd finished and was unsure if her sudden flush of warmth was from the sherry or his glorious hospitality.

Finally, it seemed only natural to pack their bags and leave the rolling hills of Tipperary. Equipped with Seamus's dreams of freeing Ireland, and Betty's desire to escape the humdrum rural life, they were married in a small church in Bray to the sound of seagulls squawking and the waves crashing into the pier.

Betty had known that there would be restrictions until Seamus finished his violin apprenticeship, but living in the squalor of a tenement was something she had never envisaged. In Middle Abbey Street, cultured neighbours were as rare as well-bred horses. Their home was close to the infamous Monto region where the ladies of the night made their living. She was all agog when she saw one of those shameless girls from Monto, her face covered in cosmetics, as she passed by one Sunday evening.

That first week when Seamus tried to speak to her, she reminded him of his promise. 'Until May at the very latest,' she said. 'Five months.'

'Is that all you're going to say to me between this and then?' he asked. 'This is all we can afford right now!'

'We'll be lucky if we last until May,' Betty said, pointing at the hole in the floor which was stuffed with broken glass to keep the rats at bay. They'd gnaw on the glass and eventually bleed to death.

Seamus tried reasoning with her. 'I didn't bring you here deliberately. It was you who suggested Dublin, you who insisted I finish my violin apprenticeship. What more can I do?'

'There must be better homes to rent!' Betty said, refusing to look at him.

But Seamus insisted they must live within their means. 'Betty, you have no idea of the value of money. Since our wedding, I've watched you spend money as if keeping it was a greater burden.'

Betty knew she couldn't return to the morning she made her decision to marry Seamus against her mother's angry protests. While Maureen threatened her with everything from a beating with an ash plant to 'expulsion from the family home for all eternity', Betty gaily packed her suitcase. She was proud to be heading to Dublin where her beautiful blouses and brooches would be appreciated. She couldn't wait to embark on the first step of her new life and spend the rest of her days with Seamus Hopkins.

Maureen had rapped the table impatiently when Betty said those very words. 'Wilful and thoughtless!' she declared. 'You'll rue the day, my girl.'

'It's a disgrace to all of us,' her Aunt Úna said, as if she was accepting responsibility for a family scandal she could have prevented. 'He was raised in a cottage with a crowd of fighting men. How would he know how to treat a woman? As for his limited education, that poor boy has nothing to offer you.'

'Seamus has kindness and honesty that will carry him farther than most of our educated family,' Betty countered. She ignored her aunt's incredulous expression at the notion that one of the Hopkins could have better breeding than her family.

'We are the O'Fogartys,' Úna said, as if that finalised the argument.

Betty ignored the insinuations that Seamus was nothing more than an ignorant mountain peasant not worthy of their kin. She deemed their old values useless burdens. As far as she could see, to them anything that implied happiness was almost immoral. She desperately wanted to escape the life of self-inflicted hardship that her mother endured. Unlike other villagers, her parents were not poor. As well as her father's workshop, they also had a small holding of land. Yet Maureen insisted on toiling from morning till night. She turned her hand to everything, from feeding calves to washing clothes, and baking as if she was feeding an army. Her work seemed endless, and some of it unnecessary. It was as if each welt on her hand was another badge of honour. She believed suffering in this life would find its reward in the next. Such balderdash, Betty thought. Who could wait that long for a reward?

Chapter 2

As Betty sat crying alone during her first week in Middle Abbey Street, she couldn't help thinking how her proud aunts would surely die of embarrassment if they ever saw where their niece – 'a direct descendent of the O'Fogartys' – had ended up living.

Seamus refused to acknowledge how upset she was.

During those days she thought incessantly of her home. Each night at seven she knew her mother and father would kneel to say the Rosary. Afterwards her aunts and neighbours would walk the short distance to her home where they'd play cards or talk by the large fire. Maureen would hold court in the most central position while her reserved father Jim was more inclined to listen – a gentle observer in the background.

Betty recalled the morning of her departure when her father discreetly met her and Seamus at the bus station. He had two envelopes in his hand, one for Betty with a nice sum of money 'in case she ran into difficulties' and another for Seamus with the name and address of a workshop in Dublin where he could get employment and finish his violin apprenticeship.

Betty tried not to dwell on what she had left behind and thanked the Lord that at least the family didn't know her exact situation. It was too late for regrets.

Betty had never seen such poverty as she did during her first week in Middle Abbey Street. 'I can cope with the dirt and mire,' she admitted to Seamus. 'Any home can be cleaned. But the stigma of living with this class of people may not be so easy to overcome.'

'If that's all you're worried about, we'll be fine.' Seamus seemed amused. 'I won't tell anyone if you won't.'

Eventually Seamus became accustomed to her silence and retreated into his own, anger spoiling their first weeks in their new home. At night she retired to bed before him. When she rose in the morning he was up working on his violins. Refusing to acknowledge her, he never raised his head from his work – a fixated intensity that irritated her. With everything he did, he did it to perfection. Most evenings he attended political meetings. Betty knew he was a member of the secret banned society, the Irish Republican Brotherhood. Their aim was Ireland's independence which they believed could only be won by an armed revolution. He invited his friends to their home to continue with their political debates and scheming, and she'd dutifully make tea and listen in the next room as they discussed politics.

'The days of fighting the enemy with boiling water and sticks are gone,' Seamus said. 'We need to organise and arm ourselves properly. Each Volunteer must buy his own gun and bullets.'

A softly spoken man from Mayo called Digger Dempsey talked about the greed of the English. In his parish the locals were banned from collecting the plentiful oysters and shellfish on their beaches as the English landlords had claims over the shorelines.

Another man made impassioned speeches about the education system. 'The English do not deem the Irish language or Irish culture deserving of the slightest respect.'

The men would agree and their voices would get louder as they recounted stories of injustices.

On and on it went throughout their gatherings. In those early days their ultimate question was: when? When would the blow for freedom be struck? Their loyalty to their cause and their country bound them together as if they were brothers who shared a history of youth and a future filled with promise.

Betty got tired of her own tantrum. She was lying on their bed late one Saturday evening. On the corridor outside she heard a child singing one of her favourites, 'The Wind That Shakes the Barley'. Betty got up and sat inside the door to hear it more clearly. The women outside clapped and asked the boy for another. For once she wished she was part of their close-knit community and that she too could sit on the stairs for their weekly Saturday-night sing-song.

She could hear one of the mothers declare Saturday night her favourite few hours of the week. 'After a decent scrubbing the children look so fresh – it makes the week's hardship worth it.'

When another child played a melancholic song on his tin whistle, Betty softened. The music charged the air, it stilled the house of voices and replaced her fear with hope, almost reassurance. She wiped the tears from her eyes and looked around her decrepit home. There was nothing for it except to rise above it. She would learn to adapt, otherwise she might as well lie down and allow the rats to gnaw on her. The street below had lulled almost to quietness. The large redbrick house opposite was growing familiar. Maybe the tenements would also become familiar. Her little abode suspended in the sky might become home.

She placed her hands on her belly and thought of the child she was expecting. With each passing day her urgency to improve their circumstances increased. May, she reminded herself, looking around her small kitchen, wondering where to begin. In the corner were Seamus's newly varnished violins, the newness of the instruments a stark contrast to the dilapidated surroundings.

When Betty put her hand to cleaning and masking the dirty walls, it became easier. Time flew by as she made the rooms as cosy as possible. She plugged every crevice with broken glass to keep the rats away and allowed Sheila Muldoon's terrier to sniff out any four-legged intruders that might have come in through the door. Using some of the money from her father's parting gift, she bought material in Guiney's to make curtains for the two windows, some new unchipped cups and a tablecloth for the scratched table. She bought a vase in Clerys and created a bright arrangement on the window ledge. She bought fresh straw for their mattress, and real sheets and blankets. At night she made love to Seamus with the smell of DDT disinfectant rising from the mattress.

Each day when her chores were done she went for long walks and avoided her neighbours. She considered the clusters of women sitting on the doorsteps gossiping were common. She would make the most of life inside her door but would not consort with their kind.

'How'ya, love?' they'd ask. 'Settlin' in a'right?'

'Mind your own business,' she'd quietly mutter.

She overheard one of the women say: 'We're not good enough for that one.'

At least they recognise it, Betty thought with pleasure.

'Off out for your walk, love?'

Some hadn't a tooth in their heads or the price of a pair of dentures between them.

Those women represented everything Betty wanted to avoid. Everything about their oppressive hopeless lives frightened her. Their rooms were bursting with children and sicknesses, their worn faces etched with lines of hardship. Their aspirations were reduced to seeing their children washed and cleaned on a Saturday night. It seemed a far worse fate than the welts on her mother's large worn hands. More frightening was the fact that there was no escape for the tenement women. Their husbands worked long hard hours, some didn't work at all, and occasionally the men rolled up the stairs drunk. The crisp sound of flesh hitting flesh startled her more than the night she heard Mona Daly's birthing screams. Betty had not been educated to the grand age of eighteen to spend her married life yapping in doorways, dressed in rags, with fresh shining bruises.

During her free time Betty loved to walk and explore the city. Before her pregnancy became too cumbersome, she wanted to see as much of it as she could. The first time she saw the cakes in Noblett's windows with sky-blue and pink icing, her eyes were out on stalks. She never knew food could be presented so colourfully. The hats and frocks and stoles in Clerys made her hope for something more in life. The women selling flowers by Nelson's Pillar fascinated her, with their busy hands and unabashed shouting. Betty noticed poverty and wealth in extremes and side by side. The bright lights of Sackville Street with picture houses, nice hotels, ornate buildings and theatres were yards from the squalor and deprivation of the slums. She rode on the tram simply for the novelty. From the window she watched every class and creed go about their business on Dublin's streets. She visited the National Gallery and was enthralled by the stately rooms housing the magnificent paintings. Curiosity took her under the arch into the architectural splendour of Trinity College. She traced her fingers along stonework that was built to last and then sat on a bench watching the university students in their straw hats and blazers. She noticed their ease and confidence, a sense of assurance that the rest of the country lacked.

On Dame Street she saw Mr Hartmann's shop. Mr Hartmann was her father's main buyer. His violins and cellos were in the window. The small handcrafted items and first-trial violins from her father's shop went to Mr de Lacy's shop on St Stephen's Green, but the best violins went to Mr Hartmann. According to her father, Mr Hartmann was specific about his requirements and paid handsomely for the instruments.

The sight of one of Seamus's gleaming violins on display for all of Dublin to see reinvigorated Betty. At last she could breathe with ease. It removed her fears that she had made a mistake by eloping with him. It reaffirmed that she had married the best violinmaker in Ireland, a man who turned wood to music. But when she took a closer look at the violin, she gasped in disbelief. It was five times the price her father had received for it. Betty's disbelief turned to fury at her father for his inept business skills. Her uncle, Thomas O'Fogarty, had been right when he said her father was too soft to

15

ever make good money. No wonder Mr Hartmann could afford to call to their home once a year with a bottle of brandy for her father and face-powder for her mother!

That evening she could hardly wait for Seamus to return from work to tell him how much his violins were fetching.

'I have the best news imaginable,' she declared as she placed his dinner before him. She'd spent the day calculating how many violins a year Seamus could produce and what they could do with the money. At last she'd found a solution.

He looked at her curiously.

She sat in front of him, her face alive with excitement. 'I saw your violins for sale in Mr Hartmann's shop today – and selling for five times the price my father receives!'

He raised his eyebrows, surprised at the news, and then resumed eating his dinner.

Disappointed with his reaction, Betty felt the need to explain the implications. 'Seamus, we could be out of this tenement in a few weeks. I've been thinking about this all day. The best plan is to bring your finished violins to Mr Hartmann to evaluate as soon as possible.' Still not getting a reaction, she continued. 'Mr Hartmann will gladly deal with us. He knows your work.' Not only would a partnership with Mr Hartmann vastly improve their living conditions, but it would establish them as business people with a respectable occupation. 'He has buyers from America and Europe and as far away as Canada.'

Seamus cut her off. 'I won't deal with the likes of Mr Hartmann. There are plenty of shops owned by our own people. I'd rather trade with one of our own.'

'He's not an Englishman,' Betty informed him, her excitement evaporating as she noticed his stony expression. 'He's not even a Protestant – he's a Jew.'

'I don't care what he is – there are several Irish Catholic men I'd rather deal with,' he stated, ending the matter.

Speechlessly, she watched him eating his dinner. Was this the man she had packed all of her dreams into?

She recalled conversations between her father and her Uncle Thomas about Seamus. Her father Jim knew a good thing when he saw it. When he first noticed Seamus's skills he continued to give him similar assignments with complex details. To each product Seamus added his own flair. When Jim saw that Seamus's violins were as good as those of his most established violinmaker, he knew that with time his craftsmanship would not be surpassed.

Betty heard her father tell her uncle that he'd found a genius: 'He has a gift to make anything with wood and the passion for violins to sustain him into old age.'

After Mr Hartmann bought the first violin made by Seamus, he complimented his work and specifically requested violins made by Seamus Hopkins in future. He referred to Seamus as a prodigy. Jim showed the letter to his brother as validation that he had in fact found a gifted luthier. Thomas, who was more ambitious than Jim, had moved to Dublin as a young man and established a violin and instrument-making workshop which later expanded into a successful furniture business. He had an eye for the best craftsmen, and, when he saw Seamus at work, he sang his praises: 'He has the fingers and the talent that will bring him out of these mountains and see him go places.'

To show his appreciation of his work, Jim offered Seamus overtime and paid him handsomely. He also allowed him to use materials from the workshop to build his own violins. He encouraged Seamus, while at the same time not wanting to lose his best and most profitable craftsman. He confided in Betty that if his talent was ever recognised, it would bring immeasurable success.

Now Betty felt foolish. She had never imagined that the man with the gift of turning wood to music put such little value on recognition for his craft.

Chapter 3

There were only two people from their old life who knew the whereabouts of Betty and Seamus in Dublin. When, one cold February evening, Seamus brought Fr Mathew to their home, Betty cursed her husband's stupidity for allowing anyone to see where they lived. She wanted their tenement stay to be brief and unknown, obliterated from their memories forever once they escaped.

Fr Mathew was an old school friend of Seamus's from Tipperary who was now a priest in one of the nicer areas of Dublin. He seemed shocked that they were living in such circumstances and Betty squirmed when she registered his reaction. Rather than allow her shame to be seen, she behaved as if she was standing in the most beautifully furnished parlour in Ireland. She asked Fr Mathew to bless their new home. He agreed, his round cheeks flushed with embarrassment. As his stout fingers sprinkled holy water, he murmured the House Blessing Prayer. Betty didn't implore God for a blessed home but for escape from Middle Abbey Street.

On the next occasion Seamus returned with her cousin, Ursula. She was Thomas O'Fogarty's daughter and was in her final year of midwifery nursing in the Rotunda Hospital. Betty was infuriated with Seamus. It was one thing inviting his friends to their home but another thing to invite one of her own flesh and blood. That afternoon when Ursula breezed in wearing her bright starched nurse's uniform and elegant cape, Betty asked herself if she had married the greatest gombeen that ever came out of Tipperary. Any eejit would know to hide their whereabouts except the harmless clown she'd married. But, despite Betty calling their home a 'step above a pigsty', Seamus felt their rooms were a cosy little place. He remained adamant that he didn't care where they lived – any place with a warm welcome was a home to be proud of.

Seamus had brought Ursula to the tenement thinking it would be good for Betty to have a woman to talk to. Ursula could also keep an eye on her when she was nearing the final stages of her pregnancy.

When Betty got over her rage and embarrassment, she was relieved it was Ursula rather than any of her other cousins. Although Ursula's father owned a successful business and she was accustomed to the nicer things in life, status and money didn't influence her. Ursula read the papers and kept abreast of the news. She leaned on the side of the oppressed, occasionally airing radical republican attitudes: 'The poor of Dublin will remain so until they make their voices heard, by whatever means possible.'

Back in Tipperary, she had interrupted her father, uncles and brothers more than once as they discussed politics.

One evening, as the men discussed Home Rule, Ursula spoke up. 'Britain will continue to postpone Home Rule,' she said with a raised voice, across the kitchen, like a mother correcting quarrelling children. 'It's their tactic. They are trained and educated political negotiators who will push and trample on Ireland as long as they're allowed.'

Her actions had Betty's mother and aunt all agog.

'I never heard the likes of it,' Maureen said later. 'Talking up like that and interrupting the men. That one needs to be reeled in.'

They blamed the brash Dublin environment while Betty took delight in Ursula causing such consternation.

On Ursula's first visit Betty made her swear on her missal that she wouldn't tell any of her family where she lived. Earnestly Ursula swore, dramatically closing her eyes and adding an air of false solemnity to her raised voice for fun. But Betty knew there was no need to insist on her swearing. Ursula would enjoy keeping her secret. She had little tolerance for the hoity-toity notions of the women in their family. According to Ursula, they were 'more proud and idiotic than a tribe of bleating nannies'. Her irreverence was refreshing, albeit disrespectful.

'O'Fogartys, my hat! I never heard such nonsense,' she scoffed when they discussed their O'Fogarty heritage. 'The women in our family have a lot to answer for. Raking through Irish history to find some connection with a lord! How deluded can you be?'

'Well, actually, it's true – we *are* directly descended from the O'Fogartys, the Kings of North-East Munster.'

Ursula opened her mouth and guffawed like an ignorant old woman.

Betty raised her voice. 'It's in the history books. We were rulers of the kingdom of North-East Munster. Our roots can clearly be traced to the 11th Century – to the founders of Thurles.'

'Heavens above! I can't believe you share their fancy views on this O'Fogarty nonsense! Any Irish person named O'Neill or O'Donnell or McCarthy or O'Driscoll or any ancient name can trace their origins back to the ruling clans of ancient Ireland!' She sighed, exasperated with it all.

'You will get Fogartys or O'Foggartys – however, we *O'Fogartys* are a rarity,' Betty declared.

'That's, for sure, a rarity indeed,' Ursula said dryly. 'Any Irish person searching the history books for royal titles is indeed a rarity and worse than those English buffoons.'

'It's as true as we are sitting here.'

They agreed to disagree, with Betty feeling sorry for Ursula that she was so intent on discrediting her true rich heritage.

Only once did Betty refer to the shame of living in the tenements to Ursula. Ursula told her there were worse places she could be living – then, poking fun at her, added, 'It might be a bit lowly for Queen O'Fogarty!'

Betty began to look forward to Ursula's visits with her stories from the Rotunda Hospital and her outings in Dublin. She was forever going to dances and fancy hotels for drinks. She claimed to know some of the famous Dublin writers and actors.

In one conversation Ursula referred to Mr Hartmann – he was one of her father's main Dublin buyers. At the mention of Mr Hartmann's name, Betty took her missal out again and insisted Ursula swear on her life that she wouldn't tell Mr Hartmann anything about her impoverished circumstances.

'For what?' Ursula asked. 'Does it matter what Mr Hartmann thinks?'

'I don't want anybody knowing about our stay in this little hellhole,' Betty said, looking around the room distastefully.

Betty didn't reveal her intentions to Ursula. At some stage Seamus would come round to her way of thinking and sell his products to Mr Hartmann. She did not want Mr Hartmann to have any preconceived ideas about them. A man like him could use it to his advantage. If Betty's schemes went according to plan, she and Mr Hartmann could become associates. She didn't want anything thwarting that.

'Mr Hartmann wouldn't care where anyone lived,' Ursula said. 'All he cares about are well-crafted instruments to sell to foreigners with oodles of money.'

Betty thought again about Mr Hartmann's annual visit to her father's shop with his bottle of brandy for her father and powder for her mother. Each year Maureen cast the powder aside, saying it would be ideal for women in Dublin with little to do except powder their noses. Betty suspected Mr Hartmann's Jewishness was the main reason her mother rejected his gift. At some stage in the future Betty believed Mr Hartmann would be giving Seamus the brandy and herself the powder, and she'd gladly make time to use it.

Ursula was full of gossip and inside information on the Rotunda. She told Betty how some women had twenty children, with no time to recover, and some mothers were up working the next day. There were stillbirths, deformed children, children so sick they could do nothing only leave them to die. Ursula claimed she knew how to deal with every complication for a new mother and her infant.

Betty wondered if Ursula was really that brilliant at nursing or whether she was just full of her own importance. Nonetheless, she encouraged her to ramble on and found some of her stories and advice entertaining, although occasionally unlikely. Betty wasn't really interested in the sob stories – she wanted to hear about Dr O'Malley and the young nurse with whom he was having an illicit affair. The nurse was a friend of Ursula's.

Ursula told Betty that Dr O'Malley had taken the nurse for a meal in a country hotel in Kildare.

'The women wore fur coats and hats – they had white silk gloves and carried parasols with hand-painted pictures,' she gushed.

Betty suspected it was Ursula who was having the affair with Dr O'Malley and not another nurse in the Rotunda.

Each visit, Betty would pry into Dr O'Malley's affair and each time Ursula's information was too good to be second-hand.

'Did your friend tell you about the food in the swanky restaurants where Dr O'Malley takes her?' Betty asked.

'During the week he took her to a place that served oysters and crabs' claws. The sauce was so nice you could have licked it off the plate.'

Betty noticed how Ursula's eyes danced with excitement when she talked about Dr O'Malley.

'Dr O'Malley is so well educated, not only about his field of medicine but also about world affairs and etiquette. He's also quite liberated. He *encourages* my friend to drink a sherry. He says it's good to take a drink. In countries like France and Spain ordinary people drink wine with their dinner, Dr O'Malley says.'

Betty hoped Dr O'Malley was selective in whom he offered that advice to. She thought about some of the tenement women's husbands falling in the door on a Saturday night and roaring abuse to all and sundry.

Life ambled along with visits from Ursula and Fr Mathew. Betty fell into a routine of keeping house and daily walks. Each day she visited the church. In the stillness of Saint Mary's Pro-Cathedral with its long aisles and illuminated Sacred Sanctuary, she sat alone for a few minutes and thought about Tipperary. She missed her family but she knew that with time her sudden departure to marry Seamus would be forgiven. Someday she hoped to return, once she and Seamus were established in a nice home with her firstborn. Betty lit candles for her future in Dublin and prayed to the patron saint of expectant mothers, Saint Gerard Majella, for her unborn child.

Once a week Betty had afternoon tea in the Gresham Hotel, paying with her father's parting gift that remained hidden in her suitcase. Each week she chose a seat near the window and always brought writing paper and a pen with her. She always wrote a letter to her mother, telling her how happily married she was. She reiterated that Seamus was a gentleman and a decent, hardworking husband. Despite appearances, the Hopkins family were more than mountain peasants and republicans. Betty described the wonderful home her husband provided for her in Ranelagh with a large vegetable garden out back, a vestibule, a comfortable lounge and three large bedrooms. She did not tell her mother about Middle Abbey Street, the prostitutes and street hawkers, or the dung and sooty air or clusters of flies and filthy aged women sitting on doorsteps. Her mother would not be able to comprehend living in a house with a family living above her, below her and beside her, or the noise travelling between the thin partitions as sparsely veiled as their exposure to sickness. She and Betty's aunts would not be able to conceive of the notion of fifteen families living at such close proximity or a piggery at the back of the tenement attracting rats as big as Jack, their terrier. Each week she described tea in the Gresham Hotel, the delicate saucer and regal insignia on the sugar spoon. She told her parents how her pregnancy was advancing and how she looked forward to the baby's arrival.

Each Friday Betty used the same letter to light the fire before Seamus returned from work.

Chapter 4

One evening as Betty left The Winding Staircase bookstore on the Quays, she met Mona with one child in her arm and three by her side. She was en route to Middle Abbey Street.

When Betty and Seamus first moved into their home, Mona had called to Betty's kitchen to invite her to the Saturday-night singing-and-dancing session in the neighbouring tenement building. Seamus had been eating his supper and offered Mona a seat. Betty cut him off as he offered her a cup of tea. Although polite, she did not want to appear so inviting that Mona would think she could become a casual caller. Since then Betty often overheard Mona yapping at the door with the other hopeless shawlies.

'Ya like to read, do ya?' Mona enquired, indicating Betty's books as she stood on the Quays.

Betty thought Mona patronising. 'Yes, I like to read novels,' she answered, standing as far away as possible from the woman. Mona's long limp black hair, moth-balled shawl and three unkempt children made her uneasy.

'Can't read myself,' Mona confessed, folding the shawl around the baby in her arms. 'I'd say it's nice to be able to read. Ya know, to find out about foreign countries and life outside this godforsaken city.'

'I suppose,' Betty said, surprised at Mona's curiosity about the rest of the world. Their lives were so diverse she had assumed that Mona would not share her interests.

'Does your husband read?' Mona enquired.

'Yes, he can read. Usually he reads the paper but not novels.'

'Lovely fella,' Mona said.

Betty had often overheard him stopping to talk to the women when he returned from work. They knew his name and made small talk. She had suggested to Seamus that he keep his distance as they wouldn't be there long enough to establish friendships. The next day Seamus helped to move furniture for a neighbour, and afterwards they had a few pints in the pub.

When he came home he told Betty and, seeing her reaction, he said, 'Having a pint doesn't join us at the hip. Besides, it doesn't matter how poor they are – we're all Irish.'

Betty raised her hand to stop him from adding: under British tyranny.

When Mona and Betty arrived at the tenement, Mona invited Betty to join them on the doorstep for a chat and a cup of tea.

Frostily Betty declined.

'Well, enjoy your books anyway,' Mona said.

A few days after that, Betty overheard Sheila Muldoon, one of the women on the third floor say, 'Yer one reads as well. Jesus, isn't it well for her to have the time to be idlin' away on her backside with her nose in a book!'

The only thing Betty had in common with the tenement women was a devotion to Our Lady. The Holy Rosary and the Church were their refuge and solace. Each evening when Betty went to Gardiner Street Church for the Rosary she noticed Mona praying with the other women, their rosary beads mechanically slipping through their fingers, imploring Our Lady to give them strength for their impending adversities. They had an acceptance that life would always be brutal and all they needed was strength. Not necessarily strength in abundance, just enough to see them over the next hurdle. Their certainty of adversity was as definite as the existence of Our Lady, both real and side by side: life to deliver its everyday savagery and Our Lady to redeem.

Betty implored Our Lady to help her find the quickest route out of the city centre to the suburbs. Our Lady would understand that she was not born to their world. Her basic necessity was to get the strength to find a healthy safe space for her unborn child on the outskirts of Dublin. A place she could call home among her own class of people who lived for joy and not redemption. Betty murmured the 'Memorare' to Our Lady in the stillness of the church for the home she felt she deserved. Her prayers were not as basic as those of the poor of Dublin, yet they were as worthwhile. Betty felt confident Our Lady understood. She repeated the last line of the 'Memorare': '*Despise not my petitions, but in thy clemency, hear and answer me. Amen.*' Over and over again Betty repeated those words, knowing that She would help her find a solution.

In those early days of their marriage, Seamus drank only occasionally. He spent his days in the workshop and his evenings were taken up with his violins or political meetings. Betty worried about his involvement in the IRB – the Irish Republican Brotherhood – as the consequences if it was discovered would be very severe. She didn't pay much heed to his political talk – it bored her. She was tired of hearing about oppressed Ireland.

Fr Mathew saw little wrong with the poverty of the tenements.

'We are not rich by what we possess but by what we can do without,' he said when Seamus talked about the dreadful conditions he had seen since moving to Dublin.

'Maybe so,' Seamus said gently, 'but there is only so much suffering a nation can take.'

'These people have religion and God. Only when they get money and power will they question God. Finally, they will think they can do without God. Too much of anything is not good.' The priest then swallowed a whole slice of apple pie in two bites.

Betty noticed how Fr Mathew differentiated between Seamus and her and the other tenement dwellers – he knew they didn't belong there. When he called, the tenement women surrounded him asking for prayers. 'Remember me at Mass, Father?' They'd ask for a prayer for a sick child or unemployed husband. Some went as far as curtsying.

'So it's in the clergy's best interest to keep the nation poor?' Seamus probed.

'This is a poor country,' Fr Mathew agreed.

'Dublin has the worst slums in Europe and, until recently, the biggest area in Europe for –' Seamus couldn't say the word *prostitutes* in the presence of a priest, 'for those fallen women. Those who rule us are content to allow the slums to grow and grow and grow because we are nothing to them. Nothing but Irish savages who need to be eradicated. Is it not wrong to do nothing while one nation bleeds another?'

'The English ruling class you speak of might appear rich but none have the wealth of spiritualty that the poorest Irish person has,' Fr Mathew said, in the preaching tone he used on the pulpit. 'Money and affluence will test us and we must be ready. We must be ready for the temptations of affluence that lead to sin and damnation.'

Fr Mathew seemed satisfied to allow poverty to dominate yet he himself appeared to have all of the material possessions he claimed led to hell. Seamus never challenged Fr Mathew the way he debated with other men. In any case, Fr Mathew remained neutral on all matters except God if at all possible. He wanted a free country, but 'one where the clergy would take a leading role in governing the state'.

Rather than listening to Seamus and his friends, Betty made plans or thought about the future.

When alone with Seamus she read the paper to him as he crafted his violins. The only time he seemed contained and peaceful was when his hands toiled on his craft. He worked the knife so elegantly, peeling away the wood, his long slender fingers examining the indentations, a picture in his mind that only he could see. Betty was mesmerised watching him. On those evenings alone, she loved him most.

Seamus had a musician friend who was butler to an officer in the

British army who owned a Stradivarius violin. When the officer was abroad for a week, the friend allowed Seamus entry to the officer's house to study the Stradivarius. When Seamus told Betty about it, she felt it was that glimmer of hope she'd been praying to Our Lady for. She had spent her life examining violins in her father's workshop but had never held a Stradivarius. Each evening she quizzed Seamus about the craftsmanship of the instrument. She knew this opportunity to study it would advance his technique enormously.

'At least there's one single Brit good for something,' Seamus said when he returned one evening with measurements and templates of the English officer's priceless instrument.

As Seamus only had access to the violin for five nights before the officer returned to Ireland, he spent every moment of his free time scrutinising it. He studied its curves, twists and turns. He examined the patina of its varnish and considered the possible constituents of Stradivari's long-lost varnish recipe.

With Seamus's next completed violin, Betty persuaded him to enter the instrument-making category of the Royal Dublin Society's craft competitions. She hoped some of his focus would shift from his fanciful nationalist obsession to a more profitable worthwhile one. Initially he was reluctant until she volunteered to enter it for him. When he won first prize he was dumbfounded and grateful his wife had suggested it.

'I told you,' she reiterated. 'You're gifted.'

Inspired by his win, Seamus worked harder at his craft. Betty watched as he compared his old violins to the newer ones. He made comparisons with the weight of the newer violins, he studied the improved interior, the peg-box and strings. He attended music sessions in neighbouring houses to test the sound. Occasionally he made adjustments.

To Seamus a violin or any musical instrument made from wood was almost a living thing. 'It's a tool filled with wild nature, its God-given elements waiting to be released.'

When he made such outlandish statements, Betty pretended to

agree with him. She had never given any instrument that much thought. She was more interested in the value, particularly the value of her husband's violins.

Although the city was crowded with people of every description, there were times when Betty was lonely. She'd wish there was a house where she could call and drink tea by the stove with a friend. It was the simple pleasures of familiar neighbours that she missed. She was friendless and lonely.

One morning when Ursula arrived, Betty was reminded again how much her life lacked the gaiety and busyness that was ever-present in her cousin's life.

'I feel so neglected with a husband who's more concerned with freeing Ireland than freeing me from this squalor!' she moaned to Ursula.

Instead of responding frivolously as Betty expected, Ursula suggested that she could 'do her part'. She said: 'Coming together is the beginning and working together will bring us closer to our objectives.'

Betty almost laughed aloud at Ursula's gullible pretentious words – she was sounding as big an eejit as Seamus.

'You should consider joining the Cumann na mBan after your delivery,' Ursula said, referring to the Irish Republican women's organisation.

Betty was about to dismiss the idea when it occurred to her that she might meet women with whom she could make friends. It would be wonderful to have a girlfriend who'd like to go to Wynn's Hotel for tea on a Friday. Or to go to a picture house when Seamus abandoned her for his military activities.

'What does it involve?' she asked. It would be worth pretending to be another misguided fool trying to free Ireland if she could develop a few friendships outside of her disease-riddled tenement abode.

'It's a support network for the Irish Volunteers. We fundraise by knitting or sewing or arranging dances.'

Betty couldn't help thinking that Ursula was as impressed with her own little role against the Empire as Seamus was. Why did all those republicans think they were the bee's knees? It must be the element of danger, she mused.

'We also attend lectures, we do courses and give training in first-aid and other such matters.'

Immediately Betty knew those women were too dedicated to idle away an afternoon in Wynn's or attend the theatre.

'No, thank you. It sounds as if it's brimming with old fogies.'

'Then you should join the Irish Citizen Army. Gender is irrelevant and it's increasingly popular with women. They partake in route marches lasting up to sixteen miles, rifle practice, and bomb-making.'

'Bomb-making?' Betty squealed. 'Dear Jesus, has this country gone mad?'

'Far from gone mad. At last it's getting organised.'

Ursula went on to tell her about the importance of the Volunteers educating as many men as possible. Betty switched off. She was tired of fighting talk from the men, their plotting and planning late into the night. Now Ursula sounded as if she too was gone simple.

For the remaining weeks of Betty's pregnancy, she found the strain of her growing bump more cumbersome. Rather than taking her long daily walks and jaunts on the tram, she remained close to Abbey Street and the confines of her own home.

The more she saw of the Dublin women's lives, the more alienated she felt. Each Monday morning, she saw them gathered outside the pawnbroker's with their coveted possessions. They chatted openly as if it were a social event rather than the humiliation of queuing for money in exchange for their meagre belongings. There was no shame in their poverty. Armed with their overcoats, clocks, picture frames or anything that would give them credit to eat for the week, their destitution unified them. People had so little it horrified her, yet gradually she was captivated by their resourcefulness. They talked about the bargains – where they could buy sheep's heads, rabbits, fish-heads, pigs' feet, pigs' cheeks, winkles and eels at the best prices. Their clothes were second-hand, bought in the Iveagh Market. The older children were sent to the bakery to buy stale bread at a cheaper price. On the street below she watched the children playing in rags, some without shoes, kicking a football made of paper and covered with an old sock. The jobless men killed time by playing cards on the street and passing a cigarette from hand to hand.

Each evening, when Betty heard Sheila Muldoon trudge down the stairs and Mary O'Keeffe bang her door closed, she knew it was time to pull her own chair to the open window to eavesdrop on the saga of their ongoing lives. Betty learned the names of all of the families and tit-bits of gossip from her eavesdropping. The ladies shared Woodbine cigarettes and clay pipes hidden under their shawls. Smoking in public was not acceptable for any class of woman and Betty was amused they took such delight in their covert smoking habits.

Sheila Muldoon always had a few extra Woodbines on account of her decent income. Kitty Doran said it was easy for Sheila to have the few extra cigarettes when her husband was a turncoat off fighting with the Brits in the Great War.

'You know the King's Penny paid for that smoke,' Kitty Doran reminded the women.

'He can keep paying for me smokes and this Saturday night he can pay for a few bottles of stout too,' Sheila quipped.

Mary Burke said Kitty Doran was a fine one to be calling someone else's husband a turncoat when her own husband was a 'scab' for breaking the Workers Strike during the 1913 Lockout. 'He did worse than take the King's Penny – he took the penny out of his neighbour's pocket and that deprived his neighbour's very own children of food in their hungry mouths.'

Patricia Mooney said Mary Burke was a fine one to be talking about taking the bit of food out of someone else's mouth. When it was Mary Burke's turn to feed the four orphaned McCarthy children, she fed them 'worse slop than you'd feed the pigs in the pen at the back of the house'. Sheila Muldoon happened to be in the McCarthys' home and saw it with her own eyes. Mary Burke turned puce when she knew she was caught. The four McCarthy orphans had lost their parents and six siblings to tuberculosis. The women took turns feeding them.

Patricia Mooney said the women should forget about the horrors of the Lockout. Peggy Moore said it was easy for Patricia Mooney to say that when she had four fine sons bringing home four fine wage packets from the fertiliser factory.

Although Mary Burke said she wouldn't call them 'fine' any more. 'They looked right peculiar when the four of them stood together for Sunday Mass.' All of the women agreed. The dust from shovelling the fertiliser in the factory had made them go as bald as eggs and the teeth fall out of their heads.

Sheila Muldoon suggested that Patricia Mooney's oldest son was 'a fella with queer tendencies on account of him being seen with Matt Be Nimble' who was known for being a man who liked men.

Betty made a note to take a good look at Patricia's son when she saw him again. She'd never seen a man with tendencies for other men, although she had heard references to the *leath-buachail*, the 'half-man'.

'Nonsense! Everyone calls to Matt Be Nimble,' Mona Daly said. 'Even Mick Daly calls to his house and there's nothing quare about his tendencies!'

The women laughed uproariously, agreeing that her husband was not a man who fancied men, after fathering eight children.

For all of their bickering, jealousies and petty feuds, Betty noticed how united the women were. Their tight-knit community was as solid as any rural community. Their charity to each other was infinite, as if sharing the daily brutality lessened the impact.

Betty was always curious about what Mona had to say. She seemed to be the head bottle-washer at the evening gatherings. When it rained the women sat on the steps outside her room, and they rarely went to the Rosary without her. They always consulted her about the bargains they got in the markets or about their problems. Several times she overheard whispering outside the Daly door. Mona was the group confidante. The close proximity of Mona's room was strangely reassuring for Betty.

Ursula faithfully called twice a week. Sometimes she was coming off an early shift from work and would arrive with fresh scones, other times she was on her way to meet a pal for an outing. To escape Dublin, she regularly went to Wicklow and Kildare with some of her many friends. Her active and independent life oozed with everything Betty wanted.

With each visit Betty always made a point of asking after Dr O'Malley. *Her friend* met some of his friends for a picnic at the Blessington Lakes, Ursula told her. The men fished while the women sat in the shade reading and chatting. Most of those present had motor cars.

Betty was enthralled. Dr O'Malley must be Protestant, she deduced. There was no way a Catholic group would tolerate one of their friends having an affair. They'd suggest that the adulterer should go to Confession and stop his carry-on. If that failed, the sinner would be ostracised by his own people and finally made leave town and start afresh.

On Holy Thursday evening Ursula called and, when she was leaving, she promised to check in on Betty over the weekend.

'If it's possible,' she whispered to Betty and squeezed her hand in a secretive manner. 'I could have a prior engagement.' She made it sound romantic and mysterious.

Immediately Betty thought Ursula was going to confess that she was in fact the nurse with whom Dr O'Malley was having an adulterous affair.

'With whom?' Betty asked, beside herself with anticipation.

'Something important is going to happen in the city over the weekend. The Irish Republicans have planned important manoeuvres,' Ursula confided.

Annoyed, Betty dismissed her ludicrous talk.

She never could have envisaged what Easter 1916 would bring.

Chapter 5

Early on Easter Monday, the 24th of April, Seamus woke Betty. When she opened her groggy eyes she saw him standing mutely at the door to the bedroom wearing his Volunteer uniform. It seemed as if he was about to speak but instead he came and sat beside her on the bed. He told her he was going on military manoeuvres. He explained that he might not be back for a few days. She was not to worry and should send a message to Ursula if she needed anything urgently.

She mumbled her response before closing her eyes again. It was too early in the morning to hear such talk. At least Seamus understood how she felt. He claimed she had been brought up to a more well-appointed life than most Irish people. Republicanism was not in her blood or her family's history. She had less cause for anger or retribution.

He tucked her long hair behind her ear.

'My beautiful wilful wife,' he sighed. 'This morning is the only time I've ever reconsidered my role. I don't want to worry you ...' His voice trailed off.

'Yes?' she said without opening her eyes.

'From the moment I joined the Volunteers a few days after moving to Dublin, I knew I was going into battle.' His voice was soft and soothing. 'My membership alone was my commitment.'

'I know,' she said.

'"*Life springs from death, and from the graves of patriot men and women spring living nations.*" I will think of Pearse's lines over the coming days.'

'Yes, do that,' she mumbled.

He then whispered two lines of a Yeats' poem into her ear:

'*We rode in sadness above Lough Lean,*
For our best were dead on Gavra's green.'

He kissed her on the forehead before leaving.

Seamus had successfully dealt with his only reservation about the war he and his comrades were about to begin.

Betty listened to Seamus trudge down the stairs. She knew he believed that what he was doing was important but she wished he was taking her to the races in Fairyhouse or the spring show in the RDS. Anything would have been better than the unseasonal heat of the city and a husband running about as if he and his friends were going to banish British rule.

For most of the day she sat by the open window, fanning her face. She wanted to open the door to allow a draught but was afraid of encouraging Mona Daly or Sheila Muldoon to arrive in on top of her. She killed time by trying to determine the sex of her baby by holding a needle and thread over the palm of her hand. The old wives' tale deemed a circular motion a girl and diagonal motion a boy. Five times the needle and thread indicated a girl and twice a boy.

During the afternoon, Betty was unsure if she heard thunder or an explosion. Later she learned it was the first aggression of the Rising. The rebels had blown up the Magazine Fort in the Phoenix Park. During the day she could hear cheering and great joviality from the women converged at the front door. For once she regretted not being part of the crew of women sitting on the steps who sounded so animated. Betty popped her head out the window for a better look.

Sheila Muldoon spotted her and called up to her to join them, 'Come on down to us, Betty! 'Tis all happening today! The rebels have raised the Irish flag on the GPO!'

Betty noticed Mona sitting among the women. She was too busy conversing with the passers-by to look up.

Betty closed the window. She spent the remainder of the day reading and prowling about her kitchen.

When she woke on Tuesday morning alone in her bed, she lay there sincerely hoping Seamus hadn't been part of the fracas. By Tuesday evening she was tempted to call to one of the other women to hear the news.

As she felt the first twinges of labour pains, she could hear gunfire. That night she slept fitfully. In her hand she held her rosary beads. With every twinge of pain, she invoked Our Lady and all the saints in heaven to bring her husband home and make the pain stop. The baby was not due for another few weeks. She cursed her rushed marriage to Seamus Hopkins and her naivety for thinking life in Dublin would offer her glamour and sophistication. She longed for the closeness of sitting around the turf fire late at night, the thick milk, her mother's homemade soda cake, salting the bacon and hanging it from the rafters, and sweet water in the spring well.

By Wednesday morning the pain was unbearable. She wiped the sweat from her brow and thought about leaving a Seamus a note: she was convinced God would take her by the end of the day. That afternoon, when the shelling of the GPO from the gunboat *Helga* began in earnest, the pain increased. Betty realised there was no hope of Ursula, Dublin's version of Florence Nightingale, travelling across the city.

Mona tapped lightly on the door. 'How'ya, Betty love? Are you a'right?'

Betty was clutching her stomach by the basin, unable to keep the tears at bay. 'Yes, I'm fine,' she groaned.

Mona rattled the door handle aggressively. 'Betty love, open the door now!' she said in the same tone she used when reprimanding her children.

Betty opened the door enough to see Mona's gappy smile.

'Thought I'd say hello, in your condition and all.'

'Make the pain stop,' Betty pleaded.

Mona soothed Betty as they paced the kitchen. When the time came she gently guided her to the bed where she had spread papers.

'It'll be over before you know it,' she said, pretending.

'I think I'm dying,' Betty gasped. 'The pain shouldn't be this bad. I know there's something wrong!'

'Whisht your whinging – it'll give the baby a harelip.' Softening, Mona added, 'It'll all be over in no time.'

As Betty's pain and birthing shrieks spiralled, so too did the gunfire. That Wednesday afternoon, the 24th of April, as she gave birth to her daughter, the GPO was hit with heavy artillery, fires raged and Dublin descended into its most destructive day of warfare.

Betty raised her head to see Mona's face as she scrutinised the infant. Her dark face creased into a big smile, revealing the three single teeth protruding from her gums like withered stakes from cracked red earth.

'She's all there,' Mona said. 'She has ten little fingers and ten little toes and a fine crown of fair curly hair.'

Day drifted into night and night extended into one long nightmare for Betty. The horror of the birth and her soreness was as wearing as the final days of pregnancy, only now the life she had borne terrorised her as much as Seamus's disappearance. When the baby cried she despaired at how to make her stop. With trembling hands, she lifted her to her sore breast and fed her as best she could, grateful that nobody could witness her poor attempts at motherhood. When the baby slept Betty willed the street below to be silent while she almost held her breath, afraid the sound of her breathing would wake her. She was in terror of the crying and feeding and winding process.

When the baby slept, Betty was left with her own thoughts. Where was Seamus? What was to become of her and her child?

Several times she thought she heard his step on the stairs, only to be disappointed. The only way she could sleep was if she told herself that Seamus would have returned by the time she woke: he would be standing at the end of the bed.

Sadly, Seamus never materialised. Her mother had said it would all end in tears and it had.

The only soul who alleviated her worry was Mona. Good old sensible Mona took to breezing in and out of Betty's kitchen. Mona was Betty's saviour and respite from the terror of her own worsening imaginings. At night she knew she'd feel better when Mona called in the morning, and she was consoled that Mona's room was right next door to hers. When the uncertainty became unbearable during the long hours of the night, she imagined Mona sleeping on the other side of the wall, right next to her bed. Mona was her only hope of a life-raft when she felt each morning she was sinking deeper into a newfound mire of despair, widowed and shamed.

'How did you get on last night?' Mona would ask.

'Very well,' Betty would lie. 'I fed her every two hours.'

She was barely mastering the feeding and making a poor job of winding whereas Mona brought with her a confidence and graciousness that she envied. She marvelled at Mona's experienced hands picking up the crying child and expertly changing her nappy without a grimace. Without Betty ever airing her fears, Mona seemed to sense her anxiety.

'There's no book that tells you how to be a ma,' she often said. 'You're doin' fine.'

Betty would try to think of something motherly and meaningful to add, but no profound words would come.

'Betty love, in a few days it'll be easier and by next week you'll be so good at it you'll be ready to have another one,' Mona said playfully.

Mona was forever rushing from one chore to another. She'd arrive hurriedly, apologising for not staying long before rushing off again about her business. Betty knew it was selfish but each time she thought Mona had a few extra moments to spare she'd try to coax her to stay longer. She'd offer her tea and some of her dwindling food supplies, and once she offered sherry.

'God bless the house that can keep sherry,' Mona said, amused.

'It's nice to have it in the house,' Betty said, thinking of her mother and how she always had sherry and whiskey to offer. 'For visitors or unexpected callers.'

'In this part of Ireland you'd be lucky to have food for your children, not to mind sherry for callers!' Mona quipped. 'Country people are a strange lot.'

During her visits, Mona told Betty little titbits of information about her own childhood in Meath Street. Mona's father was a labourer when he could get work. She knew hunger and poverty as a child.

Mona left school at nine and, apart from writing her name, she was illiterate.

'I'd like to know how to read,' she confessed. 'There's always signs up in the shops and me young ones have to read them out to me. At least me children can read and write and do their sums. Maybe I'll learn when all the children are reared, and me and Mick Daly are auld and grey and sick to death of lookin' at the sight of each other. Mind you, Mick Daly can read and write – not well but he can get by.'

When Mona referred to her husband, she always included his surname.

Mick Daly was so black from working on the coal round he looked like a black man from the depths of Africa. Betty couldn't imagine how long he'd need to soak in water to find his white skin. But, during those uncertain days Betty almost wished she could move into Mona's crowded home with Mick Daly and the infinite layers of coal dust covering his skin. She'd have liked to stay under Mona's stoic arm for the rest of her days. Occasionally she would ask herself how her life had become so terrifyingly bleak that she enjoyed the company of a coarse woman from the Dublin slums. But, regardless of what Mona was, Betty never needed anyone more than she needed her for those few days. She brought reassurance and common sense and Betty tried to soak up anything that would rescue her.

By Friday morning Betty's food finally ran out.

Mona shared what little supplies she had. 'Sorry, love, it's the best I could do,' she said, leaving a bowl of watery stirabout on the table. 'Everything is closed in the city. No milk or butter or bread. Not a thing can be got.'

'What about the Volunteers?' Betty asked, wishing for news of Seamus. 'Are they in trouble?'

'Volunteers?' Mona scoffed. 'Every woman in Dublin is fit to kill those eejits.' She told Betty how the public had turned against the rebels. 'Sheila Muldoon and all those wives and mothers can't collect their Separation Allowance. They're starving.'

Betty thought about the thousands of families whose husbands, fathers and sons were fighting in the trenches in France, their families in Ireland dependent on their weekly allowance collected in the GPO. Unable to get provisions or leave their homes for the last few days, it was no wonder the Dubliners were gunning for the so-called Volunteers.

Each snippet of news increased Betty's anguish. What had become of Seamus? They were so principled and selfless in their quest and so foolhardy and naïve. None of them could have foreseen the outcome.

'It's unlikely we'll be able to leave our homes for another week. Everything is shut down,' Mona said. 'Mick Daly couldn't go to work these last few days. If he doesn't get out from under my feet soon, I'll shoot him myself.'

Betty forced back the welling tears. What was to become of her baby? A fatherless child raised in such poverty? Mona Daly's and Sheila Muldoon's children would know a wealth her baby would never see. The mouth-watering cakes in Noblett's window on Sackville Street and the grand hats and frocks in Clerys had given her notions, unchristian greedy notions. God had other plans. Was this part of his plan?

The dying flames of burning buildings danced in the distance, suffusing the kitchen with a surreal orange glow.

Betty questioned Mona about one of her limited options. 'Where is the poorhouse?' she asked her.

During the night Betty had been thinking about the poorhouse. As a means of survival it seemed like a reasonable option for a woman whose husband had disappeared and had probably been killed. At least she would be fed and safe. She could retreat there for a few weeks or months with her daughter until she thought of something else.

'There's only a few left in Dublin. There are two in the city and one out in the country.'

'Do they let anyone in?' Betty asked.

'As long as you can work, you can walk right on through the doors. In the poorhouse there's little else to do only work, then go to Mass and do what you're told.'

'That's not too bad,' Betty said.

Mona looked at her incredulously. 'It's like hell on earth. Families are separated, women are at one side and men the other side. Even the children aren't spared – they work until they're sick or dead. It makes the tenements seem like a walk on a sunny strand.'

Betty was horrified. 'Did you ever know anybody who went to the workhouse?' she asked.

'There was a family from Summerhill who went into one. Mick Daly said he saw the father after a couple a months and he was like a ghost. He said they starved him and treated him worse than an animal. They work from sunrise to sunset for their bed and barely enough to survive. He never saw a drop of milk when he was in there – it's all buttermilk! They say the wife got a hunchback from polishing floors. Ever after the poor woman would get crazy if she smelled a certain type of floor polish that she used in the poorhouse. She was mental in the end. That's what Mick Daly said.'

Betty's face fell. What was she to do?

'Betty love, you're not that hard up,' Mona said after a few moments. 'You should be more concerned about getting churched by the priest and your baby christened as quick as be damned.'

Betty hadn't given a thought to any of this or even considered a name for the child. At the moment surviving seemed more of a priority.

Mona added, 'If this bloody uprising ever ends. Don't know what's to become of this godforsaken town. Clerys and the Imperial Hotel have crashed to the ground – the fires are still burning.'

'Are we safe?' Betty asked.

''Tis the fires we can't see that worry me – the inferno in our own men is fiercer than burning buildings.'

Betty watched Mona's tough face by the window, her hooded eyes looking uneasily onto the street. Although she wasn't very much wrinkled, the lines she had were deep, like gullies etched on the weather-beaten earth.

'Boys will be boys is all well and good except it's not much good for us left without food,' Mona said in an unusually quiet tone.

They remained silent, both thinking about their destroyed city, the loss of life and uncertainty.

Mona broke the silence by speaking in the same quiet tone. 'The Brits are searching every house for any man they think is a Sinn Féiner.'

Betty's eyes opened wide in surprise.

'Listen to me, Betty – if them Brits come, be sure to tell them that your husband is fighting the Germans in Flanders.'

Mutely, Betty nodded.

'You don't want them blasted fellas coming back a second time and finding anyone,' Mona warned. 'Especially now when they're bloodthirsty for revenge.'

Betty understood the implications. Throughout the last few days Mona had never asked where Seamus was. The silence between them confirmed what was not spoken.

When Betty retired to bed, her mind raced with anxiety for her daughter. What would become of them? She thought of Seamus's unsold violins. Most were finished with the final layer of varnish and ready for sale. Not for the first time it crossed her mind to find out how much they were worth. Quickly she dispelled the idea. Selling his violins was a ludicrous idea. She thought of the bookcase in the good room at home in Tipperary. One shelf was devoted to books her kindly uncle, a priest in England, sent to her mother. One such book was by his friend Fr Bernard O'Reilly: *The Mirror of True Womanhood.*

It said: '*No woman animated by the spirit of baptism ever fancied that she had or could have any other sphere of duty than that home which is her domain, her garden, her paradise, her world.*'

The only women comfortable wheeling and dealing were the flower sellers by Nelson's Pillar and the fruit sellers on Moore Street. She was not that kind of woman.

Returning to Tipperary would probably be an easier solution than facing the rest of her life working eleven-hour days weaving baskets or making rosary beads in the poorhouse. Her mother and aunts would never allow her to forget her final act of defiance, but at least in Tipperary she could grow old with fresh air, good food and a healthier form of hardship than ending up like Mona's friend with a curved spine from polishing floors. Beside Betty's bed was her prayer book, the Nine-Day Novena tucked within its pages. She'd begin a novena in the morning. Nothing less than a nine-day novena to St Jude, the Patron of Hopeless Cases. She'd fast too. She'd only take bread and water. She'd offer it all up, she'd offer up any suffering to save her from a life of destitution. With every spare moment she would pray and plead and implore every saint in heaven to help her find a solution.

Chapter 6

Mona arrived on Saturday evening, bursting with news.

'It's all over,' she declared, clunking down a large pail of water. 'All the rebels surrendered.'

Betty got to her feet. 'Are there many alive?'

'There were a few hundred of them arrested and the Brits made every last one of them parade down Grafton Street to disgrace them. Some of the women threw rotten vegetables at them and called them "starvers of people".' Mona paused to catch her breath. 'Mick Daly said they'd their chests out, not a bit ashamed of the caper they caused.'

'A few hundred men,' Betty asked, hoping Seamus would be among the living.

'Yes, a few hundred men and one woman. That Constance Markievicz was dressed in a man's uniform. When she surrendered she made a big show of kissing her revolver before handing it over. Can you imagine the boldness? Kissing her gun! 'Tis only a mad English toff would go on like that.'

'She's Anglo-Irish, Mona, not English.' Betty had heard before about the flamboyant lady from Sligo who had been presented to Queen Victoria as a girl and had married a Polish count in Paris.

'Same thing if you ask me!'

'What will happen to her?' Betty asked.

'Only God knows. At least now we'll be able to get back to normal.' Mona looked at the baby as she slept soundly. 'Did you rest?'

'She woke three times and didn't want to feed or sleep. I don't know what was wrong with her.'

'Yes, I heard her crying,' Mona admitted. 'I was going to come in to you but I was afraid I'd frighten the living daylights out of you. I'm scary enough during the day, never mind at night.'

Betty was too preoccupied with her troubles to enjoy Mona's humour. She only got respite from her worry for fleeting seconds, then Seamus's absence tumbled on top of her like an impending death sentence.

'We'll have to get her baptised as soon as possible,' Mona said, all business as she sat the baby on her lap. 'When is your friend, the lovely stout priest from Tipperary, callin' again?'

'I don't know,' Betty said honestly.

'We don't want any more babies going into Limbo and we'll need to get you churched too.' Mona nodded vigorously.

Betty recalled her mother and aunts discussing the churching of women after giving birth. She never knew what it meant, only that churching was as necessary as christening an infant according to her mother.

'Mona, why must women be churched?' Betty asked out of curiosity and hoping to delay her a little longer.

'It's thanksgiving and asking God to make you a pure woman again.'

'Am I impure for having my daughter?' Betty asked as she put a kettle on the stove.

'Yes – you're not really pure till you go to Fr Higgins, or your friend Fr Mathew and he'll make it right in the eyes of God.

'But I didn't do anything wrong,' Betty said. 'I've done what was natural.'

Mona considered it. 'You'll be tainted till you go to the priest with your candle and renounce the Devil and all his works.' She could see Betty was still confused. 'It'll make you a good Catholic again,' she said, thinking Betty should be happy with that explanation.

'But I never stopped being a Catholic,' Betty objected.

Impatiently Mona said, 'Just go to Fr Higgins and don't question it.' Emphatically she added, 'Whatever you do, don't go asking him what it's all about or talking about natural things and impurity. He roared the head off Deirdre Nolan when she went to Confession and said she wouldn't lay with her husband any more cos she didn't want any more babies.'

'What?' Betty looked at her incredulously.

'Yes, and Fr Higgins sent her home to do her duty and told her never in a million years to darken his confessional with such a sin against God.'

Betty had forgotten about the implications of making love to Seamus. It was not God but the act that would send her more children, and more and more until there would not be enough food to feed them. Their long shared nights of pleasure were far removed from her current crisis. In the unlikely event of Seamus's survival, there would be more nights where they could enjoy the intimacies of marriage. Accordingly, her home would fill to the brim like Mona's with children and mouths to feed. She too would be dividing her home with sheets draped across the room for stolen moments of privacy with her husband. It was a greater injustice than the O'Sheas being evicted because the owner of the house wanted it as a tuck shop. The tenement family problems were becoming her problems. The invisible wall that Betty thought rigidly separated them from her was dissolving fast, and she was one of them now. Her years ahead loomed like an eternal torrential downpour. The saying '*The Church is a good mother but a hard mother,*' resonated with her.

Mona noticed Betty's perturbed expression. 'I know. Deirdre Nolan was always forward. Imagine her thinking she could control such matters, not to mind looking for absolution for a sin she hadn't yet committed. That's a bigger sin than committing the sin and then looking for absolution after it's done.'

'Did she have more children?' Betty asked.

'No, she done somethin' far worse – she went to see a nurse on the North Circular Road who tells you how to stop havin' babies.'

Seamus still didn't come home. Nor did he come on Sunday. Betty's worst fears were being realised.

On Monday morning she counted the remaining money tucked in the back of her suitcase. There was enough to pay two weeks' rent. She needed to find a solution or else she could be joining the Dubliners queuing for the pawnbroker's. Maybe she could get a job. Fr Mathew might know someone who could assist. She could get a job in an office. If she wrote to her father he would furnish her with a letter of recommendation. She knew how to manage his office – she had bookkeeping skills, shorthand, and excellent handwriting – something most women did not have. Surely she could survive without returning home? Could she manage her own life in this turbulent world? Lesser women than her had managed. She would have to find a solution – all this dithering was wasting precious time.

Rather than allowing her home to imprison her, Betty decided to get fresh air to buoy her faith and help her think. At least the streets were safe again, she thought as she walked down Middle Abbey Street, her baby held close to her chest. She walked to Sackville Street and joined the city dwellers who were cautiously emerging from their days of confinement to find a city so decimated that they were all shocked by a scene they would remember till their dying day. The crumbling buildings and smouldering fires transfixed her. The windows were smashed on every shopfront; there were mountains of rubble clogging the pavement. At her feet was a lump of molten metal with bits of glass embedded in it. It seemed as deadly as the madness that had engulfed the city. Betty imagined that the Europeans in the thick of the Great War must find similar sights each day. She hoped not; she hoped no person would ever wake to find their city so annihilated. The streets were thronged with people, the air of hysteria tangible. There were Red Cross nurses whizzing by on bicycles, their white cap-ends floating behind, giving them a magical other-worldly quality. There were carts carrying dead horses, fire brigades, ambulances, harried priests rushing by to prepare the sick for death. All fervent in their acts of mercy.

'It's like the end of the world,' a man said, echoing Betty's thoughts.

Beneath her feet she noticed drops of blood, dark stains leading onto the road. She allowed her eyes to follow the path of blood. A few feet away there was a large dark stain. It was as if a man had lain and leaked blood until death found him.

It was all too much to take in. Her fear for her husband, the anxiety of not knowing where he was or what had happened to him made her feel weak. Her sense of urgency to escape became overwhelming but every ounce of strength seemed to evaporate. She leaned against the nearby wall. She needed food, a meal as good as her own mother would provide, sustenance that would keep her strength up. Aware she hadn't eaten a proper meal for almost a week, Betty resolved to find an open butcher's and fill her saucepan with good meat and plenty of it. Her mouth watered when she thought about a large satisfying bowl of coddle, a traditional Dublin dish. She'd buy a variety of meat, potatoes and vegetables. For once she'd dip into the money hidden in her suitcase. The thought of preparing the meal would occupy her mind for a few hours. At least she would think better on a full stomach.

Betty noticed the confident swagger of an approaching man. He swung his ornamental walking cane, oblivious to the carnage of his surroundings. He was a strange dot of elegance among the mountains of rubble and the decimated city. There was something vaguely familiar about him; his gait and shape were distinct. Suddenly it dawned on her. Betty turned her back and tilted her hat to hide her eyes. She would recognise him anywhere. Only a man like Mr Hartmann could be immune to Ireland's crisis. His Jewishness kept him neutral and line of business kept him earning. The Americans, who were not as affected by the World War or Ireland's crisis, would continue to be Mr Hartmann's main buyers. As he approached, Betty could hear the click of his shoes. She watched him pass her by.

Betty was breathless when the thought occurred to her: Mr Hartmann would be her saviour.

Mona confessed that she thought she was hallucinating when she smelled the food. On the table in Betty's kitchen was the finest saucepan of coddle she had seen in ages.

Betty was stirring another big saucepan on the stove. 'You can take this pot in to your family,' she said, 'and hopefully there will be enough for all of you. There might even be enough here for the McCarthy orphans.'

'Jesus, there's enough here for my lot and the McCarthys for the rest of the week!' Mona gasped, staring into the large saucepan bubbling with oodles of meat, rashers, sausages, thick broth and vegetables. 'Ah, surely you can't afford to give all this away!'

'I didn't buy it,' Betty lied. 'I met an old acquaintance of my family on Sackville Street this afternoon. He knew how affected we were due to the uprising and insisted on buying me some food.'

Mona looked at her agog before finding her voice, 'God bless him and all belonging to him and his decency!'

'I need a letter delivered to Mr Hartmann's shop on College Green,' Betty said. 'Will your young fella be able to do it? I'll pay him.'

Mona dipped a spoon into the pot to taste the coddle. 'There's eatin' and drinkin' in that pot!' She hollered for her son. 'No need to pay him – money is scarce.'

'I'm calling to see the same man and his wife at some stage tomorrow. Do you think you might be able to look after my little one for an hour or so?'

Mona looked at Betty's exhausted face. Although she continued to dress as if each day presented her with an occasion, the city was etching its mark on her already. The young fresh-faced beautiful girl who had moved in a few months ago was disappearing fast.

'Don't be doing too much – it's still early days for you,' Mona said. 'Course I'll look after herself.' She hoisted the pot from the stove, and made for the door, then hesitated and turned back. 'My sister's husband was one of the rebels in Boland's Mill. He came home safely to her last night.'

Betty acknowledged what Mona had said without admitting Seamus's involvement. 'Anything is possible,' she said, only for something to say.

The families of the arrested and the dead were being informed by the authorities. That was Betty's only evidence to suggest that Seamus was alive.

Chapter 7

When Betty stepped over the threshold into Mr Hartmann's shop she felt as if she had left behind the troubles of Dublin. The cool interior gleamed with polished musical instruments. There was no suggestion of the war-ravaged city on his doorstep. Betty compared Seamus's violin to the items within the many glass showcases. She knew the tools used on each item. She could hear the hum of the saws in her father's workshop and smell the gathering sawdust. The last violin Seamus had made for her father was on sale. She recognised the varnish – it was slightly redder than the violin next to it. When she looked she saw her father's label with his initial and surname, tagged to the inside lining. Seamus had been working on that very item when she slipped him a note agreeing to marry him. They had arranged to meet secretly later that day and finalise their plans. So much had been lost since then. If Seamus had been spared, he could have gone to great heights with his talent rather than dying in vain for a country that would always be a small rebellious dot on the Empire's map.

The shop boy led Betty into a backroom with bookshelves from floor to ceiling. She refused to be intimidated by her surroundings. In preparation for her appointment she had scrubbed her body from head to toe and washed her hair three times, hoping to rinse the wreckage of the last week from every pore in her body. It was more than just the last week that she wanted to wash away – she wanted to wash away any suggestion of desperation. She wore her best jacket and skirt, with her new blouse fixed at the neck with a little gold-and-pearl brooch. On her many afternoons in the Gresham she had noticed the ladies wore small delicate brooches rather than large cheap trinkets. She was careful to lightly dust her face with powder and only apply the smallest amount of rouge.

Mr Hartmann stood to greet her. 'Miss O'Fogarty,' he said, 'I was so pleased to receive your note that you wished to see me. What brings you to Dublin?'

Over tea Betty remained affable yet business-like. She explained that she was now Mrs Hopkins and was living in Dublin with her new husband.

Mr Hartmann interrupted her. 'I hope you were not affected by the dreadful mêlée during the week?'

'Well, actually, that is one of the reasons I'm calling to see you,' Betty said. 'My new husband is Seamus Hopkins – the luthier who worked for my father and who made the violin in your display cabinet.'

'Oh yes, he won the Royal Dublin Society's craft competition in the instrument-making category this year, did he not?'

'He did indeed.'

'Congratulations on your marriage, Mrs Hopkins. Your father must be so proud.'

'Of course he's delighted,' she said, irked that he was distracting her from her rehearsed proposal. 'Well, my poor husband was hit with a stray bullet the day the fighting began. Our home in St Stephen's Green was badly damaged but thankfully I was not harmed. My husband is recovering with our friends in Ranelagh.' She was thinking of the nice houses where Fr Mathew was a priest. She did not want to mention the birth of her daughter as that would distract from her main objective.

'How awful! You poor, poor child! You must have been terrified.'

Betty noticed the concern in his large brown eyes and the way his black moustache turned down with worry. She was mildly touched. Then she thought of Seamus's pieces selling for five times the price her father received and became less emotional.

She brushed off her husband's injury as a minor inconvenience. 'Yes, but thankfully the city has resumed normal life and all that palaver is done with.'

He agreed with her. Betty noticed how he remained neutral. He didn't either criticise the Volunteers or suggest the British should relinquish power.

'Actually, I'm here on business,' Betty went on. 'My husband has produced some fine pieces since we moved to Dublin. He was going to call to see you himself except I've forbidden him to leave the house until he is fine and fit again.'

Mr Hartmann listened without commenting. It was as if his conviviality was tucked in a drawer until he needed it again. Betty was aware that he was a shrewd businessman.

'I brought you one of his violins to evaluate. Would you like to see it?'

'Please.' He indicated the table.

As he examined the craftsmanship he asked where the bullet had hit Seamus.

'In the leg.' Betty was not going to mention any part of the body that might affect his woodwork. She continued talking while he scrutinised the violin. 'I passed your shop a few times since I moved to Dublin. I also saw Mr de Lacy's on Stephen's Green.' She knew de Lacy was his main competitor.

She noticed him react to the mention of de Lacy's name. She had passed the shop and dawdled by the window. His stock was inferior and, unlike Mr Hartmann, he had little appreciation for the craft. While looking into the window, she had overheard two men, who were leaving the shop, commenting on how thin Mr de Lacy had become.

She continued, 'Mr de Lacy has lost a considerable amount of weight.'

On her Uncle Thomas's visits to her parents, she had often

overheard the adults gossiping. As Thomas's instrument business was well-established, he was privy to gossip in Dublin. Betty learned that Mr de Lacy and Mr Hartmann had been friends some years back but had had a huge row. It was rumoured that Mr de Lacy had approached Mr Hartmann's suppliers and offered them more money for their pieces. He had also instigated a rumour that Mr Hartmann regularly bought stolen instruments and resold them. Her uncle also referred to unforgivable gossip about Mr Hartmann's personal life. Her uncle wouldn't reveal anything while Betty was there. She guessed it had something to do with his sexual relations. Naturally Mr Hartmann and Mr de Lacy's friendship soured. Betty had never met Mr de Lacy.

'Oh, you've met him?' Mr Hartmann seemed surprised.

'I was acquainted with him through my uncle, Thomas O'Fogarty from O'Fogarty Instruments in Fairview.'

Mr Hartmann tilted his head slightly and looked at her thoughtfully. Each was gauging the other, their feelings disguised with affable smiling expressions.

'What would you like?' he asked.

Betty didn't answer immediately. She wanted to find common ground and build on it. When she had all of Seamus's six violins sold, she would go to her father and offer to fetch a higher price for the instruments crafted in his shop, even if it meant dealing with de Lacy rather than Hartmann. She would not perish in this godforsaken city. But Hartmann was the business associate she needed, with his expertise and reputation.

'I would like half of the price that you receive.'

'I couldn't do that. There are many expenses in my business – the upkeep of my shop, my trips abroad, my time examining prospective craftsmen.'

Betty continued as if he had not spoken. 'There are several more pieces almost finished, two of which are the most remarkable items to date. Your business will grow stronger from your affiliation with my husband's products. In fact,' Betty held his surprised gaze, 'I am a woman and I know my place – however, my husband is influenced

56

by my opinions. I will persuade my husband to deal only with you, Mr Hartmann,' she smiled, 'and you alone.'

Mr Hartmann finally sat back in his large chair with a slight grin. Betty was unable to establish if he was amused or deemed her bartering more vulgar than that of the women selling flowers at Nelson's Pillar.

'Mrs Hopkins, you are as rare and exquisite as your husband's finely crafted wood but, you may not have noticed, there is a war raging in Europe and our city has been destroyed. Money is short all over the world.'

'Your prices are the same now as they were when I first moved to Dublin,' Betty said.

He exhaled loudly. 'No, 50% is impossible.'

'Well, thank you for your time,' Betty said with a smile. She placed her handbag on her lap as if she was preparing to leave.

'However,' he began, 'I will give you 35% of the price.'

Betty listened.

'I will give you 25% of the price now for this violin.' He placed his hand on the violin, as if he had no intention of allowing it out of his possession.

Betty noticed his large clean hands and long fingers spanning the waist of the violin.

'I will give you the remaining 10% when I sell it. I will gladly do the same for each violin you bring me.'

'I think 45% is a more reasonable figure,' Betty gently coerced him.

'I couldn't possibly do that. At a stretch, 37%.'

It was turning into a game, Betty thought, as she smiled into his large dark eyes.

'Mr Hartmann, I'm too delicate to enter into this bargaining,' she sighed, 'but 40% is a more rounded figure. I will accept 25% now and 15% on the sale of the stock.'

He conceded with a discreet nod and smile.

Betty spent the remainder of the day elated. Her day was not only about receiving enough money to pay rent for weeks in advance, eat lavishly and take the train to Tipperary where she could reclaim the rest of Seamus's stock when she wanted – it was so much more. She had enjoyed selling the item, there was a thrill in her bargaining. To be honest, she had also enjoyed the way Mr Hartmann looked at her. It was a wonderful feeling to be appreciated in her finery, even if he was not her husband. She thought of Fr Bernard O'Reilly's book on *Instruction for Women in the World*. His Reverence warned against vanity. Women were warned against pleasing any eye other than that of their husband, or to value any praise on dress or personal appearance but what fell from his dear lips. Nor should a woman wish for any amusement that was not shared by her husband. Fr Bernard O'Reilly's concepts held little sway over Betty now.

Later that night she examined Seamus's remaining pieces that she had tucked safely into a corner of the bedroom. Five of the pieces were as immaculate as Mr Hartmann demanded his stock should be. There were a further two violins that required another coat of varnish. Betty would not dare touch them until later in the week when she was less exhausted. Even then she was not the right candidate to apply the final coat. Any flaw in the product would diminish their value.

Over the previous few days, Betty had heard that the Royal Irish Constabulary and British soldiers were raiding homes and taking anything of value. Rather than risking the loss of the violins, she knew she needed to hide them. On the landing outside her door there was a small cubbyhole. It was stuffed with useless items, including a cracked bucket, a single worn boot and a statue of Our Lady with one of her arms and her nose missing. Useless things nobody took responsibility for throwing out. Betty wrapped the violins in strips of an old sheet she had torn up and, in the dead of night, slid them as far inside the cubbyhole as possible. They fitted snugly and she cushioned them with straw and rags. Then she haphazardly arranged the other items in front of them. As an afterthought she stood the damaged statue in front and prayed that

Our Lady would protect the violins for her. At least they were warm and close enough so she'd hear if any of the neighbours went rooting in the cubbyhole.

With the violins safely hidden, she lay on the bed and drifted to sleep, content that she had more time to toy with a few ideas on her survival.

It was not yet bright outside when Betty woke with a start, still dressed in her clothes. Unsure what had woken her, she sat up and lit the lamp. In the street below she could hear horses' hooves and voices, then silence. She peeped in at her daughter who was sleeping contentedly in her cradle, her pale little fingers a contrast to the dark blanket. She was tempted to stroke her cheek but fear of waking her and enduring the penetrating sound of her cry was a greater deterrent.

Then Betty heard shuffling feet on the stairs. She left the bedroom and listened behind the kitchen door. She knew the door was locked but, nevertheless, she quietly retrieved a chair to wedge under the handle. She held her breath as she fumbled with the chair and willed the sound of feet to continue up the next flight of stairs.

The door was kicked twice. '*Missus, open up!*' a man whispered loudly.

Betty couldn't find her voice.

A second kick jolted her to react. 'Who are you?'

'Your husband is with us – he's injured,' came the whisper.

She discarded the chair and swung open her door. Seamus was propped up by two men. She wrapped her arms around him and clung to him until one of the men suggested they let him lie down. The two men helped him into the bedroom and sat him on the bed. In the lamplight she could see that he had a dirty bandage on his head and all three of them were covered in what looked like flour.

'It looks worse than it seems,' the taller man said.

'I'll be grand in the morning,' Seamus muttered, swaying. 'I need to sleep.'

Then he noticed the cradle by the bed. Betty picked up the baby and held her out to him. He brought his trembling finger to the baby's cheek.

'It's a girl,' Betty said regretfully.

'She brought us luck,' he smiled, alleviating Betty's anxiety that she had not given him a son.

One of the men helped her move the cradle to the kitchen before he returned to the bedroom to sleep. As Betty closed the bedroom door she saw Seamus was already asleep, his two comrades on either side of him.

Betty sat alone in the kitchen with her daughter in her arms and waited with impatience for her husband to rise.

She could not predict the role that Seamus's two sleeping comrades would play in her life and the future generations of her family.

Chapter 8

Tuesday 2nd May 1916

During the night while the men slept and between feeds for the baby, Betty dressed in the kitchen in one of her nicer blouses and skirts. She fastened a brooch with a sparkling green stone at the neck of the blouse. She wanted to appear fresh and unscathed for her husband.

She had been thinking of her agreement with Mr Hartmann. Now that Seamus had returned there would be no need to sell his violins or enter into an arrangement with Hartmann. It was not her place; Seamus would be her provider. A wife did not assess her husband's productivity any more than she interfered in his working day. Her role was as black and white as a woman not having a vote. Her voice would be her husband's; it was wrong to assume she was anything other than a homemaker. With Seamus's safe return she would resume her duties as his wife.

She was feeding the baby when one of the Volunteers emerged from the bedroom next morning. She was taken aback. The previous night she had been too overwhelmed with Seamus returning to take too much notice of the other men. Initially she thought the third man was very short but what stood before her was a child. A little boy covered in what looked like white flour. He looked a sight.

'We had to hide in a flour mill,' he said.

'You're only a boy,' Betty said, aghast. 'What kind of people employ the service of little children in war?'

'Ma'am, I'm eleven,' he said crossly.

Betty smiled at his indignation. She remained seated as she fed the baby.

'I'm big for my age.' He stuck his shoulders back and stretched his neck. 'I've been fighting with men,' he added, his voice high with elation.

Betty noticed he was indeed tall for his age, a cute little fellow with a mop of black hair, wide hazel eyes staring out from a pretty oval face.

'I'm a real soldier,' he said, then emphatically added, 'A *real* soldier fighting a *real* war.'

He stepped into boots that were several sizes too big. Betty watched as he dragged his feet across the room to the looking-glass by the window. He glanced at his reflection then began to dust his clothes with his hands.

'Use a wet cloth for your face and hands.' Betty pointed to the window where some were drying.

He poured some water into a pan, wet a cloth and began to wipe his face.

She found him captivating. After five restless nights and tentative days with her new baby, the boy's vigour was a breath of fresh air.

'What's your name?' she asked.

'Conleth Salmon, missus.'

'And where do you live, Conleth?'

'In the best part of the city,' he smiled. 'Thomas Street.'

From his answer she guessed he spent a lot of time with older men who gave a similar reply.

'Were you in the GPO during the shelling?' She looked at him closely to see if he appeared altered or upset by the horrific scenes he'd no doubt witnessed.

'I was there for some of it,' he replied, unperturbed. 'I was everywhere. I was at the Four Courts, Marrowbone Lane, St. Stephen's Green. Everywhere. I went home for a few hours then Phelim sent word he and Seamus were hiding in Mr Mahon's flour mill. I brought them food and then we came here last night.'

So the other man's name was Phelim.

'Who did you fight in your war, Conleth?' Betty said, pretending to be ignorant.

He looked at her aghast. 'We're fighting the Brits. Do you know anything, missus?

'Where did they find a great soldier like yourself?'

'My brother Phelim said I'd be useful for carrying messages.' He gestured towards the bedroom door again.

'Did you carry messages?'

'I carried loads of messages. I was able to fit in the window of Liberty Hall and then go to the GPO with more messages. Then I went to the Four Courts. I ran the whole way and when I got there I saw two dead men and a dead horse.' He was quiet for a few moments. 'He was lovely and brown with a white nose. He was lying across the footpath. I wanted to rub him but the Brits were everywhere and I had more messages.'

'Did you cry?' Betty asked.

Quickly Conleth snapped out of his sombre mood. 'No, I did not.' He clopped around the small kitchen to stand in front of her. 'No crying from Volunteers like me.'

'Where did you get the boots?' she asked as he almost tripped.

'At the GPO.'

'Let me help you.' Betty decided to do the little fellow a favour. She told him to remove the boots and take two rags from Seamus's tool kit – he used them to clean his violins. She told him to roll them into tight balls.

'Stuff them tightly into the toes of your boots. That will help them to fit you better.'

She watched his small hands scrunching one of the rags into a ball.

'Stick it right down to the toes,' she told him.

He did so with vigour and repeated the process for the other boot. Then he placed his feet into the boots and tried them out. They didn't slide as much.

'Commandant Pearse gave me the boots,' he explained, admiring the improved fit.

'Pádraig Pearse?'

'Yes, he told me Ireland can't have her soldiers fighting in bare feet. He gave me these boots and a cigarette. He said if anything happened to him Ireland would be in great hands with me.'

Betty was fascinated. She'd heard Seamus refer to Pearse with almost boyish adulation. 'What does he look like?'

'He looks like a man,' Conleth said. He regarded Betty, confused by such a question. 'A man like Phelim,' he said, slowly pointing towards the bedroom as if she might not know what a man looked like.

'What else did Pearse tell you?'

'He showed me how to march with my shoulders back and no slouching.' He demonstrated as he spoke, holding his head up, unconsciously pouting.

'He did a good job,' Betty said, watching him as he paraded around the perimeter of the kitchen.

'He's a great singer too,' Conleth said.

'Did he sing in the GPO?' Betty asked. 'In the middle of all that bombing?'

'No!' He laughed at her surprise. 'He sang in my house.'

'Pearse was in your house?' Betty asked, thinking it highly unlikely an esteemed scholar like Pearse would associate with the poor of Dublin.

'He came in the middle of the night with Phelim. My ma got up and made him sandwiches. He stayed until it was bright and sang a few songs while Phelim played the flute. My ma loved him singing 'Bold Robert Emmet'. She said he sang it like a paid singer in the Abbey Theatre.'

Betty knew the song – her father used to sing it:

'The struggle is over, the boys were defeated
  Old Ireland's surrounded by sadness and gloom . . .'

Betty couldn't help thinking of poor Robert Emmet and how little had changed in one hundred years. Her father would sing that song when alone in his workshop: it was his quiet expression of his nationalistic views. God only knew what her father would have made of the Rising. If he had any idea of the state of Dublin, he would want his daughter home. A trusting man like her father who was accustomed to fresh air, open spaces and plenty of food would never be able to comprehend how much the city dwellers had to endure over the last week.

'Where do you live?' the boy suddenly asked.

'Here? Why do you ask?'

He turned from the mirror to look at her. 'Because you don't look like you live here.'

'Do I look like a thief?' she asked playfully.

He shook his head. 'You look different. Your hair, and your clothes and the way you talk is different.'

'Different in a nice way, or different in a bad way?' she teased.

He looked at her, his face perplexed. 'I can't understand why you're here in your fine clothes and your strange way of talking and,' he pointed his finger, 'your hair.'

Suddenly he blushed and turned away from her.

'Where do *you* live?' she asked.

He didn't hear her – he was looking at yesterday's stirabout on the stove.

'Would you like something to eat?'

He nodded, his eyes fixed on the food.

She told him to pour some stirabout into a smaller pot and heat it while she winded the baby. Jokingly she added, 'Or are soldiers not allowed to eat?'

'Of course soldiers eat but sometimes it's hard between battles,' he said.

She was amused at how seriously he was taking the rebellion. 'Did you manage to eat yesterday or did the battle prevent you from eating?'

'I ate the day before yesterday.'

'The day before yesterday?'

The boy didn't hear her. He was concentrating on the food, licking his lips as he stirred the heating stirabout.

'I think it's hot enough now,' he said.

She pointed out the bowls to him and he filled one to the brim.

Betty had never seen a boy eat so hungrily. When he finished eating he used his finger to wipe the bowl.

'Where did you have your last meal?' Betty couldn't fathom how any child could last two days without eating. The entire city seemed immoral.

'I ate in my house before Phelim sent word that he and Seamus were hiding in Mr Mahon's flour mill and my ma gave me a parcel of sandwiches to bring to them.'

'Your mother sent you?' Betty wanted to be sure she'd heard him correctly. What class of a woman would allow a boy of his years onto the streets amidst such chaos?

He nodded, eyeing the bread on the shelf over Betty's head. She told him to help himself to a few cuts of bread and butter.

'Your poor mother is probably out of her mind with worry. You should go to her immediately.'

'She knows I'm with the men or that I'm dead.'

'Dead?'

From her few short months in Dublin she was aware that the Dublin women had more children than they could feed but sending them directly into the raging battle to be killed seemed an immoral way of solving their problems. Was Mona capable of such callousness? Maybe Sheila Muldoon might do it in a fit of rage, but even Sheila wouldn't be long pulling them back in by the scruff of the neck. The more she saw of the city, the less she understood.

Conleth returned her gaze, wondering if he had said something wrong. He responded in an old man's tone: 'My death is bound by God and not by the English.'

'Who told you that?' Betty asked, surprised at such patriotic words flowing from the mouth of a boy.

He continued to gaze at her, one hand hesitantly on another slice of bread.

Aware she was making him self-conscious, Betty resumed feeding the baby.

'Was it your teacher in school?' she asked.

'No – my ma and da.' He returned to eating and spoke between mouthfuls. 'Last Monday morning when Phelim and me were called to take part in the Rising, Da said it – before that he said it to us lots of times.'

'What else did your parents say?'

'They just said they were proud of us, proud that we were willing to die for our country.'

Apart from tales of the 1798 and 1803 rebellions and a general discontent at the English running her country from the gilded halls of Westminster, Betty had never been exposed to such extreme nationalism. Seamus often suggested that fellows like Betty's father made poor republicans. People like them, he said, had everything they needed – they did not know poverty. Regularly he referred to the unwritten seating arrangements at Mass. The first few pews were reserved for the business owners, the teachers, the doctor, while Seamus and his family had to stand due to the shortage of seats. Seamus said the poor would be the dominant class to fight for Ireland's freedom because they had nothing only their humble lives to lose. Maybe he was right. Until now she viewed his hardliner republican opinions as romantic sentiments passed on from his notorious Fenian uncles. Glorious martyrs appeared attractive to young men.

Conleth finished eating and gestured to the baby.

'What's her name?' he asked.

Betty hadn't even thought about a name. At last there was an enjoyable chore to be done. But no name jumped into her mind when she studied her daughter's small round face. A five-day-old baby couldn't look like any name.

'I haven't thought about a name,' she confessed.

'What's your granny's name?' the chirpy little fellow asked.

'Molly.'

'Well then, it must be Molly,' he said as if that finalised the matter. 'The first daughter must be called after your mother's mother.'

Betty was aware of this naming tradition that also demanded the first son must be called after the paternal grandfather. Betty thought of her other grandmother, Bridget, a giant of a woman who sat in the most comfortable seat in the house. Although she was fond of her, Betty had no notion of sticking to such a silly tradition that had half the country called Paddy, Mick and Mary. Betty wanted something better for her daughter, something elegant that would set her apart. She liked the name Amy but wouldn't risk it as local priests refused to christen girls with a name which was not that of a recognised saint.

'I might call her after myself,' she said thoughtfully. 'Elizabeth.' But, as in her own case, the name would inevitably be shortened to Betty, Eliza, Lizzy or Beth. But what about a variation of it like Isabel? That was one of those pretty names like Grace or Maeve. 'Isabel.' She tried the name aloud. 'It's a nice name.'

'I've never heard that name. It's not a real name,' the boy said.

'Of course it's a real name.'

Conleth shook his head. 'Well, it's not an Irish name.'

'I don't care,' Betty declared. 'She looks like a pretty little Isabel.'

She was jolted back to reality when the baby began to cry. The child's crying was a regular event after feeding times. 'Oh, now,' she mumbled before awkwardly resting the child on her bosom. Cautiously she rubbed her back, then patted it gently as Mona had taught her to do. She noticed Conleth watching her intently. She felt the need to explain her obvious anxiety. 'She's a new baby – it's my first.' She changed position but the baby cried even more. Then there was a sudden pause as she inhaled only to release a further torrent of cries. Betty gritted her teeth against the piercing din.

'Trapped wind,' Conleth declared.

Betty was surprised when he leaned closer to take a better look as if he was a doctor diagnosing the illness.

'Put her up higher on your shoulder,' he continued, unfazed by the crying.

Betty ignored his suggestion. Not only was he a brash young Dublin boy, he was far too vocal for a lad his age. For all she knew, he probably stole those very boots off one of the dead soldiers.

She stood up and began to pace and rock her infant.

'I told you, missus, it's trapped wind.'

'How would you know?' Betty snapped. She knew he was right, of course.

She wished the little boy would leave her home and take his brother who was still sleeping in her bedroom with him. They were the very culprits every soul in Dublin wanted to lynch. God only knew what the consequences would be if they were found in her home.

'Give her to me and I'll show you.' He opened his arms.

Ignoring him, she walked in circles and tried to rock the child.

'Give her to me, missus. I know what to do, I promise.'

'Dear Jesus, you're only a child yourself.' But she passed the infant to him, choking back her frustrated tears.

Conleth took the child as confidently as Mona Daly. He placed her sitting on his knee, facing him, holding her under the arms. He began rocking her up and down gently. 'There, there,' he soothed.

Betty stood watching, thinking it absurd.

Suddenly he smiled. 'She's very windy.'

Expertly he then held the infant high on his shoulder, patted her back and rotated his hand in circular motions. When the baby burped loudly, he continued to pat her back, all the time quietly shushing into her ear. Much to Betty's astonishment, the cries subsided to a whimper. Occasionally the baby would erupt into another crying outburst and Conleth would revert to rocking her on his knee. Then she released another volley of burps and he continued to soothe her until her eyes grew drowsy.

'How do you know how to do that?'

'My sister Aideen has babies. I help her. Phelim says I shouldn't cos I'm turning into a right old woman.'

Betty sank into the chair opposite him, more relieved and grateful than she could ever express.

Eventually he passed the baby back to her. She almost laughed out loud when he gently raised her elbow. 'To support the baby's head,' he explained.

'Where are you off to now?' Betty asked as she watched him prepare to leave.

'Soldiers don't have to explain,' he said with a serious expression, 'but I'll tell you. I have to go home and give my ma and da the news. Then I'll see where I'm needed by the men.'

'Your brother is still sleeping,' Betty said.

'I don't want to wake him,' he said, taking one final look at his reflection in the mirror. She watched him brush his hair with his hands.

'Do you know the way back to your parents' house?' she asked.

'Missus,' he said in a surprised voice, 'I'm beginning to wonder if you're the full shilling.'

Betty stared at him. She didn't know whether to rebuke him for insolence or laugh. She'd never heard such talk from a child.

'I know every part of this city, and are you forgetting,' he paused, 'I am a soldier. Soldiers know lots of things.'

'Conleth, you're the best soldier that God Himself could have sent me.'

He smiled, appearing pleased with her compliment. Then he saluted her before rushing off and clonking noisily down the stairs in his too-big boots.

Conleth Salmon had never heard the name Isabel and doubted it was a real name, nor had he ever met a woman like the child's mother, Betty Hopkins. A woman who didn't know what to do with her baby's trapped wind and was dressed in fine clothes. He was captivated by her strangeness: a pretty smile that poked fun, her straight back sitting high and mighty in her chair, lending a strange richness to the room. The loose hair from her bun draped down her long white neck and onto a fresh white blouse. Her peculiar bold attitude and strange accent sounded odd in the Dublin he knew. He couldn't fathom where she had come from. Betty Hopkins sitting in her tenement reminded him of a fur coat he'd found outside the Shelbourne Hotel. When Conleth brought the long elegant coat home, the women ogled the rich thick fur. His mother compared it to hot milk with a roaring stove on a cold day. The women tried it on but none could carry it off like the rich ladies who frequented the Shelbourne. Mrs Hopkins looked as out of place in her surroundings as the fur coat did in his ma's house, lost among the rags there.

Conleth loved his city, the capital of the whole country. He loved the thousand-year-old history of Dublin with its invasions by Normans and Vikings. He loved being from The Liberties, the same place as Strongbow, the great feared warlord entombed in his patch. Conleth loved to swing off the lampposts and run when the policemen came to reprimand the boys because of the dangers. He loved when his mother sent him to the pub to bring home a gill of porter. She'd put the hot poker into the porter to give it a good head, and smoke Woodbine within the confines of her home. Swinging off lampposts and playing toss would have to end, now that he had found his calling. The missionary priests had come to his school to talk about the rewarding life of a priest. Until the Rising, working as a missionary in a foreign country had seemed like the best idea. His imagination spiralled at the thought of foreign countries and jungles filled with wild people he'd tell about Jesus. He'd save their damned souls and secure his seat in heaven at the right hand of the Lord.

Clumping up Sackville Street in his big boots, he realised he'd found a better people to save: his own country needed him now. Like Pearse said, they needed great young soldiers like him to finish what the 1916 Volunteers began. The uncivilised black people of Africa would have to find someone else to save their souls. When he saved Ireland Mrs Hopkins might realise what a great soldier he was and the important role he played in the Rising. As he removed his shoes to enable him to run, he was careful not to lose the rags she had made him stuff into the toes.

Throughout the morning his thoughts returned to her strange green eyes. Her white hands and clean face.

Shortly after Conleth had left, a knock on the door heralded the arrival of Ursula. Betty had rehearsed what she'd say to her when she saw her again. Her cousin was supposed to be all things caring and kind, yet she had left Betty alone in her greatest hour of need. Now, when life would resume as before, Ursula arrived like a fair-weather friend wearing her nursing cape, effusing self-importance.

Ursula rushed to her and wrapped her arms around her. 'Thank God, at least you're alive!'

Betty remained seated and composed. She watched Ursula gently caress the baby's face with her index finger.

'Boy or girl?' Ursula asked, her face crinkled with affection for the new child.

'Girl.'

'How was the birth?' Ursula asked.

'I'm lucky to be alive, between bombs and giving birth and the subsequent starvation. I thought Our Lord was taking me from this mortal soil.' She waved her hand dramatically towards the ceiling.

Ursula rolled her eyes. 'Nice to see your sense of humour wasn't blown to smithereens like parts of Dublin.'

It was easy to be playful on such a morning. Forgiveness and humour came easily today. At last Betty could return to normality. With Seamus's return she would be spared getting a hunched back from overwork in the poorhouse. There would be no need to return to her family with her tail between her legs, obliged to spend the rest of her days repenting for her act of defiance. The prospect of living in the tenements with her husband was no longer the worst fate. She thought about Seamus's remaining five violins that she had hidden, and tried to banish the thought of Mr Hartmann. Of course her husband would provide. Yet she'd leave the violins where they were and allow time to pass. It was as if he had forgotten about them after the stress he'd been through. When he asked she'd return them. Now that she knew their value she was reluctant to hand them back to Seamus who'd rather give them away or allow them sit gathering dust.

'Tell me everything about the birth,' Ursula said. 'How did it go?'

Betty put a finger to her lips, then pointed towards the bedroom. 'We'll go out for a stroll and I'll tell all about it.'

Ursula looked towards the bedroom door. 'Seamus?' she asked softly.

Betty nodded. 'I need to arrange a christening for the baby,' she said. 'Then I'll tell you everything.'

Chapter 9

Tuesday 2nd May 1916

Betty and Ursula met a priest in the Pro-Cathedral who asked them to return two hours later when he'd baptise the child. They sat for two hours in the back of the church, whispering their news. Betty revealed every detail of the last week. She told her how she gave birth at the height of the shelling of the GPO. She took great delight in hearing Ursula gasp with horror at her ordeal.

Ursula was extremely impressed with Mona's generosity and support.

'Tenement women are the salt of the earth,' she gushed. 'The disregarded backbone of society.'

Betty told her about her days without food or milk for tea, fearing Ursula was more impressed with Mona's generosity than her own suffering. 'I was at the stage of feeling faint with the hunger,' she said. 'Now I know what it is to starve, almost to death.'

'These are the conditions we must learn to endure for independence,' said Ursula. 'There's more to come. We must be prepared.'

'Well, I've done my bit,' Betty said, relieved the two-hour wait was almost over as Ursula was getting into her political lecturing mode.

Betty was home with her newly baptised baby before Seamus finally woke from his sleep. Ursula had been puzzled at Betty's urgency about the baptism but Betty had told her she was terrified that the baby might die and be condemned to Limbo. Ursula said no more but Betty wasn't at all sure if she believed her. The truth was that, once Betty had settled on the name, she didn't want to give Seamus the opportunity of choosing dreary names of dead relatives or Gaelic martyrs. She didn't see the point of burdening her daughter with some other victim's abysmal history before her little feet even touched the ground.

Seamus and Betty stood quietly in the kitchen holding each other, both fully aware of their utter good luck that he had been spared. Betty felt his grasp tighten. Slowly she became aware of her ebbing terror. Relief swept into every bone of her body as she soaked up the strength from his warm grip. His return was her deliverance from a life of loneliness and destitution. He tried to speak but stopped when his voice quivered. Instead he slowly ran his fingers over her face. He unpinned her bun and wrapped his hands in her long soft hair.

'Every free moment I prayed that God would spare me just to see your face one more time,' he said, his eyes welling with tears.

When they stepped apart she held him at arm's length to examine him. 'What in the name of God are you wearing?'

Seamus was wearing overalls that were too small. The legs were too short and the arms were only down to his elbow. He was coated in flour.

He pretended to take offense. 'Do you not like my outfit?' He assumed a feminine pose with his hand on his hip.

'You'll always be handsome to me, even if you're wearing a midget's overalls,' she said, smiling.

'Well, you won't have the pleasure much longer,' he said with a grin. 'I need to wash all this incriminating flour off immediately and get rid of the overalls. We've been hiding in a flour mill.'

'I know! That extraordinary child Conleth told me.'

She sank into his arms again, resting her head against his chest. In the silence she sensed how broken he was. She would right him, help him overcome the awfulness of the last week. More than anything she wanted their own simple life to resume. She would do whatever it took to get him well. She would support him until he returned to the full of his health.

'Will her eyes ever see a free Ireland?' he asked, gazing into the cradle at his firstborn.

Betty was too relieved at his safe return to find his continuing obsession with a free Ireland upsetting.

'Isabel Mary is her name,' Betty announced, adjusting the blanket around her infant's shoulders.

'What kind of a name is that?' he asked, startled at its foreign air.

'It's French,' Betty said, immediately removing any affiliations with England. 'She founded the Poor Clare Monastery at Longchamp near Paris.' In fact, the priest had complimented her on calling her daughter after such an exemplary saint. 'I was afraid she'd die and spend an eternity in Limbo. I had her baptised the first chance I got.'

'Isabel Mary,' he whispered, 'we lost the battle but we'll win the war.'

Quietly Betty removed Seamus's bandages. She tried not to gasp in horror when she saw two deep cuts in his head. She fetched hot water and disinfectant and began to clean his wounds as best she could. He hardly reacted. His dull eyes told her nothing but wretchedness.

'What happened?' she asked, broaching the subject gingerly.

'I'm too worn out to think,' he sighed. 'A series of blunders destroyed our chances. The Chief of Staff cancelled the Rising the day before. Only a fraction of the men turned up, the rest of the country thinking it was cancelled. Very little happened as planned. We fought hard but their reinforcements wiped us out in the end. The ports and communication depots should have been destroyed. We lost some great brave men.'

Betty had been thinking only of Seamus's safety. Now she began to see how the horror of battle would have affected him. He would have witnessed appalling deaths.

'Was it awful?'

'I could never burden you with the horrors of it.'

The morning of the Rising on 24th April Seamus bought a football in a shop in the city centre. He joined over thirty Volunteers in the Phoenix Park, the site of the British Army's principal armoury in the city. Their mission was to destroy the Magazine Fort. The thirty men said a decade of the Rosary together and shook hands in case they would never meet again. With Seamus's ball and dressed in their civilian clothes, with their pistols hidden inside their jackets, they pretended they were having a football game. Gradually they moved to the front of the fort, continuing with their charade by kicking the ball from one to the other. The only sentry on the gate was overwhelmed when the rebels rushed them. They laid mines and blew up the Fort then raced to the city centre to join Pádraig Pearse, James Connolly and their waiting comrades in the GPO.

When the offensive began there were very few men prepared for what followed. Only a fraction of the Volunteers turned out after Eoin McNeill, the Chief of Staff, cancelled the Rising. Those present fought with determination. They fought as united Irishmen, each bullet going towards severing all connection with the British Empire. The adjoining buildings caught fire. The initial fires were small yet the glare made it difficult to detect movements. It was easy for the enemy to attack, retreat and then re-attack in greater numbers. The British used shrapnel shells, filled with molten wax which steamed on the ground when it fell.

While the GPO was shelled Seamus Hopkins kept his men optimistic, returned fire and showed fearlessness in the face of death.

Over the course of the following day Sackville Street was set alight by incendiary shells from the gunboat *Helga* which blasted everything in sight from its position on the Liffey. The raging flames caused a beautiful but terrifying spectacle that could be seen from far outside Dublin. In the GPO some of the men were heartened by the blazing furnace while others were so unnerved they almost turned their guns on themselves. The blaze stretched up to the dark sky as if the flames themselves were caught in the frenzy. Throughout the explosions, the bursting glass, collapsing walls and the roofs caving in, Seamus rallied his men. He told them to take delight in the great magnitude of the rebellion, he told them it would change the position of Ireland forever, that if a Rising could be carried out with so few men, 'with the might of the country behind us we will achieve independence'.

A ricocheting bullet grazed his head, and the crude bandage hurriedly applied was red with blood, yet passionately Seamus reminded them that their eyes were the first to see the flag of a free Ireland over the GPO.

'Our dead are with us,' he pointed to the empty street below, 'and even Daniel O'Connell is still with us.' The *Helga* had not knocked the statue of the great Daniel O'Connell, 'The Liberator'. It was a reminder to the Volunteers of the years they'd waited to strike, the years of oppression and being second-class citizens in their own country, the years of being denied political and economic equality.

During those bloody days, boys and men who had never before touched a corpse or fired a gun were kept going with the words of the proclamation: '*The right of the people of Ireland to the ownership of Ireland.*' These words helped the boys to fight on through the suffering and death all around them. It was a week when dreams were almost realised and boys became men.

The GPO caught fire, forcing the rebels to abandon their headquarters. As the roof caved in, Phelim was knocked unconscious and a burning beam of wood fell on his arm and hand. His clothing protected his arm but his exposed hand was burned. Seamus pulled him from beneath the burning wood and carried him out to the adjoining street where the battle still raged. He'd always remember the coppery smell from the burning flesh of Phelim's hand. Staggering under Phelim's weight, he moved down the street in a hail of gunfire. In desperation he hammered on a door and was lucky enough to find refuge in a sympathetic house. While the remainder of the men were surrounded and later captured, Seamus was hiding in an upstairs bedroom with the still unconscious Phelim. He watched an old man, who was beyond the stage of taking part in any battle, step outside his door. He was shot in the crossfire between the Volunteers and the British army, but not killed. He remained on the street all night, crying out for water. For those excruciating hours they listened to his pleas for help, his voice getting weaker as the night progressed until finally his call expired with his life.

Apart from the man's pleas for water, the stillness was terrifying. There was nothing to do but pray and wait to be captured. Regret, self-disgust and aversion to the horrors consumed Seamus. He could only think about death and those they'd killed, the killings they'd witnessed, their hands stained with the blood of so many of their own innocent people – most of all the old man pleading for water.

The following morning the remainder of the Volunteers surrendered to stop the slaughter of Dublin citizens and in the hope of saving the lives of their followers.

Phelim had regained consciousness and they were moved to a storeroom in a flour mill. Phelim sent word about his whereabouts to his family, via a sympathetic republican. His young brother Conleth arrived with food and lay low with them, waiting for the storm to pass.

Betty was relieved her husband didn't relay the events of the previous week. She needed to find the light, something to drag him from his desolation and help him to gradually return to normality.

'Sit down – you need rest and nourishment,' she said, setting a plate of stew on the table. 'Is your friend awake? Is he hungry?'

'Let him sleep for another while. His hand is badly burned – I hope he doesn't lose it,' he said mournfully as he glanced at the door of the bedroom.

'I'm sure you did all you could – I've no doubt you fought gallantly,' Betty said, tenderly placing her hand on his cheek. Thank God it was over, she thought, and the Volunteers who were not captured and marched off to cross the Irish Sea to Frongoch internment camp in Wales could resume their lives. Those who had survived could count their blessings and eventually have a great story to tell their grandchildren. 'It's all over now. You're safe again.'

'Until we get our independence it will never be over,' he said, raising his eyes to meet hers.

'Has there not been enough killing?' she asked in disbelief. 'Do you want more? What's the use of it all?' She thought of the bloodstained footpath and the city razed to the ground. Foolishly, she had not given any thought to her husband's continuing republican ideals.

'You ask what's the use of it? Has your life been so comfortable that you have never asked why a foreigner is running your country? Do you never question why an Irish Catholic working in an Irish country in the exact same job as a Protestant man gets half his pay?'

Betty knew there were no Protestants in Seamus's job, so why was he so troubled? He had done his bit for Ireland. Let the single men without families continue the fight for their cause.

Seamus continued, his face paling with indignation. 'We are ruled by Englishmen, Protestant English and Scottish men who discriminate against me and my fellow Irishmen. These same Protestant Scottish and English men rule in the interests of England rather than the interests of the native Irish. There is no fair competition in their economics. They teach Irish children a doctored version of English history and make them learn the poem "A Happy English Child". You and I,' he waved towards the infant in the cot, 'and our child are second-class citizens and we have no voice and no equality! Ultimately we are ruled by a parliament in London most of whose members have never set foot on Irish soil!'

Betty had heard it all before and she was tired to death of it. 'What about your life? You're a father and husband. Do you want your blood staining the streets of Dublin too?'

'There are worse things than bloodshed, and slavery is one of them,' he said with finality.

Only then did Betty realise how endless her own war was. Without ever forming a political thought of substance, she was as involved as her husband and his sleeping comrade. Like the countless grieving families, there was more to come. The realisation that she was not immune was as insistent as the shelling that struck the GPO . . . ceaseless.

Chapter 10

Phelim Salmon had made little impact on Betty the night he arrived with Seamus. The first time she met him properly was the following afternoon when he emerged from the bedroom while Seamus was having a bath in the tin tub he had carried in there.

She turned from the window and saw him standing there. He nodded politely. He seemed awkward, unsure what to do or say. She judged him to be a few years more than Seamus's twenty-three. She noticed his height, his broad expansive shoulders blocking the light. Like Seamus, he was covered in a fine film of flour. She wanted to take a wet cloth and wipe it away from his face and hands. It coated his hair and eyebrows, and overalls. His hand was crudely bandaged. She offered to see to it, but he declined. So instead she invited him to sit at the table where she served him up a plate of stew which he ate ravenously. While she made tea he went to the cradle to see Isabel. He stood there, looking at her in silence for a long while.

Betty felt he didn't want to talk. She poured tea for both of them and they sat quietly at the table, waiting for Seamus to finish his bath.

Ursula called later that day with news that three of the 1916 leaders had been executed by the British. Pádraig Pearse was shot at 6am after a secret court-martial. Later in the day Thomas Clarke and Thomas MacDonagh were shot.

There was little said while Ursula cleaned Phelim's wound, each digesting news of the deaths of their comrades. In silence Betty watched as Ursula removed a crude bandage Phelim had wrapped around his hand. Betty gasped, breaking the silence, when she saw the burn on the back of his hand and top of his fingers. It looked inhuman, like a shrivelled hand belonging to a smaller man. It appeared as if a triangle-shaped iron had been placed there. Then as Ursula removed the dead skin and treated the hand, Betty turned away.

'Infected,' Ursula finally said.

For a moment Betty thought she was referring to the state of the country.

'Your hand is badly infected. I'll have to go and get you ointment.'

Later that day Ursula called again with ointment and bandages. She advised Betty how to change the dressing and care for his wound. Betty said nothing. She was full of resentment. It was all right for Ursula, the gallant nurse who could return to her comfortable bed in a nice home that was not filled with men on the run.

When Betty began to change the bandages, Phelim would sit facing the window as if their closeness made him uncomfortable – yet he didn't move when she dabbed on ointment that should have stung. Despite the unsightliness of the burn, once Betty started administering the treatment, she wasn't so repulsed by it.

'You're a very good patient,' she said.

'You're a great nurse, Mrs Hopkins,' he replied and then pretended he was about to faint.

They laughed, a welcome light moment to relieve the tension.

For three days the men were confined to her home. Two days after the first executions of the 1916 leaders, John McBride was shot.

During those three days when the May sun blazed through their window, filling the small home with uncomfortable heat, the executions were the only topic of conversation. The more it was talked about, the more incensed her husband appeared.

At least Phelim was a calming influence on Seamus's rage, for which Betty was grateful. The tall imposing figure was the voice of reason.

'Nothing changes overnight,' he said, to pacify Seamus.

Betty noted how informed Phelim was. He could reel out statistics at will. He had facts about the tenements: 3 generations in a single room, and 26,000 families in tenements. Of those 26,000, 20,000 were in one-roomed homes.

'There is nobody fighting their corner because none of our representatives care,' he said.

Phelim had a clear picture of what he wanted. He didn't retell the stories about his grandparents and uncles fighting the might of the English with boiling water and sticks. Nor did he dwell on every injustice committed by the English in every parish in Ireland. He wanted to build on what they had. He wanted a progressive country, one that could use its natural resources. He gave a deep sense of his aims in a quiet unassuming manner.

'The country is economically underdeveloped due to political repression. We need to reform the education system and build up the spirit and pride of our people.'

He referred to the signs of imperialism that so few Irish questioned: the symbols of sovereignty on every street in Dublin, the royal crests on buildings, the flapping Union Jack, the familiar red post boxes and the ever-present picture of the King of England.

'Nobody notices or questions,' he said.

Unlike his brother and most of the tenement dwellers, Phelim's accent was more refined. He was a national-school teacher, having won a number of scholarships. When Betty heard that Phelim won his first scholarship at sixteen to attend Blackrock College, she wasn't at all surprised. While there he won another scholarship to a teacher-training college. She assumed his improved use of the

English language was gained from his education and the fact that he was such an avid reader. He had perfect grammar, was articulate and was a fluent Gaelic speaker. But it wasn't only his education that set him apart. He was confident and assured in a quiet manner. His face had an air of austerity with defined bone structure and large brown eyes. He was comfortable with silence; he didn't need to fill every lull with conversation. When he did contribute, what he said was valid.

Finally, when it was deemed safe, he left their home, with Ursula pretending to be his wife. When a man was in the company of a woman, there was less chance of harassment or arrest. A few days later when Phelim returned to their home, he looked like a different man. He wore a well-cut suit and carried an umbrella. Betty thought he looked quite the gentleman.

The normality Betty wished for was drifting further away from her. Occasionally she had a glimpse of what they once were. The scene was a tranquil picturesque countryside – she could smell the fresh air and remember the texture of the early morning dew on the grass. But it belonged to someone else now. Just as Seamus belonged to another cause, his great intentions to be a provider and protector for his family ideals belonging to a simpler time and a different man. Their long tender nights were a thing of the past.

Seamus's new fury at the enemy took up every moment of his time and was fuelled by the shootings and events which followed the Rising.

On the 12th May Seán MacDiarmada and James Connolly were shot. Within twelve days from the end of the Rising, fourteen of the rebel leaders had been executed by firing squad in Kilmainham Gaol, their bodies thrown into a pit in Arbour Hill Detention Barracks. Each snippet of news was like blood trickling from behind a closed door. The people were breathless with abhorrence and fear.

James Connelly's execution was the most difficult to understand.

On 12th May he was carried to the firing squad and placed sitting in a chair as his leg had been shattered by a bullet and he was unable to stand. Betty imagined Connolly with his Scottish accent trying to reason with his captors. Did he beg for clemency or was he resigned to his death? These were not questions she could ask Seamus. Several nights after she retired to bed she thought about Connolly and his death, fighting the sense of sympathy that was creeping into her mind for the rebels. She did not want to take on another man's troubles – keeping her husband calm was enough of a new war. During quiet moments of the day she thought about Connolly, Pearse, Clarke, and the rest of the fourteen executed leaders. She knew each of their names and who they left behind. Their deaths seemed so senseless. When she cradled her daughter she cursed the country and swore she'd save herself.

All around the country Volunteers were rounded up and escorted to Richmond Barracks. There were 3,500 arrests including 79 women. A large number were innocent and were released, while the remainder, including several hundred blameless Irishmen, were shipped off to England's prisons. Those thought to have organised the insurrection had been held in Ireland for trial – 190 men and one woman, Constance Markievicz. In ninety cases the court's verdict was 'Death by being shot'. These verdicts were later commuted — all but the fourteen already executed leaders.

Those who escaped lay low, not knowing when the city would be safe again. Seamus didn't leave their home. He stayed up late at night alone. She'd hear him walking the floors and see him peering out the window. In the mornings when she entered the kitchen, the plate that served as an ashtray would be overflowing with cigarette butts. Whenever she left for a walk, he was in a fever of anxiety until she returned safely.

When Betty was alone with Ursula she expressed her impatience with her husband's constant presence. 'I want the house to myself. I'm tired of making pots of tea for these men who talk about Ireland's struggles till they are hoarse. When will we get back to normal? When will Seamus return to work and earn a living?'

'You'll be waiting a long time,' was Ursula's curt reply. 'Life as we know it is over.'

'Is Seamus in trouble?' Betty asked naively.

'If Seamus is spotted by the Brits, he'll be locked away in England with the others. His fresh wounds would arouse suspicion.'

Betty tried to understand, listening as Ursula explained, speaking slowly as if to a child: 'Seamus must exercise caution. They are arresting men for anything from marching to speeches, and anything that may be likely to excite the populace is banned. We are not allowed to organise any public political meetings. There are harsh consequences if anyone is caught with literature relating to promoting Irish politics. One false move and you may not see your husband for quite some time.'

Betty finally understood.

She tried to have patience when Seamus pounded the table or cursed the Brits for another injustice.

'We are a country filled with able men ready to retaliate, so why not now?' He wasn't speaking to anyone, his mind awash with unfocused vengeance.

It was during one of the men's discussions that Betty learned of Ursula's involvement in the Rising and the death of her lover Dr O'Malley. Phelim and Seamus were discussing women's role in a free Ireland.

'It says it in the Proclamation of the Republic – it guarantees *"religious and civil liberty, equal rights and equal opportunities to all its citizens"*.'

'Why then did Eamon de Valera turn the women away from Boland's Mill during the Rising?'

'Did he?' Phelim was surprised.

'When Ursula went to Boland's Mill, de Valera told the women to go away, that it was no place for them.'

'That's surprising,' Phelim said, 'Maybe he just thought it was too dangerous.'

'Some of the women went home but Ursula went to the Four Courts. Dr Martin O'Malley was shot dead on their way. Ursula had a narrow escape.'

Suddenly Betty saw Ursula in a new light. Not only had she lost her fancy man, she couldn't mention it to a single soul. There would be no offerings of condolences. She was forced to carry her cross in silence. There wasn't one soul who'd pray for her if they knew of her sin with her married doctor. No wonder she was a dry boots since the Rising. Regardless of her adulterous carry-on, Betty vowed to offer up a decade of the Rosary for her that night.

Betty wished Seamus could return to work or their normal lives could resume in some way. Instead he only had time for talking about politics with the many callers, or writing notes. At night he was like a disinterested stranger in her bed. He never acknowledged her when she inclined towards him; he was too absorbed in his world of war to make love to his wife.

Conleth, the little boy in the soldier's boots, was another regular in their home. He arrived at all hours of the day delivering messages, or carrying letters and parcels. He would be dispatched with more letters and return only to be sent out again, always eager to do what was asked.

Fr Mathew called when he felt the city was safe enough to venture out. He spent his first visit sitting in the chair furthest away from the window. 'Terrible times we're living in,' he kept repeating. He was clearly petrified at the talk of murder and death and killing. Instead he offered to hear the men's confessions, and afterwards his hand trembled when he accepted a glass of sherry. 'Awful business,' he muttered, at the sight of Seamus's wounds. He warned them about arrests and beatings and took his leave, fearing he too could be a marked man for associating with die-hard republicans.

Chapter 11

In May, Betty returned to Mr Hartmann with a second violin. Initially her conscience bothered her. Seamus had not missed the violins or looked at his unfinished pieces since returning. Trying to justify her actions, she felt it would be a worse sin to allow a good instrument to lie idle in their basement when she could use the money to feed her family. It was pivotal that she keep up her pretence that Seamus was producing a violin a month. Dealers liked consistency – they favoured an established means of increasing their income rather than sourcing new craftsmen. A good craftsman could only improve if he worked. Mr Hartmann asked after her husband and how his recuperation was going since the 'stray bullet'. Betty always reassured him that Mr Hopkins was right as rain, eager as ever to improve with each instrument.

When Seamus's temper improved or when he noticed the missing violins, she would think of something to tell him then.

To buoy her own sanity, Betty wrote to Reverend William Meredith Morris, an expert in violins. He was based in Tonypandy in Wales. He was the author of a dictionary entitled *British Violin Makers*. Betty had heard his named bandied about by her father and uncles. She remembered her father becoming so enthusiastic about Seamus's work that he sent an earlier violin to Reverend Morris, hoping he would include Seamus in his dictionary. Rev Morris had responded to her father's correspondence with a complimentary letter. In his estimation the boy's work was not quite ready yet, although he felt confident that at Seamus's age and evident talent so far, within a few years he would be included if he refined his craft and continued to work at it. The violin that Seamus completed before the Rising was his best yet. Betty sent it to Reverend Morris. She wrote the letter and signed her husband's signature. Fr Bernard O'Reilly's book, *Instruction for Women in the World*, was clearly not penned for a woman who had ambition for her husband.

Balderdash to Fr O'Reilly, Betty thought.

Betty could hear Seamus's raised voice as she climbed the stairs after posting the letter and violin.

'We'll spare our bullets to execute them like they did us,' he said angrily.

Phelim explained calmly to Seamus that some of the executed leaders had signed their own death warrant. 'When our comrades put their names to the Proclamation of the Irish Republic they *knew* they were going to die.'

'There were only seven signatures on the proclamation, so why did they kill another seven?' Seamus demanded. The strain of confinement and grief for his dead friends had taken their toll.

'Some were shot because of the roles they played, others were familiar to the Dublin Castle authorities.' Phelim shrugged. 'Revenge in some cases. They can justify it by simply saying that each of the fourteen men fought in the Rising.'

In the same calm tone, Phelim told him all was not lost, that the public were revolted by the executions and arrests.

'The moderates are now sympathisers,' he said. 'As a country we are unified against the British. It's an opportune time to finish what we began.'

'Unless it happens soon, all will be lost,' Seamus said. 'There are millions of English squaddies fighting in France against the Hun. They've been blooded by war. When there's nothing left to destroy in the killing fields of Europe, England will send them to our streets. They'll want my blood, and yours, your young brother's blood and my child's blood.'

During those weeks there were times when Betty felt she was playing a role in a theatre production. It was not her life – this absurdity belonged to another's.

She knew when Conleth was approaching, from his loud clunking on the stairs. He continued to wear the soldier's boots. He would arrive breathless, bursting with the latest news.

'Them Brits are searching the river for arms and ammunition – them squaddies are all over the quays with boats and nets.'

'*Those* Brits,' Phelim would say.

'Mr Whittle, my teacher, never corrects me like you does.'

'Because Mr Whittle is a Unionist who likes to keep the Irish ignorant and wants all of us to use poor grammar and remain uneducated. And it's like I *do*, not like I *does*.'

Wild-eyed with rage over another assault on the rebels, Seamus would look from one to the other, as if unsure which was taking precedence, the boy's grammar or Ireland's fight for freedom.

Those words could lead to a full-scale discussion on the poor education system in Ireland and how best to deal with it when they achieved independence. Betty was struck by how the men were always so certain that Ireland would get independence from Britain. At night when she retired to bed, she could hear Seamus and his friends talking and debating late into the night. She could hear most of their conversation but she had to strain to hear what Phelim said, his gentle voice provoking or dissuading the men from rash actions.

One evening she returned after her walk to find Seamus playing his violin and Phelim attempting to play the flute, their legs jigging in time to the music. Phelim's hand and fingers were not healed enough to play well.

'You'll get there,' Seamus said encouragingly when they'd finished.

'Hopefully,' Phelim said, trying to stretch his fingers.

Many more times he played the flute in their home. He carried it in a little wooden box, and slowly he'd put the three-piece instrument together. Betty would watch him as he'd remove any dust by wiping it several times with his hanky. There was a thoughtful elegance about him.

Fr Mathew roused Seamus when he could, encouraging him to return to work and keep his mind occupied. Seamus eventually returned to full-time employment as a violinmaker with a man called Mr Andrew Perry. Fr Mathew got him the job. After his first week he confessed how much he had missed his work.

When Betty heard his cheerful voice at the main door and his sprightly step on the stairs when he returned from his day's work, she felt life would resume as before. Seamus was animated as he discussed his day; he talked about the wood he used, the improved tools, and told little anecdotes about his colleagues. Each snippet of news increased her urgency to bring Seamus round to her way of thinking. He would make so much more money by producing the violins and selling them directly to Mr Hartmann. While Seamus worked for another man, his employer's seal would go onto Seamus's craft. He was giving away the very gift that she knew could provide them with a comfortable life. It made it all the more frustrating when Mr Hartmann was eager to buy Seamus's stock. Sundays were the only time he worked on his own violins; every other hour of the week went to Mr Perry or his nationalistic cause.

'Seamus, I need to tell you something.' She wanted to tell him before he asked. 'It's about your violins. I had to sell some of them.'

His looked at her, bewildered. Silently he waited for her to continue.

'After the events of Easter Week we were hungry,' she said. 'I sold two of them and hid the remaining violins in the small disused room at the top of the house.'

'Which ones did you sell?'

'I sold the last two with the darker varnish. The authorities were raiding houses and taking anything of value. I can only assume that they stole the remaining violins.' Betty crossed her fingers behind her back. Seamus might as well believe they were all gone. 'I've been so disturbed about them it's all I could think of. Maybe somebody in the house took them, I don't know.'

'Who did you sell the two violins to?' he asked, his expression still one of incomprehension.

'I sold them to Mr Hartmann,' she sighed. 'He gave me a very good price for them. I think he knew my predicament.' At all costs she wanted to make Mr Hartmann appear like a man with a heart. 'I'm sorry, Seamus, but when you didn't return after the Rising, we were hungry. I wasn't the only one who was hungry, the entire building was starving.'

She could see him soften. She placed the remaining money on the table before him. He picked up one of the notes and as quickly tossed it out of his hand in anger.

Betty continued, 'Mona was so good to me after Isabel was born that naturally I shared the food with her, and the McCarthy orphans. The little girls were weak with the hunger.'

He nodded as the news sank in. 'It galls me to think of some Brit getting one hour's pleasure out of my violin. Anyway, at least you managed to sell two of them and the money did more good that I could imagine.' He sighed loudly as if still absorbing the news. 'They're gone now.' There was an air of disappointment in his tone.

He removed the outline cutting of a violin from his satchel to examine it. He rubbed his fingers the length of the template to inspect the grain of the wood, then held it up to the light. 'Mr Perry uses high quality wood but not as good as this. Your father understands the need for wood from old trees.' Then he added mournfully, 'He used to allow me to take the material to make violins of my own.'

In the pocket of her apron Betty had Reverend Morris's response with the good news that Seamus would be included in his dictionary of violinmakers. It read: '*This is to certify that I have this day examined and tried a violin made by Mr Seamus Hopkins in 1916, and that I consider the instrument to be a first class instrument with the most superior craftsmanship and brilliant tone.*

The instrument is worth fully thirty pounds. The maker is certainly in the very front row of modern artists.' Reverend Morris went on to say he would include several passages on the life and work of Seamus in the next edition of his book.

She would bide her time and return to Mr Hartmann with a different proposal.

Betty noticed that Seamus didn't even ask how much his violins fetched. It was never more blatantly obvious that she had married a man with an ocean of talent and no regard for money. She loved him for it but could never be like him.

Chapter 12

For the remainder of 1916 the British did their best to suppress Irish Republicanism. They introduced further restricting laws to curb the nationalists. Rather than suppressing the movement, it had the opposite effect. Like molten lava erupting through the earth, in every pocket of Ireland sentiment changed to support the Republican movement, and their members grew with the shifting tide. The old who thought change would never happen in their lifetime recognised the lost opportunity of 1916. They could not allow their slain leaders to turn to dust without examining the possibilities of change. 'The Soldiers Song' was sung ardently, their fighting passionate hearts matching its every beat. Seamus and his comrades worked fervently. During the day he worked in Mr Perry's violin workshop, but every other waking moment was divided between the Republican Party and furniture-making with a difference.

When Seamus arrived home with the first item of furniture, Betty thought that at last he was showing an interest in something other than politics. It was a large 8-foot wardrobe, with double doors, and it took four men to carry it upstairs. He had built it in the evenings in the house of one of his republican friends.

She admired his handiwork, the heavy and expensive wood with elaborate etchings on the doors. She had never seen a wardrobe as beautiful.

'I didn't really build it for you,' he admitted, 'but you can use this part.' He opened the doors of the wardrobe.

'What other part is there? I'm hardly going to sit on it!' She pointed toward the ceiling.

He showed her that the wardrobe had another purpose. On the floor inside were concealed small box-like drawers in each corner. There was a groove that allowed you to lift the base of the wardrobe to access the boxes. Seamus used the secret boxes to keep his private correspondence for the Irish Republican Brotherhood.

At the right-hand side was another hidden panel concealing a compartment big enough for Seamus to hide should the Brits come knocking. The hiding space had to be small enough not to arouse suspicion. The panel door, similar to the rest of the wardrobe, was elaborately decorated with carved ferns and shells. When the secret panel was open, the decorative shells and fern jutted out; when closed, they knitted perfectly into the main part of the wardrobe, hiding the fact that it was a door. Beneath one of the shells was a small groove to lock it from the outside. Betty thought it was ingenious.

Testing the wardrobe as a hiding space, Seamus stepped into the small compartment. It was two feet wide, he informed her as he squeezed his body into the narrow opening. They couldn't stop laughing as he manoeuvred his body to fit. When he was in place she closed it and locked him in.

'Damn it,' he said, 'I should have put the lock on the inside.'

Both of them erupted into convulsive giggling.

'You can open it now,' Seamus said.

Betty stood looking at the wardrobe without releasing him.

'Quick, Betty, I can't breathe.'

Betty didn't open the door immediately. Instead she leaned close and began to sing the love song, 'When a Man's in Love'.

'*I gently tapped at my lover's window – Would you rise and let me in?*

Slowly the door unlocked and slowly I drew in.'

Continuing to sing, slowly she opened the doors. Seamus remained where he was, and she extended her hand as if they were performing a song on stage.

'Her hands were soft, her bosom warm and her tongue it did gently glide

I stole a kiss, thought it no miss and wished her for my bride.'

When she finished the last line, slowly he slid out from the wardrobe and kissed her. He cupped her face with his hands, then kissed her again, intent and urgently. He held her tightly and then peeled away the layers of her clothing, standing back to gaze and touch her body as if seeing her nakedness for the first time. Only then did Betty realise how much she'd missed him, his naked firm chest and his hands that explored her.

As the evening sun flooded their bedroom, they unlocked their hunger and resumed their marital pleasures where they had left off before the Rising. The worst was over, Betty thought as he entered her with an insatiable attentive craving, and she as hungrily accepted him, each thrust shedding the months of loss.

Mr Perry, Seamus's employer, invited him into his office for tea. As Seamus revealed the details about their little chat, Betty suspected that Mr Perry had recognised Seamus's flair. Seamus was the loyal type of friend and employee – if Mr Perry showed any signs of kindness towards him, he would remain working for him until his fingers were old and brittle. Ideally, Betty would prefer it if Seamus didn't like Mr Perry, or if he was even suspicious of him. At least, then, working for himself would seem more attractive than taking orders from a boss he didn't like.

'Did he invite the rest of the craftsmen to take tea in his office?' she asked.

'No. I got a right slagging for it off the rest of the lads,' he said good-humouredly.

'What did you talk about?'

'He wanted to know if the tools were all right, that sort of thing.'

Perry had certainly recognised his flair. Every moment he spent making money for other men galled her.

'Remember,' she said, 'he is a black Protestant and we all know where we stand with them.'

Seamus looked up at her, surprised. 'My lovely rebel wife! Has our cause finally caught up with you?' He smiled, amused at her choice of words.

Betty pretended to concede. 'After everything that has happened, of course I am.'

When Seamus was singing the praises of Mr Perry's instruments and workshop, Betty raised the topic of moving house again.

'One thing at a time,' he said.

Although she knew it was futile encouraging him to seek a better part of Dublin to live in, it was important she did not give up on the matter altogether.

'We're only getting back on our feet,' he said, then added, 'Surely you'd miss Mona if we moved now?'

Although amused at his delaying tactics, she was not about to give up. 'Seamus, the only thing the English have told the truth about is written on their recruitment circulars for the British army where they say *The trenches are safer than the Dublin slums*. They know it and we know it. More infants die in Dublin's tenements than anywhere else in Europe – remember, Phelim said that the other day. Two dead children were taken out of Number 82 last week.'

The families of the children were too poor to afford coffins. They were wrapped in bedclothes, one little child small enough to fit under his father's arm as he cycled to the cemetery to bury him. Their humble burial was another reminder of the precariousness of life for the poor.

He looked forlorn. 'I know.'

Phelim and the boy Conleth called regularly. They'd come and go with papers to be deposited or taken from the wardrobe. Betty left them to their own devices.

Phelim called without fail each Thursday. In the bedroom he worked on papers while he waited for Seamus to return from work. Seamus then usually left with Phelim – his republican activities were taking up what little time he had left outside of working hours. There were times when Seamus didn't return home at night. The following morning, he would arrive to change his clothes and apologise for his absence. He'd curse the job for tying him, before rushing out the door, hoping Mr Perry would be late himself. In time Betty accepted it. She did not ask where he had been. His life revolved around his republicanism. A few times Seamus was gone for two days at a time. Conleth would bring a note. "*Won't be back for two nights. I am sorry, duty calls. Lots of love to my girls.*" A few times there was a note requesting Betty to go the wardrobe and remove a bundle of papers from the bottom and give them to Conleth. She usually made the boy a bowl of porridge and gave him tea.

To make conversation, she once asked Conleth where was he off to with the papers from the wardrobe.

'You needn't worry your poor head about that, missus,' he said.

She giggled at the authoritarian tone coming from a child's mouth.

He was raging when she told him it was strange to hear a child speak an old man's words. He told her he was a man.

'Look at the size of me,' he said, standing in front of her with his shoulders raised to add to his height. 'Don't you think I've grown since you first saw me?' He was almost pleading for affirmation.

Betty hid her smile and agreed. 'You're a great man. The boots must be fitting you now.' She knew it would take years before his feet would stretch to wear them comfortably.

He nodded. 'Maybe in a few months.'

She agreed, tickled by his childish and hopeful response.

Ursula continued to call. Betty always examined her face for signs of grief for Dr O'Malley. Instead of inquiring, she decided to be as kind as possible.

Then for the first time she noticed Ursula pass an envelope to Seamus.

Betty and Ursula went for a walk to the Pro-Cathedral to Mass. It was the 1st of November, All Saints Day and a Holy Day of Obligation. As All Saints Day was a commemoration of the 'faithful departed' who had not yet been purified and reached heaven, Betty would have liked to ask Ursula if she was praying for Dr O'Malley's soul. Instead they lit a candle and sat quietly praying. Rather than praying for the dead, Betty said a prayer for Ursula. Since the Rising she had been quieter.

When Ursula was leaving that evening, Betty noticed Seamus leave another envelope beside her handbag. It was probably happening all the time but only now did Betty become aware that Ursula was also playing a role in the struggle for independence.

Mona was still popping in during the day. She never stayed long as there was always a chore to be done, food to be prepared and a room to be scrubbed or a corpse to be washed. War did not stop nature from taking its course. Mona would sit by the window smoking a Woodbine and chatting as if she hadn't a care in the world.

'She's getting bigger by the day, God bless her.' Mona always scrutinised Isabel with her head tilted to one side. 'With the help of God, she'll soon have a sister or brother to keep her company.'

'Please God.' Betty pretended to agree only because she knew it was expected. She did not want another child until she could think of some way to get Seamus round to her way of thinking. Mr Hartmann had sent a note via Ursula to contact him.

'By all accounts she'll have the vote,' Mona informed Betty.

'Do you really think they'll give us women the vote?'

Mona's simple ramblings were a relief for Betty, compared to the talk of death and killings she heard from Seamus and his friends.

'Mick Daly said a woman in England flung herself under the King of England's horse during the races in the hope he'd give women the vote. Imagine killing yourself so other women could vote! She's as daft as that Constance Markievicz!'

Betty was horrified. 'Why would any woman be that desperate to vote?'

'I said the very same thing. Mick Daly said it happened. Seemingly these mad yokes have been chaining themselves to railings, setting fire to mailboxes and going around England smashing windows. Pure idle hands, if you ask me. Imagine all those people who write their letters to their families bein' set on fire by them English lunatics. It takes Mick Daly so long to write a letter, and then to think of it going up in flames!'

'They must be very desperate for the vote,' Betty said, not giving a fiddler's if she ever got it. There was so much more to be done apart from becoming well versed in politics.

'If we get the vote it only means that the normal election results will be doubled cos women will vote the way their husbands and fathers vote. Codswallop if you ask me,' Mona said.

'Codswallop is right,' Betty said.

'We'll all end up voting for a free Ireland,' Mona said. 'Even Sheila Muldoon has started singing "Boolavogue" and "The Rising of the Moon".'

Betty was surprised. Sheila Muldoon had been one of the most vocal haters of the rebels.

'She's saying "The Wearing of the Green" is her new party-piece. She's trying to sing it. Lord bless us, she'll drive the English home it's so bad."

"True. Poor Sheila hasn't a note in her head.'

Mona stood up. 'Are you in need of anything?' She always asked this before she left.

With the war there was a shortage of fuel, food and other items. Somehow Mona could source anything that Betty required for a small payment. She was as discreet in offering products as she was about Seamus's activities during Easter Week.

'The only thing we need is a new bicycle tyre for Seamus,' Betty said.

'I think I'll be able to get one,' Mona said, knowing full well she had access to any amount of requirements.

'I'd be most grateful if you happen to come across one.' Betty played along as if it were luck on Mona's part.

Throughout the conversation Betty had been conscious that Phelim was in their bedroom, waiting for Seamus to return. Later she went to him with a cup of tea. Phelim was sitting on the floor, beside him a small bundle of envelopes. He smiled at her as she placed the tea beside his envelopes. She noticed how his appearance had improved since their first encounter. With the summer sun he had a golden tan, and his hair was not as tightly cut. He had a few black curls falling onto his forehead. As time passed he was more relaxed in her presence. His large brown eyes were less guarded and more expressive.

'On second thoughts,' he said, placing his hands on the envelopes, 'are you a suffragette in the making? Is my post safe?'

She laughed while he pretended to guard his post.

Occasionally he asked her to post his letters. He had distinctly clear, even handwriting. The "g" was not curled, the "t" crossed modestly. There was a tinker woman in her village who maintained she could tell a person's character and their future from their handwriting. The first time Betty queued for stamps for him, she traced her fingers over his perfect handwriting and tried to see what the tinker woman saw. She imagined it conveyed a man who was determined, a modest man who would not feel the need to curl his "g". A selfless unwed teacher who remained living in his crowded family home among his own people. A scholar with a great deal to offer. Before posting the letters she got the whiff of his cigarettes from them. She imagined him sitting in their bedroom beside the great wardrobe as he wrote letters and read documents for the Irish Republican Brotherhood. She imagined him methodically placing the documents in the concealed drawer in the wardrobe, his shirtsleeves rolled up and his brown contemplative eyes double-checking everything.

In October 1916 Betty returned to Mr Hartmann with the last violin and a plan of her own.

'A pleasure, Mrs Hopkins.' He held her chair while she sat. His quaint manners were touching. 'How is Mr Hopkins?'

He always asked after Seamus, she noted, another confirmation that he wanted his violins.

'Very well, thank you.'

Sitting in his presence in his beautifully furnished office, Betty was very much at ease. She liked to think that someday she too could have an office and pleasant surroundings like Mr Hartmann's.

'Are your buyers pleased with my husband's products?' Betty asked.

'You will be pleased to hear that I have an order from England for your husband's next two violins,' he said pleasantly, as he examined the violin. 'How is work advancing on the instruments?'

Betty didn't answer his question immediately. If Mr Hartmann knew of Seamus's republican activity or if he knew that Seamus worked his fingers to the bone for Mr Perry's reputation and bank balance, he never pretended.

He looked at her, waiting for a response.

'Mr Hartmann, I would like to continue my dealings with you indefinitely. However, we cannot move forward without establishing a stronger footing and a revised payment scheme. You might also like to read this certificate from Reverend Morris.'

Mr Hartmann read the letter and looked at her. His black eyebrows rose slightly with impressed surprise.

Betty remained composed.

'If you and I find a common ground, it can last a lifetime and benefit both of us enormously.' She was aware she was coaxing him. 'My husband is from a working-class background. He is intimidated by men in nice suits and polished offices.'

Mr Hartmann nodded as if accepting a compliment.

'I can act as a go-between, however.' She delayed a moment to ensure she had his full attention. 'Unlike my husband, I know the value of good stock. I have no issue with dealing with men in nice offices and I will get the price my husband's violins are worth.'

103

From the sale of the last two violins Betty had ordered spruce wood from Switzerland. She remembered her father and uncle talking about the wood from the Jura Mountains. The trees there grew slower and gathered more strength. There were less knots which made the finest violins with the greatest resonance. The maple wood made it possible to create a low-weight instrument with the best acoustic properties. Betty gave Mr Hartmann's address as the delivery point. Ursula had told Betty that there was a disused workshop behind the hall where she practised her reels with Cumann na mBan. Betty could store the wood there.

If Mr Hartmann was not amenable, then she would find some other way. She would find another dealer – if not Mr de Lacy, then another dealer in Wicklow or Kildare. She could travel to London. There were other avenues to explore. There was always an alternative route. Maybe it was wrong to be wishful for too much but what was her alternative? If she stayed any longer in the tenements, it would become home, a place she might even miss eventually. She would not become a bystander in her own life and accept her cruel conditions without a fight.

Mr Hartmann's eyes remained on hers as his fingers stroked the f-hole of the violin.

Part two

Chapter 13

On the 1st of January 1919, Sinn Féin MPs gathered in Dublin, to establish the First Dáil Éireann and adopt a Declaration of Independence. On the same day, the first shots of the Irish War of Independence were fired, killing two Royal Irish Constabulary men at Soloheadbeg in Tipperary.

Betty heard the news in her new home in Ranelagh. Phelim, Conleth, and Seamus were having tea at the kitchen table with two more rebels, Digger Dempsey and Johnny Red. They were on a break from digging a concealed bunker beneath the floor of the shed at the bottom of the garden. As the news was relayed, Seamus and his comrades pulled their chairs closer to the wireless. They stared expectantly at the grid as if they were seated in the front row of the Abbey Theatre, waiting for the scene to be re-enacted before their eyes.

'*The two Royal Irish Constabulary men were shot dead when they refused to surrender a consignment of gelignite they were guarding in the rural setting of Soloheadbeg in County Tipperary.*'

Seamus leapt to his feet with his hands raised victoriously above his head. '*The day for passivism is gone!*'

Digger Dempsey joined him, '*Match them gun for gun!*'

'I'll lay money it was our own Dan Breen,' Seamus said, referring to a Volunteer from the Tipperary Brigade who lived very close to the vicinity.

'Tipperary is doing us proud,' Johnny Red said. He too was a Tipperary native.

'I'll buy him a pint if I ever get to Soloheadbeg,' Digger said.

Phelim remained seated. When the men's theatrics died down, he said, 'You know this is the beginning of it?'

Seamus looked at his friend. 'I know,' he said quietly.

'The only tactic now is guerrilla warfare,' Conleth said.

'You taught him well,' Johnny Red said, impressed with Conleth's adult words.

'The real war begins now,' Phelim continued in the same indifferent tone.

The men in the kitchen gradually realised that Dan Breen's actions would start a war with the British. In shooting the RIC officers, they had attacked and killed the enemy. England could only retaliate. The objective of the rebels was to paralyse the civil administration and undermine and demoralise the British army, until they rendered Ireland ungovernable. The killing in Tipperary would spark a chain of events that could never be undone. The men looked from one to the other, elation and fear peppering the air. They realised the inevitable consequences of what they had just heard.

'It could take months or years,' Phelim said, 'and a lot of men will die. One of us, if not all of us in this room, could be dead within a few months.'

'We don't need to be afraid,' Seamus said. 'We didn't sign up to quit when we're this near.'

There was silence as they thought about it.

'Another thing,' Seamus said. 'I hope you boys know the Act of Contrition.'

The laughter in the room relieved the strain. Beneath the hilarity, the fear was palpable. Each knew their country was on the cusp of something momentous.

Betty left the men. Over the months of conflict, she had learned to remove herself from their talk of war. She found it difficult to shake off the sense of looming dangers. Instead she sat in her back garden under the warm summer sun and admired her home. With the proceeds from Seamus's violins, Betty and Seamus had the down-payment for a home within two years. Much to Betty's frustration, they could have moved sooner except Seamus kept dipping into their savings to give to the Volunteers.

Even when they had enough money for a down-payment, Seamus continued to stall. 'The tenements haven't killed us yet,' he reminded her, his blue eyes filled with defiance.

There were times when she thought he was going against her deliberately. He claimed to be a working man and wanted to remain living among the working men. The salt of the earth, as he saw it. He spoke in flowery language about the joys and taste of life in the heart of the city. All the while Betty wanted to whack his thick head with the sweeping brush. Instead she gently cajoled him.

Finally, Fr Mathew told them about a beautiful house in his parish. "Large and solid, and going for a song" was how he described it.

Twice they viewed the house in Roseberry Gardens in Ranelagh.

Phelim thought it would be a great location to hide arms. 'The Brits would never suspect a house like that.'

Only when Kitty Doran's daughter, who was the same age as Isabel, died did Seamus relent.

When Betty first moved into her new home, the little things no longer bothered her. When Seamus returned after a few nights' absence, exhausted and elated, or frustrated and silent, there was enough space to let him to his own devices. When the men moved their meetings from the shed to the lounge below her bedroom, Betty didn't care. When their voices were raised in animation, keeping her awake, she didn't mind because she had the comfort of her own home. She had a large bedroom, and three to spare. They had their own toilet and didn't have to queue or clean another person's mess. In the early days of her new home, she could tolerate anything.

When Mona first saw her house, her reaction was a let-down.

''Tis grand. A bit big but grand,' she said vaguely.

Despite the great joy of the new home, Betty missed Mona. She missed her pottering in and out of her home and her quaint simple ways and that air of reassurance she effused.

'A bit big?' Betty repeated, aghast at Mona's mild criticism of the size of her house. 'Wouldn't you like to live here?' She needed to see a flicker of want in Mona.

'Shure what would I want to live here for? I'd end up getting notions about myself,' Mona said, spitting out a flake of tobacco as she spoke.

'What would be wrong with getting notions? We all need to have a little pride,' Betty said.

'Irish people with notions is only tuppence ha'penny looking down on tuppence,' Mona said as if the idea of snobbery was beneath her.

Like Mona, Seamus was not comfortable with his new surroundings. He treated his new home like a countryman uncomfortable wearing his Sunday clothes. The size overwhelmed him and he was irked by his neighbours' accents.

'Their auld grand voices annoy me,' he complained.

'You'll be speaking like that soon enough,' she teased him, wishing he'd wear nicer suits and take more pride in his appearance. It was as if he felt that by changing he was reneging on his past.

'There's only room for one deluded grandiose clown in this marriage and it's not me,' he retorted good-humouredly.

Seamus's brothers did not help matters. Initially, the Hopkins boys were not very impressed with his new surroundings. They viewed the well-to-do as people who remained content to allow British rule. 'Slave-minded,' was how they called those who didn't question. They were concerned that their brother was turning into 'one of those eejits who starts acting like he's English when he makes a few bob'.

'Not for me, boys,' Seamus said. 'The house is an IRA haven in disguise.' Proudly he showed them the items of furniture he had made with hidden panels. Since moving into their new house, Seamus had furnished the house with pieces made by him alone. Every single item he made had hidden panels. The coffee table had a two-inch concealed space to hide documents, the kitchen cabinet had a concealed back panel behind which hung several guns. The legs of each of the beds were hollow. Betty couldn't keep up with the secret places in her home.

But Seamus was not put off by every man with a toff's accent. Betty prevailed on him to meet Mr Hartmann and, the first time he met him, he liked him. Betty pretended to tutor Seamus on what to ask Mr Hartmann, like how much the violins would fetch and how many he would produce a year. She had already prepared Mr Hartmann, hinting that he should be discreet about his dealings with her. Mr Hartmann met Seamus in the less formal environment of Davy's pub. According to Seamus, Mr Hartmann insisted on buying him a pint and drank one himself. As well as discussing his workmanship and the luthier craft, they discussed politics.

Seamus said later, with utter surprise, 'Reading between the lines, Mr Hartmann could be a bit sympathetic.'

Just then Betty wished she had been a fly on the wall during their meeting. Maybe Mr Hartmann knew more about their lives than he led her to believe. It was clear he wanted Seamus's business, even if it meant behaving like a working-class man swigging pints and quietly praising the rebels.

More determined than ever to turn their money into more money, Betty got to work on her next plan. She walked the length and breadth of Dublin visiting every furniture shop. She inspected the layout, workmanship, products, pricing and manner of the assistants. She scrutinised the quality of the household furniture and compared the quality of wood. She wrote to timber merchants to find the best prices. Lastly she viewed shops available to rent in the city. Once she established exactly the type of shop she wanted, she waited for the right opportunity to discuss it with Seamus.

When Betty overheard Seamus and Phelim discussing the constant difficulties for the Irish Volunteers with the continuing draconian laws, she felt it was an opportune time. Sinn Féin, the Irish Volunteers, the Gaelic League and Cumann na mBan remained banned organisations. Men were continually stopped and harassed, and their pockets and jackets rifled by the RIC.

Seamus lamented that shortly they'd be banned from speaking to each other on the street. 'Where will it end?' he asked.

'I know an easier way to continue your fight without coming under their notice,' Betty said when they were alone. 'We can benefit ourselves, and help the republican movement to advance without harassment.'

She proposed to Seamus that they establish their own cabinetmaking business with a workshop attached where Irish volunteers could work. They would employ republicans, which would help the cause. Not only would they would have money to donate to the cause, it would be a location where covert republican activities could carry on freely. They would be free to transport anything across the city under the guise that they were delivering furniture. Betty told Seamus about the furniture shops she'd visited recently, the shoddy workmanship and price of the products. Seamus realised that Betty had been right about making the violins for Mr Hartmann. He also knew she was clever and, with the success of Mr Hartmann's venture, he thought she was his lucky charm. A lucky charm with a lot more ambition, Betty thought cynically.

When Seamus was confounded at the notion of the paperwork involved for setting up the business, Betty told him she would take care of that side of things. She explained how she had done it for her father. She knew where to source the wood and material that Seamus preferred. She also promised that she would look after the bookkeeping and all of the administrative side of the business.

'All you have to do is keep making the violins,' she said.

'I'll be like the boy on the workshop floor?' Seamus said.

Betty trod carefully. No man wanted to think his wife was his puppeteer.

'My role is the easy one. Without you there would be no workshop floor, no house, and no nice dresses for Isabel.'

Mr Hartmann reiterated Betty's points. Seamus brought him to their home one evening. Formally she shook his hand and was careful to allow Seamus to take the leading role in their conversation about the business. Mr Hartmann played along as if she had again tutored him in how to behave. He really was a shrewd old owl, she realised – not for the first time. After that, he called to their home occasionally in his pony and trap. Theatrically he would pull a little toy from his hat for Isabel then smoke cigars and drink tea.

Mr Hartmann told Seamus if he never reached old age he was already leaving a magnificent legacy behind with his completed violins.

'You have made a name for yourself and your business.'

Betty had to stop herself from waltzing around the kitchen with exhilaration at his compliments, while Seamus remained unfazed.

Chapter 14

When Betty was established in her new home and the business was ticking along, she set to work on forming her own friendships. Her only female company was Mona whom she employed to work in her home, minding Isabel and housekeeping each day, while the women of the tenement took care of Mona's own children.

For a while Betty was concerned that Mona might tell the new neighbours that they'd lived side by side in the tenements. The thought of people finding out brought Betty out in a cold sweat.

'Don't mention it to anybody,' Betty said. 'You know, that we lived in Middle Abbey Street.'

Mona looked at Betty as if she wasn't the full shilling. 'But you did live in the tenements in Middle Abbey Street.'

Even to hear it said aloud irked Betty. 'That's not the point, Mona.'

'So you want me to pretend we were never friends and you and Seamus and little Isabel never lived in Middle Abbey Street,' Mona said slowly. 'You want me to act like it was a child's dream?'

'Of course we're friends,' Betty said dismissively. 'Just the part about living in Middle Abbey Street.' She was certain that Mona knew exactly what she meant but was enjoying highlighting Betty's little bit of pride.

'And, am I really here now?' Mona continued. She was washing clothes at the sink, 'Am I really here washing your drawers or is this like a child's dream too?'

'Of course you're here,' Betty said and left quickly, ending Mona's opportunity to ridicule her. In fact, she was confident Mona would never reveal the truth. Mona knew every woman's secrets in the tenements yet she never divulged a thing to Betty.

Betty needed to find her own like-minded friends. She noticed how Ursula was forever going to the theatre and calling on various friends who were clearly not downtrodden women. They were the class of women who went on day trips to the country or shopped in Clerys for style. Unlike Betty, Ursula was never sitting at home alone, trying to deny to herself how lonely she felt. Betty realised she had misjudged Ursula's friends from Cumann na mBan. Its members were independent ladies – some owned their own business, and most were from educated backgrounds. Betty knew about Countess Markievicz and also Kathleen Clarke, one of the widows from the Rising – her husband Thomas was one of the seven signatories of the Proclamation of Independence. Betty was very curious to meet those two notorious women.

Ursula took her to her first meeting in Parnell Street. Hidden in Ursula's hat she carried a sketch of a British Army Officer's home.

'How do you know which room is their bedroom?' Betty asked, recalling her "friend's" clandestine relationship with Dr O'Malley and suspecting her cousin was up to her old tricks.

'Because I delivered his wife's baby in the bedroom last week.'

'What will Cumann na mBan do with that information?' Betty asked.

'You'll find out soon enough,' Ursula said.

Betty was immediately disappointed that the Cumann's president, Countess Markievicz, was not present. She was in Cork Gaol for making a seditious speech.

Betty was introduced to Mrs Jennie Wyse who owned her own restaurant and shop, the Irish Farm Produce Company, at 21 Henry

Street. Betty had heard about the formidable old lady and her resistance to the British.

Later in the evening she heard one of the committee members discuss the sketch of the RIC officer's house. 'We must know the enemy. Collins will be glad of this,' she said, popping it into her handbag.

During her introduction Betty was told the role of the women was to assist by every means. They were to act as organisers and recorders in the Republican Courts set up by the First Dáil in 1919. They assisted in distributing pamphlets, posting handbills and organising public meetings. The members were also active selling Dáil Bonds and in other fundraising activities such as organising dances, concerts and campaigning on behalf of political leaders. Betty's head spun at the prospect of the dances and stylish people she'd meet. She tried to seek out at least one moderate woman to befriend who'd rather having tea or attending the movies. She'd have to bide her time, she thought, as she saw the brooch of the Cumann na mBan: a rifle framed with the initials of the organisation.

It was some weeks before Betty learned about the dangers involved in many of the other roles the women played. They provided safe-houses for men on the run, served on prison relief committees, provided practical assistance for the prisoners' families, sourced employment for them upon their release, collected petitions, protested and maintained a prayerful presence at executions. Betty played along. She promised Mrs Wyse Power and company that she would do all she could for her fellowmen and country. All the while Seamus was bursting with pride that his wife was playing her role in the nationalist movement. He was more proud of her Cumann na mBan membership than her prowess at business and accumulating money.

Betty spent most of her day in the newly acquired shop in Dawson Street, with Isabel in Mona's safe care at home while Seamus continued to make his violins in the workshop at the back of their house and occasionally made items of furniture with secret compartments for the house. Admittedly, they were well-crafted items that Betty was proud of. In any case, she was not concerned what Seamus did as long as Mr Hartmann received his violins each month as agreed.

Betty loved their Dawson Street shop. Their name over the door, *Hopkins Furniture*, inspired her to work harder. She appraised the men's work. Their products needed to be the best. She enjoyed her busy days, meeting people and showing the fine quality of her products to prospective buyers. There was a wonderful joy in selling the goods. Bartering distracted her further from the increasingly troubled country. Betty knew the value of every single product in her shop and was determined to get the highest price possible. It was like a game where she learned how to speak to people. She began to recognise their taste by their appearance, and it was a game that she was confident she would always win.

Each night Betty returned home to Seamus and informed him how much they had sold in the shop that day and what profit had been made. She always led him to believe that he was the one who conceived the idea of establishing the business, and underlined the fact that it was his creative genius that had saved them from disease and death. When he gasped in awe at the accumulating money, Betty reiterated that without him none of it was possible. It was his flair, his commitment to his workmanship that started it all. She reminded him that everything was his.

As long as Seamus was kept happy, there would be no interference.

With each item sold, there was a receipt written. If Seamus ever asked, Betty would show him the grey receipt book. She never told Seamus about the second receipt book, the colour of the receipts slightly darker. She kept that receipt book safely tucked away along with all the money she accumulated from the products that Seamus was too busy to notice. Her conscience was so clear that she felt no need to justify her actions. The way he handed out money to the Volunteers, they'd never know a rich day if he had control of all of the money. And he was happy to let her manage everything. He was too consumed with the daily accounts of gaol breaks, arrests, and imprisonments without trial, assassinations, and assassination squads, men dying slowly on hunger strikes, reprisal killings, and death squads. On the rare occasion when they were at home alone he would read out newspaper articles and rant about the endless incidents of the war. In the end Betty ignored him. Like a child clawing for attention, Seamus focused on Mona, only because she feigned a vague interest.

'The Lord save us!' Mona would gasp on hearing about another killing.

Betty knew Mona couldn't have cared less – she had her own struggle to keep her and her brood alive.

Mona and Seamus were prolific smokers. If Seamus was present when Mona arrived, he'd accept a cup of tea and give her a cigarette.

While Mona ironed their clothes she'd occasionally say, ''Tis shockin', Sacred Heart, completely shockin'.'

Encouraged by her reaction, Seamus would continue reading the atrocities from the newspaper in a raised incredulous voice while Mona ironed and puffed cigarettes.

On those mornings, Betty was glad to leave them in their cloud of smoke.

Seamus's working hours became increasingly erratic. Sometimes he'd arrive home early in the morning and go immediately to his workshop in the back garden. She would bring him his meals. He was so absorbed in his own troubled world he barely acknowledged her. Once a month Mr Hartmann called to see how work was progressing and to collect the completed violins. Mr Hartmann was Seamus's only friend who was not an active member of the IRA. Their conversations mainly revolved around music, instruments and concerts.

Mr Hartmann encouraged Seamus to try his hand at making a cello. 'You would master it very quickly and make much more money.'

'I've barely the time to eat my meals,' Seamus confessed.

As the months passed, Seamus's face changed. The soft curves of his face hardened and the glint in his eyes died.

'Where will it all end?' he'd sigh.

She dreaded to think how exhausted his mind must be. She saw so many indications of the strain on his mental health. The loaded revolver by the bed, another by the bath, a book with the inside cut out holding a grenade. His ever-vigilant eyes scanning the road outside their bedroom when he opened the shutters each morning. To reinforce his safety, there were three bolts on the front and back doors, another to the entrance from the basement and finally a bolt on their bedroom. She thought his security measures unnecessary until she woke one night as he returned. There was blood on his clothes. The tremor in his left hand as he tried to unbutton his shirt was a stark reminder how involved he was. She was aware he carried a burden so great it would cripple him entirely if Ireland did not soon find peace.

The only time her mind was still was during Phelim's visits. Several times each evening Betty looked towards the special cup and saucer she used for his visit. He didn't request that particular cup, but had once admired the picture on it of two Irish Red Setters. It was sitting in the kitchen cabinet awaiting his arrival. He liked his tea strong with one sugar and two Jacob's biscuits. He called a few evenings a week with messages for Seamus. Most of the time he came alone with documents to be hidden or removed from the wardrobe in their bedroom. In the early days, he declined the offer of tea. His visits were brief. If Seamus was not home he had no reason to delay. His formality kept him at a clear distance. But, as the months passed, his brief words with Betty grew longer. His reasons for delaying increased until finally he always accepted the offer of tea.

They'd chat in the kitchen as he lingered over cold tea. They talked about their lives. Betty thought his occupation as a teacher made him interested in all aspects of Irish life. He'd ask questions about her parents' home in Tipperary, about their garden, what fresh vegetables they grew or how many cows they had. The size of the school and ratio of teachers to pupils. He was easy company. The quiet type who preferred to listen. Betty regaled him with stories of the characters she'd known: Kitty Connors and her hunger for bad news, the headmaster who brought his greyhounds to school and appointed two boys to walk them during lessons. She described in detail her midlands village, the landscape and her father's workshop.

During those evenings as they sat by the stove in her kitchen, he told her about his crowded two-bedroomed childhood home in Christchurch which he shared with his unwed brothers and sisters, and his parents. The five boys, including Phelim, slept on makeshift beds in the warmth of the kitchen, the three remaining unmarried girls in one of the bedrooms and his parents in the other bedroom. He told her the first up in the morning lit the fire, the next boiled the water and from there on it was a hub of activity for the day. He described with pride his hardworking mother and invalid father. He told anecdotes about his life as a teacher, kept her up to date on the school and his colleagues.

Those evenings alone with him slipped by so peacefully yet there were times when she felt she was doing something wrong. On the rare occasion when Seamus arrived home when he was present, Phelim would go to the lounge and work on the documents. Without ever saying it, both sensed they were doing something wrong.

Chapter 15

1920

When Betty's parents eventually made the trip to Dublin in March 1920, Betty wanted everything to run smoothly. It had been over four years since she'd laid eyes on her family. A time so far removed from her current life. There were days when she felt she knew no other existence but a bustling life in a torn city she'd grown to love. At last she could invite her parents to a house she was proud of. The furnishings were testament to Seamus's craftsmanship, each room containing furniture that he crafted in his workshop at the back of their house. Betty just hoped her mother would not be curious enough to go fiddling with the bedside locker – God only knows what Seamus had hidden there. A gun or maps or lists of names could come tumbling out. More than anything, Betty wanted Seamus to appear untroubled, a man contented with his home and business. Her parents would think his nightly ritual of bolting the doors with three locks highly irregular. For the previous few weeks he insisted on closing the shutters to their bedroom, afraid a shaft of light would betray which room he slept in. Each night before retiring to bed Betty would hear him obsessively rattle the handle to see if it would give.

'A closed window won't keep the Brits out,' Betty said. 'If they want to come in they'll blow it to pieces.'

'At least this will delay them,' he replied, placing a beam over the window shutters.

Although her parents would expect more vigilance with locked doors in the city than in their own rural home, if they saw his angst while rechecking the locked and bolted doors and windows, they would think Seamus had the nerves.

The day of their arrival, Betty left Isabel in the care of Conleth, while she and Seamus went to Kingsbridge to collect her parents and Aunt Úna. Of course Mona could have minded Isabel. Instead Betty gave Mona a few days off and explained that her parents were coming, and she hadn't seen them for a few years and they'd need a bit of privacy to catch up. Mona would have been delighted to meet Betty's parents. No doubt she'd question them at length about the train journey to Dublin and marvel at the rural life in Tipperary. She would probably be honest enough to admit she had never been to Tipperary, never been anywhere except the confines of this godforsaken dirty city. Betty didn't want her people to see the likes of poor Mona. Then they'd want to know how Betty made Mona's acquaintance. Betty visualised Mona sitting back with one leg hoisted on her knee like a man, the nearly toothless grin as she smoked Woodbine and spat out the stray flake of tobacco. "Ah, shur me and Betty go way back!" Although Mona knew not to mention the tenements she'd probably say they knew each other from the pawnbroker's. There was enough to worry about without adding that to the mix.

When Betty's parents and Aunt Úna saw their home in Ranelagh, much to her satisfaction they couldn't stop oohing over its size.

They gazed at it from the back garden.

''Tis bigger than Thomas O'Fogarty's house,' Aunt Úna said, referring to the most prosperous member of their family.

Her mother suggested laying drills of cabbage and beetroot. Maybe plant an apple tree so as Betty could make apple tarts and apple jam. She told Betty about Aunt Helen's secret recipe for the best apple jam in Ireland. Betty silently thought that while there was so much money to be made in furniture, someone else could make her apple jam.

They admired Seamus's carpentry dotted throughout the house.

Her mother ran her fingers over the giant wardrobe. 'The whole lot of us would fit into it.'

Her father Jim scrutinised the timber and carvings on the wardrobe. He opened and closed the door and examined the hinges.

'Utterly flawless,' he said. 'It'll last hundreds of years.'

'Thanks, Mr O'Fogarty,' Seamus said, embarrassed with the compliments.

'Jim. No more Mr O'Fogarty – 'tis Jim,' her father said, clapping Seamus on the back.

When Conleth returned with Isabel shortly after the visitors' arrival, cabbage drills and apple tarts were quickly forgotten. For once in her life Betty's mother was silenced. Although there was no reference to Betty's sudden departure from Tipperary, when they saw the child each silently acknowledged that a lot had happened in a few years.

Betty watched her mother's large frame lean forward. Her stout face, framed with grey hair pinned in a bun, beamed as she extended a warped arthritic hand towards the child.

'Will you sit on your grandmother's lap?' she said in an unusually quiet tone.

So used to a full house of strangers, Isabel never made strange. She obliged, sat on Maureen's lap and sang part of a song when asked. All agreed Isabel should be on the stage.

'She'd win the Feis Ceoil,' Maureen said, referring to the competition for traditional singing and dancing.

The men retreated to Seamus's workshop in the back garden while the women cooked. They told Betty all the news from home. Funerals, deaths, births and marriages and of course the state of the country. Her mother said they nearly had welts on their feet from walking to the church praying for the bedlam to stop.

'Kitty Connors says it's a sign the world is coming to an end,' Aunt Úna said.

'She's flinging holy water around the house every time she hears a motor car approach,' her mother added.

'I was only after having my hair set when she was sprinkling holy water at me,' Úna said. 'I said to Maureen, she's reading the newspapers looking for more misery.'

''Twas quiet for a few days and nobody was being shot,' said Maureen. 'I said to Úna, "If she doesn't hear about a killing in the next few hours, she'll surely take the shotgun and kill someone herself!"'

As her mother and aunt regaled Betty with stories, she realised how much she missed home. Although she loved Dublin and was aware there remained a great deal of hard work to be done, the prospect of going home for a holiday pleased her. For those few days in March 1920, it was the first time in months that Betty didn't think about the business.

On the surface Seamus appeared relaxed. Separately both women whispered their approval to Betty. She noticed how they no longer referred to him as a mountain peasant.

Maureen said, ''Twas only that Seamus's father fell on hard times after his wife died and him left with the job of raisin' all those boys by himself.'

Úna added, 'We'd forgotten that Seamus has a cousin who's a priest in Africa and another cousin of his mother's a priest in America.'

They didn't retell the story about the priest in Africa. He was so unrefined from his years of working in the wilderness that he removed his false teeth and licked them after eating. Now that Seamus was married to one of their own, that story would never again be told.

Although accepting of Seamus, they were not generous enough to allow Isabel to resemble Seamus's side of the family.

'She's an O'Fogarty! She has Granddad John's eyes,' Aunt Una said.

Maureen echoed her sister's thoughts. 'I noticed that myself.'

They held Isabel in their arms and looked at her feature by feature, claiming everything from her blonde curls to her gamey glint.

Digger Dempsey and Johnny Red called on Saturday evening. So too did Phelim. Seamus introduced him as one of Dublin's finest. As always, Phelim was ill at ease in a room of strange women. He was more comfortable in men's company. Her mother was impressed with his teaching profession and nice manners. Betty was going to tell her mother how patriotic Mrs Salmon was by sending little Conleth into the streets during the rebellion, but, afraid she'd prejudice them against Phelim, she didn't say a word, only told them about Phelim's scholarships and achievements.

That night Ursula, her brother and her parents joined them for a sing-song. Everybody sang and Seamus accompanied them on the violin while Phelim played the flute. When Phelim played a slow version of 'Castlekelly', Betty felt the heat rise to her cheeks. She was as affected by his presence as by his music. When he and Seamus played a reel she danced with Ursula's brother and clapped loudly when it was over.

Betty could see her mother looking at the scar on Phelim's hand. Afterwards she asked about it. Betty told them how nobly he'd fought in the GPO, how selfless he and each of his family were in their fight for freedom.

'Another lovely boy who'll probably die before his time,' her mother observed.

It gave Betty great satisfaction that her parents liked him. She thought him very handsome in his tweed jacket and slacks.

'He'd be a grand fellow for Ursula,' Aunt Úna said when everyone had gone home.

'No, absolutely not,' Betty said categorically.

With Betty's reaction, her mother and aunt were curious to know if there was news about Ursula. Was she walking out with a man? Why not Phelim?

Betty dismissed the notion adamantly. 'No, they'd never be suited. He's too refined for her.'

On Sunday morning Seamus and Betty took their guests to see

their new shop on Dawson Street. They had lunch in the Gresham Hotel where Betty had compiled so many letters to her mother only to burn them in the evening. Afterwards they took a tour of the city. Her parents were agog to witness the British troops searching the men's pockets as they stepped off the trams. Betty was accustomed to the daily harassment of Dubliners. Each time Seamus witnessed it, it reinforced his determination to fight.

Betty pointed out all of the notable features: the Abbey Theatre, Mr Hartmann's shop, the GPO, the hotels.

But when the cab took them up Abbey Street, Betty remained quiet. As they passed their old home with Mona Daly and the women sitting on the steps, Seamus glanced at his wife who remained tight-lipped.

'A shocking poor area,' Betty's mother said, breaking the silence. 'Dear Jesus, we're so blessed!' she gasped, at the sight of the children in rags and the density of the crumbling houses.

If Seamus's brothers were on the tour, he'd tell them that the children were poor but united. He would stop the cab to introduce him to anyone he knew and tell them how Mona Daly looked after his wife and infant. He'd tell them that Betty shared her food with these people when he was in the GPO. His brothers would be delighted to meet Seamus's old neighbours, and insist on buying them a pint. They'd see the tenement dwellers as the salt of the earth. It would be another interesting part of their brother's story to be proud of. Whereas Betty's family would be left with a sense of shame that one of their own had spent time in a tenement.

'It's not as bad as it looks,' was as much as Betty could manage to say.

The day her guests were leaving, Betty promised to return to Tipperary for a weeklong holiday.

Seamus sent a parcel to be delivered to his Uncle Bart. 'It's freshly cut steaks and a bottle of whiskey,' he explained to Jim lest he thought he was delivering IRA correspondence or weapons. 'My Uncle Bart is a stubborn old fool who won't take money from me.'

Jim understood. 'I'll be sure to deliver it.'

Everyone knew Bart, a bachelor who lived for music and nationalism. The men shook hands.

'I'm very grateful for the violin,' Jim said. 'The men in the workshop will enjoy examining it.'

It was only then Betty realised that Seamus had gifted one of his violins to her father. She hoped he was not going to make a habit of giving their violins away as well as their money.

On their way to the train station, Maureen said she'd pray for them, for prosperity for their business and the poor children who lived in rags. Betty realised her mother was delighted with her trip to Dublin as she also included Seamus's nationalist movement in her prayers although she thought their fighting was all in vain.

'For five hundred years men have tried to get a free country,' she continued. 'If you and your men can achieve that, my hat is off to you. But I don't know how it's possible.'

Betty squeezed Seamus's arm to stop him from entering a debate with her mother. Politics was always only a spectator sport for her family. They saw Seamus and his comrade's fight as a movement propelled by romance rather than reality. Death would be the only reward and life would continue, regardless of whether they fought or not.

'I'll pray for your girls' movement too.' Maureen meant the Cumann na mBan. 'Put your might behind the men and you'd never know what might happen,' she added unconvincingly.

'Don't forget –' Betty was about to request to be remembered in the family Rosary when she was knocked forward, almost falling off her seat.

Their cab had stopped suddenly to allow an influx of soldiers to march into the station. Everyone stopped to look at the strange new recruits. A few hundred soldiers passed before them, wearing an odd mixture of khaki British Army and rifle-green RIC items with black berets. Even the Dubliners who were accustomed to marching soldiers stopped to look at this peculiarly outfitted lot.

Chapter 16

The soldiers they saw that March evening were a new mercenary force of temporary constables recruited to assist the Royal Irish Constabulary. They were rushed through the training process and lacked an official uniform. Their mismatched uniforms earned them the nickname "The Black and Tans"

Seamus was apoplectic when he discovered what the English had sent to Ireland. 'They're riff-raff ex-soldiers, men insane from fighting too many wars.'

With the arrival of the Black and Tans Ireland saw a new wave of violence. Men and women were shot for nothing other than being in the wrong place at the wrong time. Families were burned out of their homes, young men were executed. In September 1920 a force of 150 Black and Tans assaulted the town of Balbriggan in County Dublin, killing two men and burning 49 houses.

There was also a new Auxiliary Division created to assist the RIC, and these were as violent as the Tans.

On November 21st, fourteen British undercover agents from Dublin Castle were shot dead, some in their homes, some as they left their homes and others outside Dublin Castle. From early that morning, Betty heard animated talking from downstairs. At the sight of the bloodied shirt that Mona Daly had steeping in the kitchen sink, Betty asked no questions. Rather than thinking about it, she thought of the kitchen sideboards she'd sold during the week. The grain of the wood was appealing.

Later that day, during the All-Ireland Hurling final between Tipperary and Dublin, the Auxiliary Division interrupted the game by firing into the crowd. They killed thirteen spectators and one player and there were countless wounded.

A few weeks later when a Tan was killed in Cork, they burnt down more than 300 buildings in the city centre and afterwards the Black and Tans proudly pinned pieces of burnt cork to their caps. Betty closed her mind to that atrocity too. She directed her energy into the shop. She had a new kitchen dresser painted cream with the shelves painted olive-green. She placed it in the window display.

An 18-year-old medical student, Kevin Barry, was executed for participating in the killing of three British soldiers. Part of Betty's duty in Cumann na mBan was to take part in a vigil outside the prison. Betty knelt to pray aloud with the other women, imploring God to intervene. There was such strength in the mass of women that Betty thought Kevin Barry would get a reprieve. The morning that he was hanged, Betty understood what it felt to be part of the movement. For those few hours that she knelt and prayed, she was drawn closer to the Cumann na mBan women. There was an air of desperation and hope, and death and cruelty strengthened their sense of comradeship.

Mrs Wyse Power told Betty how Kevin Barry said, 'It is nothing, to give one's life for Ireland. What's my life compared to the cause?'

Betty closed her eyes but, instead of thinking about Kevin Barry, she tried to recall the type of clientele that stopped to admire the cream-and-green cabinet.

A few days after Kevin Barry's death the Black and Tans arrested two men from the Lec cinema. One of them was a boy that Betty and Seamus knew from their old tenement. The next day their remains were found in Dromcondra with a bucket over each of their heads and their bodies riddled with bullet-holes. Betty and

Mrs Wyse Power called to the boy's parents to offer their assistance. It was clear that the fifteen-year-old boy had nothing whatsoever to do with the IRA. The boy's mother was drunk with grief, her few words mumbled and incoherent. Betty overheard a man ask how the English could manage to run Ireland when they sent men like the Black and Tans to govern it. In the midst of everything that day, Betty recalled what Phelim had said a week previously and realised he had been right: the Black and Tans would drive the softest pacifist to become a hardened republican sympathiser. Most Irish moderates and pacifists became sympathisers, including Betty's parents and their ilk. The rising tide of violence sparked by the arrival of the Black and Tans had precisely the opposite effect to that hoped for by the British officials. Far from demoralizing the Irish in their drive for independence, it seemed only to steel their resolve.

The cream-and-olive-green cabinet sold. She had another painted white and grey. It was placed in the window.

In Thurles, Uncle Bart's house was burned. The Tans made him stand by and watch. When they lost interest in the flames from the fire, they told Bart to put his hands over his head and run. The soldiers said they'd count to ten and chase him. Bart said his arms were too stiff to be raised above his hips – he added he'd rather see the eyes of his killers and deny any English soldier a few minutes of hunting pleasure. They shot him where he stood.

Seamus was beyond tears. When he returned from Bart's funeral he was accompanied by three Tipperary men. In their funeral suits they went straight to the shed at the bottom of the garden with shovels to dig up or bury their guns. Betty never asked.

The white-and-grey cabinet remained unsold. The colour was too dull.

For a period, gaol breaks were popular as was capturing army barracks and seizing the soldier's ammunition. Shoot-outs where bystanders were killed, abductions, torture and mutilated bodies dumped on the street were daily events. They no longer needed to make sense of killings, the time for understanding where it began had passed. News of a remotely detonated mine, a new technique, which exploded in an army barracks was a momentary talking point rather than the normal shootings and beatings.

There was little time for grief. It reminded Betty of the child's game 'Pass the Parcel'. Eventually the parcel would arrive at their door.

When Betty transported arms in Isabel's pram for the Cumann na mBan, there was an air of reckless gaiety about it. The sense of comradeship in common danger bound the women closer. It was a time when women were a vital cog in the republican wheel. Unlike the men, they could carry letters, ammunition and information and go about their republican activities unmolested. The British thought the fairer sex would not be able to cock a rifle. Betty did so much ferrying of messages and guns, there were times when she thought every woman she saw had a concealed weapon in her child's pram.

Phelim told her he used to feel the same way. 'That will pass,' he said. 'At least you don't think some of the women are going to kill you. Every time I'm stopped and searched, I ask myself, is this the moment it all ends?'

Despite hearing about houses being raided and searched for arms, it wasn't until it happened in Betty's home that she was really aware of how endangered their lives had become. Thankfully Seamus was out. When they heard the motor cars pull up outside and the first bang on the front door, Conleth fled over the back wall to find Seamus and warn him.

'We are here to search the house in the name of His Majesty the King!' an officer bellowed as he and two dozen British soldiers rushed into the house with their guns at the ready.

Regardless of the fact that Betty was constantly prepared for a raid, it frightened and then enraged her. The Cumann women had warned her to keep calm if her home was searched. Betty remained seated by the stove with Isabel on her lap. She listened to their heavy feet pounding up her stairs and barging into every room. Another batch of soldiers searched the downstairs rooms. Betty closed her eyes and soothed her daughter. She breathed deeply, conscious of a terror she had never previously felt.

As pieces of crockery crashed to the floor, Isabel began to cry, and Betty's terror intensified. She thought about a new dark wood. It would make regal bookcases and writing bureaus. A rich-coloured bureau that would make any ordinary class of a man feel he was moneyed.

The soldiers rifled her home, and pierced the beds with bayonets. When Betty was unable to concentrate on wood and kitchen cabinets, she thought of Mona Daly. Mona accepted conflict and found a way to retain her sense of humour. She met her difficulties with a peculiar elegance and dignity. With the dawning of each day such women fought a different battle, a plight that few would weather – constant grief, loss and struggle that would have driven their male counterparts to sanatoriums.

The soldiers found nothing. They stomped out the front door without a backwards glance.

Seamus was unable to think rationally when he saw the weeping child and their house with all of their belongings piled high in the centre of each room. He left only to return a few hours later with more bolts for the door. Instead of helping to reassemble the house he spent the day double-checking that his weapons were well concealed. In the afternoon he retreated to his workshop where he remained for the next day without reappearing.

Betty fought the rage she felt towards Seamus.

It was Phelim who sat and listened to the events of the previous night. She told him how she thought of Mona during the ordeal.

Phelim listened, one hand holding a mug of tea and the other a cigarette. He sat straight in the chair, his legs crossed and eyes fixed on her as she spoke. He reassured her that she had behaved like a true dignified Irishwoman.

'I don't know.' She doubted so much that morning.

'Get some rest, Betty – these are trying times for everyone,' he said.

It was the first time he had used her Christian name. It sounded peculiar. When he called her Mrs Hopkins it kept them apart.

135

Calling her Betty seemed alluring. It gave her the same feeling as carrying guns in her basket, a sense that what she was doing was ultimately right and proper yet she was treading on something dangerous.

Chapter 17

1920

For four nights Seamus was detained in Kilmainham Gaol. The locks on the front and back door proved pointless as he was arrested when entering his home. The conflict Betty experienced during his detainment was intolerable. She regretted her long conversations with Phelim, the way she anticipated his visits, contented to while away evenings in his company. It made little of Seamus. It was wrong to think and depend too much on a man who was not her husband. During those four days she thought of nothing but Seamus and the terrors he was experiencing. Already he was fragile, and she feared this would drive him further into irrationality. Each night and day she paced the floor, unable to sit still, lest her fear and guilt overcome her.

Phelim called each day, reassuring her that Seamus must be alive.

'If he was dead or if they intended to kill him they would have done it by now and you would know,' he said from across the room.

It was clear he too was affected by their closeness.

Mona Daly stayed late into the night making tea and sandwiches for callers. She reminded Betty about the many men arrested and released unharmed.

'Maggie O'Dowd's husband, Bridie O'Toole's son,' slowly Mona counted the men on her fingers, 'Joan O'Dea's husband, Annie Sullivan's son, although they should have kept that good-for-nothin' whore's melt.'

Betty thought of the men whom Mona was not counting on her fingers. The men who had been shot while in custody. She had heard the stories of arrests, beatings, torture and hate-filled badgering during their confinements at the hands of the authorities.

On the fourth night Phelim arrived with the news that Seamus was alive. In an unchecked gesture he held her by the wrist. Betty raised her free hand to hide her tears. When Phelim embraced her she cried into his chest and cursed her country and her troubles.

Seamus returned home. When he arrived he sat by the stove, breathless, with an alarmed expression. He was slow to meet her eye and jumped at her gentle touch. All of his toenails were gone: they had been pulled out with a pliers during his interrogation. Ursula bathed and bandaged his feet. At night when Betty saw the bruises on his abdomen, they reminded her of butterflies. Fluttering purple-and-blue butterflies dotted his body. When out of his sight, she cried.

Betty tried everything to resurrect the man she hoped was beneath the unresponsive mass he had become. She tried coaxing him, then leaving him alone to work on his violins. She watched him hobble to the workshop in the back garden.

Fr Mathew called for dinner each evening and finally Seamus turned to prayer. He said a Rosary each morning and one at night with Fr Mathew. Fanatically he prayed, but it didn't seem to alleviate whatever darkness he saw.

Nothing Betty said or did helped. Since his return he was unable to make love to her. He made a few brief attempts to instigate their intimacies, but as quickly turned away and slept with his back to her.

One night she wrapped her arms around him and asked if she could do anything. 'Anything?' she pleaded.

He didn't answer.

'What can I do to bring you back?' she said into the darkness.

'Don't let them destroy what's left of you, of us.'

'I'd rather be drifting through my life with everything dead inside me and closer to a free country than feel life pulsating through me with continued slavery.'

As the months passed Seamus drifted further away from her. Rather than playing records on the gramophone during their rare evenings at home alone, he would sit in silence as if caught by sudden indecision, his vacant eyes staring at hurts only he could see. During those evenings Betty would encourage Isabel to sit on his knee, hoping the child would ignite some form of life in his tormented soul. At the child's talk a vague smile would pass over his face. Other times he appeared wholeheartedly sad, as if the morning would bring damnation and there was nothing but a hell on earth waiting for his daughter's adulthood.

She found his rages difficult to handle. Unlike Betty's mother's angry tirades, Seamus was unpredictable. He could not disagree in a reasonable manner. Violently he would slam the table and shout his objections. Betty became cautious. Every utterance that fell from her lips was measured lest she upset him. Although mostly his eyes took on a glazed stare, Betty would search his face for the roguish grin she had fallen in love with. The bright dancing glint had gone from his eyes, the blue had faded, and they held nothing but the darkest seed of bleakness. Betty turned her searching eyes away from his, startled by their nothingness.

Betty knew not to ask any more was it worth it. She was all too familiar with the sacrifice he was willing to make. Ireland's problem was infiltrating the minds of men and slowly killing them. Some men were able to weather the storm more than others.

The spare room was always ready for passing volunteers. She met men from every corner of the country who were quietly fighting, men like Dan Breen from Tipperary who had cycled overnight to make a meeting the following morning in Dublin. Men who walked for miles to ensure their dispatches were delivered to safe hands would sleep for a few hours before making the return journey. Young boys eager to play their part, their eyes fresh with optimism for a country they might set free. Betty couldn't help her looming sadness at the sound of their passion, fearing that their fight for freedom would leave them detached brutal men.

Gradually Phelim and Betty returned to their old practices. He arrived in the evening when she was home from her day in the shop. It was all the more pleasurable if Seamus was out or working in his workshop at the bottom of the garden. Betty felt giddy and light prior to Phelim's arrival. His special cup was waiting to be scalded with boiling water, the empty chair by the stove was starkly vacant without him. Sometimes they would only have a few moments alone, other times it could be late into the night. Each time he arrived, Phelim would take the documents from their hiding place and lay them on the kitchen table as a woman would strategically set a placing for a dinner guest.

Each time she watched him going through the same formality, knowing he would cast the papers aside within a few minutes and direct his attention to her.

'Tea?' she always asked.

'Please,' he would reply without lifting his head from the document.

Occasionally Betty wondered if Phelim was fooling himself. Did he arrive each day with the intention of working on his documents only to pass the night away talking to his best friend's wife? Was it his way of alleviating his conscience, preparing the documents as if elbow deep in something other than conversation with Betty? Or was he using the documents only as a cover for his true intentions?

As time passed Betty needed Phelim more than ever.

'Does anyone die of natural causes any more?' she asked as she finished reading a newspaper article and stood up from the table.

The bodies of three men – Peader Clancy, Dick McKee and Conor Clune – were laid out in the Pro-Cathedral.

'It seems that way,' Phelim said, coming to stand beside her and look at the article.

'Some of the Cumann women and I went to pay our respects,' Betty said. 'Nobody should have to see corpses as mangled as theirs but it didn't really disturb me.'

The three men had been executed while in custody. Each had the appearance of being tortured. One had an enormous hole in his head, as if an explosive bullet had been used.

'I think I've become accustomed to the horrors of war and I don't know if it's a healthy way to live,' she said.

'No one is made for war.'

She waited for him to elaborate.

'The brutality will slowly crush some.' He glanced in the direction of Seamus's workshop in the garden. 'But you are so much stronger than you realise.'

'Will it ever end?' she asked. 'The older I get, the less sense any of it makes.'

She looked up at him. She would have liked to place her hand on his face, to trace her finger over his temple, down his cheeks and jawbone and over his lips. He clasped her hand and the touch gave a sense of something so much stronger than endearment.

'Stay close to the Cumann women, Betty, stay close to those who give you strength.'

Reluctantly they stepped apart.

Phelim began to talk about the first time he saw her properly in their Middle Abbey Street home. 'It was the day after Conleth and I brought Seamus home after the Rising. The first night I was too tired to notice anything but the mattress in your bedroom. When at last I woke it was to see Seamus carrying a tin bath into the room. He grinned wearily when he saw that I was awake. I lay there watching him go in and out of the kitchen carrying buckets of hot and cold water to fill the bath. Then I got up and told him I would leave him in peace to wash himself. "Your turn next," he said. Then I stepped out into the kitchen and there you were.' He smiled vaguely as he recalled it. 'I'll never forget when you turned to face me and I could see your every feature. You had a green brooch at your neck that sparkled when you stood in front of me. Your eyes were the same colour as the brooch. You had ...' He stopped mid-sentence, knowing it was wrong to talk like this.

She blushed, flattered he remembered such details.

'Without our conflict, I would never have known you,' he said.

During those evenings in her kitchen they forgot about Ireland's problems, her maimed husband and their diminishing guilt.

Curiosity brought her to Phelim's home under the pretext of delivering a message to Conleth. There she met his father, Brian, a small wiry Kilkenny man who walked with the aid of a stick. He'd worked in the docks until an accident crushed his right leg. When she met his mother, Josie, she understood where the boys got their height and resilience. Mrs Salmon was a tall well-built capable woman who managed her brood with a firm yet loving hand. Mother of ten children, Mrs Salmon was as strong as she was fierce. Betty heard how she blocked the front door when the Brits came to search her house. It took four men to remove her, by which time her sons had escaped out the back door with all of the incriminating evidence. Her objections didn't end after she was piled into the back of a Black Mariah. She continued fighting, rocking the carriage from side to side as she resisted arrest.

Betty accepted a mug of tea and discussed the state of the country with his parents.

''Twon't end too soon,' Josie Salmon said, clapping down a cut of bread beside Betty's mug of tea.

'Them Tans will keep it up,' Brian said from his chair by the fire.

All of their sons were in the IRB and all of their daughters in Cumann na mBan.

'Those evil boyos took pleasure in what they done to Kevin Barry,' said Josie.

'Evil boyos,' her husband echoed.

Betty noticed how Josie Salmon looked after her husband. With tenderness, she brought him his tea and a cut of bread. They finished each other's sentences and shared the same views. Betty pictured Phelim sleeping in the kitchen by the open fire with his five brothers, the crowded home tightening their bond.

Betty was conscious of Isabel. Nothing escaped her little eyes.

'Daddy is sad,' she said, climbing onto his lap. 'I'll sing you a song and make you happy, Daddy.' She pushed the hair off his forehead and kissed him. His jaw clenched as he tried to suppress the tears. Unabashed, she wiped the tears from his cheeks and held a hanky to his nose. 'Blow, Daddy!'

He smiled as he pretended to blow.

'That's Phelim's cup,' she said, pointing at the Red Setters on the china cup he was using.

He looked indifferently at the picture of the dogs on the cup while Betty held her breath as she gauged him for a reaction.

A few weeks after, he woke Betty and Isabel. He told them it would be safer if they slept in the bunker beneath the workshop. When Betty refused to leave her bed, Seamus dragged her and Isabel to the bunker. The following morning, she got Conleth to escort Isabel on the train to her parents in Tipperary. It was best for everybody. The city was no place for a child in the current climate. Her home was equally as volatile.

Betty took solace from her work to fill the void from Isabel's absence. Good old stoic Mona arrived faithfully to clean. Betty enjoyed her light conversation and Mona also kept her abreast of all of the news from the tenements. The latest was Patricia Mooney's son who was getting an awful name for himself as a man with queer notions for other men.

'Some of the fellas in Middle Abbey Street gave him a beating in the hope it would fix his thinking but now he's going to England and leaving his fine job in the fertiliser factory,' Mona told her.

Sheila Muldoon had a worse name for herself since she was drinking in the pubs and coming home at all hours of the night. A man was seen leaving her room after one of her nights in the pub.

That previous summer two pilots made the first non-stop transatlantic flight from Newfoundland to Connemara, County

Galway. Momentarily the country had something else to talk about apart from politics. The pilots were called 'Columbuses of the Air'. There were two Galway visitors to Betty and Seamus's home who had first-hand accounts of the plane and pilots. Mona Daly was present when the men discussed it and marvelled at the mechanics of the plane. The pilots crossed the Atlantic in three days, and there was speculation that aeroplanes would soon be used to transport people.

'Codology!' Mona said to Betty afterwards. 'How could they fit another person into the plane?'

'Maybe they'll build bigger planes.'

'Surely the plane would fall out of the sky with the weight of three men,' Mona said.

'Maybe the engines will be bigger,' Betty suggested. Phelim had made that point earlier. Throughout the conversation, she was conscious that Phelim was at the kitchen table listening. He saw the transatlantic trip as a significant occasion. 'They'll build planes that can carry fifty people at a time,' she said, quoting him. 'Then they'll build bigger planes until they'll be able to fit hundreds of people in and transport them all over the world, even to Australia.'

Mona gave it some consideration. 'How would you relieve yourself? Will they build an outhouse in it?'

'They'll build seats and bathrooms and maybe beds you can sleep in.'

'Maybe a picture house too.' Mona giggled at the nonsensical notion.

'Possibly,' Betty smiled. Mona's laughter was infectious.

'I never heard such eejit talk in my life,' Mona said. 'As soon as this war is over them planes will be left there till the next war.'

In Isabel's absence Betty established a routine to keep busy. Each morning Conleth would open the shop and wait for her to arrive before going about his chores for the day. She trusted him implicitly. He was as loyal as a protective dog. Conleth was so like Phelim, although he was a fitter, more handsome version, with finer features and a charm that Phelim lacked. From the offset she had realised that Conleth didn't have the required aptitude for carpentry or violinmaking. He was not in the slightest bit creative – however, he was clever and potentially a good businessman. Betty was training him how to keep the books and was amazed how quickly he grasped it. He could man the desk, talk nicely to customers, and he knew how to waffle about the quality of the pieces of furniture with occasional words he overheard the carpenters use in the workshop.

He was also assertive in that he asked Betty to stop referring to him as 'the boy'.

'I'm fifteen now,' he said, the sparse hair on his upper lip mocking the man he aspired to be. 'And far from a boy,' he added in his croaky voice.

'That's true,' Betty apologised. 'From now on I'll call you "the man" instead of "the boy".'

Seamus loved Conleth, once confessing that if he had a son or son-in-law he'd hope for one like Conleth.

Betty would hope for a son-in-law who would have good grammar, speak with a nicer accent, and at least be well-educated. Naturally she didn't share her thoughts with her husband who would accuse her of behaving like another eejit Irish person, 'aspiring to be British'.

When Seamus saw the professional photographs that Betty had taken of the shop and the staff, he accused her of the same.

'You're like the Whelans, lauding over your little empire,' he said, referring to the local hotelier in Tipperary. 'This could all be gone tomorrow. I could be gone like that!' He clicked his fingers.

She closed her ears to his insinuations. On her desk in the shop was a photograph of the building with the name over the door and the employees flanking her. That day the photographer also took pictures of her at her desk with Conleth and Phelim. Betty displayed all of the photos except a picture of Phelim and her alone. She wanted to keep that one to herself, her own little keepsake. She kept the photograph safely tucked away with her secret receipt book. Every evening she took a minute to look at the account of her accumulating money and admire the photograph. They both reassured her in equal measure.

Despite the distractions of work, Betty never stopped missing Isabel. There were times when she thought she was forgetting what her daughter looked like. The pain of her loss was sometimes so acute she thought she wouldn't be able to cope. Yet she knew she was making the right choice. A rural life would allow her to be a child. Every fortnight Isabel was escorted to Dublin with her cousin on the train. During those few days each month Seamus perked up slightly, yet the sadness never left his expression. He'd sit and listen to Isabel's news, stories about the dog and her pups, her cousin Elsie's goat, the greyhound Uncle Finbar was training, her friends the Ryan Dubhs, her trips to town once a week with her grandmother to shop in Kennedy's.

Chapter 18

Dublin, 1921

Betty was sitting by the stove in her kitchen, counting the days when she'd see Isabel again. The long summer days and heat of July was a time of the year when children spent their free time cooling off in the local river. Betty imagined Isabel's cousins introducing her to the summer delights in Tipperary, the same summer spots she and Seamus had enjoyed.

These were the thoughts Betty was having when she heard about the ceasefire. For years she could remember where she was sitting at the time, the smell of freshly baked bread and the flicking sound of Seamus's knife as he carved a figurine for Isabel.

The truce ended the two-and-a-half-year War of Independence. For a few months the bloodshed diminished. There was an optimistic atmosphere as the country deliberated over its future.

Business for Betty was thriving. She added pottery and delftware to her stock, arranging them in her kitchen dressers in the windows of the shop. There were days when she would not allow a punter out of her shop without selling something. Even a small cup and saucer was better than not selling anything. Each night she returned to Seamus with the book of receipts to show him how much she had sold that day, her own secret receipt book growing thicker each month.

Afraid Seamus would stumble on her accumulating money, she dispersed it in a few locations. A large portion was hidden in the shop beneath the floor. Once a week she'd lock the shop and slide the heavy desk at which she sat a few feet forward. On bended knee she'd get a flutter of excitement when adding another fistful of notes to her stash. There was a coat in her wardrobe that she never wore. The lining was packed with notes, the sound of rustling paper giving her another moment of joy. Once a month she returned to Tipperary to visit Isabel. There she hid more money. She used the same hiding place where she kept Seamus's notes during their courtship – in a cavity beneath her windowsill. While Isabel slept she'd manoeuvre off the wooden windowsill and count her amassed money.

She began to view properties in Dublin to buy.

It was pointless consulting Seamus. With the end of the War of Independence she had hoped his condition would improve. Sadly, nothing changed. He remained paranoid and remote. Each evening the official receipt book was left unopened. He was too preoccupied with the chaos of the confines of his mind to be concerned by shop business. Mostly she left him to his own devices, hoping he'd come round. He continued to write letters and pass them to Conleth or Phelim to deliver. He smoked incessantly as he pored over the newspaper, reminding Betty of an engine that was about to run out of steam. Out of her sense of duty, sometimes she sat with him while he worked. Unlike their early days in the tenements, she was no longer enamoured of his passion as he crafted his violins. They were distant independent souls and might never again find a common ground. She knew she was not as perturbed as she should have been by the thought.

The only time there was a glimmer of the old Seamus was when Isabel visited or when he opened her weekly letter. Once a month her cousin Delia escorted her on the train to Dublin and returned three days later to retrieve her. During those visits Seamus found a small vein of happiness. The little girl adored him, and never noticed his restlessness and unkempt appearance. He taught her how to play the violin. Betty marvelled at his patience and tolerance. Betty had to leave the room, the sound of Isabel's screeching violin getting on her nerves. Seamus would sit and encourage Isabel and tap his foot as if she was creating music instead of noise. As the days passed, Betty noticed that Seamus's patience paid off and Isabel did indeed improve.

Isabel loved music and like Seamus she had a determination about her. Seamus read her stories and drew pictures at the kitchen table. During Isabel's visits he could escape to the child's world, the only fragment of his life not corrupted by war.

On one of Betty's visits home Maureen asked when she would be taking Isabel back to Dublin to live, now that Ireland had found peace. Unable to discuss Seamus, Betty pretended Dublin was as unsafe with the ceasefire as it was during the war. She tried to give her mother money for Isabel's upkeep. Maureen told her they loved having the child and she had only asked as it was time to enrol her in school.

One evening Betty found Seamus standing at the wardrobe, looking into the hidden compartment where he could hide.

'You found your old hiding place,' she said.

'You can never be too careful.'

'You've grown too fat to fit into it!' Betty tried teasing him.

Seamus considered it. He thought for a moment before squeezing into the compartment. She could hear him pant with exertion. Before she slid her fingers under the secret shell and closed the entrance, he looked over his shoulder and smiled. Was this the first sign of his old self returning? It had been so long since she was intimate with him, she was startled at the prospect of it. Yet she was bound by duty. She placed her hand on the timber and traced her finger over one of the carved ferns. The detail was so intricate, only a genius could create something as complex and beautiful, yet what lurked behind it was slowly dying. Betty kept her hand on the timber. If only she could lock him out of sight.

'Let me out,' Seamus demanded.

If only it was as easy as shutting life's problems into a wardrobe or attic space, anywhere out of sight. With time they would fade or become distorted into something untrue. They would dissolve, be forgotten like old memories. Life would bring something new to replace the horrors of yesterday.

'Let me out!' He pounded on the panel from inside.

Betty leaned close and began to sing. She imagined she was about to release Phelim from the wardrobe. She thought about his arms encasing her. She relived their brief touches, his fingers brushing her, his hand holding her wrist, the open button on his shirt exposing a few sparse hairs. She always wanted to know more, to see more of him, to inhale his odour or strain to hear his soft voice.

'*Oh, a wan cloud was drawn o'er the dim weeping dawn,*
As to Shannon's side I return'd at last . . .'

Continuing to sing, slowly she unlocked the compartment.

Seamus burst out and slapped her before pinning her to bed. '*You're trying to kill me!*' he yelled. His hand tightened on her throat. 'Torturing me like they did in Kilmainham!'

Betty clawed at his fingers, and tried twisting out of his grip. Only when she managed to reach up and punch him did he let go. She rolled on her side, coughing and gasping for air. She heard his feet rush from the bedroom and down the stairs.

It took Betty days to come to terms with Seamus's outburst. Each time she thought about it she felt like crying again. She couldn't accept his sudden brutality. When she got over the shock, she thought about ways of helping him. She wanted to make him better, to return to the days in Middle Abbey Street when life was normal. The memory of his sprightly step on the stairs and his smiling face as he entered their small home were as far removed as her beginnings in Tipperary. The days when she'd delay to speak to him in her father's workshop belonged to another era. Betty wanted to believe he'd come right in the end. With a little time, he'd find his own normality.

He apologised, the bruise on the side of her face a reminder of what he'd done. She could see from his anguished expression how sorry he was. She told him she forgave him but was met with rage when she suggested he do something to take his mind off everything. She suggested they go to the seaside for a few days – the fresh air would help.

'Too dangerous,' he replied.

She pointed out the fact that the war was over.

'It's not over,' he contradicted her, shaking his head adamantly.

She looked at his grey face. Too exhausted to entertain him, she was unable to respond.

Betty tinkered with everything to fill the awful sense of dread when she returned from work at night. Once home she would find a reason to leave again.

Phelim was now only calling a few days a week rather than each day. Without ever articulating it, Betty guessed that he found Seamus's disintegration difficult. He had done all he could. More often than not his visit was brief.

When she saw him in the kitchen soon after Seamus's attack, she wanted to cry again. Finding it difficult to make eye contact, she handed him his cup and pointed towards Seamus's workshop. He nodded. She knew he was disappointed.

'What's wrong?' he whispered.

Surprised that he intuited that something was amiss, she denied it. She looked up at his anxious face and saw him looking at the fading bruise on her face. Betty's hand went instinctively to the brooch which held the neck of her blouse in place, hiding an uglier bruise that appeared worse each day.

'Nothing.' She smiled nervously and turned her attention to the radio. She fiddled with the volume. It was playing a song she'd heard only recently.

'Betty?' he asked again.

She wanted to watch him sit into the chair by the stove with a sense of relief that they were alone to talk. She loved to watch him slowly stir his tea and eat his biscuits leisurely, savouring each bite.

'Betty, tell me,' he said, gently taking her hand.

Betty stepped away from him, trying to remain composed. She took a deep breath, afraid if she started crying she would never stop.

'He's not well,' she whispered.

Phelim seemed to understand. He waited for her to continue, his eyes never leaving hers.

'If only things were different, Phelim!' She placed her hand on his shoulder. She wanted to feel happy again, to experience a sense of joy.

'I know,' Phelim said, moving closer to her.

He cupped her face with his hands and kissed her with an urgency that made her forget. They stood together, kissing hungrily to the song "By the Light of the Silvery Moon", both aware there was no turning back.

The following day she went to Cassidy's Hotel in Fairview to meet Phelim. As she climbed the stairs at one o'clock she knew with each step she ascended that she was getting further into something that she would never unravel.

At the top of the stairs, she hesitated and looked behind her down the dimly lit stairwell. At a time when so much was lost, she could not lose one of her greatest sources of happiness.

Phelim was waiting in the bedroom. He rushed to her when she entered the room and held her tightly.

'I thought you might change your mind!' he said.

She shook her head. 'No.'

He was cautious and nervous as he peeled away her blouse, the marks still visible on her neck from Seamus's assault. He kissed her neck and hurriedly they removed each other's clothes. Lying on the small hotel bed, as he pushed his way into her, she cried out with pleasure and abandonment, each thrust dissolving their pent-up pressures. Afterwards they lay together cushioned in a dreaminess. Sometime later they made unrushed love again.

Chapter 19

In December 1921, Michael Collins reached an agreement in the Anglo-Irish Treaty negotiations in London. The main points included the creation of an Irish Free State within the Commonwealth with twenty-six counties, but six counties in the North would remain with England. The Irish Free State must swear an Oath of Allegiance to the British Crown, and the British naval services would retain the use of certain Irish ports. After Collins' return, the rift was clearly visible between the nationalist factions.

The men gathered in Betty's good room late one Saturday night. There were about fifteen men forming a large circle. Some sat on chairs or the arms of chairs, some on the window ledges and the floor. The air of uncertainty was almost palpable. There was little talk of the weather or normality. They talked only of the Treaty and how the country was divided about it. Betty listened as the men argued over Ireland's future.

Ursula was also present, doling out tea and scones and so much more vocal than Betty.

'We cannot accept a botched agreement for part of a country and allow another part to be devoured by the wolves.' Ursula's cheeks were pinched with anger. 'It's utter nonsense. This is a thirty-two-county country.'

Her sentiments reflected the view of some of the men while others felt they could build on the Treaty. The latter group felt they could continue working towards reclaiming the six counties and eventually get complete independence from England.

Phelim said little. Betty thought she could see him methodically processing the news, mulling over their arguments. She could see him thinking, his eyes not focused on anyone. For periods during the evening, he listened like a bystander who was not involved, removed from the debate until he made his own decision.

Seamus was incensed with the Treaty but would not blame his friend, Michael Collins. 'Collins was not the man to negotiate with the Brits. He's a soldier, not an experienced colonial politician like the English.'

Johnny Red suggested de Valera knew what he was doing. 'He knew what the English were offering, that's why he sent Collins. He's using Collins as a scapegoat.'

'It's an insult to every one of us who fought,' Digger Dempsey said.

'The Brits are doing their best to divide the country.'

'It's the best Collins could do,' Seamus said.

'Collins is tired of fighting – the same as every man who accepts the Treaty,' another countered.

'If we don't resolve this quickly the rest of us will be dead before the year is out.'

'We've lost so much and gained so little in the last five years. Then we're left with this farce of an agreement.'

Each person thought about the men and women who had lost everything, from their limbs and lives, to their remaining shards of sanity. As the night progressed, the room divided. Some argued that Collins signed the first agreement that the English put before him.

A few argued that the Northern Unionists would never accept being part of a republic. 'We can fight for another one hundred years but the Unionists will never give way.'

Some said de Valera would never have signed the treaty. 'Even if the Unionists held a gun to his head Dev would have procured the thirty-two counties, not a half-baked agreement that split the island!'

'So why didn't he go and do that? Why send Collins?'

But some men had first-hand accounts that de Valera refused to assist Collins by ignoring his pleas from London. De Valera claimed that he was not consulted. When the content of the Treaty was made public, he opposed it only when it was too late and would create the greatest backlash against Collins. The room separated between loyalty to their country and loyalty to their republican champions.

Betty wanted to be alone with Phelim. She wanted to touch him and kiss him again. She thought about their uninterrupted day together.

'What about you?' Seamus asked Phelim.

Phelim thought before speaking. His eyes scanned the faces before him. He looked tired and weary in the dim light, as if like Collins he too had seen too much fighting.

'The Treaty states that we must continue to pledge our allegiance to the King of England. I can't do that,' he said calmly. 'This is not a choice. We have achieved nothing. The only course consistent with my republican beliefs is to continue fighting.'

Ursula nodded her head in agreement.

'Michael Collins has given us the freedom to achieve freedom,' Seamus said. 'We will accept the Treaty and negotiate with the Brits for our independence through our government and legislature. It'll give us time to catch our breath.'

Phelim accepted his friend's stance, but it was clear they were on opposing sides.

'Our friends will become our enemies,' Phelim said.

'Maybe so, it might even be our children who continue the fight when we're long gone,' Seamus said. 'I'll take the Treaty and from this day forward we'll use every political tool to get a United Ireland, even if it takes the rest of our lives.'

Whatever opinions were formed that night would decide which side of the Civil War they would fight on. In the weeks that followed, those who joined the Anti-Treaty side would come to see Michael Collins' supporters as the enemy. They would continue to fight against them with as much determination and loyalty to their country as when they fought the Black and Tans. The close-knit group of republicans would turn their guns on each other to finish what their ancestors before them had tried to achieve.

That night each man took his leave until finally Seamus stood before Phelim. They shook hands, their expressions flushed with suppressed emotion. Phelim left without closing the door behind him, his shoes resounding into the distance. His departure that night tore at Betty and Seamus's hearts, both sharing an immense love for their friend and each fraught at the loss of a different kind of love.

Chapter 20

November 1922

In the silence of the night, Betty listened. They were four months into the Civil War. Some of their dearest friends had become their deadly enemies. Their days and nights were dotted with terror that their old comrades were edging through their window with loaded pistols, eager to right the wrongs of Ireland. Within a few short months, with the same resilience the republicans used to run the Black and Tans out of the country, they were killing their old comrades. The enemy had become the friend who spoke the same language and loved the same country. Families, communities and the nation were bitterly divided and intent on destroying the other. Seamus was still alive, as was Phelim, fighting on opposing sides.

Each night Betty implored God to spare them from an early death. As the months passed, it was Phelim who was at the forefront of her daily requests.

'Listen,' Seamus urged again. He was sitting on the side of their bed, staring intently at the closed shutters of their bedroom. 'Will you listen to that?'

Betty scrutinised his face, and for once she could not see the paralysing fear that occasionally seized him. Strangely he appeared surprised, as if he found something revealing on the bolted shutters of their bedroom window.

'What is it?' she finally whispered.

There wasn't a sound, not a motor car or voices. There was nobody at the locked front door with three bolts just in case of an attack, or the back door with as many bolts and secured with a sideboard pulled before it. Assassinations by the Anti-Treaty side in the Pro-Treaty homes was a rarity, yet before retiring to bed since the troubles began Seamus locked the house as if an army would make an attempt on his life that very night.

'Not a sound to be heard.' Seamus finally exhaled sadly. 'Hard to believe there are men lurking in our beautiful country waiting to shoot us dead.'

'Is that what you woke me for?' Betty admonished. 'You big eejit!' Angrily she flopped back into bed, unsure how much more she could take.

As Phelim had predicted, the Treaty caused havoc in the country. De Valera publicly rejected it. Seamus was behind Collins, as was Conleth, all labelled 'Free Staters' or 'Pro-Treaty'. The provisions of the Treaty required a new government that would be recognised by Westminster. Despite the abdication of a large part of the Dáil, the Provisional Government of the new Free State was formed with Arthur Griffith as President and Michael Collins as Chairman and Commander-in-Chief of the National Forces. De Valera was not re-elected. Both sides engaged in negotiations to prevent a civil war. This resulted in 'The Army Document' which was signed by Pro- and Anti-Treaty officers. It called for new elections. The Collins-de-Valera Pact was created, agreeing that new elections to the Dáil would be held with each candidate running as Pro- or Anti-Treaty. The two sides would then join to form a coalition government of national unity.

Despite their efforts Ireland's Civil War began on June 28th 1922 with the 'Battle of Dublin' which was a week of street battles fought between the forces of the new Provisional Government and those of the Irish Republican Army who opposed the Treaty. It ended in victory for the Provisional Government.

Three months into the Civil War, Michael Collins travelled to Cork to meet with Anti-Treaty leaders in the hope of finding a reconciliation. He was ambushed and shot dead in a small isolated village called Béal na Bláth, a hollow between hills. His death further embittered the war and it signified the end of any hope of reuniting the victorious War of Independence forces.

Initially Betty considered taking Seamus to Tipperary to soothe his nerves but she soon learned that the country republicans proved to be more dangerous than their Dublin counterparts. The small country communities were viciously divided. Small independent military squads sprang up in every crevice in the country. These 'Flying Columns' were merciless and deadly in their attack.

Betty's brothers were Pro-Treaty, her uncle and his sons were Anti-Treaty. Seamus's brother Patrick was Pro-Treaty and was shot the previous month by a flying column whose members included Betty's uncle. It was a dangerous time when old comrades were like wild dogs set at each other. Unlike the War of Independence when the English were fighting united Irishmen on unfamiliar terrain, with the Civil War the participants knew their enemies, knew their movements, their hideouts and how they thought.

On a visit to Dublin, Seamus's brother Malachy said, 'Even the mice in the fields are taking sides.' He regaled them with a story about his neighbour taking the Anti-Treaty side. While Malachy was hunting in the fields he noticed three mice suddenly running towards him. When he investigated further he caught a glimpse of his unarmed neighbour setting traps at the other side of the ditch. Malachy dressed up the story as if the mice were fleeing from his neighbour into the mouths of two waiting terriers rather than remain with a man who was Anti-Treaty. When he told the story it was light relief from the despair within their home.

Since Seamus's brother was shot dead, Betty noticed small changes in him. For a period the old spark of his fighting spirit returned, and he attended political meetings although those meetings were normally held under cover of darkness. A few of Seamus's friends resumed their visits to their home but nobody stayed too long. Seamus was irrational, his ideas too wild. Betty monitored Seamus's outings, hoping he'd eventually be able to leave the house during daylight hours rather than darkness. She waited for him to refer to a piece of music on the radio, or for his appetite to improve. There were vague signs of an improvement – for a few days his appetite improved, and a bounce and determination returned to his step.

Betty's optimism was short-lived. On the 6th of December he left home at six in the evening with two friends. Two hours later two men brought him home. They burst into the house, pushing Seamus before them as angry parents would force a child indoors. For a moment Betty thought he was injured. Quickly she realised Seamus was distraught. One of the men forced him to sit down. Seamus held his hands to his head as his leg jigged. When he raised his head she could see his pale face and wild eyes.

'They deserve it!' Seamus shouted with his teeth gritted. 'Every last blasted one of those Salmons deserves to die!' His voice sounded inhuman.

'Enough,' one of the men said.

As suddenly Seamus burst into tears. When he took the gun from his pocket it was quickly taken from him.

'I want my gun,' he demanded through distraught gulps.

Betty stood inside the scullery door, gaping at the scene. Seamus's reference to the Salmons upset her as much as his behaviour. She closed her eyes against the thought that Phelim had been shot. *Please, please*, she implored God, *don't let it be Phelim!*

Seamus tried to speak but one of the men shouted him down. 'They're fair game – but not in front of their children!'

The room quietened except for the men's exhausted breaths and Seamus's crying.

'You're a loose cannon, Seamus,' one of the men said, in a quiet dismayed voice.

The following morning Betty felt she'd lived through the most gruelling night of her life. Between pacifying Seamus all night and dealing with the real prospect that Phelim had been shot, she thought she was going insane. When she asked Seamus which Salmon he had shot, his responses were too wild to comprehend. At one point he said he didn't know, but when she probed further he said he'd shot all of them.

When she arrived at the shop early the following morning, she learned that Seán Salmon, Phelim's brother, had been shot dead.

'Shot dead on his doorstep,' Mrs Wyse Power informed her in a by-the-way manner.

She had called by to discuss Cumann na mBan business with Betty. On the table beside her were raffle tickets to raise funds for the Cumann movement.

'So terribly sad – each day it's someone else's awful news.' Mrs Wyse Power shook her head sympathetically. 'God love them.'

Betty remained composed as a sense of relief swept through every vein in her body. Phelim was alive. God could not do that to her. As quickly her relief was lost to a new despair. The implications of Seamus's actions dawned on her. The consequences of the war were piercing her with new horrors. It was as if they had progressed into a new deadly realm of killings.

'You'd want to look after yourself,' Mrs Wyse Power continued as she poured milk into Betty's tea.

'When was he shot?' Betty asked, hoping against hope that Seán Salmon was killed by another Pro-Treaty man – a man who was not her husband. Seamus was home at eight o'clock. She remembered the clock chime a few minutes before his return.

'Yesterday evening at seven o'clock,' Mrs Wyse Power said. 'Poor lad was shot several times as he entered his home in front of his small nephews. He'd been kicking football with them.'

Betty didn't react. She needed to appear calm and unconcerned.

'His mother heard the shots. She stepped over her dead son and gave chase to his killers. Those boyos were lucky Mrs Salmon didn't catch them. She's a feisty lady – she'd have murdered them with her bare hands.'

Betty agreed with her and remained composed until she got home.

Once inside the front door she began to cry. She felt like a woman torn into many pieces. If Ireland ever found peace, would it be possible in their lifetime to shed the conflict? She saw nothing but hopelessness. They'd drag the war with them for decades and pass on the wounds to future generations. That December morning it seemed it would be never-ending.

Chapter 21

On Christmas Eve Ursula called to the shop to deliver a present for Isabel, her godchild. As Ursula sided with the Anti-Treaty side, she was unable to call to their home any longer.

'We're women,' Betty said, making light of it. 'Let the men have their little arguments over their Treaty. We don't need to take sides.'

'If I was a man, even a midget or a half-wit, I could not stand on the fence and do nothing,' Ursula said.

'Pity. Can't your Anti-Treaty side accept it?' Betty said, knowing how passionate Ursula was about republicanism.

'Unfortunately it's not that easy,' Ursula retorted. 'When a mother feeds her hungry children, she doesn't feed some and tell the others that she'll look after them in a couple of months or years or even decades. That's as senseless as accepting an agreement for twenty-six counties and leaving six counties to fend for themselves.'

'It's gone from bad to worse,' Betty said.

They were sitting behind the desk drinking tea. Christmas was almost forgotten with the carnage. The day before there were gun and grenade attacks on National Army troops in Dublin. A man in Cavan was shot dead, another in Monaghan. An IRA column raided the town of Blacklion, Cavan, looting shops and homes.

'I'm moving to London,' Ursula announced.

Betty was surprised. It was not like Ursula to leave her country when it needed her most.

'A few Cumann women and I will continue our fight from England.'

Betty didn't ask any more.

'How is Seamus?' Ursula enquired.

'Great,' Betty lied. 'He's busy plotting and planning how to kill you and all your die-hard friends.'

Ursula giggled.

Betty walked her out of the shop. They hugged, the tight clench conveying what they were unable to say.

'When it's all over, when Pro-Treaty and Anti-Treaty sides are back to killing the Brits, let's go to Tipperary for a few days and eat cake and visit all of our relatives and gossip like billy-o,' Betty said.

'I'll look forward to it.'

Ursula walked away then turned back and waved. She was wearing a fashionable blue hat that accentuated her blue eyes. Her cheeks were fresh and rosy. She radiated life and that grave gallantry that had freed twenty-six counties of their country. On her arm she carried a basket full of presents for more of her friends.

Betty blew her a kiss, not realising they would never again meet as friends.

Fr Mathew diplomatically remained neutral. Any talk of Pro-Treaty or Anti-Treaty remained an overwhelming topic for him although he admitted that his fear had abated.

'I don't know if my anxiety at the sight of constant guns and living in a city teeming with war has subsided, or if I've grown to accept my constant worry as the norm.'

'We all have our own means of adapting,' Seamus said, his face distorted with his own war.

Most nights Fr Mathew visited. Loudly he'd call from the front door and knock several times, knowing Seamus kept a loaded gun by his side.

He encouraged Seamus to eat. With his great size he made loss of appetite seem like one of life's great maladies to be avoided. After dinner he joined them in saying the Rosary. During that period the priest rose in Betty's esteem, as he tried to help Seamus to reclaim his mind. Rather than seeing Fr Mathew as a man with a constant appetite for a free meal and a thirst for decent whiskey, she saw him as a loyal friend who was as terrified as Seamus. Fr Mathew avoided talk of the war – instead he discussed recent plays or books or anecdotes. Surreptitiously he counselled Seamus about forgiveness while discussing a recent play, or the characters in a novel. He talked about a loving God rather than a punitive God.

'He is only waiting to be asked,' Fr Mathew said. 'The answer is in prayer. He is waiting for us to forgive and repent. All will be forgiven.'

Each night he guided Seamus into praying with him. They'd kneel in the kitchen, Seamus's voice quivering at '*forgive us our trespasses, as we forgive those who trespass against us*'.

Once Seamus said, 'I'm asking God to forgive the man who will kill me. There's no sense in that.'

'Forgiveness will find us peace,' Fr Mathew said. 'Don't you want peace?'

'It's been so long I don't know what peace is any more,' Seamus admitted.

Fr Mathew prayed for those involved in Ireland's troubles to find a solution, and for the mental welfare of those who remained. Betty knew he had Seamus in mind. When he implored Our Lady in Heaven to protect the countries' ladies and gentlemen from poor morals, she wondered if he had her in mind.

Seamus's only saviours were his violins, his religion and the monthly visit from Isabel. When he was not pacing the floors at night he worked feverishly, barely taking the time to raise his head when Betty called him for dinner. The pent-up frustrations went into this work. Mr Hartmann called once a month. Seamus had little to say to him. In the small paranoid cocoon that Seamus inhabited, there was no room for another occupant.

At least their daughter Isabel was relatively safe while she remained with her grandparents and extended family in Tipperary. Now that she was six, she attended the local national school. Each week her mother wrote, and included in the letter a picture that Isabel drew. She had been living with them for over two years. For the three nights of her daughter's stay with them each month, Betty was very concerned about Seamus's behaviour. Would the child see through his delirium? Would she realise that Daddy was utterly insane? Hopefully she would see his paranoia as concern: Daddy loved her so much that he bolted her into the house each night and never ventured outside the front door. Betty also feared that Isabel might find one of the many loaded guns Seamus kept scattered about the house.

Seamus began to make a doll's house similar to Betty's parents' house. He began to carve figurines from Isabel's life in Tipperary: Isabel herself, Betty's parents, Uncle Finbar, Aunt Úna. With each visit Seamus expanded on the figurines. He cut a lock of his blond hair and affixed it to the doll Isabel. She screeched with delight when she saw it. For those weekends, Seamus designated his entire weekend to revolve around his daughter. They spent long hours together in his workshop as he began crafting her cousins and callers to her grandparents' house.

Betty sensed his enthusiasm for the doll's house. In the workshop he'd sing cute songs he remembered from his childhood. Isabel's violin-playing improved. While he worked at the figurines she'd play for him. Life seemed so idyllic during her visits. When Betty watched them together she realised how much the war had taken from their family.

The killings continued throughout 1922 and into 1923 at an alarming rate. Mona Daly said it was 'the Wild West of America in the very cities and villages in Ireland'. During those months it was as if the country belonged to a different type of man, with a murderous state of mind.

Betty continued to employ Mona for one morning a week, if

anything to offer some light relief and surface chit-chat for Seamus. Mona was one of the few who knew about his state of mind. Without passing judgement or questioning, Mona accepted his mental state as she accepted the harshness of her own existence. She merely glossed over it as another one of life's cruel consequences.

'Not up to much today?' she'd say, in her inoffensive way when she noticed his vacant eyes staring into space.

Betty was surprised when Seamus would admit that he wasn't feeling great.

'I don't blame you, Seamus – it's a hard auld world.' Mona would then offer to make him tea with bread and jam. He appeared as grateful for her bread and jam as her kind words.

Betty was tired of trying to find a solution. Did men who witnessed so much war ever find normality again? Would the rest of her days be dictated by a man who oscillated between despair and paranoia? There were times when she thought Seamus a pathetic lazybones, content to allow her work while he remained at home because it was easier.

Mona was diplomatic enough not to discuss the war in Seamus's earshot.

'Men are a quare lot,' she said.

'Don't I know it,' Betty said dryly.

'It's all over a bargaining,' she said as if she had solved Ireland's crisis. 'Half the country is raging with Collins – they think he brought back a cracked agreement, the other half says we can live with it. Right?'

Betty nodded.

'Why can't the men agree and get on with it. Let them take the Treaty. We've all the time in the world to fight for the six counties in the North.'

'So you're a Free-Stater? You agree with the Treaty?' Betty teased.

'I'm nothin' at all only a mother who is wonderin' when in the name of all that's holy will the country ever get sense?'

Phelim would appreciate Mona's simplistic view – he'd find it amusing but probably be disappointed Mona hadn't leaned on the Anti-Treaty side.

Betty missed the old callers to their home, she missed wakening to the hum of voices and the countrymen who were so grateful for a clean bed and a bite to eat. Where had it gone so wrong? There were few she could confide in.

Mrs Wyse Power backed Collins, which meant they could remain friends – although her choice had less to do with the Anglo-Irish Treaty than the fact she never forgave de Valera for refusing women's assistance during Easter 1916. She said de Valera was forcing the women's organisation to the periphery. 'According to Dev, our place is in the home. We need a progressive leader to guide our country, not a backward idealist.'

Although Conleth sided with Seamus and the Pro-Treaty faction, Seamus was still nervous of him, fearing the young man would avenge his brother's death.

'Conleth is no turncoat,' Betty reminded him.

As well as being afraid for his life, Seamus was also terrified of turncoats. He was frightened that Conleth would eventually side with Phelim and shoot him. To ease tensions, and pacify Seamus, Betty asked Conleth not visit her home until the fighting died down – however, he could continue to work in the shop. Conleth understood. On the other hand, Betty felt it was pointless because no doubt Seamus would get fixated on some other old comrade who was coming to kill him. By this time, every person who passed through their home was a possible assassin, according to Seamus.

Finally, he suggested that Fr Mathew was going to shoot him.

'Don't be fooled by his profession,' Seamus said bitterly. 'That fellow would riddle me with bullets if he had the chance.'

Betty could only laugh at the unlikelihood of it.

'I know how his mind works, remember,' he said. 'He was one of us for the last few years.'

'Nonsense,' Betty retorted. 'He is too terrified to be anybody other than a molly-coddled priest.'

Seamus's wild spinning eyes stared back at Betty as he pointed to his head. 'I know what he's capable of doing.'

Although she found his accusation daft, Betty felt it was not a time to make fun of Seamus's irrational mind. During Fr Mathew's next visit, Seamus remained seated at the end of the kitchen table with a loaded gun hidden under the lace tablecloth, just in case Fr Mathew got any ideas. Betty behaved as if it was all perfectly normal. She did not believe Seamus would shoot his old pacifist friend.

Betty tried to bring some normality into their home. She suggested going to a concert or taking a drive outside of Dublin for a drink in a nice rural pub. All of her suggestions were met with adamant refusals.

Eventually his hair trailed down his shoulders but he refused to visit a barber and get a haircut and a shave.

'Are you mad?' He looked at her aghast. 'He'll slit my throat with his knife and claim it's an accident. No, sireee, not for me,' he said, with absolute certainty that every barber was Anti-Treaty.

Seamus compiled a list of potential assassins, men who knew his movements, knew the layout of the house and the workshop at the back. She asked him if he'd feel better moving to England for a few months.

'I'd be shot before I made the boat,' was his curt reply.

She asked if any of his friends had a safe house where he might feel more comfortable.

'To be a sitting duck waiting for grenades to be lobbed into my porridge? No, thank you!' He looked towards the ceiling. 'The attic is about as safe as it gets.'

As the war dragged on Seamus's Pro-Treaty friends stopped calling. They were unnerved at the sight of the cocked gun. Apart from Mona Daly, Fr Mathew and Mr Hartmann's monthly call, there were no visitors.

Seamus's brother Malachy visited to see how he was faring and warn him to keep safe.

Malachy was an animated man with a flat Tipperary accent. 'To strike at the core of the Pro-Treaty camp, the Anti-Treaty crowd need to shake the organisation from within. You are one of the stronger men, making you vulnerable to attack.'

Betty remained silent and Seamus was ashen-faced as they listened.

'Nothin' is sacred no more,' Malachy concluded.

That night Betty woke to find Seamus fully dressed, sitting on the windowsill of their bedroom, examining the density of the walls.

'You could burrow a hole in here and hide a man,' he informed her.

'How would you eat?' Betty asked, hoping he would see how far-fetched he sounded.

'That's only a minor thing,' he answered irately. 'You're putting obstacles where there's no need for them.'

Betty was too tired to fight.

Seamus continued to tap the walls. 'Just in case Fr Mathew gets any more ideas about shooting me.'

She closed her eyes and thought about the few hours she would spend with Phelim the following day. Their little safe alcove in St Stephen's Green. For that short hour she could make-believe that life's meandering stream led her to another man in another time in another country.

Chapter 22

January, 1923

On Thursdays Betty met Phelim in Buswell's Hotel. It was a popular Anti-Treaty venue and he had the use of a room for republican purposes. Only when she was with him did Betty find her voice and say what she couldn't during the week. Confiding in him was easy – he understood how Seamus arrived at his insane state without condemning him.

She was lying in his arms. Outside they could hear the noise of the city. The hotel bedroom reminded her of Middle Abbey Street, a constant hub of activity with the smell of bacon and cabbage wafting up the stairs.

'Civil war ruptures the thing that binds us,' Phelim said as he wrapped a strand of her hair around his index finger. 'There are men who will gladly kill for their country but would rather turn the gun on themselves than kill an old friend.'

'Is that what has happened to Seamus?' She needed enlightenment, someone to tell her that his condition was par for the course, that with time it would resolve itself.

'Yes, unfortunately there are a lot like him. At times like this we need to look at all we've achieved rather than dwell on the viciousness of war.'

'Do you think the reports are true? The war is at an end?'

'It appears that way,' he said. 'It can't last long more.'

They lay in silence looking out the window at the rooftops.

'How often do women wash their hair?' he asked, running his fingers through her locks.

She was tickled at his peculiar question. 'I wash mine twice a week. Why?'

'I imagine it's an enormous ordeal. You have so much hair,' he said, lifting it to his face and inhaling the fresh scent.

'What will you do when the war ends?' she cautiously asked.

He didn't answer her immediately. She looked up at him. He held her gaze.

'I always thought I would do whatever my conscience demands. Whatever is best for my country. But now things are different.'

She waited for him to continue, realising that her happiness depended on his response.

'Will you leave with me?' he suddenly asked. 'We can go away from here, away from this cursed country and start somewhere fresh.'

'Where will we go?' she asked, surprised they were talking about the future.

Neither of them had ever discussed the outcome of the war. They were so filled with surviving on a daily basis, that a future without conflict was impossible to imagine. The young were old before their time, a generation had grown up only knowing war. Ireland's men and women were tired of death shadowing them.

'I'm going to England next week. I'm leaving. For good.'

His words left her stranded. Without Phelim life would be impossible. Even if the war was over and Dublin found some semblance of peace, she needed him. His presence changed the scenery of her daily life. He was the rock who buoyed her faith. She was in love with him, more in love with him than she'd ever been with Seamus.

'Can you not stay?'

'No. Nothing is certain here.'

They lay together silently.

Betty was aware of rising panic. The mere thought of even a few days passing without Phelim's presence was unbearable.

'I'd need a few weeks to tie things up here,' she said.

Her head was suddenly full of conflicts. She had to consider Isabel who had spent so many years away from her. Her daughter was like a stranger. Despite the country's conflicts, her business was doing well. She had her eye on a business premises in Anne Street. There were so many more plans for the business. Hopkins Furniture was like a child she had nurtured. It was at the stage where it had grown, and would keep growing. Nothing pleased her more than when customers returned, or when they referred their family and friends. It affirmed that she had established a business to be proud of. She was known in Dublin. She was somebody, albeit the wife of the shop-owner, yet she was business class. How could she abandon it now? Seamus was another obstacle to Betty's departure. She was still his wife and would be until death. Although she would not be the first woman to leave the country with another man, she would need to ensure there would be no scandal. What would become of Seamus? He'd probably spend the rest of his days dipping deeper into the cauldron of insanity.

'You're definitely leaving next week?'

'After everything that has happened I can't stay. This damned war over a compromise will govern our country for years to come.' He sighed, disappointed with the gridlock Ireland had arrived at. 'Wherever I go, I hope you will come with me. You, Isabel and I can start somewhere else.'

So he intended that Isabel should go with them. And take her away from Seamus and her grandparents?

She could not go with him immediately. It would take a few weeks or months to get prepared. She needed a little more time.

He lifted up her chin to see her. 'If I could find an easier way, I would gladly.' He kissed her. 'I need to drown in your emerald eyes to feel alive.'

'Give me a few weeks to get organised. Isabel and I will join you then,' she said vaguely. It was suddenly daunting.

'Weeks?' he repeated.

'Yes, a few weeks.'

It was easier to say weeks rather than months. She didn't know if she was consoling herself or consoling Phelim. How could she put a timescale on Seamus's illness? It might take weeks or months, or even years before he found a resolution. She didn't want to think about it now.

Betty kissed him slowly while he ran his fingers down her neck and held her breast firmly. She loved his great height and size, his broad chest and strong muscular arms. She swept her hand down his abdomen and felt his penis hardening in her hand. He smelled of fresh salty sweat, his maleness aroused her.

He rolled on top of her, pushed her hair from her face. With utter tenderness he kissed her again. He placed his hands behind her head, entered her and kissed her again. The walls of her mind and the enduring tension dissolved with each thrust. Their matching rhythm momentarily subdued the conflict and impending loss.

The day of Phelim's departure Betty couldn't stop crying. Unable to hide her tears, she left the shop early, leaving Conleth to lock up.

When he asked if she was all right, she wondered how much he knew. Had he figured out she was crying over his brother's departure? Of course he had – he was a clever fellow. It was arranged that over the coming weeks Conleth would receive Betty's letters from Phelim. Although she guessed he was aware of her infidelities, she knew they were safe with him.

'I'm fine,' she said, holding a hanky to her red swollen eyes. 'After you've locked up, bring the receipt book to Ranelagh. I'll meet you by the canal at seven.'

At home Betty's crying did not subside. She told Seamus she was crying because she missed Isabel.

''Tis a bit late for that now,' he said.

He was sitting at the table with his back to her, paring a piece of wood with his knife. His hair was hacked from Mona's attempt at tidying it.

174

'It's time you brought Isabel back to us,' he said.

Betty continued crying.

Phelim sent his first letter. It was filled with news of his daily life. He'd landed a job as a sports reporter for an Irish newspaper. He attended horse meetings and football games and he lived in digs with three Welshmen. He wanted to know about her daily life – *'every single minute detail, regardless of how small it appears'*. Reading between the lines, she could see how lonely he was. It filled her with hope that he would not stay in England. A man as culturally rich in Irishness would never last in a country he abhorred. She missed him terribly – the gap in her life unsettled her.

Chapter 23

Dublin 1923

Conleth delivered two letters a week to Betty from Phelim. Each letter had an account of his day, the trips to work on the Underground railway, the English sense of humour and his job as a clerk in a newspaper. He avoided the Irish areas and pubs. Until tensions were less strained he felt the distance was necessary. In a follow-up letter he provided a forwarding address. The name he was using was Dominic Harris. He explained that he changed his surname to his mother's maiden name, Harris, and the second name on his baptismal form was Dominic. With so many reprisals since the end of the Civil War, both in Ireland and as far away as Chicago and New York, Phelim felt he was at risk. When Betty read that, she sincerely hoped he was not heading in the same direction as Seamus. She kept Phelim's letters and photos in a hiding place in the shop. Rereading his words once a day increased her anticipation until their next reunion.

A pattern developed. Every month Betty went to London to visit Phelim. As Seamus never left the house he would never find out. Once her feet touched English soil she felt invigorated. It was more than the prospect of seeing Phelim. Post-war London was

177

something different. Although large parts of the city were decimated, there was an optimism she adored. The sound of jazz from the hotels added a bounce to her step, and the stylish women made her feel less confined. The fashionable ladies wore shorter dresses with pleats that swung freely as if matching time with the jazzy music. The gay atmosphere reminded Betty that Ireland was not the only country crawling out of a long turbulent period. London was roaring and had an infectious vibrancy that she thrived on. Contrary to what she heard about the enemy country with its pagan ways and bullish people, it was a relief to bask in something other than struggling devout Ireland.

On one of her first trips, she asked Phelim to take her to Mayfair. It was easy to locate Willems' Violin Shop. She had learned that Mr Hartmann sold Seamus's violins to this shop. She had heard about Mrs Willems from Mr Hartmann himself. She was a woman in her late fifties who managed her father's business.

Reminded of her first time in Dublin when she saw Seamus's violins in Mr Hartmann's window, Betty stood gaping into Willems' window. At the sight of her husband's instruments she was tickled with glee as much as the first day she saw them on Dame Street in Dublin all those years ago. It wasn't Dublin any more but London – they'd came a long way, she thought with pride.

For a few months Betty had been thinking about Mr Hartmann's role. He was the middle man taking a fine cut for himself. It would make more sense if she introduced herself to Mrs Willems and removed Mr Hartmann and the fine slice of the value of Seamus's violins he took. Each time Mr Hartmann called for the last few visits, Betty gave him feeble excuses that Seamus was too busy, too unwell or too disinterested. Until she established a link with another violin shop, it seemed pointless continuing to deal with him.

On Betty's next trip to London she took Seamus's most recent violin and introduced herself to Mrs Willems. She made a similar arrangement to the initial agreement with Mr Hartmann. She'd supply one violin per month at a far higher price than Mr Hartmann gave her.

Mrs Willems said she was happy to pay for good stock; she had her reputation to uphold. When she said that, she made her only reference to Mr Hartmann. She mentioned his first name. 'Dieter is shrewd, too shrewd for his own good.'

Betty understood that Mrs Willems was happy to do business with her and remove Mr Hartmann. It soothed Betty's niggling conscience.

Mrs Willems held her hand to her chest. Three of her fingers had magnificent rings with large sparkling diamonds like nothing Betty had ever seen before. 'Business is business,' she summarised.

On each following visit to London, Betty met Mrs Willems. She wanted to strengthen their relationship, knowing how beneficial it was to do business and, besides, she was fascinated by the woman. Mrs Willems had lost her husband in the Great War. She thrived on business and appreciated beautifully crafted pieces. The Willems family was originally from Denmark; their parents moved to England to ensure their children received the best education. With war and death, there was only Mrs Willems and her ailing father, Mr Jacobs, left.

On subsequent visits Betty was invited to the living quarters over the shop for tea. Her eyes were agog at the stately apartment, the magnificent furniture and glistening chandeliers. She enjoyed their company as they discussed their diverse cultural backgrounds. Betty explained that her husband was an invalid from the troubles in Ireland and she managed his affairs. Mrs Willems gave her friendly advice, spoke to her as if advising a younger sister. When Betty looked at Mrs Willems' beautiful jewellery, stylish outfits and her short bobbed hair, she felt silly in her long dresses and quaint hats.

Betty's meetings with Phelim were carefree. They went to the movies and the theatre, they went dancing and found a pleasant routine to their time together. They sampled food in Italian, Greek and Indian restaurants. The first time they ate spaghetti, it slid off their forks as they giggled into the food. Phelim was developing a palate for Indian food; he liked the creamy moist dishes. Gradually he was learning to enjoy certain aspects of his new life, like attending race meetings and rugby games as a reporter for the newspaper.

'Rugby,' she teased, 'I thought you hated rugby.'

'While in Rome,' he smiled. 'Besides they feed and water us very well.'

He went on to tell her that he'd grown to like rugby and, strangely, soccer too. The race meetings were a grand job except when he was trying to write his article at 2am after a feed of English whisky. He told her about the men swigging out of hipflasks during the rugby matches. Most of the men he worked with were fine lads – he didn't want his past experiences of English soldiers in Ireland to prejudice him against every Englishman he met.

'It was naïve of me to assume they are all despicable,' he conceded. 'Though some are – the bigoted ones are ignorant about the Irish.'

His main friends were Welsh. His local pub was owned by a Welshman. They invited him to a party in an Irish pub but Phelim declined.

'Too soon,' he said sadly to Betty. 'Sometimes I miss home. I'd love to spend a long day fishing by a lonesome stream, and retreat with a few friends to a local pub for a couple of creamy pints and sing a few rousing rebel songs at the end of the night.'

'You'll need to find a more refined party piece.'

Their love intensified. Their lovemaking was lingering and giving. Yet she refused to make the leap and leave Ireland. Instead, each time they met she asked if he would return to Ireland.

'It was never my intention to turn my back on my country,' he finally tried to explain. 'Sometimes I feel old and tired. It's a disappointment.'

She listened, filled with sympathy for his struggle. He had done so much and gained so little. He complained that Ireland remained in the claws of a government that had to swear their allegiance to the English Crown.

'I thought so much would change once we became our own

masters. Unfortunately, the Irish government are happy to go along with further dictatorship from the Brits.'

'Will our country ever see prosperity?' Betty asked, joining him at the window of their hotel bedroom.

'Maybe Ireland will find peace, but it might take a hundred years. A future when aeroplanes will have lavatories and will carry our great-grandchildren to holiday in New York.'

They laughed, recalling Mona Daly's thoughts on airplanes.

'I miss you so much,' she said. 'Every time I pass Trinity I think of our meetings by the secluded oak tree. When I see Buswell's Hotel I'm reminded of you and the smell of bacon and cabbage. I wish you'd come home.'

'And be your little man on the side?' he said, showing his hurt that she had not come to join him.

'The scandal,' she said, unable to imagine how her parents would survive such a thing. 'My parents.'

'Don't tell them you're meeting me.'

'What about Seamus?'

They lay in silence watching the mist gather on the window as it distorted their view.

Chapter 24

Towards the end of May 1923 Betty went to Tipperary to take her mind off Phelim. Isabel was overjoyed to see her yet she noticed how attached Isabel had become to her grandparents and cousins. Her friends lived close by; the house was always busy with visitors who adored her. Isabel called Maureen 'Mother' in the flat Tipperary accent of her cousins. They didn't pronounce the 'th': 'Moder'. She had her chores. After breakfast each morning she filled the basket by the fire with turf, ran down to the farmyard to check the calves and cows. She told Betty how she was learning to milk the cow, demonstrating with her hands tugging in mid-air. Betty was fascinated as she watched her little hands mimic the movement of milking.

After supper Isabel sat beside Maureen on the arm of the chair. When Betty sat on the other chair by the fire, Isabel left Maureen to sit beside Betty. It was a natural thing to do, yet Betty was relieved that her child was still bound to her.

Isabel knew each visitor by name. While they took their seats by the open hearth she helped make tea and dished out cuts of bread and scones for the callers.

'How's the boss?' Betty's brother Finbar asked.

'I'm fine,' Maureen said. 'Pains in my old feet today – 'tis the weather.'

'I wasn't talking to you,' he said. 'I was talking to the dog.'

The terrier on Maureen's lap leaned her head forward as Finbar patted her.

'This is the boss of the house, and Isabel is the nicest boss,' he said.

Isabel laughed as he gently tickled her.

When alone with her, Maureen asked Betty how she was. Betty was cautious with her responses, feeling her mother sensed something was amiss. Little escaped the old woman's eyes. Her mother would like to know what ailed her and how she could help. Or if she thought necessary, she wouldn't be behind the door in giving Betty a good dose of her mind.

'A little tired,' Betty answered. She watched her mother dip a cloth into a bowl of warm water with Epsom Salts. She rinsed the wet cloth and wrapped it around her knuckles. It was to ease the arthritic pain.

'You look tired,' Maureen said, eyeing Betty closely, 'and worse, you look peckish. I hope you're eating well.'

Maureen's tonic for any ailment was food: big plates of meat, potatoes and vegetables doused in butter following by large cuts of apple tart.

'I'll sleep well over the next few nights,' Betty said.

'How's Seamus?'

Betty noticed how her mother made the question sound casual yet her eyes narrowed as she looked closely at her. Had Isabel said something to arouse her mother's suspicion? Not that Isabel could have reported anything unusual other than Daddy wanting her to sleep in a hole in the ground in case she was shot dead during the night.

'Is he well?' Maureen asked, using her harmless voice.

'Yes, he's busy with his violins and of course this is an uncertain time for any republican. He's worried for his own safety.'

How could she reveal the truth about Seamus? Nobody would

comprehend how a man like him had turned into a suspicious wreck. The kindly few would want to help him, 'to fix his auld head', as Mona said. When she closed the front door of her home in Dublin to go to Tipperary, she could hear Seamus bolting the door behind her. She expected he'd spend her few days' absence barricaded inside the house. It would be an act of mercy if someone shot him. Fraught with guilt for such a terrible thought, silently she said an Act of Contrition.

'He won't have long more to worry,' her mother said. 'They're saying the war will be over in a few weeks.'

'Hopefully,' Betty said. 'We'll have forgotten how to live in a country without killings or strife.'

'How's Fr Mathew?'

'Great. He finds the war difficult. The sight of soldiers and guns continues to unnerve him.'

'Mathew was always a big softie. All belonging to him were no good to do manual labour. They'd be more inclined to talk.'

Maureen rinsed the cloth in the Epsom Salts again and applied it to the other hand. She sat back in the chair, looking at her covered hand as if she was about to witness the swelling miraculously reduce.

'How's your friend – the teacher with the scarred hand?'

'Phelim,' Betty said, trying to read her mother's line of questioning. Quickly she scolded herself for thinking her mother could know anything. Apart for Conleth, nobody knew a thing. 'He's fine. Well, I think he's fine.' She needed to pretend a distance had grown between them. 'He's Anti-Treaty so we don't see him.'

'What a shame,' her mother said. 'When Isabel first moved down here three years ago she used to play a game. Isabel would pretend she was you, I'd pretend I was Isabel, and Jim had to be Phelim drinking tea with his biscuit from a cup with red dogs.' Her mother laughed, recalling it. 'We used to love it. Like two silly eejits, your father and I were as bad as the child – we'd play any game she wanted. We'll miss her terribly when you take her away with you,' she shrugged, 'but that's life. Don't be in any rush to take her back, though. Make sure you've everything in order and Dublin is safe.'

'Any word from Uncle Maurice?' Betty indicated the picture of her mother's brother, a priest in Essex. She didn't want to hear about the child's game. It was a reminder of how much had happened.

'A letter came last week. He was all talk about the state of the country.' Maureen shook her head with a sad expression. 'These wars are an awful thing. It's a fright to God to think how our small town is torn asunder with the two sides. I've bruises on my knees from praying it will end soon.' She sighed. 'I hope poor Phelim is alive.'

Betty didn't want to say that Phelim had emigrated. She didn't want to discuss him at all with her mother. It was a surprise that Isabel remembered him after her departure.

When Betty woke the following morning she heard that the Civil War was over. Her brother Finbar was reporting the news from town. A few neighbours called, all animated and filled with renewed optimism.

Isabel looked at her mother expectantly.

'You'll come to Dublin with your cousin in two weeks for a few days.' Betty couldn't bring her back now. She'd wait to see how Seamus took the news. Before she left Tipperary she counted the money she had hidden under the windowsill in her bedroom. She thought about the business premises in Anne Street, then she thought of Phelim. There was enough money there to start all over again in England. But might he now come home?

When Betty arrived at her Dublin home, she waited with impatience on the doorstep as Seamus removed the sideboard from inside the door and unbolted the many locks. His ashen face peered out at her, and then he looked over her shoulder suspiciously. Betty was in no mood for his nonsense today.

'It's all over,' she declared jubilantly, pushing past him into the kitchen. 'You can come out of your lair and return to living like a human being.'

He looked back at her with disbelief, his wild hair and patchy red-and-blond beard making him look like the untamed ape-man from the movie *A Blind Bargain*.

'It's far from over,' he said calmly, following her into the kitchen.

'It's in the papers and on the wireless. Seamus, it's all over,' she said, laying the *Irish Independent* on the table. The big bold headlines declared the end of Ireland's Civil War. 'Go on, read it.'

'I told you it's far from over,' he repeated.

'For a man who doesn't leave the house, read the papers, listen to the radio, meet one single solitary soul,' she said, hoping he would realise how daft he had become, 'how in God's name would you know?'

He tapped the side of his head. 'I know,' he said with conviction.

Betty was annoyed with herself that she was foolish enough to think Seamus would suddenly revert to his old self with the news.

As the weeks passed, the war was officially over yet sporadic killings continued.

Betty found a list of possible assassins that Seamus had written. Conleth's name was scrolled in large angry capitals. Underneath that was Fr Mathew's.

The following week she found Seamus rooting in her handbag.

'Are you looking for my hairbrush?' she boldly asked. 'Because you're turning into a woman with that long hair.'

She knew it was only a matter of time before he began suspecting her.

He suggested she should remain in the house rather than spending time in the shop. He made it clear to her that he was not accusing her of anything – however, he was adamant that the Anti-Treaty side were manipulative.

'They could make it sound like you're doing the right thing,' he explained.

The thought of spending her days holed up within the strained walls of her home unsettled her as much as his accusations did. He wouldn't be happy until he had his family hiding beneath the floorboards.

Each evening she put off returning home for as long as possible. She couldn't bear the stifled predictable air. It drained her and left her feeling wholeheartedly pessimistic in a time when she should have been rejoicing. How could she bring her child back from the country to a man who mistrusted the insects in the earth beneath his feet? Life would have been easier if he lived somewhere else. There were nights when she would have welcomed his death. Richmond District Lunatic Asylum was full of saner men than her barking mad husband.

'Next you'll be thinking that the enemy has broken into our house at night to poison the food.'

Seamus shook his head. 'Not possible. I'd hear them.'

Irritated by his response, Betty continued in the same angry vein. 'Or you'll think that Isabel is a runner for the Anti-Treaty lot!'

At that his eyes widened then he shook his head.

Throughout his last year of delirium, his daughter was the only thing he trusted and depended on. Each week Betty posted a letter that he had written for Isabel which her grandparents would read aloud to her. He kept her up to date on the figurines he was carving. Isabel would write back telling him about her friends and cousins and requesting yet another figurine. It was only while he carved the miniature people that his mind was somewhat eased. In the last letter he told her that the doll's house was completed with all the requested grandparents, uncles, aunts, and Maureen's new dog, Winnie. He told her how it took pride of place in his workshop and would remain there until her next visit. Betty always read Seamus's letters.

'Do you not see there is real danger?' he said.

'The only man you need to be concerned about is Mr Hartmann,' she responded.

For the second time he gaped at her with such wild terror that she almost regretted saying it. Yet she wouldn't undo what she'd said. Throughout Ireland's troubles and her husband's worsening mind, his craft never diminished – if anything, it improved. Now that Betty had come to an agreement with Mrs Willems, she wanted to keep Mr Hartmann and her husband apart until she found an opportune moment to tell Mr Hartmann his services were no longer needed.

'Do you think?' he asked, his eyes pleading for clarification.

She was suddenly pained to see the real agony etched on his features.

He approached the bed and stepped over the slash hook on the floor which he insisted on sleeping with. 'Tell me,' he said again in a quiet alarmed voice.

Death would be easier than living with his delirium.

'By all accounts,' she added quietly, sticking to her plan of separating her husband from Mr Hartmann.

The eight unsold violins were stored in solid cases for safekeeping. Each time she visited London, she called to Mrs Willems and disposed of one violin. It was vital to keep her husband's work in circulation. By day Betty silently swore that her husband could turn into Ireland's biggest lunatic but she would save herself. She would not stop working or making money or allow her mind to be drawn into his vortex of paranoia.

Chapter 25

A year since the end of the Civil War and nothing had changed. If anything Seamus was a more terrified reclusive than he had been during Ireland's worse periods of conflict. Betty confided in Mrs Wyse Power who put her in touch with a doctor. Seamus was furious when she suggested they meet the doctor to discuss the problems in his head. He suggested everyone else needed a head-doctor except himself. Fearing she would go behind his back, Seamus locked her into their bedroom for the day.

When Betty relayed the events to Phelim, he appeared more sad than angry.

'I know it's wrong but I often pray at night that God will take him,' she admitted. 'Sometimes I see him polishing his gun. He keeps it by his side at all times. I often expect him to shoot me.' She laughed when she said it, but as quickly she began to cry. 'His condition is worsening all the time. I do believe he will kill me.'

Betty didn't know why she needed to paint such a horrid picture. Most of the time she ignored Seamus. There were many days when they would not meet. He'd sleep when she went to work and at night when she slept he worked on his violins and figurines for the doll's house. To some extent she had learned to live with his madness. At night when he'd wake her to ensure the light beneath the Sacred Heart was still burning, she recalled her stolen days with Phelim. When Seamus went hysterical at the thought of a gap in the shutters, she would escape his accusing eyes and retreat to her memories of Phelim. Her respite was Phelim. The mere thought of him offered her sanctuary. The prospect of their encounters gave her the courage to sustain life with Seamus. The sin of their hungry flesh lessened with her growing realisation that Seamus was unlikely to find peace.

Phelim stood by the window, listening.

'He's terrified of your family. He thinks he should kill your brother Conleth before Conleth kills him. He thinks Conleth or one of your Anti-Treaty brothers will avenge Seán Salmon's death.'

Phelim stared at her disbelievingly. His expression changed from concern to hurt. Slowly he sat down on the chair by the window.

Betty continued speaking as if she didn't notice his sudden sadness. 'I had to pretend that Conleth no longer works for me. But that doesn't stop him questioning me and locking me into my room if he's dissatisfied with my responses to his interrogation.'

Suddenly Phelim went to her. He held her hands in his. 'Stop,' he said firmly. 'I don't want you to say any more.'

He took her in his arms and soothed her as she cried.

When her tears subsided he got a drink from the bar and brought it to the bedroom. They sat in silence and watched the rain pour down, the overcast day reflecting their despondency. Finally, Phelim drained his glass, placed his chair in front of Betty and took her hands in his. He took his hankie and gently wiped the remaining tears from her face.

When he had her full attention, he spoke. 'Next week, possibly Friday or Saturday, don't go to work.'

Betty nodded like a child as if she was following basic instructions to a simple task.

'Stay at home for those two days. At some stage on Friday or Saturday, Conleth will notify you closer to the time. He will tell you the time when you must leave the house. You must not lock the door. Leave it on the latch.'

Betty listened. She knew he was finding a solution. Albeit an unorthodox solution. It was best for everyone.

'Leave the door on the latch,' he repeated.

She nodded.

'That's all you need to do,' Phelim whispered.

It was early November and the frost remained on the ground till mid-morning. It was the following week that Mr Hartmann called to Betty's home. When she saw him at the door breathing fog, she was daunted at the prospect of dealing with him on that day. She was focussed on waiting for word from Phelim.

She hesitated, afraid Seamus might spot him. So she didn't invite him in but stepped outside and held the door ajar.

With a solemn expression she told him that her husband was not well. 'He was injured in a farming accident in Tipperary.' Even as she spoke the words, Betty felt foolish. Yet she would rather feel foolish than reveal the truth.

Mr Hartmann did not appear surprised. 'Will he recover?'

'Only the dear Lord in heaven knows the answer to that.'

'May I ask where he was injured?'

Betty would like to have said her husband's head was injured. The vault that kept his sanity was shattered. Her once glorious husband was like a putrefying corpse sucking the fragrance from her daily life. As well as hiding his remaining eight violins in solid cases, Betty realised she was also hiding Seamus. Not only did he look like a caveman, she feared he might shoot the first person who looked crooked at him with the loaded gun he carried everywhere. With the exception of Mona and Fr Mathew, there was nobody who knew the extent of her husband's craziness. Keeping his peculiarities hidden was as much a burden as managing his disorder. Rumour of a mental issue was as damning as illegitimacy and epilepsy – all were indicators of a corrupt bloodline. It would never do to inflict that kind of stigma on their daughter. There was courage in death, courage in fighting, there was courage in losing but no courage was reserved for the men in the mental asylums.

'His chest, close to the heart.' Betty quivered when she said that. It wasn't intended – she'd wanted to appear stoic, dignified. When she thought she was going to cry she hid her face in her hand and turned to go inside, indicating they'd nothing more to say.

'I don't expect we'll meet again.' Mr Hartmann extended his hand. 'I'm leaving the country.'

She looked at his proffered hand, shocked at the sudden news.

Everything was changing so suddenly. Mutely she looked at his hand and back at him. 'Where are you going?'

'America,' he announced, sounding very proud. 'The land of the free.'

'What about your shop, and your business? You've been building it up for years,' she said, taking his hand and feeling in some way rebuffed.

He sighed loudly. 'I have a buyer for my business. This opportunity may not present itself again. It's time I moved further afield,' he said with finality.

Just then she imagined America. The gigantic buildings in the crowded cities, the vast prairies where the white man stalked the Indians, the roaming buffalo, the heat of Hollywood where they made movies. Their broad accents and sun-kissed complexions. She envied Mr Hartmann.

'It's well for you. If only we could do the same.'

He smiled at her. 'I'm sure you'll be fine,' he said. 'Seamus's stock will always be in demand, as well you know from your trips to Mayfair.'

His reference to Mrs Willems' violin shop confirmed that he knew Betty had been deceiving him for the last few months. She didn't feel the need to defend her actions. As Mrs Willems said, 'Business is business.' A shrewd man like him would do the same if he was in her position.

After he left Betty sat alone in the sitting room, watching the ticking clock. She thought about America. How easy it was for Mr Hartmann to uproot and move on. That afternoon she believed that sometimes you have to let something die to let something else live. Seamus's heart might as well have been pierced; their lives would never resume as before. A man like him would never find peace again. The man she loved was gone forever; there would have been greater dignity in his death. Betty sat on the settee, crying loudly into her handkerchief. The years of remaining strong, finding a means of living through the hell of war, always active to stay just out of reach of the claws of death and sinking under the debris of conflict, seemed to dissolve into bitter tears that flushed through her like a gully at the side of house taking the excess water and carelessly dispersing it on lower grounds. Betty couldn't remember when she had cried like that – maybe as a child, certainly not in the last few years. It left her drained yet relieved. Even the imminent sense of sadness was dispelled when she thought of Seamus who was working in the workshop behind the house. Shortly he too would be relieved of his suffering. At last the windmills that constantly rotated despairing thoughts would stop and he would find peace in death.

That afternoon, on the 7th of November 1924, Conleth came by, telling her it was time to go.

'Leave the door on the latch,' he said and left without delaying.

Betty took her coat and hat from the stand by the door. She didn't speak to Seamus before she left. She didn't want one final glance at what was left of her decaying husband. As arranged the door was on the latch. She would not pull the trigger of the gun that would kill him but she would not stand in the way of his enemy who chose to take his life. As she made her way into town she passed the postman doing his rounds, a nanny walking her charge in the direction of the park, a woman seeing her husband off at their front gate. All normal everyday life swelled around her, each a consoling reassurance that life for her would return to normality. Betty was aware it would not happen overnight. She'd give herself three months to sell off the remaining stock in the shop and her home. By spring she would be living in London with Isabel and Phelim. With God's help they would begin a life of peace and prosperity without long-suffering Ireland snapping at their heels.

Chapter 26

January 1925

Seamus's death, on the 7th of November 1924, coincided with a general amnesty for acts committed during the Civil War. Several names were bandied about, and she did not dissuade them from suspecting Mr Hartmann. A man bearing his description had been seen in the locality, a Jewish violin dealer. Betty pretended this news added to her grief.

The Free State soldiers formed a guard of honour and fired their guns over the graveside. She acknowledged the hundreds who attended the funeral, her eyes fixed on the future when she would be reunited with Phelim in England. By the graveside she imagined their home, their sense of united freedom that they could move on from troubled Ireland. The darkest period of Irish history was over. And, as the guns were fired, it signified the end of Betty's darkest period. The horror of the last few years was over for her. At last she could plan for the future.

As a young widow it was assumed she would return to Tipperary immediately.

'You're a woman after all,' Fr Mathew advised. 'Let your brother take care of the sale of Seamus's house and business.'

Her mother shared Fr Mathew's view. In one of her letters she suggested that Betty return to the country immediately and be a good parent to her daughter. Her words were, '*Finbar is willing to go to Dublin and take care of matters from now on. Come home and stop your tomfoolery. The little girl needs you. You might need her too – little Isabel will help you through this difficult time.*'

One week after Seamus's burial Betty opened a bank account in her name and deposited most of her hidden money in it. There was enough money to flee to America like Mr Hartmann and begin again. But Betty didn't want America. She wanted Phelim as they were during the war when he'd sit in her kitchen and dunk his biscuits into his milky tea. He'd been distant in his last letter. Betty understood – a great deal was about to change in both of their lives – it was a daunting prospect.

With a dogged determination, she tried to clear the wreckage of the past few years. When she thought of Seamus, she was occasionally disturbed by the events of his death but quickly reasoned that the best course of action had been taken. As yet she did not know who the actual assassin was, nor did she want to know. Of course Phelim had played some part in it; he probably had got one of his associates to end Seamus's life. It need not matter any more. It was utterly pointless reliving those events. She wanted to start anew.

At night when she was left alone with her own thoughts, she imagined living in London with Phelim, the sounds and smell of his crowded city. The idea of starting again as somebody else's wife in another country invigorated her. She would continue making money and living in Dublin until a respectable period passed. Then she would join Phelim in London to begin again.

Mona Daly helped Betty remove all of Seamus's clothing, books and IRA correspondence from the house. They made a fire at the bottom of the garden and burned everything.

Mona wept for Seamus while Betty fed the flames.

'Jaysus, Betty, 'tis a bit soon,' she pleaded. 'We're not over the shock yet.'

'No time like the present,' Betty said as she scoured the house to ensure nothing was left. She wanted no reminders. The only item she kept was a display case containing one of Seamus's violins. In time, that too would be removed.

'It's not right at all,' she heard Mona mumble.

With the glow of the dying embers from the fire still in the back garden, Betty packed her suitcase. In the morning she would take the boat to England with another violin for Mrs Willems and to see Phelim. It would be her first time meeting him since the week prior to Seamus's death. She had been so desperate for his presence over the last month that she could think of nothing else. Although his letters were consistent, Betty tried to ignore the gnawing sense of uneasiness that all was not well. It was not the content of his letters that disturbed her but the missing intimate pieces of Phelim that she loved. No longer was there a reference to the picture he kept by his bedside, or his wish to be reunited with her and smother her in kisses. She compared his last letter to reading a roundup of the week's sporting events. He included the outcome of the rugby game and mentioned the weather. They reminded her of the obligatory letters she wrote to her uncle the priest, stifled with formality.

Even more troubling was his reference to Ursula. He mentioned he'd bumped into her at the Horseshow, and then met her again at a race meeting outside London. Betty sent him a letter of caution that Ursula might reveal his whereabouts to the Irish community. She'd like to have mentioned Ursula's inappropriate relationship with Dr O'Malley. Instead she'd tell him when they met. Phelim was a lonely man in London, clearly disturbed by the recent events. A vulnerable man who could find refuge in the first familiar face he encountered. Disappointed after his last letter, she brought it close to her nose, hoping to recapture a sense of him on the page. There was nothing, not even the smell of his cigarettes, only his even handwriting.

By the time Phelim arrived at the hotel bedroom she'd fallen asleep on the bed in her clothes. She woke to find him sitting in the chair smoking a cigarette, looking at her. He did not go to her when she woke and extended her arm. He regarded her with a vague smile and looked away as quickly. He asked how she was. It was asked in the same tone he would use for a girl serving him in a shop.

'Why didn't you wake me?' she whispered, drowsy from sleep.

'You were dreaming.'

'I've missed you,' she said, extending her hand again.

He remained where he was, sitting at the table in the corner holding his drink. He looked away from her. Sensing his reluctance, she went to him.

'Life can only get better,' she said. She knew she was coaxing him, trying to bring them back to the closeness they shared during the wars.

She climbed onto his lap, removed his tie and undid the top buttons on his shirt. She ran her hands through his hair, sat higher on his lap and kissed him again until he was more attentive. He lowered his eyes to her breast. Without speaking, he undid the buttons on her blouse and roughly pushed his hands through her layers of clothes. Aggressively he held her breast and dug his teeth into her neck. She opened his trousers and reached in to find him erect. He stood up and pushed her onto the table, knocking his drink onto the floor. He reached under her clothes, ripping her petticoat. Greedily he clawed at her body like a man on the verge of imploding. Suddenly he stopped, and wiped his mouth with the back of his hand. She was strangely aroused by his aggression. He remained clothed, his erect penis exposed. Roughly he clenched his teeth and thrust himself into her – angry rapid thrusts. She flinched before finding the pain a welcome release.

They had lunch in an Italian restaurant the following day. It was Betty's idea. They made a half-hearted attempt at recapturing what they first had. Phelim glanced at his dish of spaghetti as if eating it was a chore. She watched the steam rise from his dish, conscious of the rising conviction that Phelim did not want to be with her.

'How is Isabel?' he asked, making it sound casual.

'Children are resilient.' Betty felt the need to make Isabel seem less damaged by the incident.

Because Isabel had witnessed Seamus's death. It was too daunting for either of them to dwell on the miscalculation of that afternoon.

Isabel had been due to arrive in Dublin on Saturday, the day after Seamus's death. But Betty's brother Finbar had an appointment in Dublin on Friday, so she travelled with him and arrived a day early. He left Isabel in the care of her father before departing. Not long afterwards the neighbours heard gunshots. Isabel's fingers had to be prised off the legs of the table under which she had been hiding in the workshop where she witnessed Seamus's death.

'Isabel . . .' Phelim whispered and momentarily closed his eyes.

Betty noticed how he referred to her daughter by name. Most people asked how 'the little one' was. Just then she was reminded that Phelim knew Isabel as a baby. Until she was dispatched to Tipperary at four years of age he regularly saw her.

That was their last and only reference to Seamus's death.

'You miss the old sodden soil?' she probed.

'Of course. There are very few happy Irish emigrants. We make the most of it, struggling with our daft melancholy.'

'Are you growing fond of London?'

'The anonymity suits me right now. It's a good time to take stock.'

'Any classy English ladies turning your head?'

He didn't smile at her attempt at humour, only shook his head. No compliment followed.

'Do you meet any Irish?' She tried to sound casual, 'Ursula, how is she?' She tried to make it sound as if she had only thought of her then.

'She's in fine form,' Phelim said and smiled at the mention of her name. 'She's working in a hospital for soldiers injured in the army. She was quite comical about spending so many years with murderous thoughts for the men she is now nursing.'

'Are you not concerned she will reveal your whereabouts?'

'Not at all,' he said dismissively. 'She's a fine friend, she understands.'

Betty nodded as if she too understood.

'Ursula's lonely too,' he added.

'You don't need to be lonely,' she said, taking his hand.

He acknowledged what she'd said with a noncommittal nod.

Betty spent another two nights in London with Phelim. They travelled on the Underground and went to a jazz club. Betty bought a doll for Isabel which she kept out of Phelim's sight. When she smiled, he returned her smile and held her hand when she reached for his. There were periods when she felt like an adult prompting a child to respond with manners.

Chapter 27

On Betty's return to Ireland, she went to Tipperary to bring Isabel back to Dublin to live with her. Maureen and Jim were heartbroken at losing the child. Her mother described the last five years as the best time of their life. She said she knew the day would come when they'd lose her – nonetheless it didn't make it easier. With an air of resignation, she went through a litany of Isabel's routines and preferences. Her normal bed time, how she liked thick gravy and didn't like carrots. Lukewarm milk, not cold milk.

'Watery tea as a treat when she wants to feel like an adult.' Maureen smiled indulgently when she said that.

Betty wanted to ask her mother if she'd lost the run of herself. Maureen was one of those pragmatic women who reared her children with the ethos 'they'd eat whatever was put in front of them'.

'I must tell you about the nightmares,' her mother began. She exhaled a long sigh as if about to undertake a laborious task. 'Sometimes they're over quickly and she returns to sleep, other nights the crying seems to go on till the morning.'

Betty had stayed the previous night, sharing the bedroom with Isabel. When Isabel woke screaming, Betty was startled at the piercing pitch of the scream. Maureen came into the bedroom, wrapped her arms around the little girl and soothed her for a while. Eventually Isabel returned to sleep.

'Last night it was over grand and quick,' Maureen continued. 'When Isabel has a routine like school days, the nightmares aren't as bad. Some nights there are no nightmares. It'll take time, but make sure she has a solid routine and feels safe.'

Much to her mother's consternation, Betty was reluctant to take one of the terrier pups back to Dublin with her.

'It'll give Isabel great comfort,' her mother protested.

'It'll give my house fleas, shedding hair and that awful dog-smell,' Betty countered.

'It's time to put your child first and leave your airy-fairy notions behind you. The child needs the dog and anything else that'll give her poor soul comfort.'

Betty and Isabel got on the train loaded with Isabel's belongings, including Patch the dog. As the train pulled away from the platform Betty could see her father wipe the tears from his eyes with the back of his hand.

Isabel's nightmares were taking their toll on Betty. When she heard the first shrill scream the first night home, she woke with a start. A pang of guilt left her breathless. Quickly she dispelled those thoughts. Enveloping the child in her arms, as she'd seen her own mother do, did little to pacify Isabel. For most of the night she held Isabel in her arms, the little girl's face wet with tears.

During the following sleepless nights, as Isabel lay in her arms, Betty thought about Seamus's death. Every argument brought her back to the same point. Death was a welcome release for Seamus. She pacified the Hopkins men when they swore to avenge their brother's death. They mentioned several names of Anti-Treaty and non-political men including Mr Hartmann. So enraged was he at his brother's death, Malachy said he'd go to Chicago or Boston to find Hartmann, 'and blow him to smithereens'. Betty thought it interesting that the Hopkins men were so intent on finding a culprit, they would consider a harmless non-political violin seller like Mr Hartmann. Intent on keeping the blame away from Phelim Salmon or his family, Betty never encouraged or dissuaded the Hopkins from accusing anyone, including Mr Hartmann.

To establish a routine, Betty hired Mona's daughter Margaret as a live-in housekeeper. At seventeen, she was young and capable, but not anywhere as strong as her mother Mona. Betty enrolled Isabel in the local school and each morning Margaret would walk her to its gate. Betty worked in the shop each day and collected Isabel at the school in the afternoons. They walked home and ate their dinner together. Then Betty returned to work for a few hours in the evening, leaving Isabel in Margaret's care. Mona continued to call two evenings a week and do small jobs for Betty. Her presence gave a sense of security to Isabel, and occasionally an added strength to Betty.

Since returning to Dublin Betty noticed Isabel avoided the sight of Seamus's workshop. She had not stepped outside the back door and kept her head down while passing the windows at the back of the house. So, two weeks after Isabel's return to Dublin, Betty got a few men to tear down Seamus's old workshop. From the kitchen window she watched the men. First the roof, and then they attacked the four walls with their hammers. A horse and cart spent the day removing the rubble. Every few hours the cart returned to be piled high with more rubble and moved off again. The horse's clicking hoofs sounded laboured. Finally, there was a small mound of dust. As darkness fell she saw the men clean their boots and tools at the tap by the wall. They shared a cigarette as they shielded their eyes when the wind forced the dust to move.

Let that be the end of it, Betty thought.

That night when Isabel woke screaming, Betty went to her room. She took Isabel from her bed and brought her to the window overlooking the garden. Holding the child in an upright position until her hysterics subsided, she opened the curtains. From the light of the moon Betty pointed to the vacant corner of the garden and sighed with relief – she had done it to remove the incident from her mind as much as Isabel's. Ignoring her daughter's limp body, Betty used all of her strength to keep Isabel on her feet. She waited until the child was as calm and alert as possible.

'Look, it's gone,' Betty said. 'It never happened.'

The child looked at her, wild-eyed. Betty forced her to look into the dimly lit garden by moving her head. Tightly she wrapped her other arm around Isabel's shoulder.

'It's gone forever,' she said adamantly.

Isabel uncoiled her body from her mother's before sliding to the floor. Her eyes were not frightened or pacified – they were dull – two vacant blue eyes.

There were times when Betty felt she was walking against a strong wind. Looking at her daughter was like a tunnel leading her straight back to the Seamus. She found herself thinking other thoughts. It seemed as if Phelim was also battling her. Once a month she went to London to see Mrs Willems and to spend time with him. With each visit, he was more reticent. When he asked how Isabel was, Betty always reassured him that she was fine. She placed the emphasis on their future, a life when they could be together, as free as possible from the past.

Seamus was never far from their minds. In Piccadilly Circus a man passed them, his entire body shaking. Betty tried not to look while the man put one shaky foot in front of the other, using the wall to steady himself with an equally shaky hand.

'Shellshock,' Phelim explained.

Since coming to London she'd seen men with missing limbs or lame steps or badly scarred faces but had never seen a man tremble so much.

'Some men cannot overcome the inhumaneness of taking another man's life,' Phelim added as they watched the man attempt to walk.

Now he never asked her to join him in London.

Once she broached the subject by asking when would be the best time to move.

'Not yet,' he said. 'I'm possibly changing to a different newspaper over the coming weeks.'

She held his hand and smiled through her growing realisation that so much had changed.

She received one brief letter before his correspondence abruptly ended.

'*A great deal has happened over the past few weeks. That old war and all the horrors that accompany a war are ever present in my thoughts. I must take responsibility for what I've done. I don't want to trouble you with the difficulties of a man's world. Over the coming weeks I will be in Dublin. I will call to see you and explain.*'

Betty responded with a short understanding letter. She would not appear to pursue him at a time when he found comfort in distance. She told him she would look forward to his visit. Instead of allowing her disappointment to consume her, she kept busy with the shop. She noted how much money was in her bank account but didn't view any business premises. She felt Phelim would come round, in time.

There was no visit from Phelim and no letters from him followed. When Betty's time came to travel again to see Mrs Willems, she wrote to Phelim notifying him of her arrival and departure dates. She kept the letter short. She did not receive a reply. From the moment she boarded the boat to London she could not stop thinking about him. Without the distraction of work or Isabel, Phelim consumed her.

On Saturday when she finished her business with Mrs Willems, she took the tube to his digs. Betty hadn't formulated a solid plan, she merely put one foot in front of the other until she arrived at his digs. It was an ugly large plain red-bricked terraced house. While she waited for the door to be answered she noticed the cheap netted curtains. They were plain without any pattern. Betty had never seen such ordinary curtains.

An elderly unfriendly Englishwoman answered the door.

Betty smiled hoping to win her over, 'I'm looking for Ph–' She was about to asked for Phelim Salmon when she remembered his English alias. 'Dominic, do you know what time Dominic Harris will be in?'

The woman shook her head. 'He's moved on.'

Betty was taken aback. She waited for the woman to elaborate. 'Where to?' she asked when she was met with silence.

'We don't give out forwarding addresses,' the woman replied in the same unfriendly manner.

'I'm his sister, you see,' Betty began, 'there's been an accident at home and I need to contact him urgently.'

'I can't help you. I'll try and get word to him through one of his pals tonight.'

Before the door was closed Betty noticed the net curtain move from the downstairs window. Phelim would not do that to her. He would not hide from her like that.

For the remainder of the day she was numb. It was as if Phelim no longer existed. There was no correspondence, no address and clearly he wanted it that way. Gradually her numbness gave way to a wave of dreadful loneliness. She cried throughout the journey back to Ireland and the following day was unable to leave her house, her outbursts of sobbing were so intense.

Chapter 28

Dublin, 1925

One month after her last visit to London, Betty returned to see Mrs Willems and took Isabel with her. Glorious London suddenly seemed lonely and empty. The usual excitement she felt when she disembarked from the train was gone. She felt like a woman in mourning for Phelim yet there had been no death. For a change she booked into a different hotel. It was in the same street as Phelim's office. Each day she saw droves of men dressed like Phelim make their way to work with newspapers tucked under their arms. Robotically her eyes scanned the faces beneath the men's hats for Phelim's brown watchful eyes.

There were times when she forgot about him. She saw the sights of London through Isabel's childish eyes. She hoped the excitement of London would invigorate her daughter. It would give the child a different aspect to life. It would allow her see there was more to her little world than her rural grandparent's humble homestead. Betty watched Isabel closely, her eyes so like Seamus's. They were not the excitable type. Isabel was more an observer than a participant.

In Mrs Willems' house Isabel gaped at the enormous chandelier in her parlour. She was polite and answered when spoken to.

'Will you marry a violinmaker when you grow up?'

Isabel nodded. 'Please God.'

Betty cringed at her daughter's flat accent and colloquial expression.

'Although I'd like to make violins myself.'

Later when they were alone Betty asked Isabel if she really wanted to make violins when she grew up. Isabel told her she'd made one violin already. Her grandfather had helped her.

'It's in Tipperary waiting to be varnished,' she explained. 'Granddad Jim said I'll be as good as my father.'

'That's marvellous,' Betty said, aware that that was Isabel's first reference to Seamus. 'I never knew that. So much has happened. That awful trouble in Ireland almost ruined everything.'

They spent that day visiting Big Ben and the jewels in the Tower of London. They peered through the railings of Buckingham Palace at the guards.

Isabel's called them 'Silly Billys' for wearing their enormous black furry helmets.

Each evening they ate in restaurants close to the pub where Phelim drank after work. They had scones and ice-cream in a café with a view of the main entrance to his office. On Whitefriar Street Betty thought she saw him, then scolded herself for being so in need of his presence. Yet she could not shake that awful sense of loss.

Each day she examined the newspaper to see what sports events were scheduled for that day. It made her feel closer to Phelim, knowing what he was doing. She pictured him filling his flask of tea in the dark cold mornings before catching a train to a race meeting. His face fixed, filled with intent as it did with everything he did.

On the last day of their London trip Betty took Isabel to a restaurant called the Continental for lunch. During her last trip Phelim had pointed it out. He told her it served the closest meal to an Irish dinner. Each floury potato made him feel as if he was sitting at his mother's kitchen table surrounded by the chorused hum of his family talking. That day Betty couldn't find any obvious sports fixtures in the paper. On days like this Phelim ate in the Continental and had a drink in the pub next door.

Isabel ate a plate of chips and sausages. It was her first time to eat chips. The greasy soggy food was a joyous discovery. She licked her lips and looked mournfully at the empty plate when she'd finished. To delay a little longer Betty treated Isabel to a sundae, another luscious delight Betty had discovered during her trips to London. Betty scanned the face of each tall man, wishing Phelim would enter. With little Isabel digging into her ice-cream he would find the setting more appealing. Phelim admitted to loving children. Their openness appealed to him. He saw newness in life through their awakening eyes.

At that point Betty did not regret what she had done. Her conscience was clear. Sadly, Phelim did not have the same matter-of-fact approach. As time passed she guessed he didn't get a third party to do the job. He was the one who pulled the trigger. By killing Seamus, she guessed that he had destroyed his sense of honour. Until that afternoon in early November, every life he had taken was done through war and love of his country. In killing Seamus, he had other motives.

'How do you spell museum?' Isabel asked. She was writing postcards.

Betty smiled and spelled it. 'We'll be home before your postcard arrives. Who is it for?'

'This one is for Mother and Jim.' She held up a postcard with a picture of the guards with their furry hats. 'This one is for Elsie and this one is for Mona.'

Isabel resumed writing, her cautious scrawl filling up the small postcard.

Betty heard Phelim's voice before she saw him. She was on the street watching Isabel put her postcards into the red post-box. Each card was individually and thoughtfully placed into the opening as if she was delivering priceless valuables rather a scrawl of speckled news.

Phelim hadn't seen her. He had stopped to talk to a man headed in the opposite direction. She turned to face him, his striking height looming ahead of her.

The other man called him Dominic. 'Dominic, put your money on Nancy's Parade for the two-thirty.'

Betty could hear Phelim thank the man and mention another horse. They parted and Phelim resumed walking in her direction.

'Phelim!' she said his name aloud to see if her eyes were betraying her.

He returned her gaze, his mouth forming her name without releasing a sound.

Instinctively she reached to touch him. She said his name aloud again as she reached for his hand.

His hands remained by his sides, a rolled-up newspaper held tightly in his left one. 'What are you doing here?' he asked disbelievingly.

'It's my usual monthly trip to see Mrs Willems. We're leaving for Ireland today.' Betty spoke quickly, trying to ignore his reaction as he took a step away from her. 'Just Isabel and me are here. We spent a few days sightseeing.'

He didn't reply.

'Aren't you happy to see me?'

She moved closer again and laid a hand on his arm. In the days following this encounter, she recalled him inclining his body away from hers.

'Betty, I don't know what to say.' He exhaled. 'I'm sorry... I've been ...' He stopped speaking, his eyes fixed on the child by the post-box.

Betty turned to find Isabel using the post-box as a prop as she slowly slid to the ground, her hand outstretched before her as if to keep something awful at bay.

Betty released Phelim's arm. She turned to Isabel. 'Get up, what are you doing?' She pulled Isabel to her feet. 'Stop this nonsense!'

Isabel stood and ran. Isabel and Phelim followed. Phelim caught up with her first. She pulled away from his grip, and stumbled to the ground. She opened her mouth and screamed. She held her hands to her ears, the pitch of her scream piercing to the passers-by who glanced in bewilderment at the scene. Only when Betty slapped her twice did Isabel's frenzy stop. She pulled from her mother's grip until she was lying on the concrete, her eyes opened and out of focus. Betty recoiled. It was as if everything within her daughter was dead, her eyes devoid of the fear or hysteria of a few moments previously.

In the weeks following their trip to London Isabel refused to speak. Betty wondered if it was a tantrum or the sight of Phelim's scarred hand that forced the memory of Seamus's death to the fore. When she thought about Isabel's reaction, she remembered it was Phelim's hand that Isabel pointed at. On the rare occasion when Betty was alone with her, she looked at Betty from under her eyelids, like a dog that had been kicked too many times. At night the dreams continued, her screams slicing the night. Isabel's inconsolable crying was followed by non-communicative behaviour during daylight hours. Each morning Margaret took her hand and led her to school like any normal girl. On the surface she appeared normal, her legs and arms worked like any normal eight-year-old's, her light blue eyes peered out from her lightly freckled face. She was like a watch that kept its shine – it ticked but never kept the right time. All it took was a short while in her company to see how haunted the child was.

One day Mona arrived when she was not expected. She joined Betty in the back garden where they sat in the shade and quenched their thirst from the June sun with lemonade. Betty could see Isabel pass inside the kitchen window. She could see her peering out, obviously surprised to see Mona on that particular day.

Mona was talking about the gossip from Middle Abbey Street. The latest was Sheila Muldoon's new fella.

'Since poor auld Richie was blown to smithereens in France she's had three different men. They stay the night. I met her latest fellow on the stairs this morning. 'Tis quare behaviour.'

'It's not that bad, she's probably lonely,' Betty said.

'How in all that's holy could anybody be lonely in Middle Abbey Street? Usin' the outhouse is as lonely as it gets.'

Betty smiled. There was something so solid about Mona that she felt safer in her presence – all those years later she continued to offer Betty a sense of security. She loved hearing the little stories from Middle Abbey Street, their ongoing lives a reminder of how blessed she was to escape the cycle of poverty.

'Maybe they're in love,' Betty said.

'Not at all! He's only after her pension from the King.'

'Would you fancy him?'

Mona smiled, knowing she was being teased. 'Not if there were diamonds coming out of his bottom would I leave me childer roam the streets like Sheila Muldoon's.'

'I expect you wouldn't.'

'If anythin' ever happened to Mick Daly I'd need me head examined if I picked up with another man. He's me biggest child.' She lit another Woodbine.

When Mona spotted Isabel hovering at the kitchen window, she smiled and beckoned to her. Isabel returned Mona's smile and came out to her, Patch at her heels.

Mona's large arms enveloped Isabel who responded to her embrace. Effortlessly she scooped the child onto her lap and asked her a few harmless questions, but nothing about London as Betty had warned her not to mention the trip. Mona pretended to ask Patch if he was a good dog. Isabel leaned in closer, appearing to melt into Mona's arms. Betty couldn't help feeling suddenly jealous. Mona had a way with children, a knack for hugging them and making them feel safe. Just for that moment Isabel appeared happy again, the happy little girl she'd always wanted.

'Do you feel closer to some of your children than others?' Betty asked when Isabel left them alone again.

Mona thought about it. 'Some children are easier to know and some children are hard to love. Our Jack is a dark horse – he'd be hard to know. Dinny is easy to love.'

'But you love them all regardless of feeling close to some and not to others?' Betty asked.

'I love them all with the same mountains of love. I probably

214

don't treat them all the same. Some children need a hard hand and others like our Dinny are natural softies who need a soft touch.'

'Are girls easier than boys?'

'Boys make a mess of the clean house and girls have a different way of annoyin' you.'

Betty was consoled to hear that.

'All children need is to feel safe. Poor little Isabel has seen too much. It will take a long time to make her feel safe again,' Mona said.

'Sometimes I wonder . . .' Betty exhaled loudly.

Mona looked at Betty. 'This is a quare chat to be havin'. Are you all right?'

'Yes, perfectly fine,' Betty assured her.

In mid-June late at night Conleth arrived at their house during the Rosary. Fr Mathew, Isabel, Betty and Margaret were kneeling. Normally when visitors called during the Rosary Margaret took them to the parlour to wait. That evening when Betty heard Conleth's voice in the corridor she went to him immediately. When they were alone he took a note from his pocket. Only when the paper trembled in her hands did Betty realise she was shaking. She turned her back to Conleth to hide her anxiety. The note was brief. Phelim would be in Dublin for one night the next week. He wanted to meet her. Betty responded with the affirmative. It had been three months since the London incident. She suspected Phelim had had time to think about their situation.

Chapter 29

In order to help Isabel feel safe and to give Betty a little breather from her daughter's accusing eyes, she allowed her to go to Tipperary for two weeks. She accompanied her on the train with the intention of spending one night there before returning to Dublin to meet Philem. She found a seat where they could be alone and during the journey she took the opportunity to try reasoning with Isabel.

'Sometimes bad things happen to people. We must pray for help when we are afraid. Each night when we say the Rosary I want you to offer it up to God for help to make you safe.'

The child nodded.

'You are safe, Isabel, you will always be safe.'

Isabel looked out the train window at the landscape flying by.

Betty spoke gently. 'When Daddy died it happened during the war. The man who . . . who sent Daddy to Heaven thought he was doing the right thing. That man is dead now. He's in Heaven too. He's not coming back.

Isabel fiddled with her hands then stroked the dog on her lap.

'How could the man who shot Daddy be gone to Heaven?' she asked.

'Because some other man sent him to Heaven. Wherever he is, he's not coming back to Ireland. You are safe.'

'Is he not with the Devil burning in the fires of Hell?' Isabel asked.

'He probably is,' Betty said. Changing the tone of the conversation, she made her voice cheerful. 'Now we must be happy. Bad things happen in life, God gives us the grace to deal with them, then we must make the most of our lives. God would not want us moping and crying and wakening with nightmares. Sure he wouldn't?'

Isabel looked helpless.

'It was Phelim. Phelim shot Daddy.'

She looked at Betty, waiting for her to agree with her.

Betty was speechless. She raised her hand to her neck and idly fiddled with her pearls as she tried to think clearly.

'I saw his burned hand. I forgot about it until I saw it in London again,' Isabel said quietly. 'When I was posting my cards, I saw his hand and knew it. When I was hiding the day ... the day ...'

Betty watched as Isabel faltered – she couldn't bring herself to discuss the day of Seamus's death.

Betty matched Isabel's quiet voice and spoke slowly. 'Isabel, Phelim was living in London when Daddy was killed. It couldn't have been Phelim. It was another man with a burned hand who shot Daddy. Lots of men have burned hands and scars from the wars.'

Isabel's eyes opened wider. Betty couldn't ascertain if it was with fear or at the fact that Betty was disbelieving her account.

'I heard him talking the day Daddy died. Phelim said ...' She stopped speaking.

'No, it wasn't Phelim,' Betty said sharply. 'I've told you. Phelim wasn't in Ireland.'

Isabel began to cry. The dog on her lap became restless and whimpered.

Betty closed her eyes and took a deep breath. 'Don't be crying,' she said gently. 'Look – poor Patch is getting upset.' She patted the dog on Isabel's lap.

218

Isabel pulled the dog closer to her.

'A man who lived in Ireland killed Daddy.' Betty didn't want to mention Phelim's name again. 'A man who is burning in the fires of Hell. We must forget all of that now and put it behind us. It was during the war. A whole load of little girls lost their daddies.'

Isabel retreated into silence.

Betty raised her daughter's chin until she made eye contact. 'We must never talk about it again. You know that, don't you? Daddy is gone to Heaven and it's all over now. You know that, don't you?'

Isabel didn't respond. When Betty removed her hand from her chin, she patted the dog slowly and nodded her head obediently. Betty watched as the dog licked her face. Isabel buried her head into the dog's neck. She never spoke and barely lifted her head until the train pulled into Thurles station.

While in Tipperary, Betty learned from her cousin Maeve that Ursula was leaving England to live in America. 'New York,' Maeve said, imitating the accent. While visiting England Maeve met a few of Ursula's friends in a Welsh pub in Temple Avenue. When Betty quizzed her cousin about the company Ursula kept, she mentioned a few Welshmen and a Dublin chap called Dominic. In a casual voice, Betty asked if Ursula was stepping out with the Dublin chap. Her cousin didn't know but went on to say how Ursula would not be suited to the Dublin fellow. Dominic was too serious for her liking. When Betty asked her if Ursula was going to America alone, Maeve didn't know. She said Ursula, being a nurse, could go anywhere in the world.

The morning of her departure Betty, her mother, two of her aunts and a few female cousins were gathered in the kitchen having tea and scones.

Betty told the women about the Dubliners she encountered. Her aunts and cousins in Tipperary deemed the crowded capital a lesser environment and the Dubliners more unfortunate people than their own honest well-bred folk with their idyllic country ways.

'They're living on top of each other,' Maureen said. 'Men hanging around with nothing to do and starving children wearing rags.'

'Too much time is a dangerous thing,' Aunt Sadie cautioned.

Everybody agreed.

'Girls and boys up to no good can lead to terrible trouble.'

'I have a girl who comes to work for me,' Betty suddenly said, seizing the opening. 'She's eighteen and expecting a baby.'

There was an audible intake of breath.

'The father of the child is an English fellow – he left a few weeks ago. Margaret wrote to him as soon as she realised but unfortunately she hasn't heard anything since. It's a terrible thing to happen to a girl so young.'

The women went on to talk at length about the morals of the Dublin girls.

'No hope for her or her child.'

'The shame she brought on her family.'

'Men are hopeless – it's up to the woman.'

Everybody nodded.

Suddenly Maeve asked, 'What will the girl do?'

'Poor Margaret will stay with me until she has the baby.' Betty smiled when she said it. 'We haven't really discussed what happens after the baby is born. I have a large basement – she can stay there.'

The women began to speak en masse, warning Betty she should do no such thing. She could not appear to condone that kind of behaviour. The girl had to pay for what she did. If Betty harboured an unwed mother and child, her house and name would get a reputation.

'It's just not done!' Aunt Úna was clearly distraught.

In the midst of their protests Betty noticed her mother. Slowly Maureen sat forward and tilted her head to the right to get a better view of her daughter. She was the only one who didn't speak. Her lips were in an angry line. Her eyes hardened and narrowed suspiciously as they lowered to Betty's abdomen. Betty would not falter under her mother's scrutiny.

When Betty later recalled her mother's knowing glare she was all the more determined to keep the baby she was expecting. Naturally her mother would never reveal her suspicions to a single soul. For appearances' sake she would be Betty's best alibi.

But a few days after Betty's return to Dublin her mother more or less said it in a raging letter. Maureen said that Betty was not the type to harbour a single mother at the risk of tarnishing her reputation. More importantly, she said she knew how Betty was the selfish sort who hated household chores. She would never do without a housekeeper while the poor girl was unable to work with her pregnancy. There were other details in the letter about Isabel but Betty was too distracted to take much notice of them.

Betty met Phelim on the banks of the canal. At the sight of his looming figure in the shade of the tree her anger abated. Just then she forgot about the rage she felt each morning when she checked the post for a letter with his handwriting. She loved him, loved him more than she had ever loved Seamus. She would sell her house and her business and live with him in England. The prospect of being parted from him again was too daunting. For the last three months she had been utterly alone. There were days when she felt it would have been better if she'd never met Phelim – then she would not know the pain of missing him.

'Thank you for meeting me,' he said as they embraced. 'I'm sorry for not writing.'

She stood back to look at him and took his hand. As soon as she touched him she could sense him tensing. She let his hand go.

'I should have contacted you,' he apologised.

'Don't,' she said. 'I understand.'

He seemed surprised.

There were so many nights Betty regretted not leaving with him when he initially suggested it. Those days in Cassidy's Hotel and eating their lunch in St Stephen's Green seemed so innocent. Their unabated love blossomed in a time when their lives were fenced with war. As she stood on the banks of the canal she felt some little semblance of hope again. He had come to meet her after all; he still held her in some esteem.

'Yes, the bloody war has almost killed what we had,' she said.

She did not want to mention Seamus by name. 'It made us old, tired and led us to question our integrity. I am more culpable than most.'

'It was I who must take responsibility. Nobody forced me.'

Betty reached for his hand again. She could not let him go.

'I am not sorry for any of my actions during Ireland's wars,' he said. 'I sought absolution for only one life I took.' He stepped to the edge of the water. At the other side of the canal they watched a motor car slowly leave a house. The driver honked the horn as a young family stood at the gate waving.

Betty couldn't think of a plausible response. In seeking absolution, he was admitting his guilt. She did not want to take responsibility or remind Phelim that it was she who coerced him. She had talked at length about Seamus's deteriorating mind and exaggerated her fear. Neither could she force Phelim to see it as an act of mercy. Dealing with a crazed comrade still held hope that someday his distorted eyes would find a lucid moment to appreciate the tricolour flapping in a peaceful wind. In killing Seamus, he had taken away even that potential pleasure.

'Each morning and night I pray for Seamus's soul.' Phelim spoke into the darkness. 'I don't pray for forgiveness any longer. It seems only fair I must do my penance for my sin. For my sin against God, my fellow countryman and against Isabel whose young eyes will be altered forever because I decided to play God and take the life of my friend.' With that he began to cry.

Betty stepped towards him.

He hid his face with his hands.

'Phelim, we have all been altered so greatly that we see the world through a unique lens. Brave men like you paved a future for us and our new country. We managed to find each other during Ireland's most troubled hour – surely we can work to find each other again? We can be happy together again. You're tired. Come home with me where we can talk.'

'No,' he said, an unusual firmness to his tone. 'I came to tell you in person that I am leaving for New York.'

'With Ursula?'

'Yes.'

'Ursula, my cousin Ursula, Dr O'Malley's mistress!' Her voice was raw with indignation.

'We're going to start afresh. We'll get married in America and begin again.' He smiled vaguely when he said that.

Betty struggled to remain poised; she could not allow him see her anger. Could she start again? Could she resume her life and look towards a future without Phelim? It stared unwaveringly, colourless and lifeless before her.

She closed her eyes and turned away from him.

'You must do what you think is right and proper,' she said quietly as she edged away from him. 'I understand you must get as far away as possible.'

'It wasn't an easy decision,' he added, following her and catching her arm.

Under the dim light of the moon she turned to face him. They stood quietly regarding each other. Beneath the veil of darkness, it was easier. It was he who reached for her hand this time.

'Do write from time to time – let me know how the land of the free treats you,' she said.

He appeared to soften.

Betty continued in the same indifferent manner, feeling it was drawing him closer to her. 'You'll learn a few new tunes on your flute and you'll speak with a Yank's accent.'

'Unlikely,' he smiled.

Gradually they moved towards each other. Betty leaned against him and he placed his arms around her. She sensed his closeness again.

'Come home with me for old times' sake,' she said. 'Just for tea and Jacobs' biscuits.'

He pinched the bridge of his nose and seemed to think. 'I have to meet an old pal now,' he finally said. 'I won't be long – about – half an hour at the most. I'll call to you at eleven o'clock.'

'Promise?' She wanted to be sure.

'I promise, eleven at the latest,' he confirmed and wrapped his arms around her.

She lay into him with her head on his chest. She could hear his heart beat and once again sensed him returning to her. In the comfort of home, she could gauge him more clearly and then she would tell him about the baby. He would stay. Phelim's desire to do the right thing was inherent.

When he did not come to her home she walked to his mother's house. Hoping to catch a glimpse of him, she lingered around his childhood home. Yet she knew he was gone.

That night Betty walked for over two hours. Finally, when her legs could not carry her any longer, she looked up at the starry sky and screamed into the warm summer night to expunge the pain of her loss.

When Betty's pregnancy registered with Mona, she sighed. 'The Lord save us, what have you done?'

She didn't wait for a response. Instead she set the iron on the fire, lit a Woodbine and gathered the pile of aired clothes.

As with the first pregnancy Mona called a few times a week. Betty felt awkward that she was not paying for these visits. So, grateful for Mona's visits, she offered her clothes and money, food and the odd item of jewellery. Mona refused everything except her wages and cigarettes. When discussing the pregnancy, they limited their conversation to the factual aspects. How much longer? What preparations needed to be made? They must concoct a story for Isabel, a plausible explanation that would suffice when she relayed the news to her Tipperary relatives.

'I've told my family that a girl in the shop is pregnant,' Betty lied. She didn't dare tell Mona that she led her family to believe that Margaret was the pregnant employee. 'I'll pretend that the girl in the shop fled and left me with her baby.'

Mona gave one quick nod of acknowledgement. 'That'll do.'

For the final two months of Betty's pregnancy she remained housebound with only Conleth, Mona and Margaret aware of the reason for her two-month isolation. Conleth called each day after he closed the shop with an itemised account of everything sold that day and any other news from the shop. They did not discuss Phelim's existence and they did not discuss the pregnancy. Her only reference to her pregnancy was that she expected discretion – however, she would not expect him to keep secrets from his brother. A little part of her hoped he'd tell Phelim about her pregnancy, sooner rather than later. She wanted to believe Phelim still loved her. She tried to take some solace in the fact that Phelim returned from England to tell her personally about his plans. So many times he'd professed his love for her, a man who took so long before he initially spoke to her. He was not the type of man to fawn insincerely or admit he was in love without meaning it. Knowing that little amount gave her hope.

Part three

Chapter 30

St Gabriel's Nursing Home, Dublin, April 2016

Isabel focused on the woman before her. She tried to follow what she was saying into the mobile phone that was tucked between her ear and chin. With her free hands the woman mashed the dessert into a pulp then tried to spoon-feed her.

'I'm in the nursing home feeding Nana,' the woman said. 'She barely touched her dinner. I mean the price of this nursing home and the shite they're feeding her. You'll have to talk to them, Eilish.'

She spoke with a clear undamaged voice. Isabel guessed she was a good singer, possibly a soprano, and a singer with a wide octave like Kirsten Flagstad. Isabel had been fortunate to see Flagstad play in the Royal Opera House in the 1930's. Her mother organised the trip, wanting her daughter to develop an interest in London's rich cultural aspects. Apart from hearing Flagstad play and a few famous sights, the sophistication of London's regal hotels and crowded restaurants did nothing for Isabel's imagination.

As the woman lifted another spoonful of dessert towards Isabel, she added regretfully, 'Although it's a bit late for that now – she won't be around much longer.'

Isabel turned her head away from the quivering jelly and ice-cream. Was there any end to it? Eating could be a struggle sometimes, especially now that life offered ample food but her appetite had shrivelled like her body. She had been tall once. Her mother always seemed grateful that Isabel had inherited her father's height. In her child's eye her father would always be tall. She remembered his wavy fair hair and the violins and the doll's house he crafted in their home. He was religious, he prayed morning and night, and sometimes he said a Rosary in his workshop at the bottom of the garden.

'Yummy yummy dessert,' the woman said, pouting as if her sultry lips would encourage Isabel to eat, then continued speaking into the phone. 'Today I found my grey knee-length Karen Millen woollen dress and dropped it into the cleaner's. Mum said black is not essential any more.' She had set aside the dessert and was nodding her head as she listened on the phone. 'Yes. I know. Actually Mum and I skyped Aunt Catherine last night. We're keeping her up to speed. She'd like to see Nana before she passes.'

Requiem æternam dona eis, Domine. Eternal rest grant unto them, O Lord. *Et lux perpetua luceat eis.* Let perpetual light shine upon them. *Requiescant in pace.* May they rest in peace. Amen. Isabel remembered her Latin from the time when daily Mass was said in Latin with the priest facing the tabernacle. Like everything, it changed. The priest now faced the congregation, ignoring the objections from the bigoted who thought it resembled a Protestant Mass, or the devout, who felt it lessened the mystery of the Mass. Without Latin it was less poetic. As always, life went on.

The woman sighed into the phone, 'There is so much to do before ...' she lowered her voice, 'Nana goes.'

Isabel was transfixed by the woman's behaviour. She couldn't be entirely sure if she heard her say "before Nana goes" yet she knew the event being discussed was her funeral. Could life have come to this? While waiting to depart to the next world we must also wait for arrivals, wait for old friends to travel and mourn and make time for nostalgia and death. For the last decade, although her mind was not her own, she was aware with each passing year that she was moving closer to death. Advancing to the final firing line, as her granddaughter Eilish boldly said.

With time the terror of her imminent death faded, and though she made previsions her resilience never subsided. Any excuse to remain longer gave her strength. She pleaded with God for another year, and then another without death, then she pleaded for seasons at a time, wait for summer with the long evenings and the smell of freshly cut grass. Hold on till autumn, the frosty mornings and dreaded ice, beg for clemency till November, the month of the Holy Souls. It was as if she was competing against her own timespan. Would the lady before her find it too unaccommodating with her cleaned grey winter dress if she died on a warm summer's day?

The woman stopped speaking and Isabel watched her head nodding. She noted that the mobile phone remained firmly lodged between her ear and neck. If she'd stop yapping Isabel would tell her that she'd get bad posture from keeping her head tilted to the side for so long. Her unusual green-grey eyes remained fixed on Isabel as she listened intently.

'Just a minute, Eilish!'

Isabel was startled when the woman suddenly leaned in close to her.

Her young heavily made-up face came nearer again, and Isabel noticed her long black eyelashes and the lipstick stain on her front tooth.

'I think Nana is having a lucid moment. She's staring at me.' The young woman gaped wildly at Isabel. 'Nana, do you know who I am?'

For years, names escaped Isabel. In the early days of her forgetfulness, she joked that she couldn't be expected to remember everyone during her long life. Her home help Oxana, a Polish girl, told her it was understandable. 'You nearly one hundred years,' she said in broken English.

Isabel admired Oxana. When she arrived in Ireland she knew little English, but after she grasped the language she enrolled in a night course and was working towards a degree. Each day when Oxana finished her cleaning, they'd have tea and biscuits. She told her stories from Poland, she talked about her family and those she left behind. Oxana was courteous and polite. She reminded Isabel of the decent girls from years ago. Mass-going good girls with morals.

When Isabel complained about her memory in a light manner, Oxana reminded her of her belief in God.

'Prayer, Mrs Salmon – you forever say to me your God will provide.'

Of course, the Sacred Heart would provide her with memory for as long as she needed it. On bended knees she'd begged Him to help her through every troublesome period of her life and He had provided. He gave her strength.

'Hasn't a clue what I'm talking about,' the woman said, returning the phone to her ear.

Doting, doddery, vague, there were so many loose terms for the terror of forgetfulness. None of them had said outright that she was losing her memory or suggested she was suffering from Alzheimer's or dementia or any other medical terms for entering dotage. Isabel thought about Mona Daly who knew the cure for every ailment. Tallow for chest problems, mustard behind the ear for toothache. For rheumatism, the grease off the goose. She couldn't recall anything for forgetfulness. Very few lived long enough to become forgetful. Seventy was considered old.

'Nana? Who am I?' the lady pleaded again.

Isabel smiled. Nobody took offense when she smiled. It staved off those indignant visitors who grabbed her arm and demanded, "You must know me? Do you not remember me? *Me?*" they'd ask wide-eyed and thump their chest crossly as if Isabel was only pretending to forget them.

Betty, Lilly, Eilish, any variation of Elizabeth was a safe bet. Isabel felt she must know her, the shape and colour of the eyes was too familiar. She had seen the same eyes in past and present generations of her own family. Her sallow complexion was different, but the deep-set green eyes and oval face were her own features, and the features of her daughters.

Isabel spoke, finally breaking the lady's hopeful silence. 'Eilish, you are Eilish,' she said with finality. 'Eilish?' she repeated, knowing it wasn't Eilish but wishing for her granddaughter's presence.

A woman's first grandchild furrows a way into her heart. When Eilish arrived in the early 70's, for the first time in Isabel's life she had empty days when she could embrace her wonderful bright granddaughter. Isabel was surprised with the abundance of love she had for Eilish, the little girl who made an impact on most who met her. Although Eilish wasn't a beautiful child, she was captivating with her page-boy haircut and expressive large dark eyes. Even her unruly behaviour was cute. A few times a year Isabel would drive to Tipperary with her granddaughter. She had wonderful fond memories of those days in the 70's when she was creating a life independent from her husband. Isabel had time for Eilish that she hadn't had for her own children. For years when the business needed her she hadn't a moment, while her children clawed at her for attention, or her husband was being demanding. Eilish was her girl, the delightful child who reignited her spark for life. Years later as an adult, it was Eilish who distracted her from the abyss of treachery and finally helped to lessen the pain of betrayal.

'Eilish? When will Eilish come?' she asked but the lady wasn't listening.

Eilish came to live with her a few times over the years. The first time Eilish lived with her was a time when both were trying to rebuild their lives. Although they never discussed their individual traumas, Isabel suspected that for Eilish it was another failed romance. During their time cohabiting, Eilish's presence and simple activities helped Isabel in a way that the girl would never understand.

According to Eilish, every woman was entitled to at least one facial a month. Isabel hadn't enjoyed the facials. She felt uncomfortable with the beautician's hands kneading her face as if it was dough she was preparing for the oven. So Eilish brought her to another sort of facial with a name that made Isabel think of freshly squeezed fruit being massaged into her face. It was more enjoyable than the kneading facial. Only once did she get a spray tan. Eilish made the tan sound essential for the frock she was wearing to a summer wedding. When the cold spray hit Isabel's body she gasped in shock. Later that night she scrubbed off the tan as it made her look jaundiced. Eilish took Isabel to a fast-food restaurant themed like a 60's American café with jive music. They went to another café and sat by the window watching people. Several times after that, Isabel went on her own. She was not embarrassed to sit alone by the window, watching people as she drank a latte and read the newspaper. They went on city breaks to Amsterdam, Milan, Barcelona and other cities whose names she couldn't think of. It was as if their roles had reversed: Eilish was the adult treating Isabel to facials and meals out and trips abroad. She brought vividness to her life, she helped her to live again.

The lady's face fell with disappointment. Irate, she relodged the phone between her ear and shoulder, 'Jesus Christ, sis, Nana thinks I'm you!'

Just then it occurred to Isabel that she was probably the other granddaughter. Her name wouldn't come to Isabel . . . it was the female version of a man's name. A silly name. What was Lilly thinking to burden her daughter with that faddish name? Isabel's husband, Conleth, thought it was too English. She was the little girl who used to hold her nose at the smell of the ever-present odour of silage in isolated rural farmhouses. Isabel wished she could recall her name. She watched her granddaughter pick up her handbag and prepare to leave.

She ended the call and tossed the phone carelessly into her oversized handbag.

Paulette! Isabel sighed with relief at remembering her name. Paulette, my granddaughter, who is entertaining with her storytelling and very vain.

Isabel watched her leave, her statuesque frame gliding through the doors, the sun giving her an enigmatic glow.

Chapter 31

Ranelagh, Dublin, April, 2016

Eilish steadied the antique wardrobe. It swayed precariously as she tried to remove her stored containers of clothes. It was made by her great-grandfather over a century before. According to her grandfather, Conleth Salmon, it was the first item of furniture Seamus Hopkins had made for his wife, Betty. Eilish traced her fingers over the decorative grooves, noticing them for the first time. The frieze below the cornice had a carved scallop of shell framed by curling fern fronds. The detail was startling. Eilish imagined her great-grandfather, Seamus Hopkins, patiently etching the grooves, the finished product testament to the pride he took in his work. As a child she was fascinated by the story of how her great-grandfather started his family business as a humble violinmaker. From that he developed a carpentry and musical-instrument business that thrived for almost a century. Hopkins Furniture employed four generations of his family for almost 100 years and saw them live comfortably when pockets of Ireland saw great scarcity.

Eilish's great-grandfather was a gifted luthier and with Betty Hopkins, a strong woman, at the helm, they achieved financial success. The business survived the universal poverty of the first half of the century, it thrived through the 60's and 70's, and saw out the cruel 80's. Eilish joined the company in 1992. Hopkins Furniture scraped through the final years of the noughties before it was declared bankrupt on a glorious sunny May morning in 2013. Eilish would always remember reading the notification with the sun blazing through the window.

There was no escaping the old reminders of Eilish's greatest failure. In the nursing home on Nana's locker was a picture of Eilish, her mother and grandmother standing inside the front door of the shop in Dawson Street. It was taken the first day that Eilish officially joined the company. She recalled driving to work in her small red Polo car and wearing a new cream suit. Her mother, Lilly, poured a glass of champagne, her eyes welling with tears as she toasted to Eilish's future and wished her father had lived to see the day. All the while Nana was impatient to get on with her day. Nana claimed to have retired at that stage yet nothing happened without her say-so. Under her grandmother's tutelage, Eilish learned everything she knew about the business. As time passed, she and Isabel mixed their ideas and saw the company thrive. During the boom years it soared. Similar to her great-grandmother Betty, Eilish knew the value of their stock. She networked with buyers, formed friendships with business acquaintances who would further her company, won contracts and made more and more money with each passing month.

At the height of the boom, Isabel regularly warned Eilish 'Don't lose sight of what it's all about.' Isabel told her that the success for the business lay not in the quantity but the quality of their violins. Every luthier could make an instrument – the secret was to find a luthier who would make an exceptional instrument. Eilish found a genius craftsman from Russia. They won competitions from Ireland and abroad for their violins. As well as the violins, Hopkins and Co. produced home furniture, cabinets, bookshelves, picture frames. To give the staff incentives Eilish gave hefty tax-free bonuses. There were work-nights out, meals with free-flowing wine and a bar tab to further encourage their efforts.

For a period Eilish thought she'd never again need to work. As well as investing, she learned to spend money. She'd joke with her girlfriends, 'This one is for Eilish.' There were Karen Millen suits and Kurt Geiger shoes, handbags and scarves, exotic holidays, yellow and white gold. She bought cars and jeeps, always choosing a leather interior, either cream or beige. She'd drink white wine and feign seduction by whispering with an exaggerated lisp, 'I get off on the whiff of my leather interior.' The girls would laugh uproariously at Eilish's theatrics. There were men but everything was fleeting. She took some consolation in the proverb 'A rolling stone gathers no moss' and thought it was wonderful how it applied to her generation and, more importantly, that it applied to women.

Her mother Lilly praised Eilish's management skills and encouraged her property investments. 'Speculate to accumulate.'

Nana was always more cautious. She was adamant that Eilish should stop 'flinging money at everything that moves' and declared that Eilish was turning into Betty Hopkins: 'She's just like my own mother, self-gratifying and unendingly indulgent.'

'Horse-shite,' Eilish muttered into her wine and raised her glass to prosperity.

For a period, she avoided Nana and continued to drive around the country examining prospective investments.

It wasn't all joy and ecstasy. There was a period when she needed anti-anxiety medication, a sweet pink pill. In the cold light of day, it was hard to believe she had to visit a doctor with chest pain and was prescribed a 'pink' to cope with her accumulating investments. Occasionally she'd get a fleeting sense that she too had blended into the leather interior of her car, that she too was a mere fashion accessory in an expensive jeep wearing overpriced suits. She was nothing more, or nothing less than her Karen Millen suit and Fendi sunglasses. In the not-too-distant future she too would be discarded like the dated suits from last year. Where would it end, this hasty rush? For those fleeting moments, she had a sense of soullessness. Her heart would race and beads of sweat dampen her forehead, she'd gasp for air and feel nauseous. She would want to stop the car but reason told her not to. When it happened she would take her 'pink', and drive at a steady pace until her racing heart calmed. There was too much to be done without dwelling on soullessness, or feeding insecure monsters.

Just as Nana predicted, it did stop.

'What goes up must come down,' Eilish remembered one of her coke friends say.

Towards the end of 2010 Hopkins Furniture was running at a loss. Like the patient wife of a troubled husband, Eilish felt she knew enough about Ireland's economics and the mechanism of business to know that it would right itself. With each passing month, her patience never waned as she descended deeper into debt and denial. Three long years after the first sign of a recession, Nana was finally placed in a nursing home. Eilish's cash was almost gone as were most of her luncheon friends. She'd wake each morning faced with the impossibility of recouping her lost money from her crumbling investments. With the exception of two apartments in Christchurch, she lost all of her money. Her remaining properties were in such negative equity and the pressure to pay her mortgages so insistent that she felt as if she was paying the money to a gun-wielding money-lender rather than a government-approved institution.

In 2013 Eilish went bankrupt. The loss of the company stripped her bare, quashed the ballsy confidence that defined her as an achiever. Overwhelmed with a sense of urgency to escape Ireland, she rented her apartment to two young men – a gay couple – and felt old as she listened to them enthusiastically discuss decor. The same month that Nana was placed in the nursing home, Eilish moved to England where she remained for three years. She worked for a kitchen company in Brighton. While there she made her accent less obvious as she went on the road selling kitchens.

At night she'd go online to read about Irish people like her who went bankrupt. She'd read how their self-worth crumbled with their businesses. Not only did she read about the bankruptcies, she read about the mortgage debts, accounts of families losing their homes, entire families living in sheltered accommodation, the litany of suicides associated with financial issues, joblessness, desperation, national despondency, increasing tax burdens. The corrupt bankers, crooked politicians earning colossal salaries, the Taoiseach earning more than the President of America, the cowboy builders. It was as if Ireland was a cesspit. She took the time to read about Brian Lenihan, Ireland's Finance Minister, who died at the age of 52, within three years of taking over the doomed role. None of the stories alleviated her sense of failure.

She tried to make the most of her time in England. She lamented the glorious boom days in Dublin. Like so many exiled Irish she could not settle. Her only consolation was that Nana was in a nursing home and didn't know night from day. The handful of Irish Eilish knew in Brighton were as miserable as she was. On the rare occasions when they met they discussed Ireland, each living through their own turmoil. During these gatherings Eilish found their amalgamated mass of hopelessness overwhelmingly negative. In the end she avoided their get-togethers. Instead she worked hard, learned what she needed to know about owning a kitchen company. She went on two lonely dates with the same guy knowing she was using him for sex.

When she returned to Ireland in February 1916 she moved into her grandmother's house under the pretext that it needed a good airing. Since returning to Ireland she'd lain low, only making contact with a handful of people. She had a plan, a small idea she wanted to keep secret. With a little work it might get her back into the game, yet so much terrified her. Was it age? The trauma of failure? Adapting to a regressive Ireland and angry nation? Where did it go so wrong?

Eilish returned to the wardrobe to enact the next part of her plan. She needed classy suits and jewellery to match the timeless picture of her on her new business brochure. Before departing to Brighton, she'd stored most of her expensive jewellery and good suits in the antique wardrobe. First she removed the small suitcase which contained her jewellery. The boxes of clothes were in two large airtight containers in the main part of the wardrobe. Before storing them, she'd had the foresight to have everything cleaned and packed away with cedar wooden balls.

She pushed aside the hanging clothes that belonged to her grandmother. Then she had to manoeuvre the containers over an internal panel. As she grappled with one of them the wardrobe swayed again. She changed tactics and pulled, in short rapid tugs. She changed angle again. Impatient to get reacquainted with her treasures she placed her foot on the base of the wardrobe to keep it steady and gave the container one final hoist. As it freed she stumbled backwards with its weight and fell on the floor.

When she heard the initial thud from the bowels of the enormous wardrobe and watched it sway, she quickly rolled out of the way. From the floor of her bedroom, she held her breath and watched in disbelief as the wardrobe crashed to the floor. It had lasted several lifetimes and took less than thirty seconds to fall apart. She remained on the floor, gaping at the mound of ornate timber and the items of clothing that were visible beneath it. She could see the sleeve one of her grandmother's blouses, a nice lilac blouse she had since Eilish was a child. Slowly she got to her feet, resolving not to make an issue of it. With difficulty she pushed the back of the wardrobe to one side. Beneath it were some of Isabel's belongings – knitted jumpers, overcoats, and woollen skirts.

Eilish picked up a jumper that must have been thirty years old. She inhaled the smell. Would Nana appreciate it now? She had an urge to hand-wash it, like Nana hand-washed anything she valued. She could bring it to the nursing home – it might revive her in some way. There was pale lipstick, the natural colours her grandmother liked. It astounded her how Nana kept everything, jars or bags that might be useful, envelopes, wrapping and bubbly paper. Not only was she a hoarder, she was frugal. When she was down to the last piece of lipstick, she'd use a brush to scrap out the inaccessible bit. She kept paper bags, thinking she'd find a use for them. Amongst her clothes, Eilish saw a necklace of pearls.

Sticking out from under an old jewellery box she saw another envelope. Unlike the envelopes that Nana kept, this was used. A large old stiff envelope with an eye-opening for twine on the flap, addressed to her great-grandmother, Betty Hopkins. Eilish picked up the envelope and opened the unsealed flap. Inside were old photographs. At a quick glance she couldn't recognise any of the faces. Maybe they were cousins of Nana's from Tipperary. Quickly she flicked through the photographs. Some were taken in London, Finsbury Park – 1922 was the date on the back. The woman looked vaguely like Betty Hopkins; the man she didn't know. They were standing close together, and there was an air of giddiness about them. There was one photo that grabbed her attention. It was torn in half. The woman was undoubtedly Betty Hopkins. A man had been removed from the photo – his hand was visible on the woman's shoulder. There was a child sitting on the woman's lap. A little girl with long fair curly hair and a startled expression. She assumed the little girl was her grandmother, Isabel.

Eilish was confused by her discovery. A few months after her grandfather Conleth's death, Isabel had cleaned out the house of anything belonging to her mother and husband. If she had seen an envelope addressed to Betty that too would have been fired into the flames.

Eilish rummaged through the clothes and timber. She tried to determine where the photographs had been hidden. She peeled away blouses and skirts, searching for a box or something solid in which the photographs were concealed. After much rooting, she found what appeared to be a small drawer measuring only ten inches long by two inches deep. It was like a narrow drawer from an old writing desk, too small for a wardrobe. Eilish never remembered seeing it before.

She thought of old stoic Nana Isabel who never revealed anything of herself. Only once did she allude to the secrets the house contained. 'I'm afraid this horrible old place will give up the truth,' she said. She had been distressed after a doctor's appointment. Under different circumstances Eilish would have asked if the secrets mattered any more. But that night Nana was upset about her memory loss. Eilish had pacified her, distracted her from the past she could not bear to talk about.

Eilish looked at the old envelope. The writing was clear and non-elaborate. Maybe Nana was right: the old house that she hated so much had not yet churned out all of its secrets.

Chapter 32

Paulette was standing by the mantelpiece examining a picture of Betty Hopkins. Westminster Abbey was in the background and her young smiling face was in the bottom left-hand corner. In another with the same background, Betty was standing beside a man. A similar photo with Betty and the same man was taken at the gates of Hyde Park, dated November 1922, London.

'Wow, did you find anything else?' Paulette asked.

'No, just those photos.'

Paulette flicked through the pictures again. She held up the photo of their grandmother Isabel as a child on her mother's lap. 'Wasn't she so cute?' she said, wrinkling up her nose. 'We could use this on the memorial card.'

All of the photos were dated between 1919 and 1924. There was a photo of their grandfather as a seventeen-year-old in his soldier's uniform: *Conleth Salmon 1922*. There was another photo of a man wearing an apron and holding tools with Betty Hopkins in the shop, and a group photo outside the shop on Dawson Street.

'This is tots amazing,' Paulette gushed. 'Why were they hidden?'

Eilish was amused at Paulette's reaction. Her sister loved conspiracy theories and unresolved family secrets. Paulette was five years younger than Eilish and the sisters could not have been more different. Paulette married a man twelve years her senior when she was twenty. She was mother to two college students, and loved cooking, home-making and all the aspects of a stay-at-home mum's life that made Eilish recoil.

In appearance Paulette was like the Hopkins women: beautiful. She was fair with soft forgiving features and large mesmerising green eyes. Men adored Paulette – they were inclined to protect her – whereas certain men were intimidated by Eilish.

Since Nana's recent sickness, Paulette's conversations were dominated by the possible scenarios. When would she die? Who'd be there? Might Nana finally talk about her life? Why all the secrecy? When she wasn't preoccupied with Nana's funeral, she considered which venue to host the meal after the burial. The Stillorgan Park Hotel was too impersonal, the Clayton too big. The jury was still out on the Beacon. Each day it changed. When finished giving the rundown on the latest hotel, she returned to Nana's life and her reasons for such 'cancer-causing unhealthy secrecy'. Paulette loved drama; she was nosy and could spent hours surmising about other people's lives. She loved to analyse people. According to her, their grandmother Isabel fought with silence, their mother Lilly was passive-aggressive, their grandfather was an egomaniac, their late father Greg was a puppet and his early death in a car accident was a possible suicide. Eilish howled with laughter when she heard that one. Paulette once suggested that Eilish tunnelled her life's disappointments into her work. Paulette blushed when Eilish asked why she deemed her life a disappointment. Paulette didn't need to answer: they were very different sisters with very different ideas of happiness.

That morning Paulette had arrived, oozing self-importance, after another visit to the nursing home. When she saw the photos she forgot about the latest update on Nana. Eilish had deliberately left the pictures on the coffee table where they'd be most noticeable.

Paulette lined them up on the coffee table as if she was playing a role in a detective series. 'What I want to know,' she began with pursed lips and using a voice laden with gravity, 'is why Seamus Hopkins is not in any of the photos?'

Eilish had also noticed their great-grandfather's absence.

'In fact, I'd say the man torn from that photo was Seamus Hopkins because . . .' Dramatically Paulette turned the photo over. The inscription on the back was halved. It appeared to say, *"To the Hopkins Family, Happy Christmas ... Hartmann"*. The Christian name was missing, as was half of the date. Paulette pointed with her long manicured nail at the image, 'This was clearly a gift to them as a family. The missing person is Seamus Hopkins. Why was he torn from the photo?'

'Well, Sherlock,' Eilish said, matching her sister's grave tone, 'I'd say Granny Betty felt he was too ugly. You know how she liked pretty people and pretty things. I deduce that Seamus Hopkins was as ugly as a Vietnamese potbelly pig.'

'Unlikely,' Paulette laughed. 'So you didn't find anything else?'

'Not yet,' Eilish said. She hadn't had time to sort through the contents of the wardrobe.

'Will I take a look to see if there's more?' Paulette offered.

'*No!*' Eilish almost shouted.

Her room was like a tip with the collapsed wardrobe nor had she sorted out her old clothes and jewellery. She didn't want Paulette poking about.

'It's a bit odd, you finding that now and poor Nana so close to the grave.'

Eilish didn't respond; she didn't want to feed her sister's dramatics.

Paulette continued, 'This house is probably filled with secrets and ghosts!' She looked around the living room as if waiting for something to materialise. 'I never liked this house. Granny Betty and Nana were too strict.'

It was a house with too many restrictions for children. When Eilish was a child her great-grandmother, Betty, owned the house. The rare times they visited they were warned not to touch a thing, inside or outside. Even their play area in the garden was limited.

245

They were warned never ever to go near the rockery at the back left-hand corner and they couldn't play near the flowers that bordered the lawn. Betty Hopkins furnished her home with the best of everything. Under pain of death they could not touch one single ornament. They'd been collected by Granny Betty from her various travels, and all were bought for hefty sums of money.

After Betty's death, Isabel and her husband Conleth moved into the house. Conleth didn't alter the house in any way. He adored his mother-in-law's expensive taste. Proudly he showed visitors the paintings and expensive ornaments. He told stories of how his mother-in-law had travelled the world and cleverly invested her money in paintings rather than losing it in shares. He'd quote Granny Betty: 'I prefer to admire my hard-earned cash on my walls rather than rereading my bank statement.'

Conleth liked to suggest he was a man of great means but the only painting he brought with him when he moved into Granny Betty's house was a large oil canvas of Strongbow, his boyhood hero. Granny Betty had it commissioned by an up-and-coming artist in the 60's. It was a reward for his service to their company, or 'a dangling carrot' according to their Aunt Catherine, Isabel's eldest daughter who lived in New York.

As if on cue, a loud knock sounded from upstairs. Slowly Paulette looked towards the ceiling then her wide eyes returned to Eilish.

Eilish had forgotten to close the bathroom window. Without moving her head and keeping a serious face, she held her sister's gaze before casting her eyes right and left.

'Stop it, Eilish!' Paulette smiled as she pleaded.

'As you say,' Eilish said in a sinister tone, 'this house is walking with ghosts.'

'Don't forget about the man who was shot in the garden,' Paulette reminded her.

When Paulette heard that there was a man shot dead in the back garden during the Civil War she refused to sleep in the house. Isabel was furious when she learned that her granddaughters had heard the rumours. She was even more enraged that Paulette was making an issue of it. Seething, she said she never wanted it mentioned again.

'How do you sleep here? It gives me the creeps,' Paulette said squeamishly.

'Easy. I recite the Irish Proclamation or a sing a rebel song before sleeping. They were all republicans who lived or were killed in this house. It's music to their ears.'

Paulette ignored her. She picked up the photos again. 'I'm amazed these few photos survived Nana's clear-out. It was weird the way she behaved after Granddad's death.'

Shortly after Conleth's death in 1989, Isabel had sold all of Granny Betty's paintings and jewellery. She dumped all of her husband's memorabilia including his IRA medals and photos. Mercilessly she swept through the house, binning artefacts her husband and mother had spent years accumulating. She also reverted the name of the company from Salmon Carpentry to its original name Hopkins Furniture. It was as if she wanted to remove any trace that the company had passed through her husband Conleth's ownership.

The only picture that Nana kept was an old framed photograph commemorating the 1916 Easter Rising. In the centre of the photo was the Irish Proclamation framed with an image of each of the seven signatories. Eilish suspected that Nana kept the 1916 painting because her father fought in the GPO during the Rising. They knew very little else about Seamus Hopkins, apart from his talent at violinmaking. They learned from cousins in Tipperary how he survived the Rising by hiding in a flour mill. From a young age, Eilish and Paulette knew never to probe into Nana's life.

'It was weird the way she'd never talk about her life,' Paulette said. 'Everything, right down to her childhood was a no-go zone.'

'Some people are private – they don't need to yap about their likes and dislikes.' Eilish felt the need to defend Nana.

Her grandmother was never one for recalling the past. During Eilish's time living with Nana, she gave only the barest details about her life. She mentioned growing up in Tipperary, her love for country life evident. She liked dogs, country sports like hurling, greyhounds and gardening. Her husband preferred Dublin, he needed the sounds of the city and choice of company that a populated environment offered. The country was grand for a visit, he claimed. Isabel accepted her lot. Reluctantly she moved into Betty Hopkins' home with Conleth after her mother's death although she was dead opposed to the idea.

Without revealing too much, Nana confessed to Eilish that it was more than the upheaval of moving that upset her. 'I'd rather this old house was sold to someone I didn't know so I'd never need to cross the threshold again,' she confessed.

When Eilish asked her why she agreed to return to live in Betty's, Nana said, ''Twas a time when women had few choices. You did what your husband told you.'

Paulette pushed the photos to one side, 'I must tell you about Nana. I've seen her every day this week. Death is creeping up fast.'

Eilish tried to hide her smile. She thought Paulette's attempt at seriousness comical.

Holding Eilish's gaze to reaffirm the seriousness of Nana's ebbing life, Paulette continued, 'She's on a second antibiotic for a kidney infection. Her colour is bad. Her face was grey today. I think there is a problem with her breathing as well. She was drawn and gasping for air, clawing at her neck as if she was suffocating.' Noisily Paulette inhaled and exhaled to emphasise how distressing the situation was. 'I told Dharfir – you know, our neighbour Dharfir, the consultant in the Beacon Hospital?' She didn't wait for Eilish to answer. 'He's from Sierra Leone, such a sweetie. I told him all about Nana last night, and he said,' she paused and pursed her lips, 'a person that age with her symptoms and infections could go at any stage.'

Eilish suddenly got up from the chair and opened the window that looked into the back garden. She took a packet of cigarettes from her pocket, lit one and kept her hand out the window.

'Jesus, I thought you were going to jump out,' Paulette said.

Eilish rolled her eyes.

'Initially Nana hadn't the foggiest idea who I was,' Paulette continued. 'Then she called me Eilish. She never really liked me. One of the nurses reassured me that they were doing all they could for her. She will not suffer.'

Eilish gazed into the wild garden. Nana was not dead and might not die for some time. Although she was days away from her 100th birthday, she was healthier than some of the women in the nursing home.

'Do you think she got dementia because she wanted to forget?' Paulette asked.

'Forget? Forget what?' Eilish asked impatiently, irritated at the way the conversation was going.

'Forget the things she never wanted to talk about – her childhood or marriage or her dead son. Did she want to keep everything private?' Paulette leaned forward, 'You know unresolved issues can be worse than a physical ailment. It can impair your life. That's why Aunt Catherine lives in New York and is so disparaging about her and Mum's childhood.'

'How could you even suggest Aunt Catherine has unresolved issues? If she chips her toenail in New York, they hear about it in Tipperary.'

'I mean,' Paulette said in an American drawl, imitating Catherine's accent, 'the linkage between the past and present is essential for a basic understanding of each race, particularly our barbaric childhood. Our mother was a demon incarnate and our father was too goddamn proud to notice how dysfunctional our lives were.'

Eilish smiled at Paulette's mockery. She was fond of Aunt Catherine despite her intensity about the past and her chosen subject of history. Catherine was a professor and historian in New York University. She was successful in her chosen academic field, had written several books on Irish-American history and was fortunate enough to travel the world giving lectures. When she spoke about Ireland's past, she appeared anti-Irish, anti-Catholic, anti-men. She could be equally as venomous about her childhood. She recounted injustices as if they only happened yesterday. And all the while her sister Lilly contradicted her account. According to Lilly, their childhood was filled with song, dance and quaint romance.

'I promised I'd keep Aunt Catherine informed,' Paulette said. 'I'd better pop in again tomorrow to see Nana.'

'If Nana's memory was intact she'd know she was dying just from the number of visits from you!'

'Now that it's all happening so quickly, you know how it is,' Paulette faltered. 'Anything could happen. I might be needed.'

Eilish nodded.

'While I was there I spoke to several members of staff and gave them my mobile number. I told them to call me at any hour of the day,' she sighed loudly, 'although I hate nursing homes.'

'I don't particularly like them myself.'

While Eilish was in London she had returned once a month to visit Nana in the nursing home. She hated it. The old men and women were propped in chairs with their mouths open, emitting a sense of resignation and rejection. As if death itself had passed them by, and their sentence was to linger in a dayroom with that wafting smell of heat and nappies. An awful sense of hopelessness lingered after her visits.

Eilish felt she'd failed her grandmother by relegating her to a nursing home. In the months before that, Isabel was found digging up the garden with her hands at all hours of the night. Initially Eilish told nobody. She'd clean her up and scrub under her nails as best she could. In the end Nana's mind was no longer her own. For the last few years she had been lost in a world that nobody but she could see. She bandied about names from fifty years ago; there were days when her mind took her back almost a century. She called visiting males "Daddy", the word sounding ill-fitting in a woman of her years. Her grandmother's mind and body were fervent with ghosts who only danced to her tune. Her rare smiles were often reserved for private conversations with those long dead.

Eilish finished her cigarette, and wrapped the butt in a piece of paper.

'Do you still think Nana is going to live?' Paulette gingerly asked. 'Mum is concerned that you've not accepted the seriousness of her condition.'

Eilish sighed, expertly tossing the paper across the room. It skilfully landed in the bin. She cleared her throat as if she was about to say something on Nana's looming death, then said: 'I'll bet you can't do that?' She crumpled a few sheets of paper and tossed them across the coffee table to Paulette. 'Twenty euro says your aim is not as good as mine.'

'It's pointless talking to you when you're like this!' Paulette said, like an exasperated parent. 'Zara is nineteen years of age and behaves more maturely than you.'

'I'll make it easy for you,' Eilish continued in the same vein. 'You can have three shots and even if you get only one into the bin, you win twenty euro. If you miss each shot, I'll allow you another concession.'

Paulette waited to hear her concession.

'You can spit,' Eilish said, her face serious. 'A good full phlegmy one.'

Paulette stood up. 'I haven't time for this.' She put on her coat. 'I'm going to call Aunt Catherine tonight, just to let her know how things are. Mum and I rang her last night.' She sighed. 'We had a good cry.'

Eilish burst out laughing. Paulette adored drama so much that even crying down the phone to her aunt in New York was enjoyable.

'*You* should have a good cry – it would help you.' Paulette was irked by her sister's insensitivity.

Eilish looked at her in bewilderment. 'You'd want to get a job now that your children are grown up. It would give you an objective in life.'

'That's something Nana would say,' Paulette said, not taking offense. 'Do you think she's going to live?'

'You sound as if you want her dead,' Eilish said in a reasonable tone.

'Jesus Christ, what sort of thing is that to say to me? Of course I don't want my grandmother dead!'

'Well, then stop making so many plans until Nana actually *dies*.'

For the last few days Eilish had fought that awful swelling lump of emotion in her throat. She was Nana's favourite. They had been friends and allies for most of her life. Maybe if she'd time, she'd do as Paulette suggested and have a good old cry. A discreet sniffle would not be enough. Maybe she'd pencil it into her diary, take a few hours to indulge in a keening session for death and the passing of time, for the loss of her youth and her beloved grandmother in the clutches of an undignified death.

'Eilish, I simply don't want to see her lingering within the confines of her own mind. Her once great mind is now her gaoler.'

That was the third time Paulette used that line. Eilish guessed she had read it in one of her self-help books or overheard someone else say it.

Paulette continued, 'Today in the nursing home, I watched Nana fiddle at the neck of her nightdress. She looked so frightened all I wanted to do was hug her.'

Eilish raised her eyebrows in doubt. Nana did not do hugs.

'I would never have thought like that if Nana was not doting on Cloud Cuckoo,' Paulette went on. 'Now that she hasn't a clue who anybody is, it would have been easier to hug her, easier to forget the teeming rage beneath her flowery nightdress and white hair.'

Like a lot of women of her grandmother's vintage, demonstrative behaviour was uncomfortable to her. Nana was capable of great kindness and sincerity, but equally she was never tactile, a no-nonsense woman who could see little sense in the likes of Paulette's behaviour. She was comfortable with her own company and a few dogs. Up until she began to lose her memory, she lived alone with two terriers. She spent Christmas Day every year in Eilish's mother's house but at the end of the night she insisted on returning to her own bed.

'I'd better go home and cook the dinner,' Paulette said. 'The children will be home from college shortly. Zara wants to know if she can stay here on Friday night? She's going out with her college friends and feels it'll be too late to come home by the time they finish up.'

'Sure, she has a key,' Eilish said.

Zara was Paulette's daughter. She was a nineteen-year-old science student in Trinity. Occasionally Eilish felt a twinge of jealousy when she thought of her niece's young life brimming with possibilities. At nineteen, she was a high achiever, earning prizes in both sports and academia. Zara was mature enough to know exactly what she wanted from life. Was she focused or naïve? Only time would tell.

Paulette was looking over Eilish's head into the back garden.

'Gosh, the garden is a mess.'

Eilish looked into the small wilderness. There used to be a little path leading through a manicured lawn. The garden was framed with colourful flowers and pretty shrubs. Now the path wasn't visible and the little shrubs had grown into looming trees and gangly weeds. She looked away. There was enough to do without thinking about gardens and shrubs.

'Just to tip you off,' Paulette said, 'Mum is really concerned that the house will not be ready for the –' she was about to say funeral, 'if anything happens to Nana. Did she mention the garden to you?'

'Yes,' Eilish confessed. 'Every day for the last week. She also mentioned cleaning the house in every conversation.'

'You have Oxana's number?'

'Actually Oxana is coming in the morning. And a landscape gardener is also calling tomorrow with a trailer to remove the shrubs and excess.'

Eilish knew Paulette would pass on that information to their mother. She'd ring the cleaner tomorrow. She'd also get a few quotes before calling her friend Sarah's gardener Cyril. He came highly recommended. According to Sarah, he was slightly expensive but the best gardener if she could ignore his foul language. While money was tight she had no notion of paying over the odds for anything, poor language or not.

When Paulette had gone she'd go to her bedroom and look through the contents of the wardrobe just in case Nana was right and the old house still contained secrets from the past. She needed to send her own suits to the drycleaner's and get cracking on selling her business. More than anything she needed to dig deep and reignite that old killer instinct for business. She tried not to deliberate over her failures yet that seemed the hardest part of her day. She looked at the photo of Granny Betty outside Westminster. She tried to imagine what Granny Betty would do if she were in her shoes. A woman ahead of her time, renowned for her ruthless business streak and successful in a man's world, would Granny Betty acknowledge her fear or wade through it like a blue-rinse warrior? Eilish got to her feet.

Chapter 33

Lilly was in Mount Jerome Cemetery. The unusual April chill was more apparent in the bleak quiet surroundings. By the time she eventually arrived at the grave she was breathless and suddenly warm. She loosened her scarf and undid the top button of her coat. She stood at the base of the grave and blessed herself before rattling off a prayer for the repose of the souls of her family interned within the small boundary. She continued to pray but couldn't concentrate at the sight of the grave. It needed a good fixing. To add to the discoloured blotchy multi-grey-coloured headstone, the weeds were growing through the cracked cement on the bed of the grave. Lilly tried to read the weather-beaten headstone. Buried in the family plot were her grandmother, grandfather, and her own father. The only legible name was her grandfather's name: **Seamus Hopkins 1893–1924.** The rest of the headstone was in such poor condition that she could barely make out the epitaphs. Lilly leaned in closer and traced her fingers over the inscription. **Elizabeth (Betty) Hopkins 1894–1981.** Beneath that was Lilly's father's name: **Conleth Salmon 1906–1989.**

Lilly thought of her father with fondness. She visualised him sitting at the kitchen table with the newspaper spread out before him as he puffed on his pipe. He'd spend hours reading the *Irish Independent* and each day he'd close it with the same line: 'Nothing in the paper today, I don't know why I buy it.' He believed in taking pride in his appearance. Apart from summers at the beach, she'd never seen her father without a shirt and tie. After drinking he'd attempt to sing 'The Valley of Knockanure'. He did not have a good voice but it never stopped him bursting into song if the occasion arose. Reciting was his forte. He was dramatic and played the role of the protagonist with such enthusiasm that his acting was as engaging as his recitations. Now that Lilly's mother's life was coming to an end, she thought about her own life and once again she marvelled at the passing of time. She did not feel like a woman in her seventies with two daughters almost entering middle age. With the country fervent with celebrations to mark the 1916 Easter Rising, she often wondered what her father would have thought of his country. Would he have remained a republican? Would he have welcomed the Queen onto Irish soil or objected with a recitation or ranted at the state of affairs?

'You may sing and speak about Easter Week or the heroes of Ninety-Eight,

Of the Fenian men who roamed the glen in victory or defeat.'

Lilly hated conversations dominated by politics. She avoided the heated debates about Pro- and Anti-Treaty sides. Unlike members of her own family who loved rebel songs, she didn't like to dwell on the hardships of Ireland. Lilly's sister would call her 'simple' for preferring happy songs. Jazz, trad, American songs, the upbeat music that burst onto the Irish scene in the 60's, invigorated her. Music she couldn't accompany on the violin. When her father drank too much, he'd request that Lilly play 'Kilkelly' on the violin, a heart-breaking song about a son writing to the mother he'd never see again. Conleth would gaze out of the window as she played and sometimes his eyes welled up. When she'd finish her piece he'd applaud and insist she take a bow. It was worth the sadness to see him smile with pleasure when she finished.

'You mightn't be the brightest spark in the classroom,' her father said, 'but you're a genius on that violin.'

When visitors arrived, at some stage of the night he'd ask his children to play a piece of music together, his chest swelling with pride. He claimed paying for music lessons for them was the best investment he ever made. His wife played several instruments – her prize possession was a violin her father made in the 1920's. Despite Conleth asking her to get the instrument valued, she refused.

'It's not for sale,' was her flat response.

When he raised the subject again her green eyes turned from his gaze. She continued as if he was not speaking. That was her way of not talking – she took on a glazed distant look. She rarely explained herself, never divulged much about her own life. Finally, she hid the violin. Conleth told her he'd find it, that he knew every crevice in their home. He reminded her that as a boy during the Tan war he utilised every single hiding place in the house. She didn't answer him. It was one of few times she disobeyed her husband. The violin belonged to some part of her that was reserved for her memory.

When Lilly tried to wipe the moss from the headstone, more of the paint flaked away. Within the next few weeks or months her mother would probably be interred in the same plot. **1916–2016** it would read. She'd like the headstone polished before the funeral. It hadn't been cleaned since her father's death twenty-four years ago. The epitaph was eroded and distorted with time, like the true account of her parents' marriage and the story that went before that, altered with accounts and opposing versions.

Whatever happened, Lilly hoped for a dignified and uneventful funeral. That was like something her mother would say. Lilly was amused how much she reminded herself of Isabel. When she thought about the coming weeks or months with her mother's imminent death, she prayed for strength and tolerance. Catherine saw their childhood from a different aspect. But, no matter how hard she tried, she couldn't understand what Catherine was referring to.

When Lilly got engaged to Greg in 1968, she was employed in the Civil Service. Catherine rang not to congratulate her sister but to urge her to postpone the wedding until the government announced they were lifting the ban on married women working.

'You need to be independent,' she urged her. 'Otherwise you will be obliged to put up with the same drudgery as Mother for the rest of your days.'

Loath as she was to admit it, Lilly hinted that she was pregnant, that the marriage must be sooner rather than later. So intimidated by her sister was Lilly that she couldn't have her knowing the truth – which was that Lilly didn't particularly like her job and could not wait a minute longer to become a housewife like most of her friends. She had no interest in her mother's business. When she married Greg in 1970 she was so happy and optimistic. She couldn't have the same perspective as her sister.

Catherine said, 'I couldn't be that kind of submissive woman, one who is transferred from her father's property to her husband's property on her wedding day.'

Lilly never saw herself as anyone's property and it never entered her head to question her role as a woman or a wife. Despite trying to explain that to Catherine, her sister continued to post her letters with the title 'Ms' rather than 'Mrs'. Lilly was pleased to be Mrs Greg Kelly. If Catherine had stayed in Ireland she would probably have been on the Condom Train with Nell McCafferty and the rest of the Irish Women's Liberation Movement. Lilly remembered being agog at their courage when they travelled to Belfast to buy condoms which were prohibited in Ireland. So much had changed, she thought. Regularly she wondered if her granddaughter's generation were any happier than she was.

Catherine was like their grandmother, Betty Hopkins, except their grandmother had a more subtle manner of winning an argument. As well as Catherine taking issue with submissive Irishwomen, the slow pace and general management of the Irish vexed her. She chided late bus drivers and the lackadaisical business approach galled her. Catherine also went through a period of hating religion, hating men. As she saw it most Irishmen were male chauvinists. Mostly she hated their father, then hated their mother, then hated their father all over again. Lilly thought it unusual she ended up marrying a man like their father, but of course she ended up hating her husband as well. Most of the time Catherine reminded Lilly of their father Conleth. His no-nonsense approach, his way or the highway attitude. Yet, for all of her faults, Catherine was wonderful. In the mid-seventies when a series of health problems affected both of their parents and Conleth's brother and nephew died around the same time, it was Catherine who flew home and took charge. She remained for weeks and did what she could in the family business, took her parents to hospital appointments, administered their medication. Catherine stayed until their parents were on their feet and Ireland became too claustrophobic.

When their father died, once again Catherine came up trumps. Lilly shuddered at the memory of her mother's despondency in the months subsequent to their father's death. Initially she behaved like any grieving widow – she visited the grave and diligently brought fresh flowers and kept the weeds at bay. Not breaking the habit of a lifetime, she wouldn't or couldn't explain what suddenly went wrong a few months later. Instead she returned to her darkened room with migraine. As soon as her migraine lifted, she emerged from her bedroom with a rage which diminished over the years but never entirely faded. Immediately she dumped or sold everything belonging to her husband Conleth and mother Betty. She refused to mark her husband's anniversary with a Mass, she refused to maintain his grave and declined all offers to have his headstone polished. Once in an angry tone she mentioned having her father Seamus's remains repatriated to the cemetery in Tipperary where she spent most of her time. There was no mention of removing her mother or dead husband from the cold Dublin cemetery.

'What in the name of God would you do that for?' Lilly was horrified at the notion of tampering with a corpse that had been dead for so long.

Isabel didn't answer immediately, then said, 'To give my father a final resting place among his own people.'

Lilly looked blankly at her mother, wondering if she had finally lost her marbles.

'Like they exhumed Roger Casement from a prison in England and buried him in Ireland which was his dying wish,' her mother said, then getting irritated added, 'You should read the newspaper instead of baking new fandangled dishes from your quare recipe books.'

Lilly didn't ask any more. Instead she asked Catherine to come home from New York, fearing their mother was going through some extreme sort of grief. Catherine arrived home and stayed for three weeks. The sisters couldn't get to the root of their mother's problem. Initially Catherine discussed depression, grief, and conditions like agoraphobia. Catherine was well read, she had seen so much more of the world and appeared informed on all kinds of treatments and modern medicine from America.

'Some say psychotherapy is a wonderful treatment but you must be open to it,' Catherine explained. 'There is no way in hell that secretive old bird would tell anybody other than her God the little secrets she's preserved.' Then she added, 'The best alternative is Prozac, and she needs bucket-loads of Prozac.'

It was 1989. Lilly could still see her sister with her newly shagged hairstyle, the sudden volume of hair looking comical and ill-fitting on her usual sleek bob-styled blonde locks.

'What will Prozac do?' Lilly whispered, fearing their mother was going to end up like one of those crazy old ladies she saw on Portmarnock Beach who were on day release from Grangegorman Asylum.

Catherine demonstrated by placing a hand at either side of her head. 'From here to here,' then she placed her hand on the top of her head and under her chin, 'and here to here, it totally fucking numbs you. Most natives of this crazy little island could do with shitloads of it.'

Whatever had happened, her mother never discussed it and, without the help of Prozac, she roused herself. Like a boxer in the ring who'd been knocked about, she picked herself up. She packed her bags and returned to Tipperary for a few months. Until her dementia took hold she lived between both houses, owning several dogs over the years, and spent her days reading and listening to music.

As Lilly left the old part of the cemetery and walked to the newer part she found the silence and rows of headstones that accompanied her into the newer section almost overwhelming. Her mother would be banished to the cold clay for ever. Life suddenly seemed so unforgiving.

Her father used to tell Lilly that if she lived long enough she'd see history repeat itself time and time again. Then she didn't understand what he meant. But with the passing of time she saw history repeat itself, not only politically but within her own family. Dealing with her distant daughter Eilish was a reminder of her own relationship with Catherine. Her daughter Paulette gravitated towards a similar life to Lilly's own life. Listening to Catherine air her strong opinions about oppression was like listening to their father towards the end of his disappointed days.

Standing over her husband's grave, she said a decade of the Rosary, imploring him for a peaceful death for her mother and a dignified funeral without tension and the re-opening of old wounds.

Chapter 34

Eilish had been awake for hours. She was in her bedroom examining the new brochures for her company. They were perfect; they depicted the type of company she needed to portray – confident and trustworthy. Yet she struggled with her new sense of apprehension. Now that the brochures and business cards had arrived, she couldn't use the lack of them as an excuse to delay her plan.

She'd had two hundred brochures printed using her grandfather's name: Hopkins Furniture. The four-page brochure was filled with glossy images of modern, contemporary, classic and rustic kitchens for restaurants. There was a list of services and a section about Eilish including a photograph. She didn't need to justify using the images of pretty kitchens from another company. It had to be done, and the chances of being found out were slim. There was a list of Eilish's qualifications. A degree in kitchen design, diploma in interior design, a finance degree and a diploma in architecture. All untrue except for the finance degree. After her first few jobs she'd use her own images for the next brochure.

The printer had stuck a post-it note over her picture on the brochure: *'As promised, I've made you young and beautiful again, Adam xx'*

Adam, the twenty-something man who produced the brochures, had promised he could turn back time with his air-brushed photography. He was not yet versed in sufficient suaveness to tell her she was still beautiful at forty-four years of age. Eilish had dark hair and brown eyes. At 5ft 9in, she was taller than most. She looked quite striking but the sun, smoking and her unhealthy lifestyle had taken their toll on her skin. Soon, she promised herself, soon she'd get healthy.

True to his word, Adam had made her ageless. Her arms were folded and black bobbed hair was freshly done for the photo. Adam airbrushed the image. Her teeth and the whites of her eyes beamed, her skin was virginal. When Eilish studied the picture, the word *pristine* sprang to mind, as if she was unscathed by life's thorny hurdles.

In the old days she'd have called Adam immediately to thank him and discuss prices for a larger order and bigger brochure. But nothing was certain any more. She was so uncertain and terrified of failing that she hid the brochures in her bedroom. If Paulette spotted them she'd tell all and sundry. Eilish didn't want that kind of pressure on top of everything else.

Then the phone rang.

At the sound of Paulette's frantic whispering, Eilish cast the brochure aside. Nana's passing could not be this sudden? Eilish was not ready. She wasn't ready for the finality that came with death.

'Nana is going in an ambulance to the hospital with a suspected kidney infection. The nursing home want someone to travel in the ambulance with her.' Paulette's voice was fraught with something like hysteria. 'Seemingly the nursing home can't afford to lose a member of staff for the day.'

'I don't understand,' Eilish said. Was this an indirect way of notifying the family? Was it only a formality, a way to gather the family together in the hospital to watch Nana's last few hours ebb away? 'Is she about to die?'

'No,' Paulette hissed impatiently. 'They need one of us to spend the day with her because she may not be seen immediately. They said that Nana could be on a trolley for the entire day and the hospital don't have the staff. They want us to sit with her in case she's agitated.'

'Why can't the hospital staff do it? Surely we'd only be in the way?'

'My sentiments exactly,' Paulette said, her voice racing with frustration. 'Cut-backs – apparently the hospital hasn't the manpower to deal with the patients. They said in case Nana wants a drink of water or something like that, that would be our job. I swear to God I'm not making this up.'

Once Eilish realised that Nana was not going to die immediately, she understood Paulette's reason for the call. She was trying to offload the job onto someone else.

Paulette filled the silence: 'When I refused, the bitch put the phone down on me – some bloody foreigner.'

'You'll simply have to go with Nana,' Eilish said in a reasonable tone.

'Dick is going to work and I need to take Zara to college. There is too much to do apart from sitting by a hospital bed pacifying our grandmother for the day.'

'Go to the hospital after you drop Zara to college.'

Paulette was emphatic. 'Not possible. I have a thousand things to do.' She began to reel off her chores for the day. None of them seemed too important.

'They called you,' Eilish said, taking some perverse pleasure out of Paulette's dilemma. Paulette wanted to be chief mourner, so let her take the gauntlet and sit yapping on the phone by Nana's bed for the day.

'It's just not possible,' Paulette said, waiting for Eilish to offer.

'I thought you were enjoying spending time with Nana? You said you were available at any hour of the day? Remember? You'll need to work something out. I've too much to do this morning. Give me a bell when you decide.' With that, she hung up.

Eilish surveyed her bedroom. It was in such a state she didn't know where to start. The contents of her grandmother's antique wardrobe were still on the floor. As yet she had not unpacked the stored containers with her good suits and jewellery. When she looked out the window for inspiration, the overgrown garden was a reminder of another pending job.

She set the needle on the old record player to listen to Albinoni's 'Adagio in G minor'. She had taken Nana to a concert in Prague's famous auditorium, the Rudolfinum, during one of their city breaks. So impressed was Nana with the Czech Philharmonic Orchestra, she spoke about it for months. After that Eilish took her to see famous orchestras in Dresden, Berlin and, Eilish's favourite, Vienna. The Musikverein Concert Hall stuck out in her memory for the performance, the entertaining conductor and the magnificent setting. She promised herself she'd return. But she didn't have the funds for those kinds of weekend breaks any more. She had to make do with her grandmother's record player in a wallpapered bedroom.

She hoisted the containers of her clothes onto her bed and opened them. Immediately she saw some of her best suits, clothes and jewellery, relics from the boom years. The cream suit she bought in Italy appeared as good as new. She held it up to the light and examined it, unable to remember the year she bought it – only that it was at the height of the boom. She and a friend went to Italy for seven days to shop, sun, wine and dine. There were periods of that holiday that she couldn't remember at all but she did remember the day she bought the suit and a real Louis Vuitton handbag.

She found her handmade shoes and Ted Baker, Michael Kor, Diana Von Furstenberg suits. Like a child rediscovering her lost toys she rushed her way through the layers of expensive cashmere, wool and silk. Next she unzipped the bag containing her jewellery. Necklaces and bracelets, gold from Dubai and a Cartier Tank watch from New York. She removed the watch from the case and tried it on. She marvelled at the diamonds edging the eloquent face. On her other wrist she placed the emerald and silver bracelet she'd bought in Kenya. Hurriedly she fogged it with her breath and cleaned it with a tissue. She examined it on her wrist and fell in love again with the emeralds, the unusual twists of sterling silver and the lobster clasp.

Within a few minutes of silently admiring her jewellery, her excitement depleted. At the sight of the sparkling diamonds she felt foolish and wasteful. The contents of the containers were another stark reminder of the money she'd made and lost. The expensive items were like relics from a bygone era. What was it all for? Her silly indulgent boom gifts to herself bought in a time when money fell into her lap. At forty-four years of age there were days when she felt she had screwed up so badly it would be impossible to shake off the sense of failure. Eilish sat on the bed recalling spending sprees and exotic holidays. There was not a country she had not visited, hardly a shopping destination where she had not flashed the cash. The sight of the collapsed wardrobe compounded her sudden despondency and Nana's music made it appear all the more tragic.

She changed the record and got to work on sorting through the wardrobe. She worked steadily, lugging bags of old clothes to the front door. Later she'd take them to the dump. She had another bag of clothes for the dry-cleaner's. By mid-morning she was down to the last few items from the wardrobe.

She noticed a tightly folded silk scarf, the colours too bright and material too good to belong to Nana. The pink-and-black pattern was dated – however, the quality of the silk was remarkable. She opened the knot to ascertain the length of it, and felt something solid between the layers. When she unravelled the long silk scarf, a concealed bundle of letters fell onto the floor. The envelopes were yellow and crisp with age. Some of the letters had Betty Hopkins' full address and the remainder were letters only with her first name.

She chose a random letter.

March 1924

My Dear Betty,
Thanks so much for your last letter and photo, especially the one with little Isabel holding her dog. Her smile will break a thousand

hearts. You, as always, capture the viewer's eye. You have no idea how much I love to hear from you. I hope you had a fine time in Tipperary. Please let me know how they are?

I'm so pleased Fr Mathew is helping Seamus to find his old self and please God with prayer he will return to the great man he is. All wars are cruel, but civil wars are merciless. It's a perilous time for a man like him. Seamus is a man of faith. Fr Mathew is a dear friend to help him through these deep dark times. I wish I shared their creed. You are so brave and cheerful under these horrid circumstances. I am sure few realise the strength beneath your elegance.

I am so looking forward to our reunion in two weeks. My days are filled with thoughts and memories of you. I think of those kisses between our tears before your departure. I did not want to wipe my face, those spaces where your tender lips had touched. In this strange city I am crushed tonight, suffocated at our parting.

Your photo is with me at all times, your letters and your words are all I have. At night I take the photo from my breast pocket and place it on my locker. When finished writing this letter to my Irish colleen, I will kiss your lips and quench the lamp.

Yours forever,

D.H.

Eilish reread the letter and then sat staring at it. She re-examined the Christmas portrait of Isabel and Betty with the inscription on the back from a man with the surname Hartmann. She compared the writing on the photo to that in the letter. They were very different. The handwriting in the letters was simple and clear, Hartmann's writing on the back of the Christmas picture was decorative.

Slowly she read the remaining letters. By the time she read the last one, it was as if she'd walked into a vault where her great-grandmother's secrets were laid bare.

Chapter 35

Throughout the following days Eilish constantly returned to the eloquent realm of the letter-writer. During each free moment she devoured the old-worldly graceful words on the flimsy paper. She googled Ireland in 1922 when the letters began. It coincided with the end of Ireland's War of Independence and the beginning of the Civil War. She tried to establish who D.H. was. In one letter, he lamented about the old sod, the state of his beloved Ireland. He was a journalist who reported on sporting fixtures. She guessed he sided with the Anti-Treaty side during the Civil War, the opposite side to her great-grandfather. She knew all belonging to the Hopkins were Fine Gael, pro-Treaty. With everything she did, she felt the weight of the letters in her bag. A window into the past was suddenly open.

Only when Eilish met her friend Sarah Willis did she momentarily forget about the letters. The intimidating prospect of starting her company brought her from the romantic 1922 letters to the pressures of doing business in 2016.

'Aren't you excited?' Sarah asked, about the two contacts she had given her. 'This could get you a footing in the kitchen and refurbishment world.'

Sarah was Eilish's only remaining friend from the boom years and the only person Eilish had confided in about her new business venture. During the boom, Sarah had her own publishing company. She produced two magazines, a restaurant guide and garden magazine. Sarah admitted that the publishing business during the boom was a licence to print money, but she too went bust. Now she was a PAYE employee for a restaurant magazine. Unlike the rest of their fallen friends from those years, Sarah and Eilish spoke openly about the recession and how it affected them. Sarah confided that she had enormous issues working for someone else. 'And as for that dreaded clocking-in-card. Imagine I'm being monitored like a schoolgirl. I'll need counselling to get over this if we ever get out of this recession,' she joked. Yet she was realistic enough to know it was a case of needs must.

'Are you afraid?' Sarah asked.

'Yes,' Eilish said honestly. 'The prospect of selling a company that does not yet exist is a little difficult.'

'You can always work for someone else. Aspire to be like me,' Sarah joked. 'Become a P... A ...Y ... E!' She held her throat as if choking on the words.

Eilish laughed.

Without Sarah's encouragement, Eilish would have remained in Brighton etching out an unhappy living in a foreign country. But Sarah had promised to give her contacts in the restaurant business. She had promised to keep her eyes peeled for any restaurateur who mentioned renovating or opening a new premises.

'You're the best woman for the job,' Sarah now said seriously. 'You've the best eye for the job. You know where to get the best material. You have that little Lithuanian carpenter. You can always get a painter and a few lads to fill in the gaps. Under your supervision it'll be the best job in the country.'

'OK,' Eilish said with a pen and paper at the ready. 'Bring it on.'

The first contact that Sarah had was a long shot. She warned Eilish not to allow that to deter her.

'Marcus Haskell. He has three restaurants in Kildare. He wants each shop overhauled and he's thinking of opening a new premises in Wicklow. He's in his fifties and knows his stuff. Don't be intimidated by him or his accent.' She gave Eilish his mobile number. 'Just do it like you did in the old days with your killer confidence and go-get attitude.'

Eilish had never been intimidated by age or class yet now so much unnerved her.

As if reading her thought, Sarah said, 'I see you found your Gucci suits and Cartier Watch. That guy is so mean, behind his Anglo-Irish accent his shoes are from Aldi.'

Renovating three shops would definitely get Eilish back into the game. At least then she could put her own pictures to the next batch of brochures and website.

'This lady is much easier to deal with – Linda Jones,' Sarah said, giving her the contact details of a woman who was establishing an organic shop in Rathmines. 'She's a real Mother Earth so tell her you use recycled materials and you love animals and you never piss in public places without considering the damage to the earth.'

Once Eilish was alone in the car, she called both potentials. If she dithered, she'd find it more difficult. She arranged her appointments for the following day.

Isabel was on a trolley on the corridor of the hospital. Despite the noise, she slept, her mouth slightly open, each wispy breath a resounding fight to remain. Eilish patted her grandmother's hand. Holding her tiny veiny hand would be inappropriate, even in death.

'It's Eilish,' she said.

When there was no response, she sat beside her and waited.

She took one of the letters from her bag and read again the author's startling reference to her great-grandfather's poor mental health.

'*He will find his way back. I laughed when I read your account of poor Seamus bolting the doors at night with eight locks on the front door and moving a cabinet to the back door. This wave of suspicion will hopefully ease soon. I know it upsets you but I feel sure that the gun and slash hook he insists on sleeping with are a mere precaution for intruders. The furthest thought from his mind is to kill you. He adores you, as I do.'*

Eilish reread that line. Her great-grandfather bolted himself and his wife into the bedroom and slept with a gun and slash hook! Nothing on Netflix was as engrossing as Granny Betty's letters.

In another letter, he referred to Seamus's 'list of possible assassins'. Eilish tried to establish if D.H. thought Seamus was stark raving cracked.

"I am not upset or surprised to hear I am at the top of his list. Although I am surprised at his other suspects. Poor Seamus is probably suffering the most dreadful delusions to think that his own brother would kill him. I don't believe Seamus will act on his suspicions. However, until such time as his mistrust abates, it would be better to dissuade Malachy from visiting.

You asked why I do not behave as Seamus does. Each man weathers his battle differently. War has monstrous consequences for some men. At night I am occasionally stalked by so many vivid dreams of dancing flames and gunshots. With the silence of the aftermath of war, it can be a more problematic time. Too much stillness is not good but when I wake in the dead of night disturbed by my memories, I think of you and sweet dreams envelop me again.

Do take care, my dear. As you say, little Isabel is safe in Tipperary with her grandparents where she can remain a child. Feel free to escape to me in England. I will always be waiting with open arms and ready to smother you in kisses."

Eilish quickly returned the letters to her bag when she noticed Nana stirring. Her hooded eyes looked out the small high window at the unusually grey April evening. Her two small hands held the top of the blanket high on her chest as if she was guarding her modesty.

'Hi, Nana.' Eilish searched for a flicker of recognition. 'It's Eilish.'

Isabel masked her bewilderment with an impersonal smile.

Eilish removed the lilac blouse from her bag that she had hand-washed and dried overnight. 'Look what I found.'

'My good blouse,' Isabel said, reaching to take it. 'Was it mixed up with Conleth's shirts?'

'Yes,' Eilish said, noting her grandmother's firm grip on the blouse and how quickly she reacted.

'You're a great girl for finding it.'

She lay back on the bed with the blouse spread out to admire it.

'Did you find Catherine's ballet shoes?' Nana asked.

Eilish shook her head.

'That's the second pair of ballet shoes that lassie has lost,' Nana said crossly. 'I don't think she wants to do ballet.'

Eilish smiled at the unlikelihood of her large loud opinionated aunt tiptoeing though a ballet in a tutu.

Nana continued. 'She's so headstrong I wouldn't be surprised if she'd flung the ballet shoes in the canal.' She shook her head in exasperation.

Eilish guessed Nana was lost somewhere in the fifties.

'How are you?' Eilish ventured.

Nana opened and closed her mouth, licking her lips. 'I'm a little thirsty.'

Eilish had been warned not to give her a drink. On her tray were small wet sponges that she could suck and use to wet her lips. Eilish dipped one in water and passed it to her.

'Anything in the paper?' Nana asked when she spotted the newspaper by Eilish's handbag.

It was always a question she asked.

'Nothing only bad news,' Eilish said, scanning to paper to read something her grandmother would find interesting.

When Eilish lived with Nana, they used to swap newspapers and read newsworthy snippets to each other. She loved Nana's reaction when she read some bizarre item of news, like the Animal Café offering visitors the chance to eat and drink alongside their pets.

Nana shook her head in bewilderment on that occasion: "Shortly they'll want official ceremonies to marry their pets."

As Nana spent several weeks at a time in Tipperary after her husband's death, Eilish had the privacy she wanted and on Nana's return they enjoyed each other's company. Two years was Eilish's longest stay. She wanted a fresh start after an affair with a married man from Wales. Feeling alone and like a drifting used mess, she returned to Nana's basement flat to evaluate her life and find a sense a rootedness that she'd lost. Each time she moved into Nana's, she pretended it was for practical reasons. She was between homes, or the house-sharing arrangement didn't work out, or she was redecorating her apartment. She never told Nana about her failed relationships yet Nana seemed to intuit when it was man-trouble.

'You find the old romances hard going,' Nana said. 'If I was a girl of your generation, I wouldn't bother with them either.'

Eilish met the doctor before his shift ended. He told her that Nana was in a precarious condition and she should not expect miracles. With each sentence the doctor uttered, she felt her last vestige of hope drain. She could not rely on her own judgement – it was too clouded with optimism and probably denial. It had been childish and foolish to hope a woman who lived a century could continue indefinitely.

'Just to keep you up to speed,' he said in a nice Dublin 4 accent as if he was letting her in on the secret that her mother and Paulette had known for weeks.

The antibiotics were not working as well as expected, there was a chest infection and possibly a urinary tract infection. The doctor told her it was the beginning of the end. As he spoke, quiet panic surfaced in Eilish. Clearly he couldn't give a definite date.

'But do you think she could last another few months?' she tried.

He shook his head. 'The next twenty-four hours will tell a lot.'

'Or even a month?' She tried not to sound as if she was pleading.

'I cannot say.'

'But she's singing!' Yet she knew it was common for dementia patients to recall the words of songs when memory and speech deserted them.

The doctor shrugged.

Before Eilish left she sat with Nana and hummed the air of a song. It was an old favourite of Nana's, 'Happy Are We All Together'. Her grandmother whispered the words, her voice getting stronger with each line, the recollection as clear as twenty years ago. The memory of music was always poignant for Eilish, and she closed her eyes against the imminent end. She remembered Nana teaching her that song in Tipperary during a windy summer's day. A sudden gale took her balloon, but Nana just shrugged when she'd bawled. 'You should have tied it to the chair. It's gone now.' Suddenly she felt like a child again, watching her escaped balloon in the wind, nature's breath taking it forever.

The doctor had told Eilish that the memory for song is facilitated by the song's rhythmic structure. When Nana first confided in Eilish about her forgetfulness, she told Eilish that music and singing old songs reassured her there was nothing at all wrong with her memory. Like a faithful old dog, the words of songs she had learned 90 years ago came flooding back. To give her a little extra joy Eilish taught her how to use an iPad. She loved YouTube and listening to the old songs her uncles and cousins sang in Tipperary. To test her memory, Isabel would type a song into the search bar, allow the first line to play, then she'd accompany the singer to the very last verse remembering every word. The music elevated Isabel to great heights – the happy memories of a simpler time with the affirmation that she was not doting.

'The memory of music is the kindest recollection of all,' Nana sighed when she finished singing.

Eilish smiled at her. A rare insight into her past.

When Eilish got home it was after six. She stood at the kitchen window gazing into the back garden – the same spot and view D.H. referred to in his letters. He described how he and Betty talked for so long that time passed quickly in a glorious haze.

'Everything we are began by the stove in your kitchen with the tall windows. Light, half-light and darkness passing unnoticed. In this enemy country I return to your kitchen so often. I am rarely

present to my English acquaintances.'

Eilish took the clearest photo of D.H. taken with Betty outside Westminster Abbey. She went to Nana's old bedroom and located her box of photo albums that were taken over eighty years. She quickly scanned the men from the black-and-white images, looking for a man similar to D.H. There were plenty of pictures of Tipperary – old relatives posing with greyhounds, clusters of people gathered at the front door of Nana's grandparents' house. There were pictures of Eilish's mother with Nana. But none of D.H. There were no photos of Betty Hopkins or Eilish's grandfather Conleth. The albums were dated, with four pictures on a page. There were gaps on some pages, the remaining stark piece of solid glue a reminder to Eilish of Nana's rage in the months after her husband's death. She'd obviously ripped any photographs of Conleth and her mother Betty from the albums. Whatever information Nana stumbled on after Conleth's death, she wanted to wipe all memory of her late mother and husband away. Loath as she was to admit it, Paulette was probably right when she insisted that Nana wanted to forget.

A woman who kept the world at arm's reach. Isabel had never chosen silence: it was as if it was engrained in her never to speak of her past. Whatever came to the surface after Conleth's death, it had propelled her to remove all reminders and never divulge her reasons. Could her mother's simple affair have prompted her to destroy any physical reminders of Betty? If there were any other memorabilia from that era, Eilish resolved to find them and censor them. It was the least she could do for her grandmother. Paulette was nosy whereas Aunt Catherine was fixated on Nana's past. If either of them suspected there were secrets still contained within the walls of Nana's home, they would take the house asunder brick by brick in their quest to find answers which might be better left hidden.

Chapter 36

A woman was sitting on the edge of the bed. Her behaviour irked Isabel, the way she patted her leg. A reassuring little clap on the thigh as if Isabel were her prize dog.

'Do you know where you are, Nana?' she asked in an overfamiliar manner.

Isabel nodded. 'Yes.'

'You know who I am?'

Isabel nodded again. She couldn't think of her name. It was the second granddaughter, the one with the man's name. The nosy one with such magnificent notions she left Betty Hopkins at the starting post.

'I'm Paulette, Nana.' Her deep-set green eyes narrowed as she persisted, 'Where are you?'

'In bed,' Isabel said.

Paulette looked at a black man standing by her bed. She laughed. 'In which bed?' she persisted.

'Dear Jesus, I'm in my own bed,' Isabel said, irritated, yet she knew it wasn't her bed in her home. The home where she never felt at home.

'Hasn't a clue,' she heard Paulette mutter to the man. 'Nana, this is Dharfir. He came to see you. He is my friend.' She spoke clearly and patted her again on the leg.

Isabel looked at the tall coloured man wearing a well-cut three-piece suit, a suit Conleth would have liked.

She thought she heard Paulette mutter, 'Go on, Dharfir – ask her a few questions.'

The man smiled tolerantly at Paulette. He appeared a little uncomfortable.

Speaking with a clipped accent, he asked quietly, 'Mrs Salmon, how are you today?'

'Very well.'

They waited for her to elaborate.

'The traffic delayed me with Obama's visit,' Isabel complained. 'I was lucky to make my appointment.'

'You're a little confused, Nana,' said Paulette. Pointing at the man at the foot of the bed she said, 'Dharfir is a doctor.'

Isabel looked at the black doctor. He would blend into Ireland's cosmopolitan city today. A far cry from a few years previously when a coloured person on Irish streets was so rare their appearance was discussed at length. In Tipperary there was one black man. He was studying to be a priest in the local seminary. Nobody could remember his peculiar name, so affectionately they called him Kunta Kinte after a black character in a 70's television series. To Isabel it seemed as if the world had come full circle: a black man running the superpower of the world was as great a sign of the change as the Queen of England visiting a fish market in Cork.

'May I ask how old you are?' the doctor asked, taking a notebook from his pocket. He appeared genuinely interested.

'Ninety-five years.'

Isabel heard Paulette gasp as if she had said something wrong.

'It's perfectly normal at her age,' the doctor said to the woman. 'Ninety-five or a hundred, there isn't a great difference.'

Isabel knew what the doctor was doing. He was checking her memory. She knew it was failing. She couldn't remember how long ago she made an appointment with a doctor in Vincent's Hospital to discuss her memory. That day when the traffic was heavy due to Obama visiting Ireland, she was lucky to arrive on time. So intent on fixing the problem, Isabel resolved to tell the doctor in Vincent's Hospital the truth, the whole damn truth and nothing but the truth. However, the words she wanted to say would not form. She'd spent a lifetime looking away, refining her habit of not telling. She did tell him about digging the garden. It wasn't that she wanted to explain the dirt under her nails – she wanted help and had no notion of wasting her time and money lying. Unable to live with the terrifying uncertainty of her own behaviour, she revealed what she could to the doctor. He asked her a series of questions. Most she could answer, others she was unable to answer. She'd learned to deny the truth for so long. "I can't recall," ended the questioning.

This doctor was asking the same questions. Isabel couldn't recall if she had requested the appointment. She assumed she had. Why else would he be asking her questions?

'Paulette tells me you play the violin. So do I,' the doctor told her. 'I'm a grade eight.'

'We didn't have grades in my time – my father taught me,' she said.

Vividly Isabel recalled those days when her father patiently taught her the strings in the workshop at the back of their house. He'd clap in time to the music encouragingly and never seemed to tire of her early dismal attempts. She remembered her father bathing his feet. His toenails were gone. Each day a woman called to their house to bandage his feet which made him walk on his heels. She went to live in Tipperary and when she saw her father again he was walking normally. She inspected his feet to find the toenails had returned.

'How old were you when your father died?' Paulette asked.

'I can't recall,' Isabel replied. 'I was a child.'

'How did your father die?' she asked.

The doctor was waiting for Isabel to reply. She noticed his pen at the ready to make a note.

Isabel remained tight-lipped. Even if God Himself stood before her she could not begin to reveal the horrid details. Her rehearsed line was easier.

'I come from a time when people went to bed and died – there didn't need to be a reason.'

Paulette shook her head as if Isabel had said something wrong.

The doctor smiled and nodded.

Isabel always answered questions about her life in the same evasive manner. She'd learned how to digress. There were times when she denied the truth to herself. It was easier to doubt her own recollection. She couldn't bear to look at the events from those years . . . the true culprit.

'You've reached a remarkably great age,' the doctor said. 'Did your mother also reach a good age?'

'My mother died in her early eighties, I think,' Isabel said.

Isabel's uncertainty was not due to her memory loss. For a few consecutive birthdays her mother claimed to be fifty-nine years old. 'Your mother will be the same age as you shortly!' Conleth said, when Betty's 61st birthday dragged on for several years. He said only a woman like Betty Hopkins could make time stand still. Isabel suspected Betty was closer to eighty-six when she died.

'Did she have good health?'

'Yes, marvellous health for a woman who liked a tipple and good food,' she admitted.

'No harm in that,' he said, returning to his notes.

With the passing of time it was the memories she tried to extinguish that pushed their way to the forefront of her mind. She saw the features and the blemishes on the hands and the contours of the faces she tried to forget. They were as clear as if they were the last people she saw before she entered the doctor's surgery. The sight of the baby in the box, the sound of clay landing on his makeshift coffin. Trickling blood. The ringing in her ears from the sound of a gun. Mona Daly and Grandmother Maureen told her the ringing in her ears was a request from a dead relative for a prayer.

'Ask her about the migraines,' Paulette prompted the doctor.

Isabel could see the doctor was reluctant. He didn't repeat the question – he knew she had heard Paulette.

'No, my mother didn't have migraines or believe in sickness.'

As the years passed, Isabel noticed how her own aging face resembled her mother's. She did not like to dwell on their fractured relationship, her deep mistrust of her mother, occasionally disdain and incomprehension at her mother's character. Betty, the kindly traitor disguised with perfume and pearls. She was someone who had planned the outcome before the argument began.

'Your accent is not a Dublin accent.' He seemed interested.

'My parents were both from Tipperary,' she said.

It was easier than explaining that she spent most of her formative years in the little piece of paradise. It was her grandparents and cousins, her uncles and aunts who were the background canvas to her life. The colour in her life was from their brushes. Humility, faith, strength, optimism, simplicity. The only little corner of the world where she was at ease.

Her husband didn't share her love of the country. Strong handsome Conleth saw little attractions in rural life. She adored him as a child and fell in love with him as a young woman. He made her feel safe again. She loved his vibrancy and good looks. It was Conleth who filled the void after her grandparents died. He helped her live again. In 1938 they had married secretly.

When Betty heard the news, she marched across the parlour and slapped Conleth' face. Isabel had never seen her mother so angry. She accused him of marrying her daughter to get his hands on the company he coveted all of his life. That December night Betty swore she'd make Conleth work for every penny he ever earned. True to her word, she did not give him many concessions – only enough to deter him from getting another job with a rival company. There were times when money was short and, like in most Irish families, there were weeks when they waited for payday to fix up the slate at the corner shop. For a period, Conleth drove a Morris Minor and the wipers worked when they felt like it. They carried a potato in the car to wipe the window screen. When it rained and if the wipers were having an off day, they'd wipe the exterior window screen with a cut potato. The starch in the potato spread the rain in smooth layers making visibility possible. According to their young daughter, Lilly, "The air in Brittas Bay makes Daddy's wipers break." Isabel thought with fondness of those times when Lilly and Catherine were small children. She and Conleth had so little and didn't know it.

On Betty's death, they inherited her large Georgian house in Ranelagh and Hopkins Furniture. Conleth was so impressed with his new acquisitions that he insisted they move to Ranelagh while the clay on her mother's grave was not yet dry. Moving made little sense to Isabel. Their children were grown up and the house in Ranelagh was too big for just the two of them. Despite its great size, the house suffocated her. There was no respite from any of the lofty rooms and the pretty lawn was as despairing. The sense of foreboding never left until she was on the road to Tipperary to relax among her own people. Conleth couldn't understand his wife's reluctance to move.

'It was a long time ago,' he said, referring only once to the incident they never discussed in their fifty-one years of marriage.

It was a long time ago . . . yet it happened. She went along with him, her proud husband. Isabel heard Conleth tell his nephew that he was a boy when Granny Betty established the house.

'Nothing more than a gopher.' Arrogantly he clapped his chest. 'Now the boy has become the man who owns the house.'

She could forgive him his little bit of haughty nonsense. Everybody had their failings. He wanted a house to reflect his position as the main man in Hopkins Furniture. Conleth was too proud and in the end he was self-seeking.

Like so many of the soldiers who fought in the Civil War, Conleth had wonderful expectations for his new free country. They felt they were on the cusp of momentous change for independent self-governed Ireland. Sadly, nothing changed with independence. The poor remained poor, the tenement dwellers remained the disregarded majority. In the new country, politics were dominated by backward fundamentalists. Over the years Conleth accepted Ireland could never develop when those in power were more concerned with keeping Ireland devout and maintaining frosty relationships with the Brits. It would remain as poor as the day he carried his messages during the 1916 Rising. Like so many of his kind, he realised the only benefit to be gained from politics was self-gain. With the right connections, he'd look after himself. He won contracts for the company, rubbed shoulders with those who had the last word. He introduced Isabel to Mr de Valera as his wife and as the daughter of the late Seamus Hopkins. It was the first time in many years that anybody referred to her father. Isabel remembered de Valera's gaze: his eyes appeared liquidated behind his thick glasses.

'How many children do you have?' the doctor asked.

'Two girls. Catherine and Lilly.'

Catherine was a fighter and Lilly was an easy child. Catherine arrived early. They'd been visiting Conleth's brother in Clontarf in the early hours of January 2nd 1941. The bombs were dropped during the night in the vicinity. The following day some of the houses were shelled in South Circular Road. When they arrived home to Harold's Cross, Isabel delivered Catherine. Conleth thought it poignant that Isabel was born in a time of unrest and his own daughter was born as the Second World War began.

Catherine was bright, too bright for her own good with facts and figures that would bamboozle a politician. She belittled her father's politics, their allegiance to the clergy. She picked holes in Ireland's politics. The Minister for Industry prohibited women working in industry as a way of reducing male unemployment. It was how it was then, but it was pointless trying to explain that to the likes of Catherine who was too quick to criticise her own country. The International Labour Organisation in Geneva placed Ireland on the blacklist for refusing to pass a law giving women equal pay. None of it surprised Isabel: in fact, she was surprised the inequality had been noted.

Catherine made it sound like the worst injustice she ever heard.

'What do you think of that?' she challenged.

'This is what we get for educating our daughters,' Conleth remarked. 'Not a grain of respect.'

Pointing out further arcane laws, Catherine would continue with her facts. 'This government was happy in 1935 to allow women to be used as cheap labour in preference to men, and now in 1965 nothing has changed.'

Vexed at her nit-picking, Isabel told Catherine that life for women would always be unfair so she might as well get used to it.

Catherine was too strong; she felt entitled to answers because she was a historian with oodles of letters and degrees after her name. She would not back down even when she knew her questioning was wrong. She was ruthless when she heard about a man shot dead in the garden. But she never did find anything out, even when she tried goading her father.

Isabel had seen a great many changes by the time her daughters reached adulthood. A man had even walked on the moon.

The doctor and Paulette were waiting for a response.

'How many grandchildren do you have?' the doctor repeated his question.

Isabel couldn't remember how many. Of course she remembered Eilish. Suddenly she felt hopeful. 'Eilish? Is Eilish coming? I think she's waiting outside? Will you see?'

'Eilish is your favourite?' He smiled. 'How old is Eilish?'

'I don't know. She's a woman.'

Isabel was tired of their visit, tired of thinking and recalling. She examined her fingernails for clay. Thankfully they were immaculate today. There was a period when she had a peculiar habit of gardening at all hours of the night. The stubborn clay under her nails was a reminder the following morning that she'd been rooting at the earth. There were times when she thought she was returning to the most troubled time of her life, as if she wanted to uproot the past from the soil, to right it in some way. There were times she doubted her own memory. If Eilish knew the way she was thinking she'd assure her every family had something to hide. Isabel would have told the doctor about digging the garden at odd hours but her granddaughter was present, waiting for her to flounder. Isabel didn't like to think about the gardening at odd hours of the morning, a pick in her hand as she rooted through the earth.

Isabel couldn't bear it any longer. Suddenly she was tired and frightened. Almost a century of hiding and she'd end up like her mother, raving for a few weeks in a hospital bed, revealing lost loves and treacherous actions. Isabel would not allow anyone to see her mother before she died, and she had pleaded with the doctors in the hospital for strong medicine to kill her mother's pain, hoping instead for silence. She would be the last one to take the secrets to the grave.

'I really must go home,' Isabel said, her eyes scanning the room for her coat.

The doctor put his notebook into his pocket. 'It was lovely to meet you, Mrs Salmon.'

She returned his smile.

Paulette stopped patting her leg and stood up to whisper to the doctor. Like children plotting a prank, they stood with their heads together, looking at her with grave expressions. The onslaught of recollection was too much. No matter how many times, or how many decades Isabel tried to suppress the memory, it resurfaced. It had more buoyancy than a beach ball held below water – it rebelled with twice as much force. Like her memory, she could never truly suffocate it.

Isabel began to sing. It was a happy song, one of Mona Daly's tunes.

'Did you ever see two Yankees part upon a foreign shore
When the good ship's just about to start for Old New York once
more?'

Chapter 37

Eilish left her first meeting with the restaurant owner in Kildare with a sense of relief. It was irrelevant that Marcus Haskell was not warm or friendly. Twice he asked if they'd met before. He mentioned a few hip spots she used to frequent during the 90's and noughties. Eilish was vague, her replies designed to lead him far away from her old haunts. During the boom years there were too many outrageous nights where anything was possible. So now, desperate for his business, she was not going to put herself at the scene of any indiscretions. In a serious tone he explained that he wanted his premises renovated. He wanted a modern-styled restaurant with lots of spotlights and his walls dotted with contemporary artwork. He was getting a few quotes from various companies – however, he liked her work.

As the meeting progressed and Eilish measured the shop and discussed ideas with him, the lingering sense of failure she'd experienced since the downturn subsided. She'd forgotten about the high she got from selling her business. Furnishings and décor gave her a natural buzz. When she saw a shop she loved to deliberate over how she'd change it – colouring schemes and wood, marble tops, textures and overall décor formed in her mind's eye each day.

During the boom, Eilish never doubted her capabilities. A tricky job was a welcome challenge. As she discussed the premises with the owner, her interest in the business overrode her lingering doubts. She gave the restaurateur a ridiculously low quote. He promised to phone her within a week.

Eilish had a much better rapport with the woman from the organic shop in Rathmines – Linda Jones. While there Eilish tasted her organic cheese and pretended it was like nothing she ever ate before. She showed interest in her stock and agreed with Linda when she talked about the great benefits of organic food. Eilish told Linda that nothing other than organic food passed her lips. Eilish didn't tell her that Ireland might be on the way out of a recession but people still had little money for such self-indulgent organic nonsense. She gave Linda Jones a quote and promised to have the shop ready in five days, a number plucked out of the sky. She vowed to herself that it would be done in three days, even if she had to roll up her sleeves and plough at the walls with a hammer beside Ivan, her carpenter. Within an hour Linda Jones phoned to offer her the job.

Eilish returned to her grandmother's house. She sat at the kitchen table and set to work on the Rathmines organic shop. She had a seamstress who'd take care of the fabric work for next to nothing, and a timber merchant in the country who'd provide the best wood. Until her new venture was up and running, everything would remain under-the-table. Needs must. She saved designs on her computer, played around with the colours and settled on three designs. She called Ivan, the carpenter from Lithuania who was willing to work without the inconvenience of tax, and told him to sharpen his tools. As she spoke she was aware her voice was animated. The whole day had been an enormous relief and an overwhelming success.

Eilish snapped her laptop shut before tackling her next job. She looked at Betty Hopkins' letters again, and was adamant if there were secrets contained in the house, she would find them. For the remainder of the evening she would comb every room in the house.

She left the letters on top of her laptop and looked around the kitchen for the old solid furniture that remained from her great-grandfather's era. She'd heard how Betty Hopkins liked to redecorate her house every few years, although she kept most of Seamus's furniture, believing his products were the most superior of their time.

'He never knew how good he was,' Betty reportedly said with disapproval. 'Too fixated on other things.'

Slowly Eilish walked around the house, seeing it with different eyes.

At the bottom of the stairs was a console table. It was made in the same style as the wardrobe. When Eilish was a child, an oriental bronze sculpture of a horse stood on it. Granny Betty had bought it in an antique shop in London. She never revealed how much it was worth, saying only that Eilish would be working for the rest of her life to replace it if she broke it. After her husband's death, the oriental statue was another item Isabel sold off. A cheap ceramic chipped ornament with the word "*Granny*" sat in the oriental sculpture's place. The "*Granny*" ornament was missing the "y". It was a gift from one of Eilish's school tours bought over thirty years ago. She examined the console, tapping on the top and base for a hollow sound. Beneath the base of the table Eilish found a secret drawer. It was empty. It didn't even contain dust.

Stealthily she walked from room to room, knocking on every item of furniture old enough to come from Seamus Hopkins' time. The lockers in her grandmother's room had hidden drawers beneath their base. The legs of the bed of the spare room were hollow – she remembered discovering that as a child. The bookcase in the sitting room had a similar drawer beneath the base which also contained nothing. Beneath the floorboards in the spare room was another empty hiding place. In the hall Eilish removed the photo of the proclamation that belonged to Seamus Hopkins. After Seamus's death, Betty gifted it to Conleth. It was the only item Isabel kept that belonged to her husband. Eilish suspected that she kept it because of her father's involvement in the 1916 Rising.

That too revealed nothing except an inscription on the inside from one of the Salmon family.

To Seamus and Betty, on acquiring your new home,

Without struggle, there is no progress,

Yours faithfully

Phelim

In the sitting room Eilish flopped into the armchair and poured herself a glass of wine. Maybe it was best that she find nothing. Who was to gain? Finding the letters and photographs was a fluke. They appeared to be the last and only remaining clues to the past. They must have been the little secrets Nana once referred to. 'Destroy anything that could lead to a scandal,' were her words to Eilish. They didn't amount to much of a scandal. A husband paranoid from war and his wife having an affair with a man who had a gift for writing eloquent letters. It had happened from the beginning of time. Poor Nana was probably caught in the middle, a child banished to the country who probably suspected or knew about the affair. At a time when sex was so sinful, it was immensely shameful. Nana probably thought they were going to the furthest realm of hell to sizzle for all eternity. Eilish had been told that Nana's father had died from pneumonia when he was a young man. His early death probably screwed up Nana's already messed-up head. Ninety years ago there were no counsellors and talking about the events would be met with disapproval. Instead Nana would have got a clap on the arse and would have been told to get on with life. She was forced to retreat into silence, her young mind conditioned to think the past was shameful. Instead of Nana realising that every family has its own dirty secrets, she believed her past was more shameful than anyone else's.

Eilish sipped her wine and regarded the only remaining violin in their family that her great-grandfather made. It was encased in a glass display box on the living-room wall. Although the violin was almost a century old, she noted how it gleamed as if it was polished only yesterday. The bow and violin stood erect and proud as if daring to be removed from their vault and played. She got up from the chair to take a closer look at the display case. That violin had pride of place on that wall 'since God was a child' as her grandmother would say. The interior of the case was lined with velvet and the case rimmed with wood. She rubbed her fingers over the edging until she found a screw. Unable to remove the screw, she wedged the screwdriver behind the wood until she heard a snap. She repeated her hacking until the glass case could be removed. She'd worry about repairing the display case later.

She sighed with utter gratitude when she peered into the violin and saw a folded piece of paper. Her act of vandalism was not in vain. She sat on the chair and took a large gulp from her wine before examining it. They were old paper clippings and a list of names wrapped within the newspaper articles. The first item she read was about a man called Bart Hopkins.

Man Found Shot Dead in Tipperary

Our Tipperary correspondent, in a telegram which he despatched last Thursday, states that yesterday night a man named Bart Hopkins was found with gunshot wounds outside his home in Borris outside Thurles. His house was set ablaze which spread to the adjoining farm shed. Mr Hopkins was in his seventies.

There was another paper clipping about Patrick Hopkins with an address in Borris. 29 years of age, shot dead while in the local bar.

Mr Hopkins was drinking a pint in Ryan's when a lone gunman shot him thrice. The deceased was from Borris and is survived by his three brothers.

The next piece was about Seán Salmon.

Unmarried, aged 22, he was riddled with bullets as he entered his mother's home in Francis Street. His assailant fired wildly

before fleeing with two accomplices. The shooting occurred on the evening of Tuesday 6th December.

The last paper clipping referred to John (Digger) Dempsey, 26 years of age.

Shot as he left Molly's Pub after 10 o'clock. He was hit in the chest with one bullet. However, it is assumed he crawled some distance for help. His hat and stained newspaper were found 30 yards from his body. He was discovered at the door of a house in Summerhill. The deceased lived in Dublin for some years but is a native of Westport, Mayo.

Eilish took a deep breath. Apart from the odd republican song and the long forgotten history she learned in school, she rarely considered Ireland's wars or those involved. The articles referred to men related to her and possibly their friends. It was unfathomable to think of small sleepy little villages like Borris being rocked by shootings. The men were so young. She thought of the man from Achill crawling for help. She found the thought quite depressing.

Eilish turned her attention to the list of names. There were nine names on the list with a number beside each name. At the top of the list was Phelim Salmon, then Seán Salmon. Seán Salmon's name was crossed out with the date of his death 6th December and note '*Instant X 6*'. Next was Malachy Hopkins, she guessed he was a relative of Seamus's – he was mentioned in Betty's letters. The fourth name was Fr Mathew – he must have been Seamus's friend who prayed with him. Digger Dempsey had a line through his name with the date of death 6th September 1922 and the words '*Slow x 1*'. Johnny Red, Dieter Hartmann and Conleth Salmon had 6th, 7th and 8th place. Lastly and most notable of all was the final name: *My Wife*.

Eilish laid the list on the coffee table. Maybe it wasn't a simple love story about her great-grandmother having torrid sex with her lover. There was no date on the list and no indication of who wrote it. The Salmons were her grandfather's side of the family. They were

Fianna Fáil, Anti-Treaty.

What intrigued her were the lines going through the names of Digger Dempsey and notably Seán Salmon. Digger Dempsey was shot with one bullet and his death was slow which Seamus also noted along with the number of bullets used. The newspaper report on Seán Salmon claimed his assassin fired wildly, and on Seamus's list he had 'x 6'. How could Seamus have known the number of shots which presumably was what the 6 referred to? Could Seamus have possibly been the assassin?

This must be the list of possible assassins that D.H. referred to in his letter. It was probably written during Ireland's civil war. Aunt Catherine told Eilish that none of those who witnessed the troubles talked about it. The following generations all claimed their grannies and granddads carried guns and blew the head off the enemy yet those involved never discussed it but carried grudges against the opposition until their deaths. There was a pub in Tipperary with a division: until the 90's those allied with Fianna Fáil drank in one side and Fine Gael in the other.

Idly Eilish plucked the strings of the violin and for the first time in many years she reflected deeply on Ireland's turbulent past. Years of fighting between an empire and an unarmed people. The ages of the dead men were a stark reminder of their sense of duty and pride in their country. They assumed responsibility for change when most had little to no education, not even armoury. Throughout it all life went on: they worked, made furniture and fought, and life ambled along amidst the tragedies.

Eilish roused herself when she heard voices from the kitchen. She put the paper clippings and Seamus Hopkins' list into her pocket. For the moment she wanted to keep her find a secret. The thought of Paulette delving into Nana's past and establishing long-winded theories seemed unfair.

Only when she saw her niece Zara and her boyfriend did she remember Paulette asking if they could stay the night.

Zara was sitting reading Betty Hopkins' letters when Eilish walked into the kitchen. Her boyfriend, Josh, was sitting in the armchair drinking a beer and fiddling with his mobile.

'Hi, Aunt Eilish, were you out?' Zara asked without removing her eyes from the letters that Eilish had left on the kitchen table.

'No, I've been here all evening,' she said, removing the rest of the letters from the coffee table. 'Thank you.' She stood in front of Zara with her hand out, waiting for the letter.

'Oh sorry!' Zara gave her the letter. 'It's a love letter. Isn't the old style of writing so beautiful?' She looked at Josh.

Josh agreed without raising his head.

Obviously she'd been reading the letters aloud.

Eilish deliberately made little of it. 'I think they belonged to a neighbour.'

Josh offered Eilish a beer. She accepted, opened the window and lit a cigarette. She was surprised Josh was still on the scene after Zara had discussed her insecurities about their relationship with her two weeks previously. Seemingly Josh was addicted to the cyber world; he had an alter ego on an Alternative Life site. Zara had to explain to Eilish, slowly, that it was a website with a 3D virtual world where users interact with each other through 3D Avatars. You create and trade virtual property and services.

'It's like normal life but they take it way more seriously,' Zara explained.

Zara thought that Josh was in love with an avatar on Ala-Lemu, the name of his island. He spent 16 hours a day during weekends on Ala-Lemu. According to Zara, Josh's conversations (when he was in reality) were dominated by news about his alternative life on Ala-Lemu. On Saturdays when they should be spending the day together, Josh spent every moment of his free time on his island.

Eilish thought it sounded the lesser of so many evils when she thought about heroin addiction, alcoholism, sex addiction, pill-popping. She tried to listen objectively to her niece's dilemma and had difficulty not to appear shocked when she mentioned their sex life.

'He slept with Mia.'

'In reality or virtual reality?'

'In reality. Mia's a college friend and knows how much I'm into Josh.'

Eilish was gobsmacked that Zara refused to dump him for his infidelity.

'Eilish, get with it – everybody sleeps with everybody,' Zara informed her aunt without a flicker of shame.

Eilish suddenly asked herself if she had become the old aunt who shrieks with astonishment at the changing times. Would she look with incomprehension at the upcoming generation and, like her mother, count her lucky stars she was not their age and wonder aloud where it would all end?

Zara joined her at the open window and lit a cigarette. It baffled Eilish why the younger generation were following suit and smoking in a time when it was known to be so unhealthy. Asking would have made her seem old.

'All set for your wild night on the town?'

'We're going to The Twisted Pepper and a house party afterwards.' Zara was never short of conversation. 'Clodagh is dating Mossy – you know, DJ Mossy – he was in my class and is *so*,' she rolled her eyes for effect, '*so* cool. He's really successful.'

Zara was like Paulette, beautiful with deep-set green eyes, long arched eyebrows and a perfectly symmetrical face. However, like a lot of that age group, she took from her beauty with faddish hair styles and outlandish make-up. Her hair was long with the right side of her head cropped close to a millimetre. She had so many piercings in her ear it was uncomfortable to look at them for too long. She was wearing mismatched clothes and workman's boots over leggings. Josh was relatively normal with thick dyed-blond hair, black roots and one eyebrow piercing. He too was pretty. Eilish couldn't help thinking in her grandmother's time Josh would be too busy fighting a war to dye his hair or play with his phone and spend every moment on a virtual island.

'Isn't it great that Aunt Catherine is coming home?' said Zara.

'Well, nothing has been decided yet,' Eilish said, recalling her last conversation with her mother.

'Didn't you hear the news?'

'I was out for most of the day. My battery is dead.' Eilish looked over the shoulder to see where she had left her phone charging.

'Aunt Catherine is coming home tomorrow!' Zara gushed. 'I'm super excited.'

The news hit Eilish like a bolt of lightning. She looked into the back garden. It would take a week to clear it out. She'd done nothing about it despite promising her mother. She thought about the state of the house, the smashed display case, the dust and cobwebs, the unwashed floors. There wasn't a thing to eat. She was not ready. Tomorrow morning, she would begin work on her first job. She needed to be focused and clear, needed to be well versed on organic vegetables and the best shop fittings for smelly organic cheese.

Eilish tossed her cigarette out the door and bellowed, '*Fuuuucccck!*'

Chapter 38

Catherine Salmon thought most cities were ultimately the same. Culturally and ethnically they differed but just below the surface every city was similar. Of course there were exceptions. The sight of New Delhi from the airport was enough to make her want to return to the empty plane, sit and wait for as long as it took to be taken back to her original destination. But after ten days Catherine found that sameness in New Delhi. In her early years of travelling she appreciated every single detail of every city she visited. Her hungry eyes soaked up the ornate buildings, the people, the style, and varying cultures. She remembered visiting Mississippi and marvelling at the rainfall. It didn't fall at any angle like a soft Irish mist but poured straight down, large raindrops bouncing off the pavement. At 74 years, she still liked to travel, regardless of the eventual sameness.

Returning to her native city of Dublin was always a little disconcerting. A sense of unease like a haze descended on her. It never entirely lifted until she was making the journey to Dublin airport to leave again yet she returned hoping to solder old links and revive happier times. Years ago she learned never to have expectations when she came home. There were always disappointments: someone had died, or their health had failed. Old friends were happy to allow their friendships to slide. Catherine was also guilty of that. Apart from her immediate family, a few cousins in Dublin and Tipperary who visited her in New York, there were very few to see. Now with her mother's death so close, a large link was about to be severed, her final obligation removed.

Catherine often wondered what life for her would have been like if she'd stayed in Ireland. When she graduated from University College Dublin as a History and English Teacher her father was overjoyed. She was made for life, he said. He marvelled that one of his children had a degree, a woman to boot. His own mother could barely read. Conleth told her where to apply for a job – he'd a bit of pull in a few of the local schools. The morning she went for her only interview, her father told her it was only a farce, 'Just go along with it – I've been assured the job is yours.'

When she received official confirmation that she got the job, Catherine was disinterested; there was a whole world to see. In May 1963 she went to America for the summer, promising her parents she'd return in September to take up her teaching post. It was a wonderful time to be Irish in America. President John F. Kennedy's election signalled the end of anti-Irish and anti-Catholic sentiment. Life in America had colour that Ireland lacked. There were so many TV stations she couldn't keep up, there was even a weather channel, quiz shows channel, pop music channel. The buildings fascinated her, the large cars with radio stations like TV stations, one for every preference.

Lilly didn't return to Ireland after the summer to take up her teaching post in Dublin, she didn't return the following year either. It was four years later when she returned with her fiancée, Flavio. In 1968 Catherine married into an Italian-American family which was like an Irish family except their language was more musical. There were no children, a decision she postponed each year. By January 1976 she was a young divorcee. She remained in America and like a spectator she watched from abroad as Ireland slowly changed. 1967 saw free secondary education. In 1974 Ireland lifted the marriage bar which disallowed women to continue working after they were married in certain sectors. The removal of the marriage bar caused great consternation for her father and the conservative voters who felt a married woman belonged in the home. In 1980 contraception was legalised, though only for married women. A bishop fathering a child and siphoning off diocesan funds to support its American mother: there were no words for that one. Scandals in the church dented the cult-like following. After ten years of fierce debates on divorce, it was eventually legalised in 1996. Same-sex marriage brought Ireland into its own in 2015. Northern Ireland found peace. The slow changes reinstated her faith in Ireland.

As Catherine passed through the city centre with Lilly and Paulette after they met her at the airport, she looked at the old familiar sights of Dublin. The regal Georgian Houses and blocks of flats side by side, the smaller red-bricked houses and pubs that had been there since her father was a boy. While they were stopped at traffic lights she watched an old lady bending to pick up her dog pooh with a black plastic bag.

'You're going to get a dreadful shock when you see Nana,' Paulette said. 'She's not eating or drinking. And she hasn't the foggiest what's going on. When I last visited, she thought President Obama was coming to James' Hospital for dinner.'

The last time Catherine saw her mother was two years before on a brief visit. She was en route to Germany to give a tour of lectures on the Irish diaspora. Prior to that, she hadn't seen her mother for four years. She had stayed two weeks on that previous visit and she had found it difficult. Her mother didn't like to have visitors for too long.

Catherine had asked her if she could do anything for her.

'What in the name of God do I need at this hour of my life?'

This was true. The little objects she depended on were a decent reading lamp, a good book, a biddable dog and a garden for fresh air. She was more comfortable with animals or rural aspects of life, her rare brilliant smiles reserved for the terrier on her lap. She told Catherine not to feel obliged to stay in Dublin with her all the time. She encouraged her to spend a few nights in Tipperary or have a few drinks in town with Eilish.

The visit upset Catherine. She had wanted to find some resolution to her relationship with her mother.

When she sat in the dayroom of the nursing home it was clear that her mother didn't know her. She nodded and smiled as if she understood and called Catherine 'dear' and 'love'. At one point she laid her hand on Catherine's. The small affectionate gesture was new to Catherine. The mother Catherine knew was not tactile in the slightest.

After ten minutes of nodding and appearing to agree, Isabel closed her eyes.

'Now, I'm a little tired,' she declared, ending the visit.

Catherine tried to discuss their childhood with Lilly when they were alone having lunch the day she was flying out. She used the same expressive words she had learned in therapy: *abandonment, rejection, neglect*. She remembered pouring her heart out to Lilly, and knowing it was not the right place and Lilly was not the right person to talk to. Yet she continued. Lilly finally finished her soup and looked at Catherine with the blankest expression Catherine had ever seen. An unreadable nothingness stared back at her.

Catherine returned to America that day swearing she'd never set foot on Irish soil again. She resumed her life and found a new therapist. For a full year, Catherine returned to the same therapist, she sat opposite the shrink and expunged everything from her mind. Gradually the memories of her childhood were less haunting. She accepted her mother's failings, and the numerous insults and disparaging remarks she received from Betty Hopkins began to fade. She accepted she too could be a tyrant like her father, she learned not only about the past but herself. Ireland grew smaller, the mystery around her mother's silence began to seem irrelevant. There were days she had empathy for her mother, a woman who never knew how to express anything except anger, and even the anger was expressed with a violent silence. The past was gradually becoming the past.

Exactly one year ago she attended a lecture on 1916 that one of her friends was giving in the Irish Centre in New York. Afterwards an old student came to talk to her. He was in his fifties and accompanied by his father who was not too many years older than Catherine.

'It's me, Ms Salmon,' he said, 'James Redmond – Irish James Redmond.'

Catherine pretended she remembered him. Thousands of students passed through her hands. There was nothing noteworthy about the small bald James Redmond with his American accent that should have made him memorable.

'Dad, this is Ms Salmon, Irish Ms Salmon from NYU.'

Nothing registered on his father's face. 'Who?' he asked.

'Salmon from Dublin. The furniture shop. Dublin violins.'

When it registered with the father, he clasped her hand as if they were long-lost friends and repeatedly shook it as he looked at her intensely. 'A pleasure,' he repeated, holding her hand even tighter. 'My father spoke highly about your family.'

It wasn't the first time Catherine met friends of her family – many people knew the shop in Dawson Street, or the Salmons from Thomas Street. Her uncles and aunts were well known in Dublin.

'My father said the Hopkins men were the best pals a guy could have,' Mr Redmond Senior said.

Catherine rarely met anyone who knew her grandfather's family and hadn't met anyone who knew her grandfather in thirty years.

The old man laughed. 'He called them "the best auld skins around",' he said, doing a good impersonation of the Irish accent.

'What was your father's name?' Catherine asked.

'Johnny Red from Horse and Jockey, a few miles from where your grandfather and grandmother are from. Tipperary people.'

Catherine was only half listening as he told her that he had visited the Hopkins home during his holidays in Ireland. He went on to tell her the history of Horse and Jockey, the oddly named village his father came from. And then he told an anecdote about his father, Johnny Red, digging a bunker in Seamus's house the same day as the first shots of the War of Independence were fired.

'My father came to America in 1922,' she heard him say.

'During the Civil War,' she said.

The old man nodded. 'It was a terrible time in Irish history when young men were gunned down by their old friends. Your grandfather – that poor guy was shot in his back garden. How inhumane is that?'

Catherine wasn't sure if she heard him correctly.

'How do you know that?' she asked.

Fearing he might have the wrong person, he stopped. 'You are one of the Salmons? Your grandfather was Seamus Hopkins from Borris? The violinmaker?'

'Yes, I am.'

He continued, happy that he was talking to the right person. 'My dad was always talking about going back to Ireland but my mom knew he was a dead man walking if he returned. She used to show him the newspaper filled with news of daily shootings and killings.'

At a time when she'd stopped searching, she found the answer. In discovering it was her grandfather who was shot, she recalled the lies her parents told her about the shooting. She had always felt they were hiding something.

Her therapist advised her not to return to Ireland and confront her mother or call a family meeting to discuss their murdered grandfather. In a nice soothing kind of way, the therapist told her she'd undo all her good work from the last year. She told Catherine she'd never find resolution until she first learned to accept. But the more she tried to accept, the less she understood. Shortly after that, Catherine stopped seeing her therapist. It was a crock of baloney.

Lilly was driving, her two hands on the steering wheel and a fretful frown on her face. Lilly never appeared comfortable behind the wheel.

'I think her respiratory system is shutting down, Aunt Catherine – she's gasping for breath,' Paulette said.

'Is she in pain?' Catherine asked.

'The staff say she's comfortable but can you believe them?' Paulette said.

'No, she's not in pain,' Lilly contradicted her.

'Mum, how do you know?' Paulette asked.

'The hospital staff ensure their patients are pain-free,' said Lilly.

'Mum,' Paulette cautioned, 'I have my doubts.'

Paulette kept patting Catherine's back and shoulder, as if she was trying to comfort her. Paulette was comfortable with touch. In the airport Lilly's hug was lame; affection was awkward for anyone who came out of their home. Catherine made a point of hugging them – she did not want to arrive at the stage of wanting to feel the closeness of someone she loved yet be too confounded to touch them.

'Mum and I could hear her breathing on the corridor, it was that loud,' Paulette said.

'Obviously, you'll notice a great difference since your last visit,' Lilly said.

'I think we've all aged.' Paulette smiled at Catherine as if waiting for a compliment.

Catherine looked away.

'You're happy to stay with Eilish in Mum's house?' Lilly asked.

'If that's OK?'

It was easier to be a guest in Eilish's home than in her sisters'. Lilly was too anxious to ensure a happy stay – her generosity was stifling. Like Isabel when they were children, when visitors stayed in their home, she was ill at ease until their departure. She would do all of the right things – dress the bed with the sheets the correct side up, all smelling like garden-fresh sheets that had been aired on a clothesline. At Eilish's there would not be a fry for breakfast or any fuss whatsoever, apart from clean matching sheets. Catherine would be free to come and go as she pleased. So accustomed to having visitors, Eilish had several spare keys on key-rings which said, "*Welcome – Wine Time is Anytime.*"

'Where is Eilish?' Catherine asked.

'She's meeting us later,' Paulette said. 'Mum and I suspect she's starting a new business since she returned from London.'

'That's great. It's not good to lie under a defeat for too long.'

Catherine was aware of Eilish going bankrupt and working in England for a period. From her few brief conversations with her, Catherine gathered it had been a rough few years.

'Eilish hasn't told us about the business. But I noticed she was at the dry-cleaner's with her old work-suits and Zara said she arrived home last night dressed for business.'

'Good for her.'

Paulette patted Catherine's back again. 'Actually, Aunt Catherine, Eilish is in complete denial about Nana. She refuses to believe that her time has come. Instead she's behaving as if nothing is happening. Mum has told her to get the house ready but Eilish doesn't want to hear a word about it.'

Catherine listened without commenting.

'You know she's moved into Nana's house?'

'Yes, I know.'

When Eilish returned from England two months before, she suggested that Isabel's house needed a good airing. Later, on the phone, she confessed to Catherine that she was broke.

'Aunt Catherine, I'd love to tell you that I've moved into Nana's to reconnect with my past and air the house but the truth is a little starker. I'm broke. I need some time.'

Eilish was strong – she was like the O'Fogarty women. Catherine's abiding memory of Eilish was at her dad's funeral. Eilish was seven when her father was killed in a car crash. She was a pretty little thing with long black plaited hair and dark eyes. In the months after the death, Lilly told Catherine that Eilish was more like an adult than a child. She assumed the adult role of rousing their spirits and comforting Lilly and Paulette. Lilly told Catherine that Eilish would appear at her bed at night with a tissue to wipe away Lilly's heartbroken tears.

As they passed the junction to Middle Abbey Street, Catherine glanced down the cobbled street. It was empty at that hour of the evening. Granny Betty had told Catherine how she came from a rural parish in Tipperary to live in Dublin at a time when children died like flies. Women gave birth year after year to children they could not feed. Catherine heard rumours that Granny Betty had lived in the tenements in Middle Abbey Street when they initially moved to Dublin, although Betty Hopkins contradicted those rumours.

'Thank God our dear Lord didn't direct us to those merciless homes,' she said with a voice of certainty that no one would doubt.

Catherine could picture her sitting in her regal sitting room in her favourite Queen Anne chair. Granny Betty drank her tea from bone china and ate in restaurants that were reviewed in the newspaper. Even in old age her grandmother remained a striking woman, radiating an air of affluence and authority, as if she'd only known a life of great privilege.

'Everybody was poor, everybody came from a small cottage or tenement but few had breeding like ours,' she'd say.

She encouraged her granddaughter to be good to herself. 'Decide what you like and spend money on it.'

She told Catherine that God did not burden women with crosses – 'Their arms were open to receive them because they wanted to be martyrs like their mothers before them.'

Long before the term *feminist* was coined, Granny Betty lived by the unwritten manual. When the debate about contraception was raised in the 70's and society cowered in fear of speaking against the Church, Granny Betty was vocal enough to advise her granddaughter that it was easy for a male-dominated Church to take their venomous anti-contraception views. She warned her granddaughters never to voice anti-cleric sentiments in the wrong company – however, she warned them 'Take care of yourself or you'll end up like the poor of Dublin, burdened with children and disease.' In 1979 when a third of the Irish population turned out to greet Pope John Paul during his Irish visit, Granny Betty said

'Women in Ireland will only find freedom when they stop fawning over the men of the cloth.'

She was many things, but was never cut out to be a mother.

'Isabel and I were almost strangers because of that damn war.'

On another occasion Granny Betty moaned to Catherine that Isabel spent too many years with the hillbillies in Tipperary. 'By the time I got her back she was uncultured, like a farmhand's daughter.'

Those few words were a valuable insight into Catherine's guarded mother.

Granny Betty lived to be eight-four. She had a stroke while having her nails painted in a beauty parlour, an unheard-of luxury for most women in Ireland in 1981. For three weeks she drifted in and out of consciousness and during that time she raved about the clay earth preserving the past and so many more secrets.

Isabel was sitting by her bed when Granny Betty mentioned this and her face burned with anger.

'Delirious balderdash,' Isabel declared to all present. 'The medication is making her rave.'

Then she ordered everyone out of the room. After that point, any utterance that left Granny Betty's lips would remain with Isabel, untold.

When they arrived at the hospital, Paulette gently squeezed Catherine's arm. Her sorrowful expression was overdone.

As they walked down the long corridor, Catherine could hear Isabel singing. It was an old song she hadn't heard for over forty years. It was one of many songs that Isabel referred to as 'one of Mona Daly's'. The voice was weak yet the words were there. With each step Catherine's anger at her mother intensified.

'*On Lough Neagh's banks as the fisherman strays ... in the clear cold eve declining ...*'

Catherine stood at the door with Lilly and Paulette, looking in, listening to Isabel singing. She waited for her mother to falter, or at least to get the verses mixed up. The song was sung in its entirety. Isabel's eyes were fixed on a small window to her right.

'*Thus shall memory often in dreams sublime ... Catch a glimpse of the days that are over ... Thus sighing, look through the waves of time . . . For the long-faded glories they cover.'*

The anger and frustration that Catherine thought had abated during her seventy-four years was as raw as the day she took her first flight over the Atlantic. Not only in dementia did her mother not see her; once again Catherine felt like the unseen child. A coiled woman who never shared anything of herself, in her near-death-like state Isabel remained unknown. Dismantling the boundaries between them would never be possible now. Even in her aged vulnerability Isabel dipped into music to find solace. Reminded of the years of disregard, Catherine was fraught with pain that she still felt it all these years later. Taken aback with the ferocity of her hurt, Catherine took one deep breath to suppress her tears. Instead a torrent of wailing erupted, the sound of her sobbing a shock to her own ears.

Chapter 39

Once inside, Eilish dropped the shopping at the front door and went straight upstairs. She could hear the hoover in the spare room. As promised. Oxana, Nana's home help, had said she would arrive at twelve and continue working until everything was done.

Eilish had been gone all day. She had returned to the organic shop in Rathmines with her designs. Linda had liked her ideas and outlined some of her own. With difficulty, Eilish ate more of Linda's organic cheese. She licked her lips and rolled her eyes as if she was sinking her teeth into a Ferrero Rocher. Afterwards she rinsed her mouth out with Coke and chewing gum. From there she drove to Wicklow to get the materials for the job, then back to Dublin and dropped Ivan to her home to repair the display case.

At noon she had lunch with Sarah, who gave her another lead in Laois. A pub owner wanted to add a kitchen to his premises. Eilish made an appointment to see the Laois pub owner the following day. From there Eilish met the seamstress in Meath Street, in Harold's Cross she met a computer guy who installed a new package onto her laptop, and finally she did the shopping for her Aunt Catherine's arrival.

'Thanks for coming at such short notice,' Eilish said to Oxana, noticing that Aunt Catherine's room was ready with a fresh smell of Shake n' Vac. 'I wouldn't doubt you,' she added, reminding herself of her grandmother.

'No problem,' Oxana said. 'I vacuum all room on that level,' she pointed to the floor beneath them, 'and change beds with sheets in cupboard on all rooms and put on electricity blanket and heating in all rooms as you said for me to do.'

'Great, that's cracking!' Eilish could have kissed her.

'Fire ready to be lit on that level,' she pointed to the floor again. 'Also kitchen is done and cleaned. I also wash Mrs Salmon's good china for visitors.'

'That's fantastic. Great thinking, Oxana.' She had to stop herself from overpraising her initiative. She herself hadn't had the foresight to think about matching plates and cups.

'Now I will finish vacuum this level.'

'Thanks so much,' Eilish said. 'But could you leave that till last, please? Instead set the side-table in the back sitting room for four people. Inside the front door are a few bags of shopping – will you put the salads on plates?'

Eilish checked her watch – she wanted Oxana and Cyril the gardener gone before Aunt Catherine and the others arrived. She'd like them to think she had prepared everything without help and that she had even thought of using the good china.

Oxana nodded and seemed to glide down the large stairs. Some people worked noisily, they liked to be seen rushing about. Others worked quietly, the finished job testament to their toil. Oxana was one of those who worked quietly; everything was done perfectly with minimal fuss, except hoovering. She was so intent on doing a good job that she practically scrubbed the floor with the hoover. Nana used to say, 'She'll come through the ceiling at me one of these days.'

Eilish showered quickly, changed her clothes and reapplied her make-up. She opened the window and waved at Cyril who had made fantastic inroads in the garden. When she had phoned him last night she had used her best sales pitch, explaining it was an emergency as her grandmother was not well and there were people coming from New York. When he arrived at 7am, she pleaded with him to remove as much as he could. At least it would appear she had finally done something about the garden when her mother arrived with Aunt Catherine.

She was so relieved at the sight of the clear garden, she blew him a kiss and closed the window to the sound of his hearty laugh.

In the sitting room Eilish was surprised to find Zara in an armchair with a towel over her shoulders and what appeared to be purple dye in her hair. Josh was nowhere to be seen. Oxana was setting the food on the table and shining the knives and forks.

'Good night?' Eilish asked Zara as she inspected the repair on the glass display case.

'Good and bad,' Zara said.

Eilish was reluctant to enter into a big confab about Zara's love-life. She was unsure what kind of advice to offer, and occasionally she was uncomfortable discussing her niece's sex-life. It seemed inappropriate. Still, she needed to show an interest.

'Is it on or off with Josh?' she asked as she busied herself arranging chairs around the fireplace.

'It was never really on – we were only having sex.'

'I thought he was your boyfriend?'

'He said he couldn't be my boyfriend – he likes me too much.'

Zara didn't seem as despondent as Eilish would have expected.

'He feels he can't commit to it and doesn't want to hurt me.'

Eilish was about to say she never heard anything so idiotic in her life – instead she tried to reason in a non-aggressive tone.

'If he can't commit to something pleasant like a relationship with a nice girl, then forget him,' she said. She was incensed that her niece would allow herself to be used by a man. 'A wonderful girl like you and he finds it difficult to commit? No staying power.'

'Well, it's me as much as him,' Zara said. 'I don't know if I could commit to him either.'

Eilish scrutinised her niece's expression.

'If I committed to him, it closes so many options for me.'

'You're young,' Eilish sighed. 'I suppose you should play the field at your age.'

'He knows I'm unsure about my sexuality.'

In the past Zara alluded to the fact that she experimented with women. Naively Eilish had thought it might have been a drunken kiss.

'I get fulfilment from a man and mental stimulation from a woman.'

Oxana left the room. Although English was not Oxana's first language, Eilish intuited she understood the conversation perfectly.

'I don't orgasm with a woman the way I orgasm with a man. Even with toys it's not the same. There's something about the physique of a man.' She stopped speaking to read an incoming email. Slowly she laid the phone on the arm of a chair. 'But a woman is so much more giving. It's almost spiritual.'

Eilish tried to digest this. She nodded her head slowly. 'Right, I see.'

'I often think it would be nice to use Josh for sex and have a different form of intimacy with a woman. A more meaningful deep love with a woman.'

Who was right and who was wrong? Eilish felt like she was the confused nineteen-year-old rather than the kid sitting in front of her with purple dye in her hair. Was their generation right? Compartmentalise your needs. The sink in the centre of the kitchen, men for penetration, the dishwasher close to the sink, women for gentle caressing and depth. Was she not doing what Zara had done? Use men for sex, hope something with substance rises from the ashes of the morning after? It sounded strange coming from her niece, abnormal. Who was more astute, the forty-four-year-old or the nineteen-year-old? Suddenly she felt sad.

'Do all of your friends feel the same way?' Eilish asked.

'It varies. Mia is a lesbian – she only slept with Josh because I told her how sexually fulfilling he is.'

Cautiously Eilish asked, 'Was Mia satisfied with Josh?'

'No, Mia doesn't know what all the fuss is about.'

Eilish nodded again. Their generation seemed to live like rock stars. Anything went. She didn't know what to say. 'You've got to find your own answers.'

'That's what Mia said. She said I'm using the wrong toys when I sleep with women.' The alarm in Zara's phone sounded. She got up from the chair. 'I've got to wash out the dye,' she said cheerily.

Instead of dwelling on Zara's complex world, Eilish went into the back garden to meet Cyril the gardener. He had a mop of curly dark unkempt hair and the beginnings of a beard. He was handsome in a rugged way. As she approached him her thoughts returned to her conversation with Zara. Maybe she'd sleep with Cyril, tell Sarah how wonderful he was, then Sarah could sleep with Cyril, then she and Sarah could sleep together. After that maybe they'd all sleep together. It seemed out of her league. This was new terrain for Eilish. Until Zara grew up, Eilish was the one in their family who dabbled in sex and drugs when most girls were sticking to Ritz beer and a grope-on-the-doorstep.

Cyril had opened the back gate and parked his jeep and trailer in the entrance. Most of the trees had been removed. His trailer was piled high with Nana's garden.

'Well done, Cyril, you've cleared most of it,' Eilish said with relief.

He began to tell her what he had done during the day. She was only half listening as he talked with colourful language about uprooting the fucking shrubs, trimming the fucking trees and spraying weed-killer on the fucking footpath.

'The old vegetable garden is so fucked up it's like something from the Amazon Jungle.'

'That's fine, strip it back and dump everything,' Eilish said.

'The trailer is too fucking full to add anything to it,' he explained.

'Can you come back over the next few days and finish it?' Eilish was not too concerned when he came back. At least when her mother saw it, she'd know Eilish finally had done what she was told.

'What about that fucking rockery?' He pointed to the left-hand corner of the garden. 'Everything's dead on it. Do you want me to plant flowers or level it?'

Eilish hadn't the time, patience or green fingers to maintain a rockery – neither did she want to incur any more expense.

'Level it,' she said.

He agreed to return the following day and finish the job.

Eilish's guests were not due for another hour. She made a cup of herbal tea, compliments of Linda Jones, her new best friend from the organic shop. Linda had recommended Oolong tea for improving skin complexion. As Eilish switched on her laptop, she wondered if Linda thought her complexion needed to be repaired. Probably. There were times in the last year when she looked in the mirror and thought she looked middle-aged.

Eilish typed in her password, resolving not to think about aging or Oolong tea until she could piece the past together. She logged onto the Census National Archives site. For most of the day her thoughts had kept returning to Seamus and Betty Hopkins. The more she learned, the more she wanted to know. For the first time she understood why Aunt Catherine was so fixated on history and her family's past.

Nana once admitted to Eilish that Catherine's constant questioning was wearisome.

'She'd be better off leaving well enough alone,' Nana said. 'She might hear a few things that'll give the poor creature more problems.'

Catherine was a young woman when she learned a man was shot in the back garden during Ireland's Civil War. Six years ago when Nana's mind was still her own, Eilish was present when Catherine raised the subject again. Nana was clearly uncomfortable with the subject yet Catherine persisted.

Nana slammed her coffee onto the table. 'Nobody came back from the dead to tell us anything new, Catherine.'

Nana's angry outburst silenced Catherine that night, yet her quest for information didn't stop there.

Eilish was present in Tipperary when Catherine visited a few of the Hopkins families. They were welcoming and hospitable until Catherine asked if they knew anything. She mentioned a violin dealer and asked who they suspected. The visit soured as they too shrugged their shoulders and sat in silence until it ended.

The Census Archive Site was easier to navigate than she expected. She opted to search the Census Archives from 1911. The first name she keyed in was Salmon. In the forename she inputted her great-grandfather Brian's name. She found them on Thomas Davis Street, Dublin 8. Each member of their family was listed under Brian Salmon's name: his spouse Josie and their ten children. The oldest child was Phelim, the youngest Conleth. Her grandfather was six years of age when the census was recorded in 1911. A brother called Seán was 10 years of age in 1911. Eilish retrieved the paper clipping from her handbag which was dated 6th December 1923. He was 22 when he was shot. Eilish returned to the oldest boy's name. Phelim, an unusual name that rang a bell. She was aware that most of her grandfather's family had emigrated. Some went to England but her grandfather told her their anti-English sentiment would not allow them settle in Tans' Country – some went to New York, and others to Boston and Canada.

Eilish retrieved the Proclamation from the hall and opened the back again.

To Seamus and Betty, on acquiring your new home,
Without struggle, there is no progress,
Yours faithfully
Phelim

The oldest member of the Salmon family, Phelim Salmon, born 1891. Eilish noticed the handwriting, neat and distinct. Like the letters from D.H., it was easy to read. Eilish took out Betty's letters from D.H. and compared them with the inscription. The clear handwriting was exactly the same.

'Bingo!' she gasped.

She compared the writing on the back of the photo of Betty Hopkins and Isabel: Dieter Hartmann's handwriting was dramatic and spidery, nothing at all like Phelim Salmon's. Seamus Hopkins' handwriting was small and appeared to be written with a heavy cautious hand.

Betty was having an affair with the oldest member of the Salmons, Phelim. It made it more complicated that the youngest Salmon, Conleth, was married to Betty's daughter. At least now she understood more clearly. No wonder Isabel and Betty had such a fractured relationship. That kind of behaviour was abhorred in old Ireland and after the wars Ireland slid from a war-torn country into the conservative grip of de Valera and the Catholic Church. Very slowly it evolved into a modern independent country that gave her generation the opportunity to have an education. Her niece had the opportunity to study in a college that was previously closed to Catholics and women. It gave them freedom to sleep with whomever they wanted without any consequences. Even the burden of sin was removed. It gave young men like Josh the freedom to flee the pressures of 2016 to alternative lives on an island called Ala-Lemu, an island where he appeared far happier than he was on the rich Irish soil Phelim Salmon referred to in his letters. She thought of her own self-indulgent lifestyle, Seamus Hopkins' bankrupt business, her spending, how she snorted a year's wages in 1999. The litany of egoism went on. How would Seamus Hopkins feel about his legacy? Almost one hundred years later his daughter was dying on a hospital trolley because the health system could not provide a bed in a ward. Eilish looked up at the violin and suddenly felt terribly sad. Ireland, a terrible beauty.

Eilish closed her laptop, hid the letters and her recent discoveries from the violin in her bedroom. It was all best left alone.

Chapter 40

When Aunt Catherine, Lilly and Paulette arrived at Nana's house, Eilish met them at the front door.

'You're as welcome as the flowers of May!' She borrowed the Tipperary greeting before warmly hugging Catherine. She took her coat and brought her through to the smaller sitting room at the back of the house.

Lilly noticed how the deep comfortable sofas were warmly arranged in front of the fire and three lamps were lighting, which lent an air of much-needed tranquillity.

'How was the flight?' Eilish asked.

'Great once I got through security,' Catherine said, standing in front of the fire. 'This is so lovely,' she sighed, flopping into the chair closest to the fire. 'You look very well.'

'Thank you,' Catherine smiled.

The conversation was stilted. Lilly hated the first hour with any family member who'd been gone for some time. It took time to forage through the formalities and niceties before finding a comfortable meeting point.

'What would you like, Aunt Catherine? Would you like a drink before we eat or eat first?'

Lilly noted the way Eilish asked the question. It was clear she wanted to drink before eating. She was standing by the sideboard with a tea towel over her arm in mock waiting-style, with a bold smirk on her face.

'It's too early for a drink,' Lilly muttered. 'Maybe in an hour.'

Catherine shook her head with a know-all smile. 'You still stick to Dad's customs, Lilly.'

'I'm only speaking for myself,' Lilly said, suddenly reminded of her sister's habit of picking holes in her routine.

In the past Catherine insinuated that Lilly retained so many of their father's customs it was unhealthy. She suggested it was like keeping a dead body in the house. Lilly never drank before 6pm on weekdays, and she gave up drinking for the month of the Holy Souls and Lent. No meat on a Friday. All healthy choices her parents adhered to, and choices that served her well. She wasn't too bad for a woman in her seventies.

'I'll bet you still read the *Irish Independent*?' Catherine said.

'Of course.' Lilly's choice of paper was the *Irish Independent* as opposed to the *Irish Times*. Not because the *Irish Times* only employed Protestants in previous years, according to Conleth, but because the *Times* was useless for the deaths.

'Scotch on the rocks?' Eilish asked Catherine as she held a tumbler to the light, examining the shine.

'Please,' Catherine said.

Paulette handed a glass of red wine to Zara and poured one for herself.

Lilly asked for a white wine and sat beside Catherine. It was nice to have Catherine home despite her little annoying habits like nit-picking over her choice of newspaper. Catherine would take charge, irking a few people along the way which never seemed to bother her. As a child, she was the one who took responsibility for the household when their mother was struck with migraine. A few times a year Isabel would retreat to their bedroom for five days to lie in uninterrupted darkness. Catherine would wear their mother's apron while preparing their meals. Although a child, she would enquire if her sibling's homework was done. She'd iron their father's shirt for the morning, prepare the lunches and finally at 8pm announce in their mother's voice, 'The Rosary, get your beads.' So intent on making the home run smoothly, Catherine would reel off decades of the Rosary in their mother's peculiar Tipperary-Dublin accent. Only once did their father say, 'Use your normal accent rather than that half-baked mixture of Culchie Tipperary and Dublin!' Years later Catherine referred with rage to those memories that Lilly recalled with amusement.

Eilish sat in the armchair at the other side of the fire and raised her drink, 'Happy days!'

'Happy days!' everybody chimed.

'Poor Delia O'Fogarty,' Catherine said, recalling Nana's cousin from Tipperary who used to use the same drinks toast.

'Zara,' Catherine turned her attention to her grand-niece, 'you're all grown up and look so ...' she shook her head trying to find the right word, 'alternative.'

'Thank you, Aunt Catherine,' Zara smiled.

'I hear Trinity has nabbed you,' Catherine continued.

'Yes, Trinity is great.'

'When I was your age, if a Catholic student wanted to attend Trinity, they had to ask the local priest for permission,' Catherine said.

'I know,' Zara said. 'Tots amazing.'

'She's more than just a pretty face,' Paulette said proudly. 'Do you see the fashion?'

'Anything is fashionable,' Lilly said, wishing her granddaughter had dressed in something prettier for Catherine's first night.

'I see that.' Catherine was looking at Zara's purple calf-high vulgar boots and purple streaked hair. 'Did you dye the hair to match the boots?'

'Kind of,' Zara said.

'We could follow suit,' Catherine said to Lilly. 'We're approaching the blue-rinse age. We'll buy blue blouses to match the blue rinse in our hair.'

Lilly laughed at the unlikelihood of it. 'I'll stick to my blonde, thank you.'

Catherine spotted a framed picture in the large mahogany bookcase her grandfather made.

'Mona Daly gazing down at us.' She got up to take a closer look.

It was a black-and-white photo of Mona Daly sitting in the back garden with Isabel. Lilly and Catherine were old enough to remembered Mona's loud cackle and her warmth. In the picture Mona was laughing, her mouth open and hardly a tooth in sight.

The bookcase contained ornaments gifted to Isabel over the years, books of all genres and old framed photos. There was a group photo of Isabel's 80th birthday, another photo of Eilish and Isabel looking at each other, their side profiles similar. A group photo taken in Tipperary. There was another photograph of Isabel with Lilly and Catherine taken at the beach when they were children.

Lilly watched Catherine scrutinise a photo of their mother. Recently she had referred to Isabel as 'that unknowable constant' in her life.

In the hospital Lilly had been taken aback by the force of Catherine's bawling. She stood staring at her sister, crying hysterically like a delirious little girl. Afterwards when Catherine had calmed down she talked about therapy in New York. She couldn't stop talking, trying to explain through gulping sobs. She said she thought the past had faded into an inconsequential few years of her long life, but at the sight of their mother still ignoring her, she felt like a disregarded child. Lilly tried to calm her. She was mortified with such wailing from a grown woman.

At the height of her distress, Catherine seemed angrier with herself than her mother. 'All the goddamn money I wasted on useless therapists, to arrive exactly where I goddamn started. Staring at a woman, hoping she'd see me. It's all fucking bullshit.'

Lilly thought it was a bit late now to dwell on childhood issues. It seemed even more idiotic paying to whine about the events of sixty years ago. Catherine had always had an enquiring mind. After she qualified as a teacher, there were further studies, culture and philosophy, ethics, a doctorate. She'd written a few academic books, but the only one Lilly could remember was about the history of Irish Music, aptly titled, *The Memory of Music*. Catherine's constant studies always brought her back to her childhood, as if she was trying to find answers to heal her present. She was as fixated on her mother's past as her mother was reluctant to discuss it. All these years later, nothing had changed.

Catherine returned the picture of Isabel to the bookcase and proceeded to examine the framed photos on the mantelpiece.

'Mum never replaced the pictures of Dad?'

Lilly sighed. 'No, she didn't.'

Each time Catherine came home, they always had the same conversation on the first night. Catherine tried to establish what had happened. She never tired of searching for clues from her mother's past. Nothing new ever came to light, they always rehashed the same old information.

'Strange how Mum behaved after Dad died,' Catherine murmured.

'Strange indeed,' Lilly replied vaguely.

They replenished their drinks.

Paulette made arrangements to stay the night in Lilly's house, which allowed her to drink. Lilly listened as Paulette told her husband Dick that he'd have to take care of things in her absence, as if the most urgent thing was eating salad and drinking wine.

'We need to get things ready,' Paulette said in a business-like manner.

Modern wives were amusing, Lilly thought as she listened to Paulette dictate to her husband.

They began to relax. Alcohol, the great ice-breaker. They talked about family members, their neighbours and extended family. Lilly brought Catherine up to speed on who had died since her last visit, those who were successful and the less fortunate. They talked about the sick and cancer victims, suicide, and births and the hopeless few.

'Maisie Salmon?' Catherine asked.

'Dead,' Lilly said.

'Evelyn Ryan?'

'Dead.'

'Molly Duane?'

'Dead.'

Eilish, Paulette and Zara started laughing.

'You're like the Grim Reaper, Mum,' Paulette said. Mimicking her mother with one arm folded under her bosom and the other holding her drink, she pronounced: *'Dead!'*

'Jessie Enright?'

'Dead!' Lilly began to grin.

'Monica Salmon?'

'Alive!' Lilly cried with delight.

'Who is Phelim Salmon?' Eilish seized the opening to ask.

"Which one?' asked Catherine. 'There's a bunch of them in Brooklyn, all related.'

'I thought one of them fought in the Rising?'

'Yes, he was Granddad's older brother. He left Ireland and went to Brooklyn. All the others are descended from him. So you could call him the 'original' Phelim Salmon.'

'Did he come home much?' Eilish asked.

'No, I don't think he ever came home,' Catherine said. 'He was a peculiar guy.'

Eilish waited for Catherine to elaborate.

'Apart from playing the flute at parties, he was a silent odd-ball.'

'Poor man probably had his own problems,' said Lilly. 'Dad told me he wasn't the only one of those brothers who left the country after the Civil War. They could never live peacefully on Irish soil.'

'Because Ireland lost the six counties?' Paulette asked.

'I think it had more to do with the brutality of the Civil War.'

'Did Granddad say that?' Eilish was curious.

'No,' Catherine said. 'He rarely discussed it – only to say who was a Free-Stater or who was an informer.'

'Or to point out the Pro-Brit reading the *Irish Times*,' Lilly laughed. 'Poor Dad, he never discussed the war yet everyone he met was categorised into the enemy or the comrade. The war never ended for a lot of those men.'

'Actually there's a book on the Rising with a chapter from Phelim Salmon,' Catherine said. 'It was published about thirty years after the Rising but was never released in Ireland because they were afraid of reprisal killings.'

'I remember that,' Lilly said. 'He kept it hidden from Mum.'

'Mum probably dumped it too,' Catherine said.

'She tried,' Lilly said. 'I kept it. I remember it was called something like *1916 Their Version of It*.'

Catherine laughed. 'It was called *1916 in Their Own Words*.'

'That's probably it,' Lilly said, disinterested. 'Anyway, when Mum was throwing out Dad's possessions she said I could take it but she never wanted to set eyes on it again. I got that book, his IRA medals – there was a lovely drawing of the Salmon family tree that Phelim Salmon's son sent from America – a few books and ledgers from his days in the shop, little office diaries with accounts of his days, that kind of thing'

'I'd like a look at those, Lilly,' Catherine said. 'It would make interesting reading.'

'Boring as anything,' Lilly said, accepting a top-up of wine from Eilish. 'They're in a box in my attic. I was so terrified of Mum stumbling on any reminders that I put them as far out of sight as possible.'

'This is probably all very boring for you,' Paulette said to Zara. 'Us yapping on about the past.'

'No, I think it's interesting. Do you think Nana was screwed up from Ireland's wars or was she, like, just always fucked up?'

Lilly winced at her granddaughter's language.

'We're not really sure,' Paulette said.

'One reason she was "fucked up" as you say,' Catherine began, 'was because her father, Seamus Hopkins, was shot dead in the back garden.'

'Nana's father was shot?' Eilish gasped.

Catherine continued, 'Nobody ever talked about it and we were fed different accounts of what happened to keep the truth at bay.'

'What?' Paulette demanded. 'He was the murdered man? No wonder this place is haunted!'

'*Oh My God!*' Zara screeched. '*This is so exciting!*'

Eilish asked, 'How do you know it was your grandfather who was shot?'

'An old Irish-American guy told me. Johnny Red was his father's name. He claims his father dug a bunker in the house and buried guns during the troubles.'

Lilly remained quiet.

Catherine looked at Lilly. 'And I believe him.'

'I thought Seamus Hopkins died from pneumonia?' Eilish said.

Catherine raised her voice. 'I always knew they were hiding something. We were all told Seamus Hopkins died from pneumonia, then my mother would say she couldn't recall how her father died. My father and uncles told so many lies, they got confused with their own lies. At one point it was suggested that the man in the back garden was killed by a violin dealer which made no sense.'

Lilly laughed recalling it. 'At one point I heard it was the violin dealer who was shot.'

'Exactly,' Catherine said.

Lilly explained, 'The reason the violin dealer's name was added to the mix is that he was the last man who called to the house the day our grandfather was shot. Some of the neighbours saw him.'

'For a while I thought it was him,' Catherine said. 'Hartmann was his name. He landed in Ellis Island in New York on November 21st, two weeks after Seamus Hopkins was killed. It would suggest he left immediately after the shooting which made him look guilty.'

'Did you look for Hartmann in New York?' Lilly was flummoxed that Catherine had gone to such lengths to delve into the past.

'Yes. I traced him to Washington D.C. Home to so many WASPS.'

'Wasps?'

'White Anglo-Saxon Protestants,' Catherine explained. 'He married an American and had three daughters, all very well-to-do.'

Exhausted by the topic, Eilish said to Zara, 'So you think you have it tough with exams and peer pressure. Imagine Ireland in the 20's when violence and murder dominated.'

'And love?' Zara asked. 'And affairs, and sex?

Lilly frowned with disapproval. 'I'd say there was little time for that. Not like now when one neighbour runs off with the other neighbour, they have a child, the mother tires and goes with another man and has a child while he has a child somewhere else. Talking about their siblings is like tracing a complicated family tree.'

'Gran, of course it was done then too,' Zara said assertively. 'Show Gran the letters that were on the kitchen table, Aunt Eilish.'

'Letters?' Eilish said vaguely. She really didn't want to produce them for scrutiny.

'Aunt Eilish, the love letters addressed to Betty. The one where he describes her pure white skin and emerald eyes.'

'Dear Jesus!' Lilly said. 'Highly unlikely.'

'What letters?' Paulette asked. 'I only saw the photos.'

Catherine hiccupped. 'Love letters to Betty Hopkins and photographs?'

'There are old photos of their first shop on Dawson Street. Pictures of Betty when she was a young woman in London with a man,' Paulette explained. 'I think Zara's right – they were having it off.'

They all looked towards Eilish for confirmation.

Knowing she would have to divulge her new findings, Eilish admitted it. 'Girls, we're going to sing a few old songs and retire to bed. In the morning, I will have the most romantic letters waiting for you to feast your wanton eyes upon.' She raised the wine bottle over her head. '*Wine time!*'

'Why? Why not now?' Catherine demanded.

'Come on, Aunt Eilish!' cried Zara. 'You can't do this to us! Show us now!"

'Eilish, I insist,' Catherine said.

'I left them in my laptop-bag which is in Sarah Willis's house,' Eilish lied. 'I'll get them first thing in the morning and when you wake I'll have the sweetest love-letters your dear old eyes ever saw waiting on this antique coffee table.' Hopefully, if they drank enough, they would have forgotten all about the matter by the morning.

Lilly tried to ignore the knot in her stomach. This digging and trying to solve matters from the past unsettled her. All of those concerned were long dead. Any conclusions that Catherine formed would always be speculative, her desire to make their mother the culprit overriding her rational mind.

Chapter 41

Eilish drove to Laois the following morning to meet the pub owner who wanted to add a kitchen to his premises. From the moment she saw his premises and heard him speak, she knew it was a waste of time. There was carpet on the floor with a thousand cigarette burns, old-styled bar stools and flowery wallpaper and curtains. The owner was a small barrel of a man in his sixties who wasn't entirely sure about adding a kitchen but knew he needed to do something drastic.

'There's no money in porter any more. Fecking smoking ban and wine drinkin' has us ruined. Even fellas my age are drinkin' wine. Can't be good for you! Sitting on your own skullin' bottles of wine.'

He wanted to retire and hand the business over to his son whom he referred to as, 'That pure fecker of mine'.

Despite her wasted morning, Eilish was amused by his quaintness. He reminded her of the characters she'd met during her trips with Nana to Tipperary. They'd sit around drinking tea, discussing politics and the world's problems. Each felt they had the solution. Their talk was flavoured by their humorous expressions.

He thanked Eilish for her time and offered her a chicken sandwich and mug of tea, 'to shorten the road'.

She accepted and listened while he talked about the state of the country.

'Pure idlers, those lads above in Dublin,' he said, referring to the politicians. 'Those Dublin boyos in their Mercedes with their drivers know nothin' about the ordinary fellow like me.'

There was a picture of Luke Kelly beside an old hurling team on the wall.

'Do you like Luke Kelly's music?' she asked, curious to know if the publican disliked all Dubliners or just politicians who worked in Dublin.

'Would you believe it, that photo was taken here, in the very spot where you're sitting. It was in the local paper, the *Tipperary Star*. Luke Kelly sang and drank here one night.' He scratched his head trying to recall how long ago. 'Feels like a hundred years ago. That isn't the original photo. A feckin' whore of a fella stole the original off the wall. So I went to Thurles library and had that printed. They've all the old *Tipperary Stars* going back a hundred and fifty years. I got that one printed up as well.' He pointed to an old group photo of a hurling team. 'I'm in that, when I had hair and could touch me toes. The Lord Jaysus, I can't even see me feet now!' He patted his large belly.

Eilish finished her tea and left. He promised if that 'pure fecker of a son' wanted the kitchen for a decent price, he'd give Eilish first refusal.

Was it curiosity or was she turning into her aunt and fixated on the past? As soon as Eilish left the publican, she turned the car towards Thurles. Within forty minutes she was in Thurles Library looking through the old *Tipperary Star* newspaper from 1924.

Seamus Hopkins' death was reported on the last week of November.

Death of Borris Native in Dublin

The death occurred of Seamus Hopkins, Borris, on November 7th. Son of Michael and the late Cissy Hopkins,

Seamus was born in Borris, attended the national school and played hurling for Borris Gaels. Until his departure to Dublin with his wife, Betty (née O'Fogarty), Seamus was employed by James O'Fogarty as a violinmaker. Shortly after Seamus moved to Dublin, he took part in the Easter Rising 1916 and found time to establish a successful business as violinmaker and furniture maker.

A gunman accessed the back garden of the house at approximately 3 o'clock on 7th November whereupon he shot Mr Hopkins dead. The assailant killed Seamus in the presence of his seven-year-old daughter who is recovering in the care of her grandparents.

Eilish reread the last line and then sat gazing at the old newspaper font, absorbing the shock. Poor Nana witnessed the shooting. She thought of Nana, her lined face and blue eyes that seemed to pause and cautiously measure everything she said. It was incomprehensible to imagine what she suffered in her early years and how it shaped her. Eilish sighed aloud. She read the news item again and wondered if Betty Hopkins' affair and Seamus's death could have been connected.

Seamus is deeply regretted by his father and his two surviving brothers, Malachy and David. Seamus's brother, Patrick, was mortally wounded one year ago.

On her return to Ranelagh Eilish was pleasantly surprised to find Cyril finishing up the job on the garden. She opened the back door and waved at him. She watched him carrying shovels full of soil to his trailer. He worked mechanically. There was an elegance to his movement, like a dancer who never puts a foot out of place. The garden was bare, devoid of any of Nana's shrubs or colourful flowers, only burned grass and the remains of the dwindling rockery that Cyril was loading into his trailer. The starkness of the garden was a daunting reminder that Nana would never be returning to fill it with her long-named shrubs and scented flowers. It was as if the house was slowly emptying of her presence. Quickly Eilish closed the door against the thought.

Aunt Catherine, Lilly and Paulette were in the living room. On the coffee table were the photographs of Betty Hopkins. All of the pictures were lined up as if the ladies had spent the afternoon having an inquest.

'Good evening, girlies,' Eilish said brightly. 'Did you all have a nice slow hung-over day?'

'We were out all day,' Paulette informed her. 'We went to the Merrion for lunch and called to see Nana afterwards.'

'Will I pour you a drink?' Eilish asked as she filled a glass with wine and kicked off her shoes.

Lilly said an emphatic no and Paulette asked for a very small glass of wine, while Catherine nodded.

'Hair of the dog,' Catherine said. 'But before you do a thing, I need to see the letters. You promised you would leave them here for us.'

Eilish was torn. She debated whether to reveal her findings, the secrets she had unravelled that Catherine had pursued all her life. It might close that chapter in Catherine's life. Yet her loyalties lay with her grandmother who never relented on keeping the past in the past. Eilish had hoped Catherine might have forgotten any mention of letters by this time. She now realised a woman who chased the past would never forget an opportunity to get a better glimpse with the photos.

For now, she'd wouldn't reveal D.H.'s identity. At least if Catherine stumbled on those details, it would confirm Eilish's suspicions. However, she would tell her that Nana witnessed her father's death. It might help Catherine to understand Nana and be less harsh towards her.

'The letters are dated January 1923 to November 1924,' she said, taking them from her bag and placing them on the coffee table.

'January 1923,' Catherine repeated. 'That was halfway through

330

the Civil War. Where was Mr Hartmann at that stage?'

Eilish watched Catherine scoop up the first letter, her eyes hungrily devouring the neat words.

Catherine examined the signature. 'D.H.? This is very confusing. The only D.H. is Dieter Hartmann.' She examined Mr Hartmann's writing on the back of the Christmas photograph with Isabel and Betty. 'Mr Hartmann's writing is very different to the handwritten letter.'

'I don't know if we should read these,' Lilly said, eyeing the letters. 'Whatever about the photographs, the letters are a different thing. Their intimacies are not for our eyes.'

Paulette was halfway through one of the letters by the time Lilly finished her protest. 'Sweet Jesus, listen to this!'

'They were hidden for a reason,' Lilly insisted. 'How would you feel if your private correspondence with your intimate feelings was discovered and passed around for viewing by all and sundry?'

'We're not all and sundry, Lilly,' Catherine said. 'We are family. Secondly, I have an academic interest. This is a slice of valuable history.'

'What good are they now? Leave the past in the past.'

'The past is us,' Catherine said without removing her eyes from the letter. 'That's why history is so significant. It defines nations, and in turn countries and smaller family units. We need to study and interpret the past to make sense of the present.'

Lilly guessed that was the way Catherine spoke when she went on her history-touring events. She hoped the audience was a lot more receptive than she was.

'All the more reason to burn them,' she said.

'Will you shut up and listen to this!' Paulette said. '*I think of your magnificent eyes and I wish you were here. I feel your absence more than the Irish soil beneath my feet.*' At that point Paulette's voice had risen to a pinnacle and she continued in the same disbelieving high tone. '*I long to touch the pale hills and valleys of your body. To abandon myself to your grooves and inlets. Without you the nothingness of this foreign country would consume me.*'

Paulette slapped the letter onto the coffee table, '*Fifty Shades of Grey*, eat your heart out!'

Lilly stared at Paulette disbelievingly and then at the letter she was holding. She began to smile. 'It doesn't really say that?'

'Look, Mum,' Paulette impatiently waved the letter, and then held it in front of Lilly and pointed out some of the words. '"*Long to touch*." There it says, "*abandon myself*".' Paulette used a seductive voice, '"*Grooves*" "*Inlets*".'

'This is terribly wrong,' Lilly said sadly.

'They're all dead so what does it matter?' Paulette said, picking up another letter and passing one to her mother.

'Maybe the letters were written after Seamus Hopkins' death?' Lilly suggested. 'She might have been a young widow and quite entitled to have her boyfriends.'

'Mum, you're totally harmless,' Paulette said. 'Look at the date, a year before your grandfather's death. Old Betty and her boyo were having it hot and heavy when the hubby was still fighting his war.'

Catherine was less enthusiastic as she read the letters. 'These are fascinating but they don't reveal a great deal. It would appear Granny Betty had an affair but with whom?'

She examined the photos again.

'D.H. could be anybody,' Lilly said dismissively. 'Our grandmother had plenty of friends whom we never heard of. I think this is ridiculous.'

'I'm not surprised that Betty had an affair,' Catherine said. 'She did her own thing.'

'Not to mention that her husband was a lunatic who slept with a gun and slash hook!' Paulette indicated the letter she was reading.

'A slash hook?' Lilly repeated.

Paulette quoted the letter, "*I feel sure the gun and slash hook he insists on sleeping with are a mere precaution for intruders. The furthest thought from his mind is to kill you. He adores you, as I do.*"

Catherine almost snatched the letter from Paulette's hand. 'Let me read it.'

There was silence while they digested the enormity of it.

'It's unbelievable,' Paulette eventually said. 'At least now we know why Nana was so screwed up.' She picked up another letter. 'Her father was a gun-toting slash-hook-wielding madman while her mother was having it off with another bloke.'

Catherine said, 'Paranoia is quite prevalent in soldiers, there's no reason why our family should be immune.'

'Sacred Heart of Jesus!' Lilly released a long laboured sigh.

Eilish placed Seamus's list of names on the coffee table and explained where she'd found it. She then picked up the letter mentioning the 'list of possible assassins' and read, '*I am not upset or surprised to hear I am at the top of his list. Although I am surprised at his other suspects. Poor Seamus is probably suffering the most dreadful delusions to think that his own brother would kill him.*'

Catherine's eyebrows shot up while Lilly looked distressed and Paulette gasped, 'Oh My God!'

Catherine picked up Seamus's list. She looked at the names, 'Gosh, he was very paranoid.' She pointed out Johnny Red's name, 'His son told me that Seamus was the man who was shot in the garden. Johnny Red was one of the lucky men who escaped. Seamus was afraid of everybody close to him, his brothers, his friends and even his wife.'

'Did Seamus Hopkins kill these men?' Eilish asked.

'Jesus, I need another drink!' Catherine exhaled. 'I've searched for information on this for decades.'

Eilish laid the paper clippings and Seamus's list side by side on the coffee table. 'On Seamus's list, he marks off the dead men with remarks about their death. The paper reports the death in a more formal fashion and with less details. Seán Salmon was riddled with bullets: Seamus's list has "x 6". Digger Dempsey died slowly. The paper reports that he was shot once and crawled some distance before dying. Seamus has "Slow x 1". Is it possible Seamus kept the paper reports on each man he killed?'

Catherine poured a large whiskey and drank a mouthful before reading the paper articles. 'It would appear that way,' she said at last.

Catherine remained silent for so long that Paulette got up from her seat, walked the short distance to the writing bureau in the corner, retrieved a box of tissues and put them tentatively in front of her, 'Just in case you need a good cry.'

Catherine never noticed the tissues or heard Paulette.

'Both his list and the paper clippings would suggest he shot Seán Salmon,' Catherine said. 'I met Phelim Salmon a few times. I thought he was a strange guy. I'm not saying it because of what I've just learned. Phelim wasn't a conversationalist, he was more of an observer. Such an observer that I remember one St Patrick's night being unnerved by him. Several times I caught him staring at me. I was married to Flavio at the time. Afterwards Favio asked if Phelim was a pervert. Looking back, I'd say Phelim was thinking of my grandfather and their shared history.'

Catherine continued to look at the paper clippings and Seamus's list. Nobody spoke. The only sound was the ice from Catherine's drink.

Paulette shivered. 'This is getting spooky. Imagine if a ghost appeared now!' Her eyes batted in anticipation.

'Hopefully he'd be a talking ghost and would answer a few of our questions,' Catherine said.

'What would you ask him?' Paulette asked.

'What d'ya think? I'd ask him who the hell killed him!'

Lilly began to laugh at the absurdity of the conversation, short rapid bursts of laugher. She'd never heard anything as foolish. From the love letters, their content, Catherine raking through the information as if her life depended on it, asking a ghost for the identity of his murderer, and she was as silly for sitting through it. It was beyond nonsensical. She laughed harder, the sight of her daughters' quizzical expressions fuelling the hilarity. Catherine looked at her under her eyebrows as if she had gone mad.

Lilly couldn't stop laughing – the more she thought about it the more she laughed.

Then Paulette too began to laugh. She repeated Aunt Catherine's response: '*I'd ask him who the hell killed him?*'

Then Eilish joined in, and finally Catherine. It was hysterical – they couldn't stop. The tears were steaming down Lilly's face. She looked at Catherine, her face scrunched into a hilarious knot which made her laugh harder.

Gradually it subsided. It lightened the air. It helped Lilly see the evening for what it was, absurd and tragic.

They sighed and wiped their laughing-tears from their eyes. Every now and then, they'd erupt into a burst of laugher and quote Catherine: '*I'd ask him who the hell killed him!*'

They resumed their digging and talking.

'Who killed Seamus Hopkins?' Paulette asked.

'We'll never know,' Lilly said. Her fit of laughing hadn't changed her view, but made the probing into the past more bearable.

'There's a lot more to come,' Eilish said to her mother.

'I know what you've stumbled on,' Lilly said. 'This is why you should leave the dead alone.'

'What? Do you know about this?' Catherine asked.

Lilly nodded.

'Who told you?'

'Dad mentioned it years before he died when he had that heart attack. He seemed troubled and mentioned Seamus Hopkins' name. He wanted me to get a priest.'

Lilly's father lived for another ten years after the first heart attack but never mentioned it again. When Betty Hopkins got her stroke she mentioned it. Isabel was in the hospital room and ushered everyone out.

'I assume this is what Mum never wanted to talk about,' Lilly said.

'Why didn't you tell me?' Catherine gasped. 'Knowing this could change everything.'

'What was the point? I was afraid you'd confront her.'

'Nana knew,' Eilish said, taking out the photocopied page from the *Tipperary Star*.

'I've seen that one,' Catherine said. 'When the *Irish Times* uploaded their archives to the net, I found it. The *Irish Times* didn't give his name.'

'This is from the *Tipperary Star*,' Eilish corrected her. '*A gunman accessed the house at approximately 3 o'clock on 7th November whereupon he shot Mr Hopkins dead. His assailant killed Seamus in the presence of his seven-year-old daughter who is recovering in the care of her grandparents.*'

'Jesus Christ, I never knew she witnessed it.' Catherine gasped. She turned to Lilly. 'How the hell could she keep something like that to herself?'

'Mum and her generation were duty bound,' Lilly said.

Catherine wasn't listening to Lilly. She was looking at the evidence before her. 'To think that Isabel knew who killed her father and never discussed it. She's a tough old bird to have survived this long. Is there anything else?'

Lilly caught Eilish's eye and discreetly shook her head.

'No, that's all I know,' Eilish said, withholding the information about Phelim Salmon.

'The will to live is wonderful. Believing in God made it easier,' Lilly said.

'They were sold a bunch of lies,' Catherine said. 'Their punitive God destroyed this country.'

'Their God was their saviour.'

'Horse-shit,' Catherine scoffed.

Lilly looked surprised at Catherine's choice of language before retorting, 'Much better than anti-depressants or ...' she stopped herself from saying "therapy", 'other false gods. Not only for our parents but for women like Mona Daly who had nothing only humour and God. But I think we should stop talking about it. Let's relax for the evening.'

'Gosh, we come from a complex time,' Catherine said, unable to stop discussing the findings.

'We turned out all right,' Lilly said. 'Even the bit of religion serves us today. I know you're really a pious old Yank eating the altar rails every first Friday.'

Catherine laughed. 'Gosh, their God was everything. Remember the night I said that religion was like a cancer. I said it corrupts societies and causes more deaths than any plague.'

Lilly nodded. 'Mum said you were worse than a prostitute from England.'

They laughed at Nana's old-fashioned slur.

'Why a "prostitute from England"?' Eilish asked. 'Why not a prostitute from Dublin or a prostitute from Mayo?'

'Because our mother's generation didn't believe that Irish girls could be prostitutes – only an English girl would resort to the oldest profession,' said Catherine.

That night her father had blamed godless America for corrupting his daughter. But Catherine had seen the wealth of Rome, the poverty in South Africa and Latin America.

In the 1970's, oppression in Ireland was as fervent as in the 50's. Catherine believed Ireland as a nation would never progress with de Valera taking political guidance from the Archbishop of Dublin and Primate of Ireland, Rev Charles McQuaid. The same archbishop who opposed women competing in the same sporting arenas as men as it was 'un-Irish and un-Catholic'. Mixed athletics were a 'social abuse' and a 'moral abuse'. In the 1940's Charles McQuaid had the power to have Tampax withdrawn from the market, fearing they would lead to immoral behaviour. When Catherine returned from New York in 1975, Eamon de Valera had been president for almost fourteen years and the Anti-Tampax cleric held the position of Archbishop of Dublin for thirty-one years. Ireland continued to be oppressed and a conflicted joke dominated by misogynists. It enraged her 35-year-old self-righteous mind.

'So you never did join the Legion of Mary in New York?' Lilly teased.

'What's the Legion of Mary?' Paulette asked.

Aunt Catherine pretended she was shocked. 'Gosh, so much has changed.'

'It's a different country.' Lilly said. She turned to Paulette. 'It's a

Catholic volunteer charitable organisation. We were all members at one stage.'

Catherine returned to the letters. 'Granny Betty was so far ahead of her time.'

Catherine and Lilly recounted anecdotes about Betty. The rare reference that Granny Betty made to the War of Independence was about the consequences for women. As a new nation, nothing changed with independence. People remained poor and unemployed, most emigrated, and women were the most disregarded marginalised bracket who suffered the greatest indignities.

'Treated like work-horses on a farm,' Betty told Catherine.

One of the archbishops said the future of Ireland was bound up with the purity and dignity of Irishwomen. 'It summed it up,' Granny Betty said. 'Have your children and shut up.'

Catherine had been present the night she lambasted the Catholic Church, and afterwards Betty gave her some advice. She told her to allow men to think that their opinion was always the correct one. 'Have your own views, no need to air them. Pretend to agree with their political opinions but secretly vote your own way.'

She encouraged her grandchildren to travel. 'See the world and learn something other than prayers and morals.'

Their conversation turned to Catherine's divorce.

Paulette asked, 'What was the big deal?'

'It just wasn't done,' Lilly said adamantly. 'It was a different era. To separate from your husband in the 70's and 80's in Ireland was a dreadful scandal.'

'Why?' Paulette asked.

'The responsibility for breaking up a family was too much.'

Catherine was about to explain how the Taliban were a sallow-skinned version of the Catholic Church but stopped at the sight of the bewildered expressions on her two nieces' faces. It was pointless.

'Why didn't you just pretend that you were still married?' Paulette asked.

'I was young and angry,' she shrugged.

By 1975, Catherine had passed through many phases. She'd discovered feminism, read every worthy book she could get her hands on, established that women would always be second-class citizens if they were willing to allow it. When she returned to Ireland for a holiday in 1976 she broke the news to her parents about her divorce. She was reading *The Myth of the Vaginal Orgasm*, an essay on women's sexuality, clitoral orgasm and female anatomy. In Ireland in 1976 a husband had the right to have sex with his wife without her consent in the eyes of the law. Women were unable to get a barring order against a violent partner, collect their Children's Allowance or sit on a jury. Naively she thought she could change a country which still revered martyrdom as a virtue.

They had a few more drinks and reminisced with contrasting viewpoints.

Catherine mimicked Granny Betty's grand accent criticising her daughter Isabel for her flat country accent. '"*Dear child, what kind of language are you speaking?*" Mum put on the country accent to irk Granny Betty. And said *push* instead of *put*, or *dash* instead of *that*, or *wan* for *one*. Mum hated Granny Betty.'

'I wish you'd let all that lie,' said Lilly.

'We'll sing "Sliabh na mBan",' Catherine announced. 'Mum loved those Tipperary songs. Sing it with me for old times' sake.'

'Which one is this?' Paulette asked.

Catherine sang the first line, '*Alone all alone, by the wave-washed strand, all alone in a crowded hall!*'

Paulette shook her head vaguely. 'I don't know that one.'

'OK, we'll sing a song that we all know. How about "The Glen of Aherlow"?'

'I know it,' Eilish said, singing the first line.

Paulette shrugged.

'"The Ballad of Dan Breen"? "Seán Tracy"?' Catherine suggested to Paulette.

Paulette shrugged again.

'What's your party piece?' Catherine finally asked.

'I don't really have one although I like Bruce Springsteen's "I'm on Fire". I know most of the words.'

'I'll be damned,' Catherine said. 'Little old Ireland is unrecognisable.'

'What's the most notable difference?' Eilish asked as she refilled their drinks.

Catherine thought for a moment. 'Nobody curses or smokes indoors, there's no Legion of Mary, no party-pieces, there are no drunk drivers – heck, you even pick up your dogshit.'

'Paulette was too young,' Lilly tried to explain.

'I know "Happy Are We All Together",' Eilish said. 'Paulette, you'll know it when I start.'

Eilish began to sing, and then Lilly and Catherine joined to sing one their mother's favourite songs. Propelled by the jovial atmosphere and alcohol, Catherine sprang to her feet and pulled Lilly up to join her. They held hands and sang with such enthusiasm Paulette felt they were shouting rather than singing.

'Happy are we all together
Happy are we one and all.
May we lead a life of leisure,
And may we rise and never fall!'

They finished the first verse to find Cyril standing at the door, his mucky boots dripping on the carpet.

'Join us,' Catherine beckoned.

'I will in my fuck!' he shouted. *'There's a fucking burial ground out there!'*

They stared at him.

'I'm after digging up a fucking baby's coffin and some yokes buried with him.' He spoke to Eilish. 'I want my money, I'm outta here.'

Chapter 42

Eilish went outside with Cyril, followed by Catherine and Paulette who walked towards the end of the garden. It was beginning to get dark. Eilish counted out Cyril's money in the front of his jeep.

Cyril nodded his head towards Catherine and Paulette, 'That American bird isn't too steady on her feet. I hope to fuck she doesn't fall into the hole.'

Eilish suddenly felt sober with the news and Cyril's haste to hurry away. 'Not to worry, Cyril, you can hop in after her,' she said jokingly.

'It's not what's buried that bothers me,' Cyril said. 'It's the red tape and horseshit that goes with finding dead babies. This could bring the fucking Inland Revenue on me.'

Catherine called over in a nasally American whine, 'We can't see a damn thing!'

Eilish noticed how Catherine's American accent strenghtened according to the amount of alcohol she drank.

Paulette swayed, still holding her glass of wine. 'There isn't a thing down here, Eilish!'

As Cyril was thanking Eilish for the money, Catherine arrived at the window of the jeep. 'Hello, little man, do you have a torch?'

Cyril didn't have a torch. Instead he got out and used a rag from the back of his jeep. He spotted it with diesel, lit it, and then dropped it into the hole with Eilish, Paulette and Catherine watching intently. As the flame lit up the hole it took them a few moments before they saw the small skull of the baby, its little head clearly identifiable.

Zara arrived to find Lilly sitting alone in the living room with the curtains drawn, her back to the window.

'They found a baby buried in the back garden,' Lilly said. 'They've all gone out to see it.'

Zara stared at Lilly. 'Why didn't you go out too?'

'I'd rather not.'

Zara opened the curtains and looked into the garden. Just then she saw Catherine stumble away from the old rockery, pause on the path and empty the contents of her stomach.

'Aunt Catherine is vomiting,' Zara informed Lilly.

'It's not like her to waste good alcohol,' Lilly sighed. 'She must have seen more than she bargained for.'

When everybody returned to the sitting-room, they spent hours mulling over the various scenarios.

Lilly said the child could be anybody's – years ago stillbirths and infant mortality were very high. 'Every old house has the remains of a few babies in the garden,' she said, making it sound like it was normal to dump a dead infant into a hole. 'Let that be the end of it.'

Zara wished she hadn't been there with talk of dead babies and Aunt Catherine frantically scrubbing some kind of ornament that was buried with the baby. Cyril the gardener had fished it out of the hole.

'I'd lay money it was Betty Hopkins' child,' Catherine said.

'We don't know for definite,' Eilish said.

'It has to be Betty's,' Paulette suggested, 'or,' she raised a finger and looked around the room, 'the baby could have belonged to Nana. Another reason for her silence. There could be lots of dead little babies beneath us.'

Zara hated her mum when she drank too much – she looked scary with half-closed eyes. Now that she was discussing dead babies, she looked even scarier.

'No way,' Eilish countered. 'The baby could be anybody's. These houses are over two hundred years old. Mum is right, we'll never know.'

'My money is on Betty,' Catherine said as she got a tissue to clean the remaining dirt from the ornament.

It sounded like they were on teams, Paulette and Catherine versus Eilish and Lilly.

'Could be anybody's poor child,' Lilly said. 'Or it could be one of the house girls Betty employed.'

'Lilly, accept it,' Catherine said crossly. 'Accept the past. Don't run from it.'

'Nothing to accept,' Lilly said. 'You're only surmising.'

Suddenly Catherine got up from the chair and stumbled across the room towards Lilly while clenching the ornament in her hand. Zara thought she was going to wallop Lilly with the ornament until she saw her holding it to the lamp, trying to read the inscription.

Everybody waited with bated breath.

Catherine didn't reveal the inscription immediately. She looked towards the ceiling and began to count on her fingers. 'Ah ha, ah ha,' she said, appearing pleased with the findings. 'The child is Betty Hopkins'.' She read the inscription aloud. *"To Dominic, October 2nd, 1925, from Your Father."*

'Nana was nine years of age,' Paulette said, sounding disappointed.

'Granny Betty was living here at that stage,' Catherine said.

'We'll never know for definite,' Lilly repeated. 'At one stage Granny Betty had three servant girls employed.'

Catherine and Paulette spent the next hour guessing who the father of Betty's dead baby was. They mentioned names of people who lived over 100 years ago and re-examined the photos. Catherine went online to find the Irish Census from 1920's and angrily slapped Eilish's laptop closed when she realised the national archives only had the census to 1911. They talked about the scandal and impact of a child on Nana's life and discussed again who the father was.

It seemed so pointless, Zara thought. Nobody would ever really know, yet Catherine listed off the possibilities as if she would confront each man the following morning. Lilly was the only one who wanted the matter closed. In the end she insisted that Zara drive her home.

The following morning Catherine asked Zara for a ride to the shops but changed her mind as soon as they were out of the house. Instead she asked Zara to drive her to the hospital to see Nana. Zara was a little nervous while driving with Catherine. She was only a learner driver. Not that Catherine criticised her driving – she was more uptight and fidgeted. Catherine asked Zara several questions about her life. What impact religion had on her life and how she felt about Ireland? Zara tried to answer as honestly as she could. Religion rarely crossed her mind and she loved Dublin. She'd never considered her Irishness and was not affiliated with any political party. When they arrived at the hospital, Aunt Catherine tried to order Zara to park in a set-down area. Either she felt unsafe with Zara's driving or she was very eager to see Nana. Instead Zara parked in a designated car park.

Catherine said that Zara needn't bother going in with her if she didn't want to.

'I'd like to see Nana,' Zara said.

In the hospital Nana was awake. She smiled at Catherine and Zara when she saw them but Zara knew she hadn't the faintest idea who they were.

'How are you?' Aunt Catherine said, patting Nana's hand.

'Very well,' Nana said.

Then they had nothing to say.

Zara watched as Catherine stared at Isabel with two red eyes. Zara's mum had said she thought Aunt Catherine was a total dipso with shitloads of unresolved issues. Zara had to agree with her mum by the way Aunt Catherine sat by Nana's bed and stared at her, like she was on the verge of speaking but the words wouldn't come out.

'Do you know where you are?' Catherine finally asked.

Nana looked across at Catherine. 'In Mother and Jim's.'

'That's right, you're in Tipperary.'

'Jim's in the shop,' Nana volunteered. 'Finbar will be along shortly with the greyhounds. We'll slip them this evening – every second night we must slip them.'

They lapsed into silence again while Nana seemed contemplative, as if considering the greyhounds.

'Isabel, your mother had a baby?'

Nana's mouth formed a perfect circle. For a few moments she held that look and stared unblinkingly at Catherine.

'Was Mr Hartmann Betty's boyfriend? The violin dealer?'

Nana shook her head and pulled the blanket up to her neck, leaning away from Aunt Catherine. She looked around the small cubicle for escape and shook her finger, 'Enough, that's enough.'

'I think we shouldn't say any more.' Zara got to her feet and put her hand on Nana's shoulder. 'Are you warm enough?' She felt everybody asked old people that question, and she wanted Aunt Catherine to stop upsetting Nana.

'Who killed your father? We know you witnessed the shooting.'

Nana shook her shoulders angrily and cried out.

'Mum, it would help us greatly if you told us.'

Nana covered her mouth and cried out, '*No!*'

Zara couldn't help it when the tears cascaded down her cheeks. Everything seemed so horribly wrong. She put her arm around Nana.

'She's upset,' she said to Catherine angrily. 'Why are you doing this?'

'Did you know your mother had a baby?' Catherine persisted. 'Who was the father? Was it Mr Hartmann?' She placed one of the black-and-white photos of Betty with a man in London on the bed. 'Is that him?'

345

Angrily Nana swiped the picture off the bed.

'You know the identity of your father's killer,' Catherine insisted. 'Who was he?'

Nana's body relaxed. It appeared to go limp and her small frame slid sideways. '*Margaret!*' she called. Her voice was barely audible, '*Mona, Mona where are you? Is Mammy sick?*'

'Nurse!' Zara called out. 'Please, anybody, help us!'

Mona explained to Isabel that her Mammy was sick and wouldn't be able to go out for a few weeks in case she got worse. She needed to stay sitting down with a blanket for warmth. Isabel asked if the sickness made her fat and lazy and Mona agreed.

'When she gets better she'll get thin and be able to run about again,' Mona assured her. 'It's her poor auld lungs and sweet tooth. Lungs and sweets.'

Isabel knew that Mammy had done something bad. She overheard Margaret say that Betty should be ashamed of herself. Her mother never appeared ashamed – she saw her laughing and drinking tea with Mona and Conleth. Fr Mathew was not allowed into the house. Isabel wished her mother was sick with something worse than the lungs. Then she could return to live in Tipperary forever. She didn't tell anyone about her bad thoughts.

For two nights Isabel was allowed to stay in Mona's house. She slept in a bed with four of Mona's children. When she returned home the following day Betty explained that Mammy got a new baby in an orphanage. Little Baby Dominic was going to live with them in their home. Mona and Margaret applauded as if it was a wonderful thing. Even Mammy smiled at Isabel. She told her that little Dominic was her new brother. Although he was only a poor little boy from Goldenbridge Orphanage she must treat him like her brother.

'He will have the same surname as us. He will share everything with you. You must be a good well-behaved sister to your new brother.'

As they held the baby and smiled at him, Isabel buttoned up her coat. The baby could have anything except the coat that Maureen bought her in Tipperary. It smelled of Maureen's house and kitchen. Isabel loved her coat, the smell made her feel happy. Sometimes she closed her eyes, put her nose to the collar and took a deep breath. Sometimes it made her want to cry. She'd look at the sky and wonder which way it was to Tipperary.

Mammy was better. She was up and about, and apart from the new baby she was back to normal. Each day she went to work and each evening when she'd come home she'd sit looking at the baby. They said the baby was growing very fast – he was getting bigger and more beautiful every day. Isabel would peer into the infant's eyes, but she never noticed the change. A parcel arrived from America with a letter for the new baby. In the parcel was a lovely shiny flute. The holes were blocked and you couldn't blow through the mouthpiece. When Isabel asked what good was a flute that you couldn't play music with, Mammy said it was an ornament from New York that would last a lifetime. Mammy kept the flute on her dresser in her bedroom – it had legs you could stand it on. It gleamed from Mammy's polishing. She wouldn't let Isabel touch it – her paws would dirty it, Mammy said. Isabel couldn't understand how such a poor baby with no parents of his own got a present and a letter from America. Mammy said the new baby was special.

Everybody was so happy. Conleth called with a teddy bear when the baby first arrived. Each time he visited he'd stare at the baby for ages. He said a man would come home from America. Mammy seemed happy to hear about the man in America. Conleth kept staring at the new baby, and repeated that the man would have to come home now. Ireland needed him. He must do what was right. Mammy was smiling for weeks until Isabel returned from school one evening and found Mammy screaming. She cried in her bedroom for ages. Mona and Margaret sent Isabel out the front door of the house and warned her not to come in for a long time. When Isabel needed to use the toilet the front door was locked. Through the hole in the fence at the back of the house she watched

Mona and Margaret dig a hole in the back garden where Daddy's workshop used to be. It seemed like hard work. They puffed and panted while they dug, then they dropped a box into the ground and the flute that Mammy polished. With more huffing and puffing they placed several big boulders over the hole and shovelled the clay on top of that.

Isabel heard Mona, between gasping breaths, say that little Dominic would never see the face of God. 'He'll be stuck in Limbo for eternity. It's God's punishment for Betty's carry-on.'

Margaret started crying and Mona told her, 'Whisht up yer pussin' – you'll see more and worse than a dead baby in your life.'

Isabel put her nose to her coat and took deep breaths. She wished Maureen was there, or Jim, and none of this would have happened.

Mona explained to Isabel that the little orphan Dominic was sent back to the orphanage because the nuns missed him. Isabel told Mona she was glad because his crying upset Patch, her dog. Mona warned her never to tell a soul about Dominic because he might come back and would never stop crying. Mammy said that Isabel would be sent to the orphanage if she didn't start behaving and appreciate her house in Dublin. Mona told Isabel that Mammy didn't mean that – she was just sad because the baby went away.

The following morning Margaret walked Isabel to school. In the cloakroom Isabel hung up her coat. The smell of her grandmother's turf fire was fading. As she walked towards her classroom, she stopped. The looming uncertainties made her run. She ran through the gates and towards the city. She recognised various landmarks and kept going. When unsure she asked for directions to Knightsbridge Station. At the station she asked for the train to Tipperary.

When the ticket man stopped her before boarding the train, Isabel pointed towards the carriage. 'There, on the train,' she said, making no sense even to herself.

'Your parents are on the train?'

Isabel nodded before he let her through.

Only when the train pulled away from the platform did she remember her coat. On the train two nuns gave her tea and sandwiches. They told her to dry her eyes and not to worry about her coat. When they made a fuss about speaking to a conductor on the train she told the nuns a lie. She said Maureen and Jim, her grandparents, were expecting her and would meet her at Thurles station. During the train journey she said the Act of Contrition four times for forgiveness for her lie, and another time when it occurred to her that she'd lied to nuns, a graver sin again. She said more prayers. She prayed for Mona and Margaret, she prayed she'd get her coat back, she prayed for Jim and Maureen and she prayed the train driver would make the train go faster.

When she arrived in Thurles she ran most of the three-mile journey to her grandmother's.

Maureen took Isabel to town and bought her a new coat. She then sent a telegram to tell Betty that Isabel had arrived alone in Thurles.

Back home, she sat the child down in an armchair and asked her about her mammy. Isabel told her that Mammy had a sickness of the lungs which meant she had to sit down and couldn't leave the house. She was gone as fat as a cow. Maureen didn't reprimand her for using such a crude comparison. Instead she asked if she was fat in her face, or fat in her feet? 'Or,' Maureen whispered, 'was she fat in her belly?' Isabel said she wasn't sure about the belly because there was a rug covering her belly on account of being sick with the lungs and the sweet tooth. Maureen asked if Betty went to work in the shop in Dublin each day? Isabel told her she couldn't leave the house and Betty told a lie to Fr Mathew. She pretended she was at the beach with fresh air for the lungs but really she never left the house. Nobody could visit her only Margaret and Mona, and Conleth who came each evening with news from the shop.

Isabel told Maureen that she stayed in Mona's house for two nights and she slept in a bed with four other children. When she went home Mammy was better and had a new brother for Isabel called Dominic.

Maureen held onto the chair as if she too was sick with the lungs. 'Sweet Jesus – Sweet Jesus,' she whispered.

'First Mona said Mammy were very kind because she got the baby from the orphanage but then the baby was sent back to the orphanage because the nuns missed him.'

Maureen listened transfixed.

'Mammy won't stop crying, her eyes are red and she's wearing her nightshirt all day. She wouldn't say the Rosary although Mona said it would be good for her. Mona told Mammy that sometimes God chooses to carry babies' souls straight back to heaven.'

Maureen was unable to move as Isabel relayed the events. The news of her daughter's carry-on and her concern for Isabel had her wedged to the spot.

Suddenly Isabel stopped speaking, and her expression changed from one of confusion to fear. Maureen waited in silence for her to continue.

Isabel tried to hold the tears back but her voice rose with suffocated emotion. 'I know the baby wasn't sent back to the orphanage! I know he was in the box that Mona buried!'

Maureen knew the child was about to release an enormous burden. She released her grip on the back of the chair and slowly moved towards Isabel.

'I'm afraid the man who killed Daddy killed the baby.' Isabel's eyes were pleading with a terror that no child should sense.

Maureen sat on the chair beside her. She could hear Isabel's quivering breath.

'The man we met in London who Mammy knew, he killed Daddy,' the child said. 'Phelim killed Daddy. I saw his burned hand.'

Maureen put her arm around Isabel's shoulder and tried to pull her to her but Isabel resisted and continued with a raised quivering voice.

'I'm afraid he killed the baby. I'm afraid he'll kill me!' Hovering on the edge of the chair, she pointed her finger at Maureen, her chin dimpled, trying not to cry. 'I'm scared he'll kill you. He'll kill Jim.

They'll bury you in the hole!'

Maureen's eyes were wide and tear-filled as she listened.

'The man will kill Patch and bury him too. I couldn't go back and get Patch!' Her voice was raised to a sorrowful wail.

Maureen pulled Isabel from the chair into her arms and held her as tightly as she could. As Isabel unleashed a torrent of tears and cried for her dog, Maureen rocked and soothed her.

Isabel slept in the armchair for a whole day.

The shame Maureen experienced for her daughter's outrageous morals and disgusting example for her child changed quickly to an overwhelming concern for Isabel. It pained her to see such hurt and fear in a child she loved. She told Jim that she swore to herself that under pain of death she would never allow Isabel to return to live with her mother.

'Miss High-and-Mighty above in Dublin living in her own swanky house with her fancy hair-do's and mink stoles and fur coats has more interest in making money and self-gratification and despicable morals than raising her daughter.'

Maureen told Jim how she had held Isabel tightly. She thought Betty was not fit to raise a pup, not to mind a child. If Betty, her wanton daughter with her far-fetched notions wanted a battle over Isabel, then by Christ Maureen would give her one.

Isabel felt a pinch in her arm and the sound of voices.

'Nana, it's OK. It's me, Zara.'

Isabel didn't know anybody with that name. Zara, Zahara? How do you spell it, she wanted to ask.

She could hear voices, a male voice.

'We're going to make her comfortable. The antibiotics aren't working.'

'What's happening? She seemed fine a few moments ago.'

An American accent. A visitor from America. Isabel couldn't tell if it was a man or a woman. With the weight of her eyelids she couldn't open her eyes to see the speaker. She'd like to put a face to the voice. She waited to hear Maureen or Jim's voice. Uncle Finbar was out with the greyhounds or in the shop. Was it dark? He'd be home with a treat after tea. Then there'd be cards and singing, then prayers and bed.

Chapter 43

Eilish tried to ignore Paulette's questions. Eilish had called to her mother's house after spending the morning with Ivan in Linda Jones' shop, working towards her five-day deadline. She removed her workman boots and left them outside the door. Paulette was there too. It fascinated Eilish how Paulette never tired of rehashing the events of the last few days.

'Mum, she's for the birds,' Paulette was saying. 'She needs to be on medication.' She stopped talking to look at Eilish who was dressed in dirty jeans and a hoodie. 'Why are you dressed like a hobo?'

'I'm helping a friend clean her house.'

'Which friend?'

Eilish knew Paulette was fishing. As yet she was reluctant to mention her new business venture. 'Sarah.'

'I'm surprised at Sarah – I thought she'd be the type to hire a girl.'

'Some mere mortals must clean their own houses,' Eilish replied.

Eilish went to her mother's attic and located the box with Conleth's personal belongings. She brought it into the living room and joined Paulette and Lilly.

The box contained the book called *1916 in Their Own Words*. It was a first-hand account by those who'd fought in the GPO during the Rising. Also in the box were accounts from the shop on Dawson Street. Pictures, small worthless postcards, a framed drawing of the Salmon family tree. The box also contained every shop diary from 1920 until 1931. Betty had moved the business premises to Leeson Street in 1932. Eilish had read Phelim Salmon's account of the role he played in 1916. He praised the men he fought with, particularly mentioning Seamus Hopkins who saved his life by carrying him from the GPO moments before the roof collapsed. He concluded the article by saying he only regretted killing one man during his years of fighting: **"It was not a war killing."**

'I feel like Mum,' Lilly confessed as she watched Eilish remove the items from the box. 'I'd like to burn everything from that time.'

'Do you suspect Phelim Salmon shot your grandfather?' Eilish cautiously asked her.

Lilly looked at the ornamental flute that was buried with the baby and bore the inscription, *To Dominic, October 2nd, 1925, from Your Father.*

'I don't know.' Lilly exhaled. 'I never met him. We could never mention Phelim Salmon's name in Mum's presence. Granny Salmon told me that he played the flute magnificently and left Ireland in the 20's. Over the years Phelim wrote letters to my father which were not posted to his house but to his mother's house in Thomas Street. I remember being with him on several visits to Granny Salmon when she would pass him a letter discreetly. He'd read the letters outside or upstairs.'

'How do you know they were from Phelim?' Eilish asked.

'Because Granny Salmon would ask if there was any news and they'd look at Phelim's picture on the wall when they'd talk about the letters. Once or twice they made small references to his wife Ursula or mention something which identified who the letters were from.'

Lilly stopped talking.

Eilish and Paulette waited for her to continue.

Paulette prompted her, 'Share it with the group, Mumsy!'

Lilly continued, 'After Dad's death Nuala Salmon returned a box containing letters to Conleth that were in the Salmon house for years.'

Nuala Salmon was Conleth's disregarded slow niece who lived in the Salmon's home in Thomas Street. Although she was loved and occasionally ridiculed by the family, it never stopped Nuala behaving as if she was the most important Salmon family member, manning the fires at the homestead.

Poor Nuala Salmon wasn't the full shilling,' Lilly continued. 'If she'd any sense she would have realised they were kept in the Salmons' house for a reason. But she felt that they were Dad's property and she thought she was doing the right thing by returning them to Mum. I'd say the letters contained information that Dad didn't want Mum to see.'

'That's it,' Paulette said. 'The information was in the letters. We've been trying to figure it out for years and you knew?'

'I don't know and we'll never know,' Lilly corrected her. 'That is only my suspicion.'

'Why are you keeping this from Aunt Catherine?' Eilish asked.

'What's the point in telling her? It's like feeding a monster. The more she hears, the more she wants. None of it would fulfil her. She always wanted more degrees, more acclaim, more money, more drink, there's an emptiness inside in her. She ridicules Mass-goers. If she believed in some kind of God, at least He would fill a little piece of the emptiness. Instead she condemns those of us who practise.'

'Maybe historians are unfulfilled,' Paulette suggested.

'If she stumbled on that information, she'd go off to America blathering about her new historical findings. She'd write another outrageous article about her adulterous grandmother's fling with her uncle who possibly shot her grandfather. It would be worse than *EastEnders*.' Lilly tutted.

Paulette laughed loudly at her mother's comparison.

'Catherine had a piece published in one of those academic journals about the Salmons,' Lilly went on. 'She talked about their poverty, how her father and his brothers went to bed hungry and ate off the same plate because they couldn't afford crockery or food. The Salmons were disgusted with it.'

'But they were poor,' Paulette pointed out. 'Granddad told me he didn't have shoes when he was a kid.'

'Everybody was poor but nobody wants to be reminded about it. And,' Lilly said emphatically, 'the Salmons never went to bed hungry. Josie Salmon was a great manager of money and saw that every child was fed. Catherine did a few of those silly things and fell out of favour with a lot of people.'

Eilish listened as she rooted through the box of Conleth's belongings. She found the office diary from 1924. It appeared to be the main diary kept by the cash register with a list of the day's messages. The handwriting was difficult to read and the ink had faded over the years yet she was surprised that she could decipher some of the messages. Callers to the shop were logged. Most of the messages were for Conleth or Betty. The person to whom the message was addressed had their name underlined, and the message-taker's name was also noted. Betty left some humorous responses in the margin.

'9 o'clock, 2*nd* May. _Mrs Hopkins,_ Mr Thompson would like to provide the aprons at a greater discount than discussed. Mr Thompson would like to speak to you at a time convenient for you. Brideen.'

In the margin, Betty wrote, '_Brideen,_ under no circumstances will I deal with that vagabond. His samples are too small for a midget. If he calls again, get Conleth to run him. Mrs Hopkins.'

'3 o'clock, 17*th* July. _Mrs Hopkins,_ Mrs Wyse Power called in by chance hoping to meet you. She'll come back the day after tomorrow. Conleth.'

Eilish found it interesting that Conleth referred to Betty as Mrs Hopkins. She'd forgotten about the old formalities.

'4.20, 24*th* October. _Danny,_ a lady called, said she wanted a private word. Brideen.'

In the margin Betty wrote, '*Conleth, please tell Danny that I'm paying him to work, not frolic with ladies on the shop front. Third time in the past 10 days his lady friend has called. Mrs Hopkins.*'

Eilish flicked through the diary, amused by Betty's acerbic wit. As well as her humour, Eilish noticed that Betty was a hard worker who never missed a day's work. Every single day had at least one entry or comment from Betty. Eilish flicked through the earlier diaries and noticed that, apart from short holiday breaks, Betty went to work every single day since the company was established in 1920 except the 7th of November 1924, the day of Seamus's death.

Seamus was shot at 3pm. What reason could she have for not going to work on that morning? Could she have had prior notice that Seamus was going to be shot that day?

Eilish looked at the days prior to the day of his death.

On the 6th of November, Brideen wrote an appointment into the diary. '2.00, 6th November, *Mrs Salmon, Mr Fennessy has agreed to meet tomorrow afternoon. He said 2 o'clock would suit. Brideen.*'

In the margin Conleth wrote. '*Brideen, re-arrange for a later date. Conleth.*'

Eilish couldn't find any other appointments deferred by Conleth except that one time. Could Conleth have known and played some role in the killing? Did he have some prior knowledge that Betty would not be available the following day?

Eilish was about to ask her mother if she suspected Conleth played any role in Seamus's death, but she thought better of it. She thought of a nicer way of asking. 'Did your father ever confide in you about Seamus's death?'

'Not directly,' Lilly said. 'Since these recent revelations, I've been thinking about the time Dad had his heart attack. He asked me to call a priest rather than a doctor. While we waited he mentioned Seamus Hopkins – he said something like, "I didn't question, I was only doing what I was told, a silly messenger-boy."'

'He probably played a small role in it,' Eilish said. 'There was probably some reference to it in the letters that Nuala Salmon returned to Nana.'

'Oh my God,' Paulette said suddenly, sitting up straight in the armchair. 'I'm beginning to agree with you, Mum, we should stop talking about this now. Our family is littered with murderers, adulteresses, mothers dumping children in holes in the back garden – what next?'

Lilly ignored Paulette. 'Last night I couldn't sleep thinking about it. I'd hate to think of Dad killing Seamus Hopkins.'

'Well, I can tell you he didn't kill him,' Eilish said, showing her the diary entry for that date.

'2.40, 7th November, "_Brideen_, post Mrs Warby's invoice to 3 North Circular Road. Conleth." He was in the shop at 2.40pm. He was also in the shop at 3.05.' She indicated another entry.

Lilly took the diary and read the entries for the date of Seamus's death. 'At least that's a bit of good news.'

Eilish rummaged through the box while Lilly read aloud amusing entries from the diary.

Lilly laughed. '"9 o'clock, 10th December, _Mrs Hopkins_, Mr O'Meara called again re: fabric. Promises to give good price. Brideen.' In the margin, Betty has written, '_Brideen_, this is Mr O'Meara's sixth time calling. Tell Mr O'Meara nothing has changed from his five previous visits. His fabric is so coarse it might be useful to stop debris falling in the event of another world war. Mrs Hopkins." She was a tough lady!'

Eilish found postcards commemorating the 50th anniversary of 1916, and there was an old record, strangely called "The Ballad of the Teeth". She then picked up the framed drawing of the Salmon family tree. It was very artistically drawn, a tree with the Salmons and their offspring labelled on the branches. At the bottom of the tree was a sketch of a man and woman holding hands. Brian Bernard Salmon and his wife Josie Mary Harris. Each of their ten children with their Christian and middle names were above them, and their spouses on an attached branch. She noted every Salmon child had an Irish name – the middle names she assumed were the names of saints. Conleth Fintan, Seán Gerald, Aideen Brigid, Phelim Dominic.

She looked at Phelim's name: _Phelim Dominic_. The letters were signed by D.H. His mother's maiden name was Harris. Dominic Harris. It was so simple. Phelim Salmon used his middle name and mother's maiden name.

'Little Dominic was definitely Betty's Hopkins' child,' Lilly said. She was reading the dairy from October 1925, the time of the baby's birth. 'For two months prior to baby Dominic's birth she never went into the shop. Obviously she was keeping the pregnancy a secret. Less than a week after the birth, 8th October, she returned to work.' She flicked the pages forward. 'On the 27th October she didn't go to work and remained away for two weeks. I imagine that's when the baby died – he lived for four weeks.' Lilly closed the diary and returned it to the box.

'So we're not surmising any more?' Paulette said.

'No, it's there in black and white,' Eilish said. 'So too is the fact that Betty didn't go to work on 7th November 1924.'

'Although Seamus wasn't shot until 3pm,' Paulette said.

'The office diary, 1920's version of Big Brother.' Eilish returned the Salmon Family tree to the box and slid it to one side. 'I'd better go,' she said, getting to her feet.

'So what we've got is,' Paulette began by holding one finger up, 'Betty Salmon had an affair with Phelim Salmon.'

Eilish wondered what Paulette would do when all the drama passed. When Nana eventually died and Aunt Catherine returned to New York and life resumed as normal, Paulette would have withdrawal symptoms. That morning she had revealed that her husband Dick asked her if she was moving out because he saw so little of her. She was indignant at his insinuation.

Paulette continued, 'They had a baby that is buried in the back garden. A boy,' she pointed at the ornamental flute and raised a second finger, 'called Dominic,' third finger raised.

Eilish noticed her how mother appeared disinterested. She looked tired. Just then it occurred to Eilish that she personally knew those involved and loved them. It was not pleasant to hear the information that had been regurgitated over the last few days.

'Before all this, Phelim Salmon came home from England to

shoot your grandfather,' Paulette's expressive eyes opened wide, 'shoot him dead.' She lapsed into a moment's silence for impact. 'I suspect Conleth knew about Phelim killing Seamus.' She had five fingers raised.

'This is all terribly depressing,' Lilly repeated.

'Then Phelim moved to New York and wrote to his brother Conleth,' Paulette went on. 'At some stage he discussed Seamus Hopkins' death. Nana read about it when Conleth's letters that were kept in his mother's house were returned to her by Nuala Salmon. Then she realised that her husband played some role in her father's death. A death she witnessed at seven years of age. Then Nana tried to wipe her husband's memory from her life by throwing out any reminders of him.' Paulette had ten fingers raised. She opened and closed her hands three times to emphasise her ten discoveries. 'This is better than anything you'd see on *Who Do You Think You Are?.*'

Lilly sighed. 'I'm exhausted after the last few days.'

'I agree,' said Eilish. 'Case closed.'

'And not a word of this to Catherine,' Lilly said, 'or anybody else in case we end up in a history journal or *Who Do You Think You Are?.*'

They sat in silence. There was nothing more to be said.

Paulette was sitting sideways in the armchair, her legs swinging over the arm.

'I was thinking,' she began.

Eilish knew from the way Paulette spoke that she wanted to drag on their analytical conversation for the rest of the day. Eilish would return to Rathmines to help Ivan work on Linda Jones' shop. She didn't care what she had to do – even if she broke every nail lugging timber back and forth, the organic shop would be gleaming within the five-day deadline.

'Do you think,' Paulette paused and wrinkled her nose as she looked from Eilish to her mother, 'that Aunt Catherine's a lesbian?'

'In the name of God, no!' Lilly was incredulous. 'As if we haven't enough to deal with this week!'

'Mum, are you homophobic?'

'Stop that talk.'

'Her big laugh and her deep voice,' Paulette paused to think, 'and the way she drinks whiskey – it's all very mannish. I notice she needs her upper lip waxed. She has way too much testosterone I think.'

'She was married,' Lilly said as if that confirmed her as a heterosexual. 'Although she didn't stay in the marriage a wet week.'

'What was the husband like?'

'I only met him a few times – very handsome and fashionable, Italian, dark and tall,' Lilly said. She paused as she recalled it. 'He wore a pink jacket and had unusual glasses. They were two-tone. We didn't have glasses like that in Ireland. Fashionable.'

'He obviously had the wrong prescription in his two-tone fashionable glasses,' Paulette said. 'She even cries like a man. Eilish, you should have seen the scene in the hospital.' She jumped off the chair to act out Catherine's hysterical crying. She held the door of the living room and pretended to loudly bawl. 'Oh dear Jesus,' she said in an American accent, in a man's voice, 'all my goddamn therapy!' She moved her theatrics to the armchair. She rocked back and forth. 'And I end up back here! It's all fucking bullshit!' She wailed, waving her arms in the air.

Eilish would always remember where she was when she realised Nana's death was almost upon them.

The ringing phone interrupted Paulette's performance.

Her mother's changing face as she listened on the phone signified the ending.

Chapter 44

Isabel drifted in and out of consciousness but remained tight-lipped despite the American urging her to speak.

'Are you awake? Is there anything you'd like us to know?'

Someone took Isabel's hand in theirs. It was a strong hand with a sharp ring that scratched her finger.

'Mum, can you hear me?' The American accent was there again. 'Is there anything you want to say?'

Isabel remained silent.

She remembered the morning that Nuala Salmon arrived with a shoebox containing items belonging to Conleth. It was exactly three months after Conleth's death, May 3rd 1989.

'It's rightfully your property,' Nuala explained. 'When I found it last night I said to myself I'd wait till the morning and bring it straight to you at the shop.' Her lips were pursed with self-importance as she handed over the old shoebox with Conleth's name on the lid.

Graciously Isabel accepted the box and glanced inside. She noticed a pipe and buttons. She thanked Nuala for returning it. 'You did the right thing.'

Assuming the box only contained silly boyish memorabilia, it was several days before Isabel looked through it. There were letters from America from Phelim to Conleth, and one letter from Ursula Salmon, writing to Conleth imploring him to ask Betty Hopkins to refrain from writing to her husband.

'Phelim is a married man, his life is in America with me and our son. Although Ireland defines us, it and the sorry state of affairs remain in our past. I enclose Betty's unopened letters and ask you, as your sister-in-law, to intervene. Please ask Betty to desist with her tomfoolery. We have found a degree of happiness and would like to be left alone to enjoy it.'

Isabel read the letters, each letter that Ursula returned, penned by her mother.

Betty was beseeching a married man to leave his wife and return to her. She referred to him as her 'darling'. She wrote about the birth of her son, how she could begin again. There were more letters after the baby's death, Betty clawing at the man to return in an inappropriately honest manner.

'I had hoped to begin again after Baby Dominic's birth. With each new day I was renewed. The prospect of a second chance at motherhood energises me and all the more as it is your child, your son. There is no war or reasons to send our son to the country like I was forced to do with Isabel. It is a wonderful time to be Irish.'

Betty also wrote to Phelim to inform him that their son died. When Isabel read Betty's account, she tried to see it through the empathetic eyes of a mother but she couldn't see beyond her sense of disgust at her mother's undignified craving.

One of Betty's unopened letters to Phelim was dated 29th October 1925.

'The afternoon I found his cheeks cold and his body limp, my plans crumbled so violently. The little thing that gave me so much hope had turned to ice, its little body interned in the back garden to dissolve into nothingness. I am shocked it has had such an impact on me. It was as if something in me died the afternoon I found him dead. I fear with the death of the baby boy, my remaining connection to you, my darling, is severed. Your initial letter was full *of hope. You wrote about the apt time it is to have a son born to a young promising country like Ireland. You vowed to pray and write often. Regardless of your marital status, you would do what you could for our son and would always be bound to me. I could never have imagined how quickly it would end.'*

It was a strange experience to read the intimate thoughts of the woman who had almost ceased to be part of her life once she had fled to Tipperary.

The most damning letter of all was the letter in which Phelim discussed Conleth's role in the event on the afternoon of the 7th November.

"*No amount of prayer will ever remove my guilt for Seamus's death. Not only my own actions but I deeply regret involving you. I hear you say you were only the messenger boy who notified Betty of the time, I am the culprit who involved you and am deeply sorry. I have made my peace with God, today I try to live by his creed. On Judgement Day He will decide.*"

Conleth's role sickened Isabel the most. Her saviour and sanctuary was as corrupt as Betty and Phelim.

There was only one sanctuary where she was utterly loved. Maureen had told her that she would never return to Dublin, that she would live with them forever. Only when Conleth arrived with a trunk filled with all of her belongings and her dog did Isabel really believe she would remain in Tipperary. For a short time she feared that her mother would reclaim her until one night she overheard Maureen telling Jim that she'd sent a letter to Betty now that Betty's health had returned after the death of the boy. She told Jim that in the letter she said she knew about 'her carry-on' and that it would best if Isabel was raised in a 'good home'. She said she informed Betty that Isabel lived in terror of being returned to Dublin. And if Betty made matters worse for Isabel, she'd gladly sacrifice her family's decent reputation for the sake of Isabel's happiness. 'I told her I'll blather to the world what she did to Seamus, how she frolicked with his killer and lost an illegitimate child.' Those words stuck in Isabel's head despite the fact that she didn't really understand them.

Isabel remembered Betty visiting Tipperary but never staying too long. As time passed, Isabel became more at ease with Betty yet her mistrust never entirely faded. There were periods when Isabel was in awe of her. The style and Betty's new motor cars were wealthy in a time of continued poverty. The stories Betty told from her travels and her winter tan were exotic when many in their local community had never been to Dublin. Isabel listened as she talked about the Leaning Tower of Pisa, the Colosseum and Vatican City, the Louvre and the Eiffel Tower in Paris, Chicago, Boston. She spoke with a grand accent and dressed in the finest clothes. The friends she referred to had strange un-Irish names like the Belangers, Lynn de Jonker, Dean and June Claxton. Betty talked in a strange way about other countries, referring to 'mesmerising architecture' and another country as having 'an unoppressed culture'.

Maureen always raised her eyes to heaven when Betty went on like that.

Isabel knew she was a disappointment to her mother. Ideally Betty wanted a daughter who shared her interests, a daughter who appreciated the nice shops in Dublin, who spoke properly, attended a recognised boarding school like the children of Lynn de Jonker and the Claxtons. She'd like a daughter who'd appreciate the theatre and have a curiosity about travel. Instead Isabel couldn't be pried away from her grandparents' house, basic and crude as it was in Betty's opinion.

'Wouldn't you like to see Venice?' Betty asked Isabel. 'There are no roads or streets, only canals and boats.'

'Maybe,' Isabel said noncommittally.

The only cultural attribute that Isabel had that her mother was proud of was her natural ear for music. She sang beautifully and could play to the air of any tune. When Betty saw her playing music she was silenced.

'She's like her father,' Jim said. 'Lost to the beauty they create.'

Mutely Betty nodded, the colour draining from her face.

When Isabel's grandparents passed away, Betty enticed her to Dublin. They were never entirely comfortable with each other. Isabel's courtship and hasty marriage to Conleth left Betty raging and claiming that Conleth had deceived her. Conleth and Isabel got on with their lives. They bought a house in Harold's Cross and lived happily with their little family of two girls. Isabel missed the country and returned as often as she could, taking her little family with her for weeks during the summer holidays. They were happy most of the time. As the years passed they learned to accept each other's small failings. They swam on the changing waves of life.

The bickering of politics continued. The Anti-Treaty and Pro-Treaty sides becoming entrenched in Fianna Fáil and Fine Gael. The Second World War came and went. Hitler shot himself although Mona Daly reckoned he was alive and well.

'That fecker didn't die in any bunker. He's off sunning himself in California,' Mona told Isabel and Betty as she ironed clothes with a cigarette dangling from her lips. She said she knew it was a fact. 'As sure as I'm standin' here. One of the missionary priests said he knows a fellow who sees Hitler day-in-day-out singing German songs in a pub in California and swigging out of a pint.'

When the electricity came to her house, Mona refused to touch the light switch.

'It makes everything look dirty and it's not safe,' she said, gaping at the bulb. 'We don't know who's sending it.'

Until the mid-50's Mona continued to work a few hours a week in Betty's home. Isabel suspected that Betty did not need Mona's work, merely her presence. Mona Daly was the only solid constant who remained in her mother's life. At Christmas and occasions throughout the year Betty looked after Mona financially. One year she gifted her a gramophone and old records she no longer listened to. Mona would learn the songs with her grandchildren and sing a few bars without much encouragement. Her new favourite was "Remember Me", an eerie Frankie Lane song with the chorus repeating '*Remember me, remember me, remember me . . .*'

Isabel could see Betty smiling when she'd hear Mona singing the song as she went about her chores.

'There are few who would forget you, Mona,' Betty said.

Mona was the only person who spoke her mind to Betty.

Occasionally, when Betty overdid her quota of Dubonnet and Gins, Mona would scold her when she'd see her nursing her hangover. 'Ya auld eejit, you know only men can drink like that.' Mona would cook Betty black pudding with strong tea. 'The only fix for too much porter.'

Once Isabel heard Mona refer to the men in Betty's life.

'Your romances won't last till you make your mind up that all the other romances you've had are long dead.'

Suddenly Mona grew thin. Within a few weeks she was lost in her jumpers and held her skirt up with a man's belt. Betty insisted she visit a doctor who sent her for tests. Mona wouldn't believe in the doctor's methods.

'That chancer was only making it up as he went along,' Mona informed Betty and Isabel. 'First of all he put a plastic square picture onto a white box with a light and told me he was looking at me lungs. Then he tells me I had TB years ago without knowing a thing about me. He tried to tell me he could see scars from TB on me lungs that was in the picture on the white box with the big light. How could he take a picture of something that's inside in me? 'Tis all rubbish talk.'

'It's an X-Ray, a new way of seeing under your skin,' Betty told Mona.

'I never had TB,' Mona protested. 'Then he starts telling me they'll cut me open and cut out me lungs.' Her voice rose incredulously. 'I says to him, how will I breathe without me lungs? Then he changes his mind and says they'll only cut off some of me lungs. I thanked him for his time. Then I left as quickly as my two feet would carry me with me lungs still inside in me.'

A few weeks later Mona was not able to get out of bed. Betty, Isabel and Catherine called with a bottle of whiskey and a few packets of Woodbine. Mona was propped up in her bed, so thin she was unrecognisable. Without a flicker of shame at the dilapidated surroundings, she beckoned the visitors into the bedroom. There were a few neighbours and family gathered round. Her son gave Betty his seat and filled glasses of whiskey for everyone. Mona gave a rendition of "Remember Me".

As she sang, Isabel knew her mother was about to lose her oldest friend.

The night after Mona's funeral, Betty drank too much and muttered sadly, 'A shawlie from the tenements who taught me about dignity.'

After Mona's death, Isabel noticed a change in Betty. She reminded Isabel of a child unable to sit still. She returned early from her holiday, bought a new car and sold it as quickly, had the kitchen redecorated only to have it repainted weeks later. Betty returned to her religion and went to Confession. The lively spark faded and instead she became despondent. Suddenly she looked older. Mona's daughter who was Betty's housekeeper confided in Isabel that she was worried about Mrs Hopkins.

'She's stayin' up half the night sipping her Dubonnet and Gins and reading old letters from that boyo.'

Isabel never asked which boyo but had her suspicions when Betty went on a holiday to New York.

Isabel pieced the closing chapter of Betty's love affair from tit-bits she heard from the housekeeper, from her daughters and during Betty's final three weeks when she rambled at length. She talked about rereading Phelim's letters over and over. She wanted to find a blemish in their love, something that would make her feel idiotic to have loved him for so long. Rather than finding fault, it reaffirmed that they'd shared the most immense kind of love. For the first time she thought about the circumstances of Seamus's death – it was catalyst of change between her and Phelim. God had lain her at this lonely junction where guilt was etching its way into her mind. She went to Confession, admitted she was sorry. The priest absolved her.

But her curiosity increased. Rereading his letters fed her curiosity.

According to members of the Salmon family whom she met at Isabel's home, they were getting on fine in America. He'd had five sons and one daughter with Ursula. They were still living in Brooklyn, and education was a priority for their children. Several of Phelim's sisters and brothers, nieces and nephews emigrated to the US using Phelim and Ursula as a stopgap. Her last time in the Salmon home was for Conleth's mother's funeral. In the small living room, Betty scanned the pictures on the wall until she found Phelim with his family. It was taken sometime in the late 40's, a formal photograph with his wife and six children. Like so many, Phelim had aged. He was thin and lined, yet he remained handsome. There was another photo of him standing in front of a Christmas tree flanked by family.

Betty's ears were always pricked for an update on Phelim. It was like trying to read a placard from a train window. She only got the smallest detail yet it was enough. Through Isabel's in-laws she learned he'd stopped teaching and spent his time reading. He liked baseball and supported a team whose name Betty couldn't remember. He had a routine of Mass each morning. On Saturday afternoons he visited a used bookshop near the Children's Museum. It served coffee in a restaurant at the front where Phelim read his books. She imagined his children were like him; they'd read highbrow books and enjoy in-depth discussions on current affairs.

In the autumn of 1965 Betty grew tired of imagining his life. She went to New York and stayed with Catherine. She found the Children's Museum. Across the street was a park and on the corner of the street was a used bookstore. It was raining the day she made the trip. She sauntered among the aisles of books. Phelim would be at home in a bookstore, his enquiring mind would always need sating. Idly Betty bought a coffee and eavesdropped on the conversations around her. She couldn't hear any Irish accents. At the other end of the coffee shop a group of three older men were chatting. They were Phelim's vintage. As suddenly she realised they were her vintage too. She guessed the men were Phelim's friends. Betty tried to imagine what Phelim would look like. It was forty years since they'd last seen each other on the canal in Dublin. That dreadful night when he chose Ursula.

Betty watched an old man shuffle in the door. He dithered over which books to select, his shaking hands and long finger lodged on one book before quickly moving to the next, as if he was feeling the texture of each cover. He picked up several books, flicked through the first few pages, wetting his fingers in a jittery fashion. As if agitated, he returned the book only to do the same again in the same harried manner.

'Good afternoon, sir,' the woman on the till said. 'We got a picture book, the ones you like.'

She retrieved a glossy book with a black-and-white cover.

'I thought of you when this one came in. It's Irish with lots of old pictures. Your kind of book.'

The man mumbled a response. He paid for the book and a soda, and then took a seat with an uncoordinated gait. Hurriedly he opened it to the first page. His head moved robotically as he scanned each page. He licked his fingers in the same hasty manner to turn the next page, repeating the rapid scanning motions.

When she saw the slight discolouring of a scar on the back of his right hand, she remained motionless, her glasses hiding her horror.

After a short time a young man came into the store and stood behind him. 'Hi, Dad, all done?'

Without answering Phelim got to his feet unsteadily and shuffled onto the street. The young man guided him into the front seat of the car outside the door. In the passenger seat Phelim opened the book again to begin the same hurried procedure of examining the old pictures of Ireland, his head mechanically moving through the pages as if he was searching for a familiar face. Despite the passing of almost half a century and residing in a world far removed from his beginnings, Betty realised he had never left his beloved country. He had never left the scene, the final curtain call on war had never closed. Like so many of their era, until death found them they would always struggle through the rubble of their past.

Betty returned to Ireland. It was a few months before her spirits lifted again. She returned to her old interests of travel and fine dining. There were periods when she grew restless, when her indulgences didn't satisfy her craving for something else. Like Phelim returning to Ireland, the scene of the crime, she too returned to his letters and photographs. She kept the best letters, the ones where he expressed his love, close at hand. She hid them in the

371

wardrobe in her bedroom, the pictures and letters remaining a daunting reminder of what they'd survived together. Their lives were controlled by war yet those days alone with Phelim were the happiest days of her life.

There were times when Isabel denied Phelim Salmons' existence to herself. She denied witnessing any shooting in her father's workshop. At the first sign of a recollection, she would think of something else. She'd work or sing or scrub the kitchen. On her own deathbed there was no work to be done and no escaping the memories.

She remembered her excitement that winter's day in November all those years ago on returning to Dublin from Tipperary to see her father and mother. She ran through the house, out the back door, down the small path and into her father's workshop. The doll's house her father had made was painted grey with white windowsills. There was a fire and turf in a basket. She marvelled at her father's ingenuity when she saw the rooms filled with her friends, a doll with a lock of real hair and a rocking chair. It was magical, her very own world on her father's worktop. He'd remembered every detail she told him.

'Is my little girl happy?' he asked, taking her onto his lap.

She never saw Phelim's face, only heard the sound of his shoes on the concrete slabs. Her father pushed her under the workbench and stood in front of it. He tried to speak but his killer fired immediately. She remembered the sound of the shotgun and the ringing in her ears. There were three shots before her father crumpled to the floor.

The speed of the blood as it seeped into his white shirt.

From her hiding place she could see the gun clasped in a wilted hand with a red triangular scar.

'May God forgive me,' she heard the man whisper before he staggered from the workshop.

From her hiding place beneath her father's workbench she stretched across the floor and held his opened waiting hand until life left him.

Epilogue

28th April 2016

Nana spent twelve days drifting in and out of a coma before dying. During those days she remained mute. She was 100 years of age and 1 day when she passed away. The day after her death they learned that she'd specifically made wishes to be laid to rest with her grandparents in Borris Cemetery in Tipperary. Everyone thought Nana's previous reference to being buried in Tipperary was a romantic passing idea, a whimsical notion fuelled by the information she unearthed in the months following her husband's death. They were not aware that Isabel had made her own funeral arrangements in 1999. Ten years after her husband's death, her anger had not waned.

When Catherine learned about the funeral arrangements, she threw her eyes up to heaven. 'She even made provisions that her remains would be interred as far away from us as possible. It's another example of –'

When Catherine was mid-sentence Lilly moved away. They were all tired, tired of waiting for Isabel to take her last breath, tired of talking about the past, and tired of each other.

Lilly found Eilish at the back door smoking a cigarette. She wondered aloud how to explain to her friends that her mother was buried 100 miles from her father.

'Tell them your parents are together in heaven – where their remains are is irrelevant,' Eilish said.

Eilish's preoccupied sad gaze upset Lilly. She wanted to hug her or put her arm around her shoulder, anything to ease the sadness in the eyes that slowly blinked as she looked into the back garden. Eilish found it difficult to suppress her tears.

'Sometimes the dead help us more than they could when they were living,' Lilly said. Her own mother had said that to her when Granny Betty died. In light of what Isabel thought of her own mother, it was a selfless gesture that Lilly always remembered.

Unlike Eilish, Paulette had not stopped bawling or bear-hugging anyone who came to the house to sympathise. Over the evening she discussed outfits between bouts of bawling. When Paulette learned that Nana was being buried in Tipperary, it was a different sort of crying, an angry wail like a child's tantrum.

'Is there even a decent hotel in Tipperary?' Paulette howled. 'None of my friends will travel to the wild country sticks for a funeral!' She was apparently more appalled at the funeral arrangements than the death.

Despite Paulette's fear of having a dismally attended funeral, Nana's cottage in Borris was overflowing with sympathisers. It was a fine country funeral that Nana would have been proud of. The small church was crowded with locals, the pipe band, the choir, her cousin's children, grandchildren and great-grandchildren.

'"*A fine box with thick sandwiches and a dignified funeral*",' Paulette said, imitating one of Nana's cousins.

Catherine was nervous throughout the proceedings. As Lilly spoke to her outside the hotel, she remained uneasy. She was flying from Shannon airport immediately after the burial. Lilly did not try dissuading Catherine from leaving that day. She continued to talk as if Zara had not told her what happened in the hospital. Through sobbing tears Zara had told Lilly how Aunt Catherine questioned Nana as if she hated her.

Making a fierce accusation as only the young can, Zara said,

'Aunt Catherine murdered Nana. She might as well have taken a gun and shot her.'

Within a few hours of hearing Zara's account, the old familiar sadness that Lilly felt for Catherine overrode her anger.

Lilly wanted to part from her sister on good terms. She felt sorry for Catherine. She had made a life for herself in New York, claimed to love the vibrancy of the city, she had status in her career, was widely recognised as an academic and historian, yet she scraped at old wounds. She was so preoccupied with the past she could not be content with the present. All of Catherine's studies led her back to her mother. Their mother's passing would not relieve her anger. She would continue to dredge the rivers of her past and her parents' past to find valuable clues she would discard as quickly until her own death.

'I fully intend on taking Nana's case to the highest echelons of the legal world,' Catherine said.

Nana died from septicaemia. During a previous hospitalisation a few months prior to the last she had contracted MRSA in the hospital.

The undertaker told Lilly and Catherine: 'A draconian system that saw a woman on a hospital trolley for five days dying of an infection she received in their care.'

Lilly pretended to agree with Catherine. 'Do that,' she said, reminding herself of their mother who assumed a passive voice when Catherine got on her high horse about something.

'Come to New York and visit me,' Catherine said as they parted.

They made promises and spoke as if they were arranging to meet the following week. Both knowing they needed to crawl back to their habitat for a long rest before they could resurface and meet again.

Eilish would survive. In the car on their return journey to Dublin, she took a call and spoke in her old business-like voice.

'My work is impeccable. Thank you for your business. I'm in Tipperary over the weekend and will call to see you first thing on Monday. Of course, Mr Haskell, you'll get a first-rate product with our company.'

When she hung up she didn't say what the call was about, only drove faster and seemed suddenly brighter as she hummed a song that Lilly couldn't recognise.

The End